FEARSOME MAGICS

EDITED BY JONATHAN STRAHAN

Also Edited by **Jonathan Strahan**

FEARSOME MAGICS

EDITED BY JONATHAN STRAHAN

EDITED BY

JONATHAN STRAHAN

INCLUDING STORIES BY

TONY BALLANTYNE

JAMES BRADLEY

ISOBELLE CARMODY

FRANCES HARDINGE

NINA KIRIKI HOFFMAN

ELLEN KLAGES

GARTH NIX

K J PARKER

JUSTINA ROBSON

CHRISTOPHER ROWE

ROBERT SHEARMAN

KARIN TIDBECK

GENEVIEVE VALENTINE

KAARON WARREN

SOLARIS

First published 2014 by Solaris
an imprint of Rebellion Publishing Ltd,
Riverside House, Osney Mead,
Oxford, OX2 0ES, UK

www.solarisbooks.com

ISBN: 978 1 78108 212 6

10 9 8 7 6 5 4 3 2 1

A CIP catalogue record for this book is available from the
British Library.

Designed & typeset by Rebellion Publishing

Printed in Denmark by Nørhaven

*For Garth, with thanks and gratitude,
for the years of friendship, the fine times,
and, of course, the stories!*

ACKNOWLEDGEMENTS

THIS PAST YEAR has been a challenging one, but I have loved working on this book and would like to thank my Solaris editor Jonathan Oliver, Ben Smith, and the whole team at Rebellion for all of their kindness, help, and consideration over the past year. I would also like to thank all of the book's contributors for letting me publish their wonderful stories. Special thanks to Garth Nix, Genevieve Valentine, Nina Kiriki Hoffman, and Kaaron Warren, who all came through when I really needed them to. And, as always, I'd like to thank my agent, the ever wonderful Howard Morhaim, and his assistant Kim-Mei Kirtland.

And, finally, an extra special thanks to my wife Marianne and to my two daughters, Jessica and Sophie, for their love and support.

CONTENTS

INTRODUCTION
JONATHAN STRAHAN

MAGIC TAKES MANY forms. In our world, and in any story set in a world that is recognizably ours, magic is either a matter of sleight of hand or a matter of faith.

Stage magicians, like storytellers, produce illusions for entertainment, using legerdemain or sleight of hand to persuade our eyes that they see one thing while another is actually happening.

Magicians or sorcerers, on the other hand, use magic to understand, experience or influence the world using rituals, symbols, actions, gestures or language. While modern magic is often about personal spiritual growth, the belief in and practice of magic as part of religious faith dates back to the very earliest human cultures and was believed to materially influence the physical world.

Magic in fiction is a more slippery thing, and even a close examination of the many, many fantasy texts published over the past hundred or so years reveals very little consistency about it beyond the fact that if magic is possible then almost anything can happen.

There is, however, one thing that every kind of magic has in common: one characteristic that is true, whether magic is practiced by a stage conjurer, a Wiccan priest or priestess, or a liberal arts graduate trying to write a follow up to *Game of Thrones*. Magic is about rules. Magic practiced on a stage has to conform to the physical rules of our world. Magic practiced as a matter of faith and belief must follow the rules and tenets of that faith. Magic in fiction, though, must only follow the rules of its creator and the rules that have been created for a fictional world. This makes a coherent structured set of rules for magic critical because magic without limitations, without consequences unbinds story, lets events run amok, and undermines dramatic power.

Each and every one of the great works of fantasy fiction that in some way use magi accepts this, whether it be Alice as she falls down a rabbit hole or Frodo, as the great ring of power drains him of his life force as he journeys into Mordor. Sometimes the driver behind a story is the consequences of magic playing out, or the consequences of not following the rules that apply where magic is practiced.

In *Fearsome Magics* storytellers take different approaches to magic and how magic manifests in their tales, but never lose sight of the importance of rules and consequences. Tony Ballantyne creates a set of eerie and disturbing rules to govern how the sick and injured pass through the wards and surgeries of his dream hospital, while in James Bradley's story rural traditions have tragic consequences. Possibly more than any other writer here, Isobelle Carmody takes rules and consequences to their limit with her mathematical tale of unbinding, while Frances Hardinge builds magical bridges that that take their builder and her passengers to their destinations, but at a price, just as Nina Kiriki Hoffman does in the strange world of twins. Ellen Klages gives us a glimpse into the behind-the-scenes lives of stage magicians while Justina Robson takes magic and politics and shows us both must follow inevitable rules. Christopher Rowe turns a tale on the clauses and sub-clauses of the written word while Robert Shearman steps through the searing stages of grief. Karin Tidbeck, Genevieve Valentine, K.J, Parker, and Kaaron Warren take their turns as well, and Garth Nix's ragged pair, Sir Hereward and Mr Fitz, look to enforce the rules of magic in one of their most thrilling adventures.

When the time came to sit down to do a follow up book to my first Solaris book of fantasy, *Fearsome Journeys*, I didn't expect to end up delivering a book that so thoroughly weighed and assessed, or indeed turned on magic. I hadn't, in truth, intended to use a consistent series title like *Fearsome* this or *Fearsome* that. Instead, I thought I might do a book called simply *The New Solaris Book of Fantasy: Volume 2*. Instead, wiser heads prevailed. My editor, the sensible and intelligent Jonathan Oliver, suggested the book should have a title that echoed *Fearsome Journeys* and it didn't take long for *Fearsome Magics* to emerge as the title of the book. That seems to have inspired writers who have turned in a series of sometimes dark and sometimes frightening, though often humorous and adventurous, stories that explore just how fearsome magic can be.

As always I would like to thank each and every one of the contributors who have stories in the book you now hold. Some were there when the project was hatched, and some came onboard in the days just before the project was complete. I'd also like to thank the writers who, for whatever reason, fell by the wayside. There are many reasons this happens, but I am always grateful to them for trying to be part of the book. Next time. My thanks too, to Jon Oliver and the Solaris team, to my agent Howard Morhaim, and my wife Marianne and daughters Jessica and Sophie.

I hope that you, as you journey through these pages, find yourselves thrilled, entertained, disturbed, and moved. That is what magic, fearsome or not, can do. And, above all, I hope we get to take this magical journey once more soon.

Jonathan Strahan
Perth, Western Australia
May, 2014.

THE DUN LETTER

CHRISTOPHER ROWE

THE JUNIPER BUSHES in front of the house had grown so high and wild they almost concealed the gray clapboard walls and even the sagging, leaf-choked gutters. The screen window on the storm door had rents in it, and the door itself was held open by half a crumbling cinder block. The cement porch had been painted red once, a long time ago.

It was the kind of house, Tansie thought, that other kids bet each other to spend the night in. It looked abandoned and haunted.

She fumbled her keys out of her knockoff Michael Kors purse and opened the front door, calling for her grandmother as she went.

"Who's that?" came the answer.

Her grandmother's voice was trembling and hoarse, as always. Frightened, as often.

Tansie turned down the volume on the television, tuned to a religious channel and blaring as loud as the old set's speaker could manage. Her grandmother sat in the same place Tansie had left her before leaving for school that morning, not facing the television but sitting to one side, so that her good ear was as close to the set as possible. The old woman looked anxiously out into the room with milky eyes, worrying her heavy oak cane with arthritic hands.

"It's just me, Grandma," said Tansie. "Just Tansie, home from school."

"Tansie? Where's Eileen? Do you want me to make you something to eat?"

These were the same questions her grandmother always asked. *Tansie,* with a hint of *who are you?* And *Where is my daughter?* And *Can I feed you? Make you warmer? Make you safe?*

"It's you needs something to eat, I bet," said Tansie. "Did you eat the lunch I left set out for you?"

But she could see into the kitchen and the plate covered in aluminum foil still sat on the counter, undisturbed. Sighing, Tansie walked over and peeled back the foil, revealing a baked chicken leg, canned peas, fried potatoes, all leftovers from the dinner she had made the night before. She took the plate and a glass of water into the living room and set up a tray in front of her grandmother.

"Here, Grandma," she said, taking the old woman's hands and guiding them to the water glass and a fork. "It's the same thing we had for dinner last night, set out the same way. Do you remember?"

Her grandmother did not answer, but set down the fork and lightly ran her fingers over the food, knocking a few peas rolling onto the tray. She found the chicken leg and took a healthy bite. Tansie was thankful again at how careful her grandmother had always been with her teeth. She didn't think she could deal with dentures on top of everything else.

The next-door neighbor's dog started barking wildly, in the particular way that meant the mailman was working his way down the block. Tansie went out to the porch and was disappointed to see that Mr. Stevens, the usual carrier, must have been sick or on vacation. A slight woman she'd never seen before, wearing uniform shorts and shirtsleeves despite the cool and damp of the autumn day, picked her way daintily through the weeds that cracked the front sidewalk.

Usually, Mr. Stevens would pause for a few minutes and ask after Tansie's grandmother, and maybe tell her a corny joke. A few years before, she had told him he should save the candy he used to give her for other children on the route, but he still called her Little Miss.

This sharp-featured woman, shorter even than Tansie, who was not tall, unshouldered her leather bag and nodded in a quick way that reminded Tansie of the parrot in the biology lab at school. She held out a bundle of envelopes and sales flyers expectantly, but did not speak.

"Thank you," said Tansie. Then, "Is Mr. Stevens sick?"

The postwoman narrowed her eyes. "Mr. Stevens?" she said. Her accent was odd to Tansie's ears, like someone from public television, but pitched strangely low for such a small woman.

"The usual mailman," said Tansie. "The man you're substituting for."

The woman sniffed. "I substitute for no man," she said, and turned on her heel.

Tansie shook her head at the rude response, and carried the mail in to the dining room table, where she did her homework and kept all the household correspondence. They had only used the dining room on holidays even when her grandmother still did the cooking.

She flipped through the sales flyers first, looking for sales on groceries. She regretfully tossed the coupons for pizza places into the bin filled with paper she used to kindle the woodstove. Tansie loved pizza but could never figure out how to make the checks her grandmother received from the government and from her late grandfather's pension fund stretch to cover much more than the monthly bills. She had to be satisfied with the greasy rectangles the school cafeteria called pizza every other Thursday.

There were two bills, water and gas, and she put them at the bottom of the stack on the edge of the table. That was her method. She paid them in the order they arrived, timing the payments according to how much was in her grandmother's checking account on any given Monday night, which was bill night.

There was an offer for a credit card addressed to her grandfather, who had been dead for over ten years, and an assortment of advertisements for magazines, cable television (something else they couldn't afford), and a plumber. Most of these went into the woodstove pile as well, but she set the plumber's flyer aside, just in case. It said 'free estimates' and Tansie had noticed that the water was taking longer and longer to run hot when she bathed her grandmother.

She looked back into the living room. Her grandmother was using her fingers and fork to chase peas around her plate. The bone of the chicken leg was on the floor.

Finally, she looked at the last four envelopes, the ones addressed to her mother.

Urgent. Your attention is needed. Final notice. To be opened only by.

The first one was from a law firm that sent letters which arrived regularly every Tuesday. The second and third were from collection agencies with generic sounding names. Tansie only knew they were collection agencies because they had called constantly when the phone was still connected.

The fourth letter was unlike anything Tansie had ever seen.

The paper of the envelope was thick and felt rough to her fingers. Its color was like the edges of a coffee stain on a white dishrag, somewhere between brown and gold. There was no return address, and neither was there a stamp. The address read simply 'Eileen Abnett' followed by the name of the street without the number, then the city without the state or a zip code.

Tansie turned the envelope over. There was a smear of red wax holding it closed, and a seal had been pressed into the wax that looked like letters in some alphabet she didn't know. All together it was like something out of one of the Regency romance novels her grandmother used to read to her at bedtime.

Normally, Tansie put all of her mother's mail into brown paper grocery bags beneath the table to turn over if she showed up for Thanksgiving or Christmas, and this was what she did now to the first three letters. She didn't know why she left the fourth one laying on the table when she went to clean up after her grandmother.

LATER, AFTER HER grandmother was bathed and settled in to watch the television for the evening, Tansie returned to the dining room to decide what homework she was going to do. She was on an at-risk track at high school because of her grades and her 'family situation' as the counselor put it, which was code for students who didn't live with their parents for one reason or another.

For some reason, being at risk meant they expected her to do *more* homework than the other kids as far as Tansie could tell. And it meant bag checks at the beginning and end of every school day to assure that she had carried all of her books home.

She pulled them out of her book bag and sat them on the table one by one.

English III. This semester English was just reading stories, and she liked that well enough.

Algebra II. A battered book with half its paper cover torn away. Tansie always felt like she should be better at math because of paying the bills, but it turned out algebra was only partly about arithmetic. She would do what she always did and copy the homework off Greg Barnett in study hall before lunch.

Keyboarding. Tansie could already type 80 words per minute and didn't know what else she was supposed to learn in this class, or what the homework was supposed to be. Neither did Ms. Troutman, apparently, because all she ever assigned was 'finger exercises.'

Home Ec. II. She flipped through the workbook. They were in a unit called "Household Budgeting" and the exercises looked like the kind of arithmetic she knew how to do. It was also the kind of workbook that had the answers in the back, so you were supposedly graded on *how* you got the answer, not just *whether* you got it. Mrs. Burton never checked, though, so Tansie would just fill these in.

And World Civilization I. Which was fine in class, when it was just Mr. Campbell telling more stories, but the homework would be reading a long chapter and then answering the study questions at the back.

She put the Keyboarding and Algebra books back into her bag, then quickly went through filling in the answers to the budgeting questions. The English and History books still sat on the table when she was done. She heard the program changing on the television in the next room and could tell by the theme song that began to play that it was eight o'clock. She would put her grandmother to bed in another hour, and go to bed herself around midnight. There was no reason to get started on the real homework right away.

The envelope still lay on the table, and Tansie picked it up again. When she shook it, she didn't feel any movement at all. When she held it up to the dining room light, none shone through.

She idly wondered how long she would take to talk herself into opening it.

There had been a time when she opened all of her mother's mail, along with that addressed to her grandparents. She had even tried to pay one of the bills that came, once, one of those addressed to Eileen *Kincaid,* which was just one of the three married names her mother had taken in the years since she left Tansie with her grandmother. That had proven to be a mistake, because it proved impossible to keep up with the payments and meant that even more bills for her mother had found their way into Mr. Stevens' mailbag. Once, a deputy had even come by the house looking for her mother, but Tansie was able to truthfully say that Eileen Abnett hadn't lived at the house for as long as she could remember, and that she hadn't seen her in over a year. The deputy left a business card with a number for Tansie to call the next time her mother visited, but Tansie tore it into dozens of tiny pieces.

So she had stopped opening her mother's mail, and started putting in her grandmother's information under 'or guardian' on any forms she had to fill out for school. Since her mother had stopped by out of the blue a few days before last Christmas to drop off matching Body Works gift baskets for Tansie and her grandmother, there were only three of the brown paper sacks under the table. Last December her mother had left the house burdened under the weight of more than twice that many, because it had been a long time since her previous visit. Tansie remembered hearing the lids of the neighbor's trash cans being lifted and replaced one by one as her mother threw away the bags before she drove off into the night.

She picked up the letter again, and examined it even more closely. She didn't know how it had been delivered with only a partial address and no stamp at all. Some sort of mistake at the post office? That didn't seem likely, but she didn't know how else to explain it. Everyone wanted money to do anything, even if it was just the price of a stamp.

She wasn't aware of making a conscious decision to open the envelope until she found herself in the kitchen pulling a serrated steak knife from the back of the silverware drawer. She never fixed anything that needed a knife to cut, so she had to dig until she found something sharp.

Back at the dining room table, she laid the envelope face down on the table and put the cutting edge of the knife up against the edge of the wax seal. She tried to work the blade under the wax, but wound up cutting into it and spreading a gritty mess of red flakes over the rough paper. She stopped and gently blew the flakes away.

How would her mother even know if she opened it? When had she ever looked at her mail?

But still, something kept her from just tearing the envelope open. She turned it over and read the address again. *Eileen Abnett.*

That wasn't her. That wouldn't ever be her.

WITH HER GRANDMOTHER in bed and the house finally, blessedly, silent, Tansie took up the envelope one more time. She turned it over and over and then shrugged and ran her finger beneath the fold on the back and tugged. The seal gave way without tearing.

Then she saw why there had been no movement inside the envelope when she shook it. It wasn't an envelope at all, but a large, single sheet of paper, folded this way and that so it was a letter that made its own package. Tansie thought of the geometry problems she sometimes saw Greg Barnett laboring over in study hall.

All unfolded, the sheet was almost twice as long and wide as a piece of notebook paper. The address was written in the center of one rectangular fold among many rectangles and triangle creases. She turned it over.

The writing was so curled and looped that she almost couldn't read it. But then she made out what she supposed was a date at the top, 'The 451st day of the 1,918th Great Year of Our Reign.'

And on below:

To the human, Eileen Abnett, these letters are writ.

Our advisors have brought a matter of great importance to our attention. To our eternal regret, our beloved seventh son Killian, while visiting the earthly realm, lay with you. His seed quickened and you gave birth to a daughter of the elves. To his shame, Killian concealed this matter until he lay on his deathbed, having fallen to the cursed blades of the treacherous Dökkálfar.

Now this child, who has lived in the ignoble mortal world for far too long, will be given to us and elevated as a lady of our court. A knight will be sent when the seal of this order has been broken and, on your release, recover her to us.

I set down this writing
Ilinana, Queen of the Ljósálfar

Tansie let the letter roll back flat on the table and read it once again. She was always conscious of how lightly her grandmother slept, but she couldn't help it. She laughed out loud.

It had to be some kind of weird love letter from Greg Barnett, who spent the time in study hall when he wasn't doing his homework or hers reading fat fantasy paperbacks. He'd lent her more than one, and she'd taken them out of gratitude for his help with the algebra problems, but she'd not been able to get into any of them. Too many made up words, for one thing, not much in the way of girl characters for another, at least not in the ones Greg favored.

"Dock*al*far," she said aloud, trying the word out on her tongue. She had no idea how it was supposed to be pronounced. The little tick over the 'a' might mean a stressed syllable, she knew that from Spanish last year, but she didn't remember any little dots like over the 'o.' Not that she'd done that well in Spanish.

She was trying to decide whether she thought the note was weird-and-cute or weird-and-creepy when she thought to question why Greg Barnett would have addressed a love letter meant for her to her mother.

But then who else could have written such an oddball letter? Maybe her mother had dated the adult version of Greg Barnett at some point.

There was a slamming sound at the back of the house. It sounded to Tansie like a car door, but there was no way for a car to get into the weed choked back yard. She made her way back through the kitchen to the door that led out back and flicked the light switch, even though she knew the bulb in the outside fixture had needed replacing for years.

The door from the kitchen to the back yard had a narrow window running from above the doorknob to near its top. Tansie couldn't see anything through it, just her reflection and the kitchen counter behind her. For some reason, her gaze focused on the clean plates in the drainer, and then she realized it was because they were moving.

No, not the plates, something white on the other side of the window. It was a hand, curled into a fist.

Tansie jumped back, just as the slamming sound came again. This time she recognized it as someone knocking hard on the screen door outside. It was a single blow, sounding like a bat swung hard against a sheet of metal.

"No way," said Tansie, then louder, "No way! I'm not opening the door! Go away!"

When Tansie's grandparents had bought the house it had been in what her grandmother called a 'decent, working neighborhood.' Time and circumstances had changed that, though. The house directly behind them was abandoned, which Tansie was actually thankful for given what was rumored to go on along the backing street. Could whoever was knocking have jumped the fence from back there?

Again, the slam.

"I'm calling the police!" said Tansie. 911 always worked, didn't it? Even when you hadn't paid the phone bill?

A voice, muffled by the door, answered her. "Are you the Lady Tanistasia Killiansdottir?"

Tanistasia? No one had ever called her that, not even her mother. Tansie had only ever seen the name once when she dug out her birth certificate for some paperwork that had to be filled out when she started high school.

"I'm calling the police!" she said again, with slightly less conviction, though she did walk over to where the old yellow phone hung on the wall.

The voice was clearer this time, as if whoever was outside had opened the screen door and now only the kitchen door stood between them. "Are you the daughter of the mortal woman Eileen Abnett?"

Mortal woman. This was the letter writer, then.

"She's not here!" Tansie said. "She doesn't live here! Go away! Why are you in the back yard?" She said it all in a rush, and realized that her heart was beating fast.

"You must be she," said the voice, and Tansie now recognized it as a man's, speaking in a strangely familiar cultured accent. "The glamour I cast has caused any without elven blood hereabouts to slumber. I am opening the door now."

As soon as he said it, Tansie picked up the receiver and punched in 911. Holding the old corded handset to her ear, she looked around frantically for something, anything, to fend off whoever might be coming through the door, even though she was sure that the door was locked.

She saw the old iron skillet her grandmother had used to make cornbread when she still cooked and took it up in her right hand. It was heavy.

There was no sound on the phone, no dial tone, no voice saying, "What is the nature of your emergency?"

What *was* the nature of her emergency, anyway? She looked at the door, and saw that the doorknob was turning, even though yes, the deadbolt was thrown. But somehow, the door swung inward anyway.

Tansie screamed "Go away!" and dropped the phone so that she could grip the skillet with both hands.

The man who came through the door held up his open palms. "You greet me with cold iron? Are you giving challenge, my Lady?"

He didn't look like Tansie's idea of a home invader. In fact, he didn't look like anything she'd ever seen or imagined before.

He was about her height, or even less, which would mean he was barely five feet tall. His long hair and his skin were milk white, like an albino's, but his eyes were huge and green instead of tinged with pink. His chin and nose and ears were all sharply pointed, and he wore the most extravagant clothes Tansie had ever seen, a knee-length coat with brocade and epaulets of gold over puffy pants gathered at the knee above high red boots. His shirt looked like the kind of blouse her eighth grade music teacher had always worn, except that it had a lace collar. And, of course, Tansie's eighth grade music teacher had never carried a sword.

The blade was thin and gleamed in the light of the overhead fluorescents, but then practically everything about the man gleamed, from his clothes to his boots to the rings he wore on every finger. He caused the tip of the blade to move in a lazy figure eight, and said, "The honor has been given me to—"

He stopped talking when Tansie threw the pan straight at his face for all she was worth. It caught him in the forehead edge on, and he folded to the ground in an almost prim fashion, blood pouring from a huge welt above his white eyebrow, and, Tansie had to be imagining this, *steaming* as it flowed freely into his fluttering eyes.

Tansie stood still for a moment, waiting to see if the man would rise, but he appeared to be out cold. *Dead?* She couldn't think about that.

Instead, she rushed through the living room and into the den where she'd moved her grandmother's bed when getting her up and down the stairs grew to be too much trouble. She expected to find her standing in her nightgown, searching for her canes. But she was still under the hand-pieced quilt, softly snoring. How could all that noise not have woken her when a car driving by could be enough to make her cry out?

Tansie took her grandmother's stout oak cane from its place leaning against the nightstand. She cautiously walked back through the living room with it held out before her in two hands like a softball bat.

The blood on the kitchen floor *was* steaming where it pooled around the skillet. But where was—

The man stepped out of nowhere, his arm moving so fast it blurred. Pain shot up from Tansie's palms and wrists where his sword came down on the cane, not just knocking it from her grasp but slicing it cleanly in two.

"No more of that, half-breed," he said, his voice low and threatening. He held a dishrag to his forehead in the hand that did not hold the sword to her throat.

Tansie leaned back from the point of the sword but the man simply took a graceful step forward. She felt the steel tip graze the hollow of her throat where her collarbones met, and then a lightning fast jab like a vaccination shot. Involuntarily, her hands went to her throat, where she felt the welting of a drop of blood.

"Now we have each wounded one another," said the man, "and I need not kill you unless you carry on attacking me." He didn't lower the sword.

"I won't," whispered Tansie, terrified. "I won't attack you."

The handset of the phone still lay on the floor where she'd dropped it, and it suddenly let forth with a loud, repeating beep. Showing his uncanny speed again, the man whipped his sword around, severed the coiled yellow cord, and brought the blade back to bear on Tansie, all in the space of a quick breath.

"A talking machine, yes?" asked the man. "You meant to call for aid. But, Lady, you have nothing to fear. I am the knight of the Queen's message, sent here only to escort you to your new home."

The Queen's message. The letter.

"The letter was to my mother. I... I opened it by accident."

The man cocked his head to one side, and at that moment Tansie realized that the reason his accent was familiar was that it was the same as the strange postwoman's from that afternoon. "This is of no import," he said. "You are Tanistasia, the daughter of Prince Killian of blessed memory, borne by the human woman Eileen Abnett, yes?"

Tansie lifted her gaze from the sword to the stranger's green eyes. "I'm Tansie Abnett. I don't know who my father is." Then, "If I don't have anything to fear why are you pointing that sword at me?"

The man cocked his head in the other direction, and Tansie thought of eagles or owls. For a moment, she was afraid he was going to stab her again, but then he stood up straight and moved the tip of the sword so that it nearly rested on his chin. Then his tongue, as black as his skin was white, darted out and touched the blade's point. His nostrils flared and his eyes widened. "Yes," he said, with an odd hissing noise, "it is polluted by mortality but it is the blood of my Queen in your veins."

He backed away from Tansie, spread his arms as wide as he could in the galley kitchen, and bowed. Then, not turning his back to her, he stepped back and kicked the bloody skillet through the still-open back door. It made a dull clang when it hit the brickwork walk.

"Iron is an ugly thing," he said. "Not often wielded by a princess."

It occurred to Tansie then that the man was completely insane.

"Are you one of my mother's ex-husbands?" she asked.

The man opened his mouth as if he were about to answer, but then closed it again. He blinked very slowly, twice.

Then he said, "I am Gothwiddion, the Primrose Knight."

Tansie studied the man's elaborate clothing again and decided he probably wasn't her mother's type. Aloud, she said, "Are there any little dots over your name?"

The man's smile was not pleasant. His teeth were white but looked like they had been sharpened with a file, and his gums were as black as his tongue. "Prince Killian was a jokester and a player of games, as well."

Killian. Her supposed dead father.

"So your queen is my other grandmother?"

The man nodded. "Ilinana, Queen of the Ljósálfar and Lady of the Realm Beyond, most beautiful of the High Fey and immortal ruler of us all. And the mother of your father of blessed memory, yes."

Tansie thought about her grandmother's gentle snoring and, for some reason, realized just then she had forgotten to pick up the chicken leg from the living room floor.

"And you're here to, what, take me away to fairyland?"

Again, the discomfiting smile. "You say the word like you can imagine it, Lady, but I assure you, you cannot. Compared to this sad world, the glory of the Realm Beyond is the fire of a thousand suns next to a dying ember. The life that awaits you is exalted beyond anything any human has ever lived on the mortal plane."

For some reason, this reminded Tansie of the stories she had heard about foster care from some of the kids on the at-risk track. It was always advertised as going someplace better by the people taking you away from your home. Gothwiddion the Primrose Knight sounded like he worked for Child Protective Services.

She examined the strange man more closely and realized that there was now no sign of the bloody wound that she had opened above his eye with the iron skillet. Why was that the most frightening thing that had happened yet?

"What if I don't want to go?" she asked him.

The man shrugged. "My charge was to await the breaking of the seal and then retrieve you. No mention was made of your desires." His voice had taken on that edge again. But then he relaxed, and said, "Life at court is nothing but an endless round of pleasures."

It sounded like the kind of place her mother would like.

She thought of what he had said before about the seal. That was the wax on the back of the letter, the letter to her mother.

"'On your release...'" she said aloud.

The man narrowed his eyes. "My release?"

"The letter from your Queen to my mother. It says that you'll take me... wherever, *on my mother's release.*"

The man sheathed his sword, but she remembered how fast he could draw it again. He reached into one of his voluminous sleeves and pulled out a sheet of paper rolled up into a scroll, the same color as the letter to her mother. He unrolled the sheet, read it quickly, then thrust it back in his sleeve.

"What of it?" he asked.

Gothwiddion the Primrose Knight seemed like somebody who liked rules.

"Well, maybe my desires don't come into it, but that's an order from your Queen, right? Doesn't it say you need my mother's permission to take me?"

An incredulous look crossed his face. "You are maneuvering to *stay* here?" He gestured, the sweep of his arm taking in the dingy kitchen, the falling-down house, the sketchy neighborhood, the whole wide world. Again, he said, "*Here?*"

Her house, her world.

She wasn't her mother.

The man made a scoffing sound. "Then I will go to your mother and obtain her release," he said. "Where is she?"

It was Tansie's turn to shrug. "You're not the only one who wants to know."

The man waved a hand at her, disgusted, then, unexpectedly, let out a high whistle. There was a sound of something very large moving in the back yard. Tansie supposed if he was some kind of knight, he must have some kind of mount. She was afraid to go see what it might look like.

"Now I must quest across the mortal world to find this woman," he said. "You could have won an ally this day, Lady, instead of making an enemy."

Tansie didn't think she needed allies like this man, but as he started to leave, she held up her hand and said, "Wait."

When he paused, she rushed into the dining room and scrambled under the dining room table. He was still in the kitchen when she returned, so she thrust the paper bags full of bills and notices and summons into his arms.

"Take these," she said.

HOME IS THE HAUNTER
GARTH NIX

THE CANNON WAS one hundred and twenty-five feet long and its rifled bore tapered from six feet in diameter at the breech to two foot nine and three quarter inches at the muzzle, using the old measures of the Mergantz system. Cast in bronze, the vast weapon's entire length was adorned with cryptic writings and fevered drawings of tormented souls, acid-etched into the metal. Never designed to be moved at all, the great gun was currently being transported upon a dozen carefully-lashed-together ox carts, the whole being drawn by six mokleks, the shorn and gentled draft animals that were not to be confused with their wild cousins, the hairy mammoths of the icy wastes.

Sir Hereward was seated inside the howdah of the lead moklek, resting uncomfortably on the slightly-padded shelf that was supposed to be a seat, and might have served as such for a shorter and slighter man. He would have preferred to be astride a battlemount or a horse, but their last horse had died the week before, and their last battlemount a few days after its final meal of horse.

The mokleks would go next, Hereward thought, though their most pressing need was for water rather than food. He could then survive on moklek meat and blood for a considerable time thereafter, but without the draft animals the cannon would have to be abandoned here on the featureless steppe, the interminable grassy plain that he had loathed from the start of this ill-fated journey.

They were taking a route that his companion Mister Fitz had claimed would cut weeks from the more usual way between Low Yalpen and Jeminero. That followed the switch-backed road up and through the passes of the Kapoman range. Though they would have needed even more mokleks to make the grade, the high road had no shortage of springs and wells and even several well-spaced and highly hospitable caravanserais.

Hereward's dry throat instinctively swallowed at the thought of arriving at one of those grand hostels, to be met at the gate with a silver ewer of chilled wine, as was the traditional welcome to important travelers. But the high Kapoman passes, the caravanserais and the chilled wine were regrettably far distant. Here, there was only the sea of yellow grass that stretched ahead of him so monochromatically, till at the horizon it met with the downward-curving expanse of an equally featureless sky of endless blue.

The knight sighed and shifted the carbine off his legs, so that he could stretch out and push his feet against the front wall. But the thin pink-lacquered timber, hardly thicker than parchment, promptly splintered under his boot heels and the rear of the howdah began to bend behind him, requiring him to sit up straight again.

"Please do not destroy our accommodation," called out Mister Fitz as he climbed up the ear of the moklek. The ears were the only parts of the animal left unshorn, and a plaited and knotted rope of hair hung from each lobe to allow their mahouts an easy way to climb aboard.

"You will be glad of it when the rains begin," continued the puppet as he continued up onto the high roof of the howdah, which was made of thick canvas, painted with an oily concoction—also pink—that supposedly would repel any rain short of a tropical cloudburst. Not that there had been any rain, and in fact there was not even a single cloud to take the sting out of the sun. Even this late in the afternoon it still burned fiercely hot.

"What rain?" asked Hereward. He spoke to the puppet's shadow directly above him, showing through the pink canvas roof like a dark stain. "I keep hearing promises of rain, but I believe there is some requirement for clouds to be in the sky first."

"The rains are some days late, it is true," agreed Mister Fitz. "However, I do not believe it is a matter of concern."

"Possibly because you do not need to drink. However, I and the mokleks do, so if you have any thoughts about finding water, I would welcome them."

Above Sir Hereward, Mister Fitz's pumpkin-shaped papier-mache head slowly swiveled around a full three hundred and sixty degrees before finally stopping as his gaze focused ahead and somewhat to the right of their line of march.

"I do not believe it is a matter of concern," repeated Mister Fitz, "because we shall shortly be wading through the stuff. I expect you will then curse the abundance of water, rather than the lack."

"Wading? Through what?" asked Sir Hereward. He shielded his eyes with his hand, and looked where the shadow of Fitz's arm pointed, but all he could see was the heat haze shimmering off the yellow grass.

"The Shallows, as the folk hereabouts call them," said Mister Fitz. "You will see them in a few more minutes, when we reach the crest of this rise."

"Rise?" asked Sir Hereward. He looked behind and scowled. He had thought they were making slow progress for flat country, but now he saw that the ground behind did slope away, albeit very gently. The ubiquity of the yellow grass and the heat haze had disguised the lay of the land, and he was disappointed in himself that he had not noticed it. As a soldier he prided himself on his awareness of any advantages or disadvantages the ground might offer if, as was often the case, battle was suddenly joined.

"Yes, a rise," said Mister Fitz. "We have climbed some sixty-eight paces in the last league. Assisted by the haze, an increase in altitude sufficient to mask the Shallows, even from the back of a moklek. Ah, look ahead now."

Hereward grunted as he turned about again and put another dent in the howdah with his elbow.

"Do be careful," chided Mister Fitz.

Hereward did not answer. He was gaping at the suddenly transformed vista that lay ahead. It was like one of the trompe l'oeil shows of the Participatory Theatre of Hurshell, where backdrop after backdrop slid away to reveal new scenes and worlds. Admittedly, the panorama of clear water and reedy islands ahead lacked the fornicating nymphs and satyrs of the Hurshell, which were possibly the real reason the theatre flourished, not the scenery behind the frolics.

"It seems unusual, topographically speaking," said Hereward. "A freshwater lake shallow enough to wade through—why does it not dry up?"

"It is the relic of a god," said Mister Fitz, in his instructional voice. "Some two thousand years ago, a benign entity known as Ryzha the Twelve-Wheeled, who since time immemorial had roamed the steppe, was partially subsumed by a much more aggressive intruder from the Beyond. The resulting entity, which became known as Yeogh-Yeogh the Two-Headed, was driven mad by its conflicting natures and wreaked great destruction before, with a little assistance, Ryzha managed to assert itself for the several minutes required to irretrievably cut its throat with one of its own sharpened hooves. A vast quantity of the godlet's blood spread across the steppe, and yet another struggle occurred as the dying godlets fought to render it into either acid or poison or something beneficial. I believe Ryzha tried to make it fermented goat milk, but instead achieved sweet water, which is preferable in any case, and certainly an improvement over the lake of extreme toxicity which Yeogh-Yeogh favoured. The sweet water has remained ever since, and so the Shallows were made."

"You mentioned Ryzha had a little help..." said Hereward, with a knowing glance at the puppet.

"Yes," said Mister Fitz. "Though not, in this case, from me. One of our own was involved, a distant relative of yours as it happens. You remind me of her sometimes."

"Oh?" asked Hereward. He smiled and sat up a little straighter. "In what fashion?"

"A certain similarity of facial hair," said Mister Fitz. "That, and an unfortunate tendency to lack forethought and allow unwarranted enthusiasms to distract you from the most pressing matters at hand. In fact, perhaps if I were to tell you of some of her more egregious follies, it might benefit your own—"

"Facial hair?" interrupted Sir Hereward. "A female ancestor of mine had a *beard*?"

"Whatever gave you that notion?" asked Mister Fitz. "Your *eyebrows* are identical, and incidentally, you have proven my statement about enthusiasms distracting you. You should have asked an improving question, not one about hair."

"An improving question?" asked Sir Hereward slowly. He was looking to the front, once again shading his eyes with his hand. "How about 'what is that fortification that lies ahead?'"

"Interesting..." came the puppet's musing reply. Sir Hereward saw Fitz's shadow lengthen as the puppet stood up on the roof. "I have no knowledge of any habitation here. It is a manor house of some kind, perhaps four or five hundred years old if I am any judge. A little newer than the most recent map in my collection."

The manor house in question was a squat, rectangular fortress some one hundred and fifty feet long, perhaps eighty wide and five storeys high, all but the highest two floors presenting a blank expanse of tightly-fitted ashlar stone. Even those top levels only had arrow slits, and there were no battlements, the whole being topped by a low-pitched roof of greenish copper.

The house was built upon hundreds of log piles, Hereward surmised, the evidence for this being a burned and destroyed lesser building some distance from the main structure, where the remnants of the piles that had once been its foundation stuck out of the water like a row of heavily decayed dragon teeth.

"A lonely house," remarked the knight. "Who would build such a place here?"

"It is not so strange," said Mister Fitz. "One moment."

He jumped down from the roof of the howdah and went to the head of the moklek, leaning down to whisper something near its ear, before he turned to continue talking to Hereward.

The moklek, who was the lead animal by virtue of being the smartest of the six, changed direction slightly, aiming towards the right of the manor house. The others followed dutifully, and the cannon trundled behind on its many well-greased wheels. Though the gun-carriage was jury-rigged from common ox carts and resembled a kind of articulated reptile of multiple segments, it had been carefully designed by Sir Hereward and put together by expert artisans, and the purely mechanical nature of its joints and bindings had been bolstered by the sorcerous intervention of Mister Fitz. No mere hole, bump, mound or minor obstacle could deter its passage, provided the mokleks continued to pull it with their full strength.

"It is not so strange," continued the puppet. "The Shallows abound with fish and other comestible aquatic life, including a weed that is dried and blended into a smoking mixture by the people of Kquq, which lies no more than a hundred and fifty leagues away. The Kquqers come three or four times a year, to harvest the weed, or at least they used to within recent memory. I would surmise that this fortification was built by some enterprising bandit with a view to exacting a suitable toll or impost upon that trade, eventually legitimizing themselves as an aristocrat."

"A weed-taxer," grunted Hereward. His bottom hurt and he was not inclined to be charitable. "Hardly a noble calling. Is there not some greater authority hereabouts who would take such carryings-on amiss?"

"None is known," said Mister Fitz. "Long ago, this was part of the demesne of the Exclusiarch of Ryzha, the godlet's principal servant, who was a semi-independent vassal of the Emperor in Kahaon. Since Ryzha's fall and the unrelated but consequent decline of the Kahaonese, dozens of petty states have temporarily exerted their control. No significant political entity claims these lands now, at least not in any active fashion."

"The house, however, is inhabited," said Sir Hereward. "Look, to the top left, there is the flash of a perspective glass in the second arrow-slit."

"Indeed," said Mister Fitz, whose odd blue orbs were keener than any mere mortal eyes. "We are being observed by a woman. Several other women cluster tight behind her, hoping for a turn at the glass, yet judging by their posture, cannot clamour or snatch, and must wait for the current wielder who doubtless is their superior... perhaps even the mistress of the house."

Hereward leaned forward in sudden attention, accidentally damaging yet more of the howdah, and searched through the saddlebags at his feet for his own spyglass, a fine instrument originally owned by a famous general of artillery. It was so well-constructed that it was the only item to survive the general's death, when the rather too short fuse of the petard he was inspecting was lit by his own cigarillo. The lenses, of course, had needed to be replaced, as did the outer case of sharkskin-covered bronze, but it was in all other respects the same.

But by the time Hereward had found it, snapped it fully open, and raised it to his eye, there was only an empty arrow-slit to look at. The womenfolk had gone.

"Did they appear friendly?" asked Hereward. "Should we... ah... skirt the place?"

Mister Fitz leaned over the edge of the howdah's roof, and neatly flipped himself over to land at Hereward's side.

"Spare me your attempts at wordplay," said the puppet. "I would adjudge the occupants as being welcoming, even receptive. Furthermore, I suggest that we stop this night within, if they offer hospitality."

"Did I hear you correctly?" asked Sir Hereward with no small suspicion. It was not like Mister Fitz to think of comfortable beds or the chance of something more interesting to eat than dry biscuit and horsemeat. After all, he did not sleep or eat.

"There is something in the air, or perhaps the water..." said the puppet slowly. He swiveled his head around in a full circle again, very slowly. "Some arcane presence is close by, though I cannot exactly place it. And as you know, I have but a single energistic needle left in my sewing desk and so I am... we are... ill-prepared for any sorcerous foe. We may need to be behind stout walls come nightfall."

Hereward scowled and also looked around, but all he could see was blue sky, the endless yellow grass of the steppe, the reflection of the sun on the water of the Shallows, and the tall manor house.

"I will load my pistols with silver shot," he said. The carbine was merely charged with lead. He hesitated, then added, "How serious is this threat? Should I get the old dagger out of the... ah... howdah-bag?"

Mister Fitz turned his head a little way to the left and then back again to the right, still questing for the source of his disquiet.

"Yes," he said finally. "It may well prove a greater help than hindrance, for once."

The old dagger was one of the two items they had been charged to deliver to Jeminero, a great and ancient city that was readying for war. The other item was the cannon, and it was not certain which of the two weapons might be more useful when the time came. Particularly as there was some question whether either of them would be any use at all. The cannon had its peculiarities, perhaps the most significant being that it was breech-loaded via a rotating chamber, and required either sorcery or two score mightily-thewed gunners and a thirty-foot high shear-legs to open the chamber, load the cartridge and shot and then rotate it back into place within the barrel again.

The old dagger, while not needing any such muscular preparation, was an entrapped extra-dimensional entity that tended towards a less than useful relationship with its various wielders. It had unique powers and, unfortunately, a mind of its own. A not very improved or civilized mind, which made it an unreliable and often unpleasant companion even when not being actively employed. When it *was* used, it became extraordinarily dangerous. Fortunately, some three centuries after its initial forging, some long-forgotten sorcerer had made the dagger a scabbard which put it into a comfortable and apparently very satisfying sleep, quietening its complaints, insults and attempts at solo forays.

Like the cannon, the dagger was a weapon of last resort.

Sir Hereward thought of this as he reached over the side and undid the straps on the topmost of the six large bags that hung down the side of the moklek in a nested cascade of pink canvas. The old dagger was the sole item in the top bag. He pulled it out, and carefully checked that the peace strings and accompanying wax seals were still in place, and the weapon secure in its scabbard.

It was a surprisingly small dagger. The blade measured less than the distance from his wrist to the tip of his index finger, and the hilt appeared to have been made to fit a child's hand. Yet in its own way, the dagger was as dangerous a weapon as the vast cannon the mokleks dragged behind them...

Tucking the dagger through his belt, Sir Hereward took out a mahogany box from a howdah bag on the other side of the moklek. It contained two duelling pistols; ready-made paper cartridges of powder; a dozen perfectly-round silver pistol balls; priming powder in a patented triangular applicator that was far less useful than its inventor imagined; pre-cut wads of thick felt that had been printed with curses and imprecations; and a serviceable ramrod that had replaced the uselessly ornate one that had been in the original set.

Hereward quickly loaded and primed the pistols and settled them in his broad leather belt. Only then did he take up his spyglass again and focus it upon the large and imposing gate of the manor house ahead, just in time to catch a flash of colour and movement.

The flash came from the wine-red dress of a woman as she hitched it up at the thighs so that it wouldn't drag in the ankle-deep water that surrounded the house. Through the glass, she appeared to be no more than forty, and comely, though Hereward could not yet make out whether she bore the facial scarifications that to him would elevate her from mere prettiness to true beauty.

She had a hand-and-a-half sword slung on her back, the bronze cross-piece almost as wide as her shoulders and the blade stretching from neck to knees. Hereward looked at the corded muscle in her wrists and knew that she could use the massive sword. The weapon was not just for show.

A dozen women followed half a dozen yards behind the tall one with the over-sized sword. They wore serviceable boiled leather cuirasses over plain linen shifts and several of them, Sir Hereward noted, carried racked crossbows with bolts in place, and all of them bore dirks in tinned iron sheaths tied to their thighs.

"Halt the mokleks," said Sir Hereward. "I would lief as not stay out of range of those arbalests."

"They will not shoot," said Mister Fitz. "Look, their chief advances alone, greatsword sheathed upon her back. You should descend and meet her."

Sir Hereward could walk faster than the mokleks' steady pace, at least when they were dragging the giant cannon, but he was not overly keen to do so. The extrémely thick, wrinkled skin of moklek might turn a crossbow bolt, but he wore no armour in the heat, his linen shirt offering no protection against anything but the sun.

"I think we need to get inside soon," said Mister Fitz slowly, once again surveying the land around them. "It is also likely these women have knowledge of... whatever is going to happen."

"Which is what?" asked Sir Hereward crossly, as he clambered out of the howdah and cautiously crawled over the flat, broad head of the moklek.

"I do not know," said Mister Fitz slowly. "Something is coming. From some other plane that intersects here, where it should not."

Sir Hereward heard the tone in the puppet's voice. Though Mister Fitz was never afraid as such, there was a certain amount of what could only be described as dread in his words.

The knight grabbed the highest knot of the dozen or so that ran the length of the strand of ear-hair, swung so as to place his feet on a lower knot, and descended knot by knot to the ground. There, he matched his pace to the moklek's, and looked back up to Mister Fitz.

"Throw down my sabre," he said. "If you would be so kind."

Mister Fitz easily lifted the weapon from the howdah, and pitched it down. Sir Hereward caught it and buckled the scabbard on, drawing the blade out a few inches and back again, to ensure that it moved freely. His hand was slightly sweaty, but the sabre's sharkskin grip was never slippery, be it inundated in sweat, blood or other fluids. Mister Fitz had ensorcelled it long ago, together with several other minor enchantments that made it a most valuable blade.

"You're sure these women are friendly?" asked Sir Hereward.

"Moderately so," replied Mister Fitz. His hand was tightly closed, but even so there was now the hint of some horrible brightness beneath his wooden fist, indicating he held his last sorcerous needle there. "I stand ready in the event I am mistaken."

Taking a deep breath, Sir Hereward settled his pistols for a quick draw, and splashed forward to meet the woman in the deep red dress, thinking that if her cohorts did raise their arbalests it would be a tricky thing to dive under the bolts without his pistols taking in rather too much water, and a sodden dash forward with his sabre would also be rather slower than desired, perhaps even allowing them time to reload and retension their weapons. In which case, he would have to use the old dagger, and this was potentially more dangerous than meeting a fusillade of crossbow bolts, even with Mister Fitz standing by with his sorcerous needle to protect him...

As he drew closer, Sir Hereward observed the women handled their weapons well and were watching carefully. But their attentions were not exclusive to him. Most of them were actually looking out across the Shallows to the left and right, as if some enemy might emerge from the waters. Nevertheless,

Sir Hereward took care to keep himself in line with their leader, so that only the flankers would get a decent shot. When he was half a dozen paces away, the swordswoman stopped, and Sir Hereward followed suit.

"Well met, good sir," said the woman, her voice evidently trained for authority and projection. "I am the Archimandress Withra. You are a most welcome guest, for this Wedding Night."

Sir Hereward instinctively took a step backward at the mention of a wedding. But his natural good manners did not desert him, and he managed to incorporate this backward step into a sweeping bow, though his eyes never left the Archimandress or the crossbows of her companions.

"Sir Hereward of the High Pale," he said. He gestured back at the lead moklek, where Mister Fitz could be seen perched on the howdah. "And my companion, Mister Fitz."

"A self-willed puppet," said the Archimandress, raising her eyebrows. The tiny jewels pasted there caught the sunlight as they moved. "It is long since we have been fortunate enough to welcome a puppet entertainer. I hope he will play and sing for us at our feast."

Sir Hereward kept his face immobile, not wanting to reveal any hint that unlike the vast majority of self-willed puppets, Mister Fitz was not an entertainer.

"We bid you both welcome, Sir Hereward, and invite you to take refuge within our convent."

"Refuge?" asked Sir Hereward.

"Indeed," said the Archimandress. She cast a glance towards the western horizon, where the sun was beginning to settle. "As a man, you have chosen an inopportune time to cross the Shallows."

"As a man?" asked Hereward.

"Tonight the Hag of the Shallows seeks a husband," said Withra. "She roams the Shallows looking for suitable candidates till the dawn. But I expect we can keep you safe inside our house."

"What precisely is this 'Hag of the Shallows'?" asked Sir Hereward. "And what does she do with her... ahem... husbands?"

"She rises from the Shallows this one day of the year, a thing of impenetrable darkness wreathed in fog and rain," said Withra, not really answering the question. "Her chosen husbands are found soon after dawn, or rather the chewed remnants of them are found..."

"I see," said Sir Hereward. He looked back at the lead moklek, which was ambling forward again. This was a conversation that Mister Fitz needed to be involved in, and the sooner the puppet *was* involved, the happier Sir Hereward would be. "And what exactly do you ladies do here, may I ask?"

"We belong to the Sacred Order of the Sisters of Mercantile Fairness of the Goddess Lanith-Eremot," said Withra. "Our convent here was established with a perpetual endowment from the Council of Seven in the city of Kquq, in order that we might protect their weed-gatherers from competitors, predators and unfortunate events. But come, the light already fails. We must all withdraw inside."

Sir Hereward hesitated. Mister Fitz had said they should seek shelter, but uncharacteristically he felt more cautious than he usually did when conversing with an attractive woman who was inviting him indoors. He had no knowledge of the goddess Lanith-Eremot, so there was a possibility she was proscribed and thus no friend to the likes of the knight and his puppet companion. Nor had he ever heard of the Sisters of Mercantile Fairness.

"I hesitate to ask," he said. "But I trust that in accepting your kind and gracious invitation, we will not be incurring any debt or entering into any arrangement beyond the mere acceptance of customary shelter, and that we will be free to leave unhindered and unharmed in the morning?"

"The Sisterhood has no ill intentions toward anyone save weed-stealers or other criminals, and it is part of the charter of the Sisters of Mercantile Fairness to offer hospitality to travellers. In some other convents there is a small charge for this, but not here, the Kquq Council of Seven having provided sufficient funds for the purpose in the original endowment. Ah, your puppet friend closes. Greetings, Master Puppet."

"Greetings," replied Mister Fitz from atop the moklek. He inclined his pumpkin-shaped head stiffly, moving slowly with small jerks and tics. This was a common practice with him, to instil in strangers a false notion of his flexibility and speed.

"This is the Archimandress Withra of the Sisters of Mercantile Fairness, who follow the goddess Lanith-Eremot," said Sir Hereward quickly, only half-turning towards Mister Fitz, at the same time calculating that he could shoot the two closer crossbow priestesses, throw his pistols down, draw his sabre and run Withra through before she could get the greatsword off her back, and then retreat holding her body up as a shield—

"I know of your order," said Mister Fitz. He pitched his voice higher and softer than usual, to enhance the impression he was one of the entertaining type of self-willed puppets. "Your good reputation travels far, and I am very pleased that we should meet such noble sisters here."

Sir Hereward's thoughts made a sharp turn away from the consideration of imminent combat and he relaxed a little. Mister Fitz would not speak so fulsomely if Lanith-Eremot was proscribed, or the Sisters an outlawed organization. But while he was less worried about the women, he was growing ever more concerned at the gathering dusk and the threat of this creature that sought a husband, or as seemed more accurate to say, a meal to be made of a male personage.

"The Archimandress invites us inside," said Hereward. "Apparently there is a... thing... called the Hag of the Shallows that will rise tonight and seek a husband, and I fear I am the only eligible prospect."

"A situation not to be envied, I apprehend," said Mister Fitz gravely. He looked around again, his tongue of blue stippled leather tasting the air, as if it had slipped out by accident.

"Perhaps if we continued on apace," said Sir Hereward. Fitz seemed undecided and he wanted to distract the priestess from the puppet. "We might remove ourselves from this Hag's hunting grounds in time?"

"I fear she ranges very widely," said Withra. "There is less than an hour until full dark, and already I feel her emanations gathering."

"Perhaps we should take shelter, Sir Hereward," said Mister Fitz, adding a quaver to his voice. "What might this Hag do to a puppet of the masculine persuasion? I am called 'Mister' after all!"

"True, true," said Sir Hereward, relieved that Fitz had come to a decision. "But first we must relieve the mokleks of their harness and let them forage and bathe. That is..."

He paused.

"Does this Hag of the Shallows molest animals as well?" he continued, thinking of their mission to deliver the cannon, which would be impossible without the mokleks.

"If they are male, of a certainty," said Withra. "However, having suffered the cut, they should be safe enough."

Hereward suppressed a wince at the thought of that cut. He had seen the thing done upon one occasion, which was more than enough. However, he did not want to reveal a weakness in front of the priestess and her womenfolk.

"If you will grant us a little time, milady, we will tend to our mokleks and then accept your kind invitation and enter your fortress," said Sir Hereward.

"Certainly," replied Withra. "Our doors are open to you, and you are welcome guests. But do be sure you come within before night falls. The gate will be locked then, and not reopened until well after the dawn."

Sir Hereward bowed and backed away. Withra inclined her head and did an about turn to slosh back to the manor house, her followers in two files behind. The sun, now setting behind the fortification, cast a red glint across everything and made the priestess's shadows long and thin and predatory, rippling across the shallow water.

It took Sir Hereward and Mister Fitz only twenty minutes to lift down the essential items they wished to carry inside, unbuckle the mokleks from their harness and slide the howdah off the back of the lead beast by means of its cunning system of blocks and lines. After a word with Mister Fitz, the massive creatures trod further into the Shallows, into a deeper pool. There, they took up water in their trunks and sprayed themselves and each other with all the gravity and deliberation that tired human workers might show upon taking a long-awaited bath after a weary day.

The cannon lay on its wagons, pointing at the north-western corner of the manor house. Sir Hereward hadn't noticed this at first, and it now irritated his professional instincts. The gun was charged, because this was the safest way to transport the arcane powder, a massive five-hundred weight cartridge bag made of seven thicknesses of calico, designed to keep out both water and stray sparks. But the cannon was not loaded with shot. In fact, it was unlikely anywhere within a thousand leagues could supply a ball of the prodigious size necessary to fit the bore, let alone one with the required sorcerous properties to complement the magic that had been infused in the weapon.

The chamber that held the charge was also kept open rather than being rotated shut in the firing position, so in the event of accidental discharge, there would be a lesser effluxion of flame and bits of calico out the business end of the barrel. But even without shot and the chamber open, Sir Hereward considered that in the event of accident the concussive and fiery force delivered would be extremely detrimental to the fabric of the building. The cannon really should not be aimed at anything but sky.

However, as the sun was now but a reddish blur on the horizon and the mokleks loosed, there was no time to put it right. He dismissed his uneasiness as mere parade ground soldiering, the kind of rigid thinking that desired everything to be just so at all times regardless of circumstance, a form of thought that he despised.

Going towards the manor, Sir Hereward spoke quietly and close to Mister Fitz, who had been silent throughout the process of freeing the mokleks, his head shifting and his blue eyes constantly searching the Shallows about them as if he had little attention to spare for harnesses.

"What might this Hag of the Shallows be, do you think? And can our hostesses be entirely trusted?"

"Judging by the emanations I perceive, the Hag of the Shallows must be a powerful inter-dimensional entity that manifests here when there is some temporary but regular alignment of the spheres," said Mister Fitz quietly. "As to the sisters, their order has a good reputation. However, an isolated house like this may not conform to the characteristics of the sorority in general. As always, we must be on guard."

"At least the place looks defensible," said Sir Hereward, as they walked up the ramp of packed earth to the main gate, which was made of the black timber called *urross*, always much in demand for gates and doors due to its strength and resistance to fire. The gate was further studded for reinforcement with steel bolts, and daubed with runes which, to Sir Hereward at least, looked ancient and powerful.

"The sorcerous protections are competent," said Mister Fitz. "Augmented by the powers of the congregation within, they should suffice to keep out a marauding godlet."

"Good," said Sir Hereward, with some relief. "That is to say, excellent."

"Yet I am still uneasy," continued Mister Fitz. "I sense the immanence, but I cannot fix upon its location. However, on the balance of probability we should be safer within than without."

Sir Hereward didn't answer, his attention caught by the inner gate, likewise of *urross*, the murder holes in the ceiling of the passage between, and the hotfoot gutters that ran between the paving stones. Not that hot oil above and below would have any effect on your typical godlet, but there were often mortal allies to be reckoned with as well, priests and soldiers and fanatical followers. At least here in a temple building it was to be presumed that the goddess would provide powerful protection against enemies mortal and otherwise, imbuing the stones and mortar with her essence, and her followers with powers of both harm and healing. Though the strength of this protection depended greatly upon the relative presence of the goddess in question.

"Where lies the locus of the goddess Lanith-Eremot?" whispered Hereward to Mister Fitz as the outer gate was shut and barred behind them by two of the priestesses, and others opened the gate within. "Close by, I trust? Not too distant?"

"Two thousand leagues or more, by a straight path," said Mister Fitz. "Longer if a mortal must tread the way."

"A long way for a godlet to exert her power," said Sir Hereward dubiously.

"The distance in this case may not be material to the strength of Lanith-Eremot here. It is possible, even likely, that this place is a point of intersection for a number of different realities, hence the manifestation of the Hag. The natural barriers which resist otherworldly intrusions were worn thin by the conflict between Yeogh-Yeogh and Ryzha, and so interdimensional connections of various kinds will have occurred."

A great hall lay beyond the inner gate, a scene of considerable bustle and noise, evidently in preparation for a feast or celebration, with an array of long tables bedecked with good linen cloth and piled with silver plate. There were many more sisters here, engaged in arranging tablecloths, plate, cutlery, salt cellars, candlesticks and floral decorations. These buzzing workers wore simple habits of bright silver cloth for the novices and shimmering gold for the full sisters, but there were also many of the warriors about, two score at least of armed and armoured priestesses, who stood against the walls in obvious positions of guard.

One of the silver-clad novices, a comely lass with her black hair coiled on top of her head, approached and bowed to Sir Hereward.

"My name is Parnailam," she said. "I am to show you to the baths we reserve for our male guests, to rest and cleanse yourselves before the feast. I regret, Master Puppet, that we were not sure whether you bathe or not, but various oils and unguents have been laid by that may prove of use to you."

"I need nothing, but I thank you," said Mister Fitz absently. His head was craned back on his spindly neck, looking up at the hammer-beamed ceiling and the dyed-paper decorations that hung there. They were of red and blue, and showed a very male figure with a great phallus entwined by a godlet who was depicted as a kind of black cloud with six, grasping tentacular arms. "Tell me, what is the feast you celebrate tonight?"

"Why, it is the Wedding!" exclaimed Parnailam. "One of our principal feast-days."

"And what does the feast celebrate, what does this Wedding signify?" continued Mister Fitz.

Parnailam looked confused.

"I am only a novice," she said hesitantly. "You would have to ask one of the sisters, or the Archimandress herself. We do not participate in the full mysteries. After I show you to the baths, we will have hot spiced milk, sing hymn number five and go off to bed. I know the full sisters stay up *very* late and are oft tired and cross the next morning."

"Ah," said Sir Hereward. He looked up at the decorations and then around at all the priestesses and thoughts of the coupling nymphs of the Participatory Theatre of Hurshell once more flitted through his mind.

Mister Fitz did not ask any more questions, but strode jerkily along next to Sir Hereward, as if invisible strings pulled upon legs and arms that had become stiff from lack of lubrication, indicating a sorcerous puppet who had lived beyond his mysterious lifespan, the internal magic winding down with every step. He was almost over-doing the deception, thought Hereward, but as none of the priestesses seemed particularly to notice, perhaps the puppet knew best. As he usually did.

The bath house the two travellers were lead to was not of the 'Most Excellent Supreme Soakwash, Scrub and Toe Cleanse' class of the Kapoman caravanserais, but it boasted a large circular hot pool with steam rising in wafts, indicating it was warmed either by sorcery or more likely by subterranean fires; a narrow rectangular cold pool to wade up and down in; and a very shallow dish-like pool for soaking feet, this last already infused with pleasant-smelling herbs. Several enormous cushions sat nearby, next to an open cupboard stacked with towels beside a low table on which were arrayed brushes, sponges and numerous bottles of scent, oil and cleansing unguents.

"Do you require someone to scrub your back, Sir Hereward?" asked Parnailam, in an innocent tone that suggested she meant precisely that and no more.

Hereward glanced at Mister Fitz, who turned his head very slightly. Not quite a visible shake but a clear indication to the knight that this offer should be refused.

"I thank you, but no," said Sir Hereward. "I must first offer my devotions to my gods before I bathe, and this cannot be done in company. Besides, you have to get to your hot milk."

"Oh, they won't serve the milk till the bell," said Parnailam. "I will wait outside in case you need anything!"

She inclined her head and retreated out the door. Mister Fitz went to it as it shut and placed one wooden hand against the timber, to sense if she was close enough to listen. Sir Hereward put down his saddlebags, put his pistols carefully on the table, unhooked his sabre and balanced it against the cupboard and then fell back into the largest cushion. Stretching out, he luxuriated in the soft embrace of good goose feather stuffing, a relieving contrast to the howdah's bottom-numbing accommodations.

But he had little time to enjoy the comfort. Mister Fitz came away from the door and signaled to him to come close. Sir Hereward obeyed, getting up with a sigh to crouch down near the puppet, their heads close together.

"There is something wrong with the sisters," whispered Mister Fitz.

"What?" asked Sir Hereward. "Isn't it enough to have this Hag of the Shallows lurking about outside, we have to have a problem inside?"

"I am afraid I may have made an error," said Mister Fitz. "I am quite familiar with both Lanith-Eremot and the Sisters of Mercantile Fairness. There is no wedding of any kind celebrated in the worship of the goddess by either her secular or ecclesiastical followers."

"No wedding," repeated Sir Hereward.

"None," said Mister Fitz. "And the goddess is never depicted as a dark cloud with tentacular arms. Or even as a human female figure. She is normally portrayed as a sort of friendly money-lending monkey atop a pile of coins."

"You think the sisters have transferred their loyalties to some other godlet?"

"Possibly. If they have, most likely it will be to this Hag of the Shallows."

"And the Hag is what you sensed outside."

"Probably," said Mister Fitz. He hesitated, then added, "Though not only outside."

"You sense something *within* the walls?"

"Yes," said Mister Fitz. "And no."

"I fail to understand you," said Sir Hereward stiffly.

"It is both within and without," said Mister Fitz. "I cannot tell more exactly. But given that it is within as well, the sisters cannot be unaware of it and most likely are complicit in its actions."

"Are you sure?" asked Sir Hereward dubiously.

"No," answered Mister Fitz, shaking his head. "They seem to all my... usual... senses to be no more or less than they present themselves. But I don't like this wedding business. We should make plans to depart."

"Depart?" asked Sir Hereward. "Need I remind you this is a fortress?"

He stood up and replaced his pistols and sabre, and nervously fingered the heavy wax of the peace seals that kept the old dagger scabbarded and slumbering, content on his belt.

"We cannot sneak out the way we came. Dozens of armed sisters in the hall, the two gates and the guards there... how wide was that arrow slit up above, where Withra looked out?"

"You could not pass through it," adjudged Mister Fitz.

"We *might* be able to fight our way out with this," said Sir Hereward, very gently tapping the scabbard of the old dagger.

"A most unreliable artifact," said Mister Fitz. "With only one needle I am not certain I could protect you when it rebounds, as it always does."

Sir Hereward frowned. He knew only an outline of the history of the dagger. But he did know that after slaying a particular number of enemies—a number it alone decided in any given circumstance, without recourse to any outside advice or reckoning—it would return and kill its wielder as well, before resuming its slumber. The only times it had failed to do this had occurred when the wielder was protected by potent sorcery, and in two other singular cases. Once when deployed by the famous inventor Kalitheke, who had launched it from a massive ballista at his rivals in conclave several miles away and had then taken ship for distant parts, the dagger failing to pursue him across the ocean for fear of rust; and the second when it was employed by the incomparable duellist known only as the Swordmistress of Heganarat, who upon the dagger's return after it had killed her faithless husband and her six paramours, parried and danced around the weapon's thrusts and sallies for seven and a half hours before it dropped from exhaustion and demanded its scabbard. The Swordmistress died of a heart attack the next day, but it was still considered her greatest victory.

"Barricade and defend ourselves here till dawn?" asked Sir Hereward, looking around the room. There was only the one doorway, but the door was mere oak and would not hold long against mundane attacks, let alone anything sorcerous or extra-dimensional.

"Even if the entity that comes departs with daylight, the sisters will still be here," said Mister Fitz.

"The pool is heated," said Sir Hereward. "There is presumably a hypocaust beneath. We can drain it, break the tiles... you, at least, might exit through those tunnels."

"Perhaps," said Mister Fitz. "Go and summon our guide. I am sure she will not be far away."

"What do you intend for her?" asked Sir Hereward.

"I will take a little blood and examine the signatures within," said Mister Fitz. "If we find evidence of an unknown godlet we will know the sisters are under its thrall and must act accordingly. If we do not... then there is a chance we will be able to negotiate with them. Lanith-Eremot was ever fair-minded."

"And if we can't negotiate?"

"I still have one needle," said Mister Fitz. "I can get us out, I think. After that, we might have a chance, if we take the lead moklek only and strike across the water. But that is a last resort, for we would certainly be pursued."

Sir Hereward nodded, his face grim. Opening the door, he looked out along the narrow corridor. Sure enough, Parnailam was standing by the doorway to the hall, chatting quietly to another silver-clad novice.

"I fear I need assistance with the removal of my boots," called out Sir Hereward. "Mister Fitz lacks the strength and I have left my jack in one of the moklek bags we didn't bring inside. Could I ask you to help me?"

"Surely, sir," called Parnailam. She came quickly to the door. Hereward stepped aside to let her pass and as she went into the room Mister Fitz jumped upon her back, ran up onto her shoulders and pressed his wooden fingers into the woman's temples. She gasped and dropped unconscious into Hereward's arms. He laid her gently down on one of the big cushions and shut the door.

As he had latched the door closed, the puppet took a very small but intensely sharp knife and a glass slide from somewhere about his person and nicked the young woman's thumb, catching a droplet of blood. Taking this to his portable sewing desk, a wooden case that casual observers presumed to be an instrument case for a clavichord or something similar, Mister Fitz smeared the blood across the slide and applied a series of alchemical fluids from small bottles. This fixed the blood in place and slowly revealed a striation of coloured lines, in the main blue and green with some yellow between, the colours to be expected from a generally benevolent godlet's presence in the bloodstream of one of its devout worshippers.

"Lanith-Eremot," said Mister Fitz. "I don't even need to check the book, I know the signature well. And no sign of anything else. It is extremely puzzling."

"Perhaps the novices and younger sisters are not part of the conspiracy," said Sir Hereward. "You recall they are sent to bed. How long will she slumber?"

"A few minutes," said Mister Fitz.

"If I draw her companion in, and we take their robes, could you cast a glamour upon us?" asked Sir Hereward.

Mister Fitz shook his head.

"Consecrated robes would resist our wearing them, and I dare not waste the power of my needle in small workings. No. Given the signature, I think—"

Sir Hereward held up his hand and jerked his head towards the door. Many feet could be heard, and not the soft swish of novice's slippers, but the boots of armed priestesses.

Knight and puppet moved quickly. Sir Hereward took one corner, levelling a pistol in his left hand and cocking it before also drawing his sabre. Mister Fitz scrambled up on top of the towel cupboard and drew out his last sorcerous needle, cupping it close in his hand, its harsh, blinding light leaking out in narrow, brilliant rays between his fingers.

There was no knock upon the door, but neither was it flung open as at the beginning of an assault. The latch ascended slowly, the door swung open, and the Archimandress Withra looked cautiously into the room, her entire body encased in a pearly nimbus indicative of some divine protective power. She saw Parnailam laid out on the cushion and her face set for a moment, but cleared as she saw the novice's breast slowly rise and fall.

"She lives then," said Withra, glancing across at Sir Hereward. "I felt her slip from my mind, and feared the worst."

"She has taken no hurt," said Sir Hereward. "We merely wished to ascertain her true allegiance."

"And how would you do—" Withra began. She stopped talking as she caught a momentary flash of the violet brilliance contained in Mister Fitz's hand, and looked up and across at the cupboard. Stepping back, a curious expression passed fleetingly across her face, one Sir Hereward could not fully read, for it seemed in equal parts anger, relief and fear. "Ah, I see. You are not an *entertaining* puppet. My apologies, Magister."

"You know me?" asked Mister Fitz mildly.

"I know *of* you," said Withra. "I had thought you in the category of long-lost legend."

Her tone of voice conveyed respect and a healthy fear. Those who knew much about Mister Fitz's real powers and experience were generally extremely wary of him. Not to mention very polite.

"What exactly is going on here?" asked Sir Hereward peremptorily. He was somewhat miffed that Mister Fitz was getting all the respectful attention. "My companion tells me there is no wedding feast in your sisterhood's usual rites, and he... we... are concerned that you have transferred your allegiance to this Hag of the Shallows."

"Never!" spat out the Archimandress. She hesitated, then added, "However, it is true that we have had to make an accommodation with the Hag. I had hoped to keep you both in ignorance of this. However, clearly this is not possible."

Withra snapped her fingers, and the pearly radiance about her disappeared.

"There is no trouble. Go back to the hall," she said over her shoulder, her words answered by the sound of shuffling boots as a large party of armed priestesses withdrew along the passage outside.

Mister Fitz replaced his sorcerous needle inside his doublet, and Sir Hereward carefully closed the pan on his pistol and uncocked the lock, before replacing it through his belt.

"You made an accommodation?" asked Sir Hereward.

"Not at first," said Withra. "When the Hag appeared some sixty years ago, she was weak, and initially believed to be merely some sort of revenant or ghost, reappearing at the site of her demise. But as time went on, this haunting spirit grew more troublesome, so the sisters tried to exorcise it, without success. It grew stronger with every year, and a number of serious battles were fought. Though it only appeared once a year and for a single night, these were very costly fights. Great damage was done—this house is the third we have built since the Hag's appearance, you must have seen the remnants of the previous buildings. Eventually, my predecessor hit upon the idea that instead of fighting the revenant, we should placate the Hag by offering up the pretense of worship. It is only one day, after all—"

"Worship would not be sufficient in itself," interrupted Mister Fitz. He jumped easily down from the cupboard and went to stand near Sir Hereward. Though his round head only came up to the knight's belt, he dominated the room. "You must give the Hag something as well. A sacrifice."

Withra nodded reluctantly, licked her lips and swallowed, as if her mouth had suddenly dried.

"We give her half a dozen men. Weed-stealers, that have been caught by us, tried fairly in Kquq, sentenced to death and sent back."

Sir Hereward looked at Mister Fitz. A demand for human sacrifice was one of the defining characteristics that would place a godlet on the list of proscribed inter-dimensional entities.

"Do you know who or what the Hag actually is?" asked Mister Fitz. "You must have had many opportunities to take its signature."

"We have," said Withra. She had shrunk a little, it seemed, her shoulders lower. From shame, Sir Hereward suspected. "It is a relict of the malevolent portion of the combined entity known as Yeogh-Yeogh the Two-Headed. It was on this spot that the godlet died, and it is here that it returns on the evening of every seventh day of Rainith, returning to haunt us."

"I am extremely surprised the Grandmother-Marshal of your order would allow your 'accommodation'," continued Mister Fitz. "Surely greater forces could be arrayed and this relict of Yeogh-Yeogh banished for good and all?"

"The matter was not referred to our principal chapter by my predecessor," said Withra. "She merely reported that the trouble with the Hag was 'settled'. By the time I came here, it had become tradition. It seemed... I believed it to be..."

"I see," said Mister Fitz. "I suspect if I took *your* blood, the striations would show the influence of Yeogh-Yeogh. However, it is not our duty to chastise you for weakness and poor choices. It is our duty to dispose of the Hag."

"Now, now, let's not rush into things," said Sir Hereward in alarm. "Just remember our current resources! And we have a very important job in hand, you know, the cannon and... we must get to Jeminero as soon as we can."

"That does not alter our principal duty," said Mister Fitz in tones that brooked no discussion. "The only question that remains is how we might best perform said duty."

"I can not let you try," said Withra hotly, her lips tight. "Our survival depends—"

"On the contrary," interrupted Mister Fitz. He raised his voice, and spoke to the air at a point above Withra's head. "I call upon Lanith-Eremot and all her followers to assist us against the intruder godlet known as Yeogh-Yeogh the Two-Headed."

"*I* speak for Lanith-Eremot here!" said Withra. "*I* say what she approves or does not—"

The words died in her throat as the pearly nimbus came back with a crack like a thunderclap and she suddenly levitated several inches off the ground. Her head jerked to the left and right, and back again, and a loud, brassy and inhuman voice screeched out of her mouth at an impossible volume.

"I do not approve! I cannot see everything all the time, but now I do, I most emphatically do not approve of what you young ladies have done and I require you to put matters to rights. Help the puppet and his knight, you hear me!"

To punctuate this speech, blood gushed from Withra's nostrils. She fell back to earth, staggered to a cushion and collapsed on to it. The nimbus blinked off again, leaving the distinctive smell of newly-printed Ghashiki banknotes, whose ink-makers used a special mixture of gall-black and balsamic vinegar. Twenty seconds later, a dozen armed priestesses rushed into the room, but they had not drawn their weapons. Instead they looked at Hereward and Mister Fitz wild-eyed, then bowed their heads and shuffled into a form of repentant choir, no one wanting to stand out among their sisters.

"Your archimandress will come to her senses in a moment," said Mister Fitz, indicating Withra. "It is a difficult thing to be the vessel for a god. How long do we have before the Hag rises?"

"I do not know, Lord Puppet," said the eldest of the priestesses, a woman with a white stripe through the greying hair atop her head, and a scar that continued on from that stripe down the side of her face. "We begin the feast at the eighth hour, and at some point soon thereafter, a black shape arises in the Hall."

"Less than an hour," mused Mister Fitz. "Possibly far less, if the Hag is already present enough to feel the momentary intervention of Lanith-Eremot. Where are your prisoners? The ones to be sacrificed?"

"We have a number of cells for penitents that are temporarily put to use for these men," said the priestess. "They are treated well."

"Until you feed them to the Hag," said Sir Hereward sourly. He turned to Mister Fitz. "I trust you have a plan, because I fear I do not."

"I have the inkling of a plan," said Mister Fitz. He tilted his head and slowly looked up and down the length of the knight.

"I already dislike this inkling," said Sir Hereward. "But tell me."

"I am formulating it," said Mister Fitz. He looked at the scarred priestess.

"What is your name?"

"Emengah. I am the Bursar of this convent."

"You heard Lanith-Eremot?"

"All within this house heard the Goddess. We stand ready to aid you, Master Puppet."

"Good. First of all, those men must be released and sent away, as quickly as possible. Give them food and money, and tell them to run as if a demon is at their backs. Which might well be true."

"As you command," said Emengah, though not without a glance at Withra, who was showing signs of returning to consciousness, her fingers twitching and part-formed groans issuing from her slack mouth. "I will see to it now."

"Good," said Mister Fitz. "Take your little novice too, and make sure the young ones are all safely out of the way."

Emengah indicated to two of her followers to pick up Parnailam, bowed to Mister Fitz and Sir Hereward and exited, the other priestesses following so swiftly they almost trampled over one another in their eagerness to go out the door.

"You intend the men to be a distraction?" asked Sir Hereward. "But we have already been told the Hag can hunt them down... oh I see... not a distraction, but a concentration, no doubt. On the one man left close at hand. That is to say, me."

"Yes," said Mister Fitz. "We must focus the Hag upon you, so that *you* are the one she pursues when you flee this house."

"Into a trap," said Sir Hereward. "But what trap could we make in so little time, and you with only one needle?"

"We have the cannon," said Mister Fitz. "And the old dagger."

Sir Hereward narrowed his eyes.

"Pray continue."

"I will go outside now to prepare," said Mister Fitz. "The Archimandress will take you towards the Hag as she manifests, as if you are the first sacrifice. You will break free and flee outside, into the mouth of the cannon—"

"The mouth of the cannon!"

"Please pay attention, Hereward. We have little time. You go into the mouth of the cannon. The Hag will follow. You race from the muzzle to the breech, and at the open chamber, you must turn and throw the dagger, instructing it to kill the Hag. You remember the words?"

"Of course I remember the words, but—"

"Next, you leap out through the open chamber, which I will then rotate and close using sorcery. I will have cocked the firing pistols already and will pull the cord as I jump—"

"I am to crawl down a fully-charged giant cannon with the

firing pistols cocked and a carnivorous godlet screaming after me?"

"Are you not paying attention? As I close the breech, you must run and take cover as best you can. Behind a moklek if one is near, I will endeavor to call them. Timing will be of the essence, if the Hag is close enough to escape out the breech before I can close it, or you are too slow with the dagger..."

"Why even use the dagger? Surely the cannon blast alone would destroy the Hag?"

"I fear that the explosive power of even that quantity of special powder will not be enough," said Mister Fitz. "We would need the proper projectile as well. However, the dagger might be strong enough to overcome the Hag in combination with the explosion. If we are fortunate, they will destroy each other."

"And if we're not?"

"Our destiny has always been to walk the knife-edge," said Mister Fitz obliquely. "It is a narrow way."

"Is this Hag, this relict of Yeogh-Yeogh, so important?" asked Sir Hereward slowly.

"It was a godlet of the first order of malevolence," said Mister Fitz. "It grew strong very quickly before, invading the essence of Ryzha. It must be dealt with before it can grow as strong again."

"Why couldn't it just be one of those little annoying things that sour wine in a single tavern or make people sneeze at a crossroads," said Sir Hereward, with a melancholy sigh. But he was already reaching inside his shirt to retrieve the brassard. Sliding it up his arm to sit above his elbow, he watched Mister Fitz follow suit with his own armband, and then together they recited the words they knew so well, and had spoken so many times, generally immediately before intense periods of mayhem, destruction, pain and death.

"In the name of the Council of the Treaty for the Safety of the World, acting under the authority granted by the Three Empires, the Seven Kingdoms, the Palatine Regency, the Jessar Republic and the Forty Lesser Realms, we declare ourselves agents of the Council. We identify the godlet manifested here as the malignant relict of Yeogh-Yeogh the Two-Headed, a listed entity under the Treaty. Consequently, the said godlet and all those who assist it are deemed to be enemies of the World and the Council authorizes us to pursue any and all actions necessary to banish, repel or exterminate the said godlet."

Faint symbols began to glow upon the brassards, ancient heraldic marks that identified empires long lost, kingdoms divided and broken, regencies ended and lesser realms grown even more insignificant. Yet still the Council of the Treaty for the Safety of the World endured, and still its executive agents prosecuted their work. And perhaps, just perhaps, the world *was* made a little safer...

"I would not help you, save the goddess commands," croaked Withra from the floor. "It is mad vainglory, and we will all be slain by the Hag."

"I have heard far worse plans, and taken part in many more badly-executed ones," said Sir Hereward, offering his hand to help the priestess up. "It offers a chance to right a wrong, where there was none before."

"If you had taken your bath the herbs therein would have made you simply sleep through the night," said Withra. "We thought your puppet would play for us, and honour the Hag, and keep his counsel, as such players do. No harm would have come to you. Now we are all doomed and the weed-stealers next season will laugh at the fallen house of Lanith-Eremot."

"A faint heart and a weak eye sees doom in everything," said Sir Hereward. He brought the priestess close and spoke with some considerable menace. "You do your part and stay true to Lanith-Eremot, and perhaps we will all survive, and you can go on chasing the weed-stealers across your shallow lake for years to come."

"I have no choice but to obey," said Withra bitterly. "The Goddess's command sits heavy upon me. Come, I feel the imminence of the Hag."

"Be sure you do as Sir Hereward instructs," said Mister Fitz sternly. He turned to the knight. "I will ensure the gates are open for you, Hereward. Need I say that you must be careful not to trip and stumble, and make the best speed you can?"

"An unnecessary warning," said Sir Hereward. "My mind is well-focused upon the matter. Please ensure you do your part equally well."

"Indeed," said Mister Fitz, and he was gone, moving so swiftly it seemed as if his shadow could barely keep up. There was no pretense now, no clicking, jerky movements. Just the empty air where he had been a moment before.

"Come," repeated Withra sourly, her manner hangdog. "If we are all to die, best we get it over with."

"You will die all the sooner if you do not play your part better," snapped Sir Hereward. He unhooked his sabre and weighed it in his hand for a moment, considering if he could somehow hide it on his person, before reluctantly laying it down and moving his two pistols and the old dagger around to the back of his belt, where they could not be so easily seen by the Hag. "You walk ahead. We will gather some of your soldiers as we go, they can march around me, and I will cross my wrists as if they are bound."

"I hear and obey," muttered Withra. She wiped the blood from her face with her sleeve and stalked from the room, Sir Hereward following very close behind. Despite the command Lanith-Eremot had laid upon the Archimandress, Sir Hereward thought there was a good chance Withra would try to betray him, and he must be ready for that, or any other development.

There were a large number of the armed priestesses at the end of the passage, muttering together. They fell silent as Withra and Hereward approached.

"Fall in to guard the 'prisoner'," snapped Withra.

The priestesses didn't move, bar some shuffling in place. Withra's fists clenched at her sides and Hereward heard the hiss of her deeply in-drawn breath.

"Do as she asks," said Hereward quickly, before Withra could speak again. "It is a pretence, no more. When the Hag moves towards me, I will break free, and you must spring away and let me go. Do you all understand?"

The priestesses nodded, but with little certainty. They seemed unclear what to do and there was still only confused shuffling until the scarred bursar Emengah pushed through from behind them.

"You all heard the Goddess," she said sternly. "We are to obey this Knight, and the Puppet. We must assist them to the full extent of our abilities and resources."

"So you fancy yourself Archimandress now, Emengah?' asked Withra. "We will do as Lanith-Ermot commands, but I still—"

"You can sort out all that later," said Sir Hereward impatiently. "For now, you will do as *I* command. You lot, form up around me as a guard. Withra, you go ahead a few paces only. Emengah, have the weed-stealers been released?"

"They have. I have rarely seen such splashes made across the Shallows with their running."

"Then please make sure I have a clear path to run from the hall to the gates and outside."

"The Puppet has already commanded the gates to be held open for you," said Emengah.

"Make sure they are," said Hereward. He crossed his wrists and held them low in front, and began to walk in step with the priestesses who now moved to surround him. "It's the kind of detail I like double-checked when my life depends upon it."

Withra snorted. "Your plan cannot work, Sir Hereward. We will all be—"

"Silence!" snapped Sir Hereward. "Do not speak hereafter, unless I give you permission."

The Archimandress cast a look of burning hate over her shoulder, but her mouth stayed shut. Walking faster, she led the group of priestesses and their ostensible prisoner along the passage, through the door and out into the hall.

There were only gold-clad priestesses there now, no novices in silver. They sat at the tables, eyes scared, the food and wine untouched. Heads turned as Withra, Hereward and his guards entered, then turned again, towards the tall stone dais at the other end of the hall. Hereward had only glanced at it when they'd passed through before, and had seen nothing unusual. Now, there was a pool of shadow there, an unnatural glob of darkness that defied the light of the lanterns hung above, and the candles in the many-branched candelabra on the tables.

Withra kept walking towards the stone dais. Hereward followed, eyes flickering to the door on the far side, calculating where he would run, the potential obstacles... he could feel his heart speeding up, the familiar surge of nervous energy that came on the brink of combat, that must be directed and controlled lest he give way to irrational fear or blustering foolishness.

Ten feet from the dais, Withra stopped and raised her arms. There was a moment of tense hesitation, before all the sisters in the hall save the guards around Hereward threw up their arms as well.

"The Hag!" shouted Withra. "The Hag!"

The third time she shouted, the Archimandress's voice was lost in the swelling roar from her sisters, who took up the chant.

"The Hag! The Hag! The Hag!"

Sir Hereward's flesh crawled as the chant was answered by the shadow atop the dais. It spread wider and then began to rise up, a column of intense darkness. Tiny arcs of lightning flashed around it, and a ring of fog began to form around the base of the dais, drops of dirty water or perhaps diluted blood dripping from the stone.

Withra advanced forward several more steps and knelt down, dropping her arms. As she did so, the chant stopped. There was total silence in the hall. It was so quiet Hereward could hear his own heart beating, beating far faster than he liked. He had to choose his moment exactly, too fast and the Hag might not pursue, too slow and it would catch him—

He started as the dark column moved again, suddenly sprouting four long tentacles and a misshapen lump atop it that perhaps was a head. The tentacles came questing down the dais and advanced across the floor, writhing and turning, emitting small puffs of fog and mist with every coiling movement.

"We bring you a sacrifice!" shouted Withra. "But hear me, Hag! It is—"

Hereward drew, cocked and fired his pistol before Withra could complete her warning. The sharp report was shocking, seemingly louder than any pistol he had ever fired before. But he paid it no heed, nor did he hesitate to gauge the extent of Withra's wounding. He'd hit her he knew, and she had gone down, the situation assessed in an instant even as he drew his second pistol and fired it straight into the shadow-stuff of the Hag. She was sliding off the dais, her tentacles racing across the floor towards him, moving in sinuous esses like a sidewinder across sand.

The silver ball was swallowed up to no obvious effect, but again Sir Hereward hadn't paused to see what it would do. Throwing the pistol aside, he jumped to the closest table, ran across the middle of it, kicking dishes, cutlery, drinks and food aside, and leaped for the door.

Tentacles lashed the air behind his back as he raced through.

"Make way!" roared Hereward, throwing himself forward, putting all his strength into his legs. "Make way!"

Guard priestesses flung themselves against the sides of the passage as he sped past, turning their faces to their wall and praying to Lanith-Eremot as the darkness that pursued him enveloped them. But their prayers were not answered. Bleached bones, shreds of human flesh, strips of leather and the metal parts of their weapons fell to the floor behind the Hag. When enraged, it seemed she was not particular about only devouring men.

Hereward ran as he had never run before. He pulled at the very air ahead of him as if he could use it to lever himself faster forward, and his knees rose almost to his chest. He skittered around the corner and through the inner gate, and for a fatal, awful second almost tripped on the first blood gutter, only just recovering his balance enough to transform a fall into a diagonal leap forward. Tentacles lashed where he had been, and a priestess behind screamed a death cry so hideous that in normal circumstances it would have galvanised Hereward to run faster still, but now there was no faster. He ran the race of his life.

Water exploded as he burst outside and into the Shallows, great sprays going up with every footfall. It was dark outside, much darker than Hereward had expected, for storm clouds had gathered over the house, blocking out the moon and stars. Yet he could not stop to get his bearings, but instead ran on, trusting to instinct, with an awful sloshing and boiling noise too close behind him the mark of the Hag's closing.

A faint blue light blossomed ahead, like a tiny falling star. It only lasted a few seconds, but the knight knew it for Fitz's aid, the least possible light to conserve the power of his needle. In those moments of scant illumination, Hereward saw the outline of the cannon and knew where its maw lay, almost straight ahead.

Hereward jumped for the cannon mouth as a tentacle grazed his back, the shadow-stuff burning like acid through his doublet and shirt and deep into the flesh beneath. He screamed but did not slow. It was only a glancing strike, the tentacle had no grip and could not pull him back.

The knight went into the cannon like a rammed shot, sliding straight on his stomach for a good six feet before he got his hands and knees under himself and began to scuttle, once again faster than he had moved in such a fashion ever before.

It was pitch black inside the cannon. Hereward sobbed and cursed Fitz, himself, the Hag, Withra, fate and all the gods and godlets who'd ever existed as he rubbed the skin off his knees, elbows and hands in his frantic passage over the thin sharp ridges of the rifled barrel. But he cared nothing for these pains, for the Hag came close behind him. He could feel the dread weight of her, and twice a tentacle lashed across the soles of his feet.

One hundred feet was too far, thought Hereward through pain and fear. He would never make it to the breech, never make it out. The Hag's tentacles would lash around his ankles and drag him back and then, then it would all be over, that fall from the razor's edge that was bound to come one day—

A blue, heatless light shone ahead, outlining an opening above.

Hereward's heart almost burst as he exerted all his remaining strength, leaping up through the open chamber to stand on top of the exposed cartridge, his bleeding fingers tearing at the wax seals and the peace strings of the old dagger, feet jumping and dancing as a single tentacle lashed across from left to right and then right to left, and he almost fell as he got the dagger free, its whiny voice piercing his head as if an icicle had been thrust through his eye and into his brain.

"Who wakes me! Who wakes me!"

"Deal death to my enemies, death to my foes, Anglar-Ithrix I command thee!" squealed Hereward, his voice weirdly pitched from exhaustion and fright, the words gabbled out so fast they were almost... almost but not quite... unrecognisable.

He threw the dagger and leaped off the cannon, even as the foremost part of the Hag emerged into the chamber, a writhing thing of darkness and fog. The dagger bounced clanging off the bottom of the breech, shouted something peevish and drove straight at the shadow.

Tentacles writhed to try and fend the weapon off, and then a great tentacle composed of blinding violet light arced over from the cascabel at the very end of the cannon, where Mister Fitz stood, wielding his one remaining sorcerous needle.

This brilliant tendril reached in and rotated the chamber shut in one swift motion, locking the old dagger and the Hag inside.

Evan as it did so, Mister Fitz jumped over the side, letting the three strings that would fire the cannon run through his open hand, and sped to his previously-prepared firing position. Though he was far more durable than a human, his papier-mache and wooden frame being heavily reinforced with sorcery, he still sought shelter behind the moklek he had made kneel down some dozen yards away.

Sir Hereward was not behind the great beast, but there was no time for Mister Fitz to check where he had gone. From the sound of the shouting and cursing inside the cannon, the godlet

Anglar-Ithrix who resided inside the dagger was getting the worst of his combat with the Hag.

Mister Fitz lay down and pulled all three strings. Two of the pistols fired, long trails of sparks spurting up from the cannon.

Then came the long second of uncertainty, the gunner's doubt. A very long second indeed, almost long enough for Fitz to pull the strings again in vain hope the third pistol would do the job, even as thoughts of spoiled powder and blocked vents whisked through this mind—

The cannon fired.

The blast was titanic, destroying all other sound. A massive jet of flame enveloped the entire corner of the fortified house, floor to ceiling. The cannon itself bucked up and backwards, smashing the carts into thousands of pieces, sending wicked splinters flying in all directions, the great long tube of bronze itself almost dancing on one end before it toppled over and came smashing down in the Shallows, creating both a minor tidal wave and a splash so great it was like a sudden, short fall of rain.

Mister Fitz stood up as the rain fell, and looked about for Sir Hereward. A great swathe of acrid gunsmoke billowed over everything, obscuring even Fitz's vision. His moklek shield was trumpeting its pain to its fellows, but the puppet adjudged it was not badly hurt. He would tend to it once he found Sir Hereward and ascertained the fate of both the Hag and the old dagger.

Sir Hereward had just kept running until the cannon blast knocked him over. It took Mister Fitz several minutes to find him amidst the clouds of thick, acrid smoke from the cannon's firing. The knight was sitting in the water, looking dazed and very bloody.

"You did well," said Mister Fitz, carefully checking over his companion's head, torso and arms for serious wounds. "Stand up."

"What?" shouted Sir Hereward. He was deaf from the blast, and stupid with weariness. Running from the Hag had taken all the strength he possessed, and then some more.

Fitz heaved him up and supported him when Hereward's knees buckled and he would have fallen again. As he did so, he looked over the lower half of his companion, noting that in addition to many cuts and abrasions, there was a small splinter buried several inches in Hereward's thigh. But it was not bleeding freely, and so it too, could wait.

"Did it work?" shouted Sir Hereward. He looked about him, blinking furiously. Even with a good part of the house of the Sisters of Mercantile Fairness ablaze and shedding light, he could hardly see anything through the gunsmoke. He took some comfort from Mister Fitz's cool wooden hands, but less from the knowledge that the puppet had used his last sorcerous needle.

"I am not yet certain," said Mister Fitz, loudly, but not loudly enough for Hereward to hear him. "I still detect some essence of the Hag... a small remnant—"

He suddenly let go of Hereward, who promptly fell onto his knees and only just managed to stop himself tilting over face-forward, to suffer an ignominious death by drowning in six inches of water.

Withra was advancing towards them, a gleaming knife in her hand. The left side of her face had been shattered by the silver ball from Sir Hereward's pistol, her cheekbone and part of her jaw bare to the elements, a wound that should have her curled up in agony. But she showed no pain, and when she opened her mouth, Sir Hereward saw why. Instead of a tongue, Withra had a small tentacle of shadow, the very last piece of the Hag still extant upon the earth.

The small, sharp knife Mister Fitz used for dissecting appeared in the puppet's hand. He crouched to spring, but before he could do so, there was the sudden whoosh of a large blade moving very fast, the flash of firelight on steel, and Withra's head parted from her shoulders. The head landed upright in the water, the shadow-tongue writhing and eyes blazing. Emengah stood above it, the Archimandress's own bastard sword held bloody in both hands.

"We take care of our own," she said wearily. "And all debts must be paid."

Fitz wasn't listening. His head was tilted, listening to a high-pitched whistle akin to the cry of a falcon speeding to its prey. It suddenly grew louder. The puppet lunged forward, quick as a snake, and snatched up Withra's head, holding the horrid remnant in front of Sir Hereward just in time to interpose it between the knight and the flying dagger that sped out of the darkness like an arrow.

Dagger and head meet with a ghastly squelch. The two were torn from Fitz's hands and went rolling off through the water, the dagger's imprecations and curses muffled by the shadow that came out of the gaping jaw and wrapped around the blade. Fitz started to walk after them, but halted as it became clear they were not going to stop, but would keep on rolling and fighting till one defeated the other. Or as was to be hoped, they both lost the strength to maintain their existence in the world and were forced to retreat and rejoin the greater part of themselves in some other dimension.

Emengah walked over to Sir Hereward and grounded her sword. Behind her, the flames from the burning house rose higher, and black smoke billowed forth to eclipse the last acrid swirls of white smoke from the cannon.

"The Sisters of Mercantile Fairness thank you Mister Fitz," said Emengah. "And you, Sir Hereward."

Sir Hereward smiled crookedly. He couldn't hear a word she said, but he knew gratitude and good will when he saw it, and the scarred Emengah with the bastard sword in her hands seemed to him to be fair indeed, a most welcome sight. He managed to stand up with Fitz's considerable help, and made a fair effort at a courtly bow before he fainted.

WAKING IN DAYLIGHT, Hereward found himself in a feather-bed in a corner of the hall that while it smelled extremely smoky, was undamaged. That could not be said for the other end of the great room, which was open to the sky, allowing the over-bright sun unfettered access past the tumbled walls of blackened stone.

Mister Fitz sat on the end of the bed, sewing up the many rents in Hereward's shirt and breeches. The novice Parnailam, clad now in an ordinary homespun habit, watched his sewing intently, marveling at the tiny, ordered stitches and the speed with which the needle moved.

"Ah," said Mister Fitz to the knight. "You wake. Good morning."

"If you can call it that," said Sir Hereward muzzily. His ears hurt, but at least he could hear again. He was not so sure about his mind, or his memory, and the many pains along his legs and arms indicated he would remain abed for quite some time. "I take it the plan worked as expected?"

"Indeed," said Mister Fitz. "Though there is a slight chance we might have to deal with the old dagger again one day. A very slight chance, in my estimation."

"I hope so—" began Sir Hereward, but he paused and tilted his head, frowning as his ears caught a distant rumble. "Cannon fire!"

"No," said Mister Fitz equably. "Thunder. The rains have begun."

As if responding to this statement, the sky darkened suddenly, the sun vanishing. Heavy drops fell through the open, destroyed part of the house, and a great fusillade of rain began to sound on the roof above.

"The Shallows... the mokleks... the cannon," blurted Sir Hereward. He sat up and made as if to get out of bed, but Mister Fitz and Parnailam together pushed him back. "We must repair, get new wagons somehow, move out before the water deepens—"

"There is no need," said Mister Fitz calmly.

"Why not?"

"The Sisters are building us a boat, in gratitude for ridding them of the Hag. We can take the cannon across the Shallows to Junum, I have a letter of credit at the Bank of The New Ingots there. We can recruit a century of ox-men haulers to drag the cannon on rollers. True, there is the small matter of the Loathsome Worms to deal with—"

Mister Fitz stopped talking. Sir Hereward had either passed out, or was feigning sleep. The puppet took up his sewing again, Parnailam sitting down to watch once more.

"You are most adept with your needle, Mister Fitz," the novice said shyly.

"Indeed," said Mister Fitz. His round head turned slowly, his strange blue eyes met Parnailam's, and his mouth quirked up in something that was not quite a smile. "But then I have had a great deal of practice, with many different needles, stitching... and unstitching."

Parnailam gulped, though she did not quite know why, and soon made her excuses to leave.

Mister Fitz returned to his sewing. Sir Hereward slept.

Outside, a line of mokleks stood happily in the rain, all of them watching a dented pink howdah float past the tumbled cannon and drift away.

GRIGORI'S SOLUTION
ISOBELLE CARMODY

It MIGHT AS well have been magic, for all that people could understand of how it worked.

Mathematics at an exalted level *is* a kind of magic.

If the fateful sum had been set down in all its inexorable and deadly perfection in the Middle Ages, it would doubtless have been regarded as a spell, and like as not the young savant who penned it would have been burnt at the stake.

And is it not a spell, in the sense that magic spells were traditionally—are still, I suppose for those who believe in such things against all modern rationality—words of power; that is, words, or in this case, numbers, which, when said, effect physical change?

To the Middle Ages magic was not a game to engage and enliven the imaginations of children, nor a literary device for writers too lazy to grasp the nettle of reality. It was regarded as a darkly potent force that might be tapped, though never without consequence.

This is not the Middle Ages and yet in the sense that the labeling of a thing as 'magic' is a primitive means of surmounting fear, it may be reasonable that some folk prefer to call that dreadful sum that has been writ 'magic', since it will affect the greatest change of all: It will unmake existence.

Despite everything, it gives me a little shiver to write those words down in my notebook. How heavy and cold they seem. How inexorable. And how strange, too, to discover at the tail end of a life full of earnestly penned words, the unimaginable extent of the power that can be contained in markings I had hitherto seen only as the bearers and vessels of meaning. I am like a child discovering the building rods he has played with for so long are sticks of dynamite.

That I heard of the sum as early as I did was by sheerest chance.

I had just settled into my room here at the Olympus, dispersing my few items of clothing from suitcase to wardrobe when I was inescapably reminded of all the times I had waited by the telephone in anonymous hotels abroad for a call from an interview subject or contact. It is odd how, viewed in retrospect, a life full of busyness can begin to seem rather empty. Perhaps this is why I had a sudden sentimental impulse to hear English and as the phone I had purchased had an application that allowed me to tune into radio stations anywhere in the world, I searched until I happened on an English voice. It was the host of a late night science program coming out of Boston and it did not take me long to discern that its main aim was not to present science but to turn science into that spurious thing— entertainment. The invited guests were the sort that spoke sensationally and none too clearly of the more speculative ends of science and the sloppiness of intellect displayed by the host was acutely irritating.

I was on the verge of shutting the application when a new guest, a young Scottish mathematician, began to speak with refreshing doggedness about something the host called the Doomsday Formula, but which the young man urgently insisted was the resolution of a mathematical problem he called Grigori's Solution. He was clearly upset about some aspect of the solution, but he lacked the slick patter and practiced urbanity of the other guests and his conversation was very technical. Nor was he entirely clear about the sum that was the center of his disquisition, for as he frankly admitted, the math involved went far beyond his considerable ability. The host soon lost interest when he could not persuade his guest to agree that the completed sum could be applied to the creation of some sort of weapon of mass destruction. Indeed, all the young man would say was that the sum itself was the thing to be feared, before again launching into labyrinthine mathematical explanations. The host managed to silence him by the simple expedient of cutting him off midsentence with a song, having no notion that the end of the world had just been announced on his trite show.

I had no idea of the magnitude of what I was hearing either, but I had heard enough to want to know more. It may be, indeed, that I was the only person listening with the right combination of an understanding of pure math and a love of philosophy to have been capable of getting some inkling of what the sum might be.

It took a little time and effort to get the telephone number of the station and by the time I called, the receptionist informed me the mathematician had left. Indeed he had left *before* the program ended, she added disapprovingly. I managed to extract his name and the information that he had an American wife, lived in Charlotteville and had left in a cab. I eventually tracked down his home number but by then it was the middle of the night in the States. I called at what seemed to me a reasonable hour the following day, only to be told by his wife that he had flown to Australia directly after the program. He had been scheduled to fly there the following week to deliver a paper at a conference at the University of Queensland, but he had altered his flight to leave earlier. Garrulous by nature, she did not have to be coaxed to tell me that her husband had been in Boston to deliver a series of lectures when the opportunity had arisen to appear on the science program. He was not normally interested in that sort of thing, but he had learned something in Boston that had got him tremendously excited and upset and he had told her that he had felt the need to let people know about it as swiftly as possible. She had no more notion than the science show host what had got him into such a state, but she said it was connected to a problem that had been solved by a young mathematician in Estonia.

She had no idea how her husband had learned of the Estonian mathematician or why his solution of a sum should have prompted her husband to speak on the radio, then fly to Australia early so that he could consult with colleagues in Adelaide. Or was it Melbourne? She thought it was Adelaide, but she had no way to reach him because the poor darling had left his mobile behind in Boston. The radio program had called her about it after his hasty departure. An email address, I suggested, rather hopelessly. She gave it to me but said her husband was unlikely to check his emails until he reached his hotel in Brisbane. Before I rang off I got the address and phone number of the hotel and the date of his arrival.

I have thought of that friendly, foolish woman more than once in these last few days, for like much of the world, her easy scorn of mathematics must have seemed cruelly short sighted in the face of the fact that humanity will face its demise at the hands of a sum. Or perhaps she and all those despisers of math merely feel vindicated in their loathing.

At the time, when I disconnected, I wondered a little at my compulsion to speak with her husband. After all I had heard only a little of the math of the sum, rendered by someone who, though a renowned mathematician, had admitted his own inadequacy. And how should a matter of world-shaking mathematical significance be announced on the radio in such a manner in any case? No one would think of announcing the cure for cancer that way. There would be a long period of testing and peer assessment and then the results would finally be announced from some dignified and reputable platform. Dismissing the matter from my mind, I told myself I had fixated on it because I was low in spirits. My disrupted circadian rhythms were affecting my sleep and appetite. With this in mind, I took a long, pleasant walk and then ate sardines in a rooftop tavern before finding the doctor whose name I had been given, to deliver to him my medical papers.

But even sitting in the doctor's office listening to him talk tediously of palliative care and what would have to be done in this or that exigency, and of the need to consider removing myself to Athens at some critical moment, the memory of the math I had heard recurred in my mind in the strong Scottish brogue of the young mathematician. I was struck anew by his dogged seriousness despite the host's attempts to persuade him into levity, and the fact that he had suddenly flown to Adelaide to consult with colleagues. Impossible to believe the possessor of that stern brogue would go to such lengths without having reason for it.

By dusk, which I observed from a small pizzeria on the very tip of Oia, having taken a bus there, I had begun to tweak the threads of my old network of journalistic connections. Those editors and sub editors and journalists who still lived were retired, and having the luxury of time, or so it seemed then, we enjoyed dissecting and lamenting the state of modern journalism and the way it had aided and abetted the rise of corporate capitalism before I finally laid the few pieces of my enquiry before them. Most were bored enough with their leisure to be intrigued. It was not two days later that I began to receive increasingly incredulous confirmation that the sum I had heard in part, *had* been solved; not by the brilliant young European mathematician with a bad haircut I had envisaged, but by a boy of fifteen living on the outskirts of a genteel Boston suburb—a mathematical savant called Grigori. But he had not come up with the problem—that had apparently been the doing of an elderly spinster; a retired math teacher, herself an immigrant, who had been attempting to solve it for thirty years.

The news of the sum was beginning to leak out to the incredulous wider world; driblets and drops of it, at least, but too little for anyone to clearly understand its significance. In my opinion it took the math and scientific community an unnecessarily long time to recognize and accept what had been done, let alone to break the news to the world at large. They are not entirely to blame, of course. Mathematicians and scientists are notoriously unable to communicate clearly, especially with the non-mathematically or scientifically inclined mind. And the lay mind is guilty of too readily closing itself to anything requiring more than the most basic digestion.

I did not understand myself what had been done until after I had finally spoken to the Scottish mathematician, Huw MacLeod. Ironically, after all my attempts to reach him, it was he who called me and, as if continuing a conversation that had already been going on for some time, told me that the math of the sum and its solution were quite simply too advanced for him *and* his Adelaide colleagues, for all their brilliance and eminence, to fully grasp. But it definitely involved some sort of ground-breaking force of reversion. Unable to help himself, perhaps, he launched into a description of math so esoteric and complex as to be completely incomprehensible to me. Perhaps sensing my bewilderment, he suddenly broke off and apologized for taking so long to call me. He had got several belated messages from me only the previous night, forwarded from the reception desk at the Brisbane hotel where he had been supposed to stay. I knew, of course, that he had cancelled his reservation and guest lecture. He had done so, he told me, in order to return to Charlotteville, to his wife and small sons. He advised me to repair at once to my own loved ones if I was not with them already, for in a very short time no one would have the luxury of choosing where they would meet their end.

I did not bother to tell the mathematician that I had no loved ones and that I had already made my choice about where I wanted to meet my end. In truth, I supposed he was making some sort of awkward joke whose point eluded me, so I simply asked him to tell me about the retired math teacher responsible for the sum.

Her name, it transpired, was Adolphine. He had got it and her phone number from a piano tuner who worked in the evenings as a doorman at the hotel where he had been put up in Boston. Discovering Huw was a mathematician on the way to the tenth floor in an elderly and very slow elevator, he had shown him a picture on his phone of a sum on a battered old blackboard, asking if the mathematician could make head or tail of a thing like that, or was it just gibberish? He had taken the picture on impulse during a break from tuning an old woman's piano, he explained, when Huw asked. It had taken fifty dollars to get the man to reveal the name and phone number of the woman.

I tried to question MacLeod about his conversation with her, but he cut me off, suggesting I speak to the woman directly, not that it would make any difference. I was pondering this aside, when he said in his brusque kind way that I had better call right away, if I was serious about wanting to speak to her. Then he hung up without saying goodbye.

Somewhat bemused, and rather unsettled by the things he had said, I called at once.

Adolphine answered and to my question about her unusual but charming accent, offered the information that she was a native Flemish Belgian. In impeccable if accented English she went on to add that, as she had told the Scottish gentleman and the Australians who had called, the sum photographed by the piano tuner had not been created by her, but by her deceased grandfather. He had spent thirty years attempting to prove Fermat's Last Theorem and had been on the verge of it when the British mathematician, Andrew Wiles, succeeded. Her grandfather's outrage had been apoplectic and he suffered an immense and catastrophic stroke that deprived him of his voice, some of his motor functions and, temporarily, his wits.

She could not say, Adolphine told me softly, if her grandfather had known what he was doing when he had scrawled the sum in the aftermath of his stroke, for he had seemed to her to be possessed of mindless rage. Certainly later, when he had regained his wits, he had no memory of composing the sum and pronounced it unsolvable quackery, yet he had never erased it and sometimes she would come upon him studying it.

"I always felt that it was not that the sum was nonsense, but that I had not the wit to understand it," Adolphine added gravely. "I think my grandfather felt the same. It was as if some other darker, more brilliant part of him had been released to a brief life by the stroke, and that part of him composed the sum."

Although she had accepted her grandfather's assertion that the sum was nonsense, the math she could understand was flawless and so she had taken the blackboard upon which it was written after his death and set it up it in the large ground room where she kept her piano. She too had found herself drawn to study it from time to time. "You see, I had begun to have the queer notion that it was a philosophical question formulated as a mathematical problem," she told me. "And that if I studied it long enough, I would understand it."

I asked how the sum had come to be completed, and she answered that one day a woman brought a boy to her for evaluation. She had been gardening, so instead of bringing them up the flight of steps from the front path to the main part of the house, she had ushered them through the piano room so that she could exchange her gumboots for the house shoes she had left by the back steps. All the way, the boy's aunt volubly proclaimed him gifted and not unteachable as the school insisted. It transpired that she was seeking the grounds to force the local school to allow her to enroll the boy to avoid keeping him home or spending the considerable funds that would be required to send him to a special school.

Although the gentle Flemish woman did not say it, I fancied Adolphine had disliked the aunt who had complained at length about the cost of feeding the grossly overweight boy, and lamented being saddled with him after her sister and Estonian brother-in-law had been killed in a car accident. This concern about money might have been less repellent had she not been granted free and full control of the boy's considerable inheritance, which would revert to her on his death, so long as he remained in her charge, save for periods away that would enhance his life either educationally or medically. Given her clothing and jewelry and the car she drove, it was evident that the aunt had been making full use of the sums at her command, and Adolphine conceded that, given this, it was quite possible she did not actually have funds enough remaining to send the boy away.

In any case, as the two women spoke, the boy wandered back down to the piano room. When they found him, he was at the blackboard furiously scratching numbers and letters with a tiny nub of chalk. Adolphine, intrigued, prevented the aunt from disciplining the boy and erasing his so-called gibberish, giving the boy a fresh stick of chalk and suggesting he remain with her until they saw what he did with his numbers. The aunt had been elated to be able to be rid of Grigori for a time without contravening the conditions of the will. Not the least bit repelled by the boy's physical grossness or his emotional reticence, Adolphine had been genuinely curious to discover what he would do with the sum, for she had been able to see that he had grasped the math immediately, and was responding in kind.

The stay of a night had become several nights and then had become a long-standing arrangement where the boy spent a certain number of hours a day and some nights with Adolphine. He had been attending her for some months before completing the formula which he had been working on steadily since that first day. He had gone far beyond her knowledge of math and although the boy seemed to have no further interest in the sum once it was solved, she had tried to interest the local university mathematicians in coming to see it. She had not succeeded and had given up. Then by chance, a photograph of the blackboard taken by her piano tuner had been shown to Huw MacLeod.

Adolphine's voice was warm when she spoke of the Scotsman, who had phoned her initially in some excitement before coming to see her to make a recording of her story and to take his own photographs. He had been very excited, saying that he thought some of the boy's math was so original that it might involve a new number. At the least, the boy and her grandfather, for he had by then got the whole story out of her, were likely to be famous.

"Not that Grigori would be much impressed by fame, and my grandfather has gone beyond the care of such things," Adolphine told me sadly. The boy's greatest pleasure was to sit with her on her porch swing and drink her homemade lemonade. "That was what he wanted to do each day when he set down his chalk, and it was what he had asked to do after he completed the sum," Adolphine said, during our last conversation.

He had also asked if he could stay with her.

"I knew I would not be able to keep him with me, but I said I thought we might contrive for him to remain with me for a week or so and that seemed to content him," she said.

Huw MacLeod had called Adolphine again, still excited by Grigori's Solution but also sounding troubled. She had been unable to get a clear understanding of what worried him, but he said that he might be able to explain better after seeing some colleagues. He had not mentioned the radio program to her and it was not until some days later when he had called from Adelaide, that he had told her what he believed the sum was capable of doing; had been doing, in fact, from the moment Grigori completed it.

He did not blame the boy, any more than Adolphine did. Indeed she had a strange theory about the sum and the boy's solution of it. She told me in our last conversation that Grigori had reacted to her grandfather's equation when they had passed by the board that first day, almost as if he perceived it as having a physical force.

"He flinched," she said wonderingly. "As one might flinch from a cry or from a slap." She added that she had supposed at the time that he had been frightened by the looming blackness of the old board in an age of pristine whiteboards. But she had thought of that reaction since, having noticed that Grigori always approached the board crabwise, leaning into it, rather in the manner of one walking into the teeth of a storm. Right up until the sum was concluded. Then the boy had straightened for the first time and had regarded the sum at length, very intently, before at last heaving a great sigh of relief and setting down his chalk.

"It sounds silly and fatuous, but I can't help but feel that Grigori had been trying to solve my grandfather's equation of rage ever since he saw it, in order to silence it," Adolphine said, more to herself than to me.

I had called her because I had become concerned about the old gentlewoman and the boy. In truth I had feared some violent retaliation as the world began to understand what the sum was doing. Certainly the first generalized reaction after disbelief was a kind of mad rage and I had been afraid that it would require a victim. I had tried, when suggesting Adolphine not answer the phone and move to a hotel or even to one of the houses nearby, vacated by people who thought they could flee what could not be escaped, not to frighten her. But Adolphine was extremely bright and understood what I left unsaid as well as what I was saying. She cut me off gently, assuring me that no one seemed to realise that *her* fat, gentle Grigori was the terrible evil genius that had come up with Grigori's Solution.

I might have guessed as much.

There were so many wildly conflicting and hysterical reports being mooted about at that stage and so much sensational misinformation, not to mention the generally melodramatic responses of various religions to the looming end of humanity, most of which seemed to revolve around how a person might deserve their version of the afterlife. And it was to happen so swiftly. What use were the dead grandfather of an elderly math teacher and a soft, fat savant Estonian boy as scapegoats, for all they had wrought an end between them? They were a strange and accidental Alpha and Omega, and I thought people would far prefer to believe the perpetrator of their end was a vicious and powerful Dark Lord.

Soon after that final call to Adolphine, even as Huw McLeod had intimated, the phones—both landlines and cell phones—ceased to operate, television stations shut down and soon after, the power went out. There had been wild and incendiary talk of the sum being an act of war, hot or cold, the successor to other attempts by humanity to annihilate themselves; but when the world went dark the orgy of paranoia and speculation petered out. For people finally understood that there was no stopping it.

They had tried, of course. Teams of experts had been flown hither and thither over the world by various governments to take part in various global think tanks aimed at trying to unmake the sum of unmaking, and there were rumours of corporations preparing to launch a select few into space in the hope that they would dodge the bullet, as the palely beautiful, sanguine young daughter of my neighbors would say.

But it all came to nothing.

The last desperate measure was the suggestion that all physical copies of the sum be destroyed. The last time we spoke, Adolphine told me that she had erased the sum from the board when the American government exhorted people to destroy all copies of the formula they might have made in any form, in a last ditch attempt to halt the process of destruction. That was after the astronomers began seeing the winking out of distant stars, or as one woman put it, quoting a children's film, the approach of the nothing. This seemed impossible, given that the light of stars is approaching us from so far away that many of them have already gone extinct before their light reaches us. Yet the stars *were* vanishing. I witnessed it myself, through my telescope. And they continued to be quenched, even after the purging of Grigori's Solution. Because of course even if every single copy that had been made was erased—and how could that be ensured in any case?—people who had seen it could not unthink seeing it, unremember it. And even if they had tried, how could someone like Grigori be made to unthink what he had created? And perhaps even if every person who had seen it, including Grigori and Adolphine, had been shot, it would still have been too late.

I saw a final discussion about the matter, just before television ceased. It was a very important program because not only did it feature two presidents, a famous actress and one of the Australian mathematicians who had been first to see the sum, but the pretty older woman hosting the program was herself famous for finding ways to get guests to reveal themselves to their detriment. I believe she honestly thought she was going to expose a massive hoax being perpetrated to some nefarious end, until the mathematician told her bluntly that there was no trick or plot. Grigori's Solution would and was at that moment, unmaking the world and there was no use in hiding in a bunker or going to the top of a mountain or flying in a plane. There was no safe place because everything was going to cease to exist; not just humanity or all creatures that lived and could die, but all inanimate matter too: the bunker and the mountain and the plane as well as every blade of grass, every grain of sand. All would all cease to be in the same instant.

For the first time, that pretty, hard mask slipped but a look of cynicism twisted her perfect lips back into place and the mask resettled itself as the hostess asked politely how the stars were being witnessed in their vanishing, if everything was to cease at the same moment. The mathematician shrugged. I fancy he was beginning to wonder why he was wasting his time in trying to explain anything. But he only said that it would require complex esoteric math to be properly explained, however the fact was that the exact process of the unmaking of existence had begun to be understood only after it was discovered that the same rate of disappearance of stars had been recorded at every observatory in the world. That was impossible since different positions of observation should have meant a difference in what was observed. *Unless the end was approaching all places from all sides at the same moment.*

He hesitated and when the interviewer remained silent, he shrugged again and said that from the point of view of a theoretical someone on one of those distant stars—the ones not already long extinct—*we* should seem to have vanished.

"Then it is an illusion, since we have patently *not* vanished," the hostess announced triumphantly.

The mathematician said he did not know how to explain it so that she would understand, without her having some understanding of math, but that she might endeavor to think of it as a personal extinction: Each thing existing until it ceased to exist, and when one thing ceased to exist, all things would cease to exist.

There had been something growing on the face of the interviewer as he spoke, and the camera panned to her face so that all who watched would have witnessed, as I did, in the sagging of her expression, her aghast realization that this was not just something that could be dissected and made jokes about after all. She was not this time to be a bystander far from the centre of destruction, who would afterwards groom herself and present a follow up story. *She* was part of the story. *She* would cease to exist at the same moment as everyone else.

She had utterly lost her larger than life glamour when she asked softly, almost hoarsely, 'So you are saying there is nothing to be done?'

The mathematician was the sort of person for whom ideas are beautiful and so he nodded calmly and asked with a slight smile if she did not think there was a sort of perfection in it; that the end of the world would come so softly and smoothly, without war or pain or horror.

I do not know how many hundreds of thousands of people saw that interview but it seemed to mark a change in how people behaved. Suddenly almost everyone knew about the sum and what it meant.

There was a shocked hiatus—a sort of false momentary peace—and then the world lurched into its brief, sharp period of madness. A few days during which people killed themselves and one another, looted and burned and fornicated indiscriminately in a mad orgy of terror and denial. I saw brief dreadful glimpses of this in cobbled-together news flashes between repeats of recent day time or late night talk shows featuring politicians making statements or movie stars offering comments, then suddenly, there was nothing but white noise until the power failed on the island. It may have taken longer on the mainland and in other parts of the world, but I have no doubt it soon failed everywhere. Who after all, would choose to man the switches in a power station for their last days of life?

There was ugliness and violence on the island too, but not as much as elsewhere. Some people killed themselves; a predictable response, though stupidly redundant. One man said to me, before he blew his head off with his hunting rifle, that it was his helplessness that was intolerable to him. Suicide, in such an instance, seemed to him to be an act of decisive courage. He was very passionate in his explanation, almost as if he was trying to convince me, though in fact I had not tried to argue with him or change his mind. He was not alone. For a time, the island seemed fairly to resound with explosions and gunshots and screams and crashes.

I was not sorry to see an end to such people with their violent and destructive responses, though I did feel sadness for the children and women and the few men deprived of choice by their partners. There were a very few murders, perhaps because vengeance and hate must have seemed pointless to anyone rational. There was one cringing little woman whom I had seen coming from time to time to the supermarket in the town, when I had been well enough to walk there. I had noticed that she always wore large dark glasses not quite dark or wide enough to hide her bruises. Electra told me coolly that she had shot her big brute of a husband before leaping off a cliff. It seems a pity she killed herself as well as her tormentor, since she might have enjoyed a few days free of terror and pain before the end. Probably that seems a rather immoral observation, but somehow most of the morals humanity has seen fit to construct seem quite beside the point now.

When all of the forceful and truculent dying petered out, a sort of great calm peacefulness descended upon us, which is surprisingly beautiful. People have grown kind and quiet and pensive. If it is not in bad taste to say so, it seems to me that humanity's finest hour might be its last.

Those that remain have turned to the business of living out their final days in whatever way seems best to them. Of course there will be other suicides, but those are likely to be more artistic and symbolic responses to the end of the world than primitive violence.

Of course, there are no more planes or cruise ships, and no

supplies of food coming in. All services ceased immediately the world understood what was happening. This would have been the cause for some alarm, if we had not understood that the world would cease to exist well before supplies on the island are exhausted. Naturally restaurants and shops have ceased to operate. People walked away from businesses and jobs. In one stroke the Sum of Undoing had laid bare the utter meaninglessness of fame and money and power.

It has become very quiet and there is little talk. People seem largely to have retreated into their own homes and heads. I do not see this as a rejecting of others, but as another form of acceptance, for is not the human condition truly to be alone at the end, even in normal circumstances? We are born alone and we must die alone—that has not changed. In truth, Grigori's Solution has found a way to unite us in our solitude, so that while solitary, we may feel ourselves to be part of collective humanity in a way that has never before been possible.

There is no fear, it seems to me.

Even quite young people like the neighbors' daughter, Electra—horrid name to give a child, I thought at first, though now it seems to fit her very well for she has a great moral decisiveness—seems to be serene in her acceptance of the end that will come. In Electra's case, it is not very surprising, for she is an unusual girl, being both self sufficient and naturally inclined to solitude. I had wondered a little if she might suddenly feel vulnerable and cling to her parents, but she has retained her distance with them, only occasionally showing the sudden touchingly awkward spurt of affection. It is they who would cling, if she allowed it, but she does not and they are too respectful of her to trespass, even at this extremity. In the main, she spends her time alone with her iPod plugged into her ears. She had the foresight to power up a number of external devices that will enable her to listen to music to the end if she wishes. "She immerses herself in music," her mother told me rather wistfully, soon after they arrived, when she came to introduce herself. She explained that Electra wrote and performed her own songs and I was curious enough to ask what sort of songs. To my surprise, she furtively brought out a computer and played one of her daughter's recorded songs to me.

I had been very surprised by the girl's voice. It was very husky and subtle, as were the words and music she had composed. I have no doubt she would have been very successful as a singer, had the world lasted long enough to allow it. Aside from being talented, she is extremely beautiful. I like to watch her for such beauty is strangely mesmerizing, though I am careful. Of course I have no sexual interest in the child, but being a man and especially an old man, I must guard myself against any seeming impropriety, even now.

I am not alone in watching her. I have seen others staring at her from their terrace. Even Oleg the Bear watched her when he carried heavy piles of tourist bags up and down the steps to and from their owners' accommodation. His head never turned in her direction, and his eyes were hidden behind his sunglasses, but I had noticed that he always stopped to rearrange his burden when she was lying on the terrace. Perhaps it is only that he was struck by the absolute contrast between them: She with her long pale, slender limbs and cool expression, her porcelain skin and sleek swath of bronze hair, and he with his hard, hugely muscular brown body, liberally furred with the same coarse black hair that mats his head. He is handsome enough for all his ferocious glower, though in a brutish way. He is only in his early thirties, but far too old for a fifteen year old girl. The Bear was her nickname for him, which I had thought a minor cruelty, until I realised that she meant it only factually and truly he did seem more bear than human with his surly grunts and growls.

I have not seen him for some days, because like all of the white clad staff of these many tourist villas and hotels, he has vanished, gone to see to his own end. The last time I saw him, he was being accosted by the odd little besuited Asian man staying at the rather shabby Atelier a little further down the hill, whose guests were also served by Oleg and his two companions in the matter of luggage transport. The little man had appeared to be berating Oleg in some incomprehensible Asian language.

I have seen the little Asian man several times since, hurrying up or down the steps always wearing his dark thin suit, looking anxious and harried. I do not know where he goes each day so early, in such a hurry, but sometimes he does not return until the following morning. He is alone in his purposefulness, however. Others move slowly, as if through water, lost in thought. Sometimes there is sadness in their faces, for of course most of them are far from the homes and loved ones they had believed themselves to be parting from only temporarily. But is it a fleeting and dignified grief, rather than the initial outpouring of sorrow that occurred when people realized they must meet the end where they were, strangers in a strange land. Those that did not choose to die grew calm, understanding as they must that this severing was only a foreshadowing of the much greater severing looming over us all.

There are many, of course, who do not understand what is happening—they are either too young or old, or, like old Maria even now in her primitive, efficient little cave of a kitchen with its coal stove, preparing dinner, too stubborn. Her refusal to leave her post means we have not wanted for good cooking, though it is Electra's parents and some of the other guests of the Olympus who have foraged for supplies. Maria accepts the offerings crossly, asking when old Mario will return to his deliveries since he would ensure she had all the ingredients she needed.

There are others who, while understanding and accepting, have chosen to go on as usual. There is a nurse at the local veterinarian clinic, who I am told continues to treat animals and there is a doctor at the hospital dispensing medications and euthanasia. There is a taxi driver who will take you anywhere upon the island so long as his supply of petrol holds out and there is a woman who is making coffee in what was once a four star restaurant, though it is on the other side of the island. There is a man who gives a free cello concert in the main square of Firostefani each night for anyone who wishes to come and hear him and a painter who sits on a terrace making sketches from morning till night.

These people have made the decision to go on doing their work, either because they have a genuine calling, or because they love what they do. Or perhaps because it is their work that will give meaning to their existence, even in these final hours.

There must be others, too.

This morning, a plane went over and everyone stopped and stared up in wonderment, for who would bother to pilot a plane now, on the eve of the end? Nor could it have been a single person, since it would take a crew to work the thing. It may be that, even now, there are things to connect us and perhaps the connection is all the more profound, being necessarily ephemeral. I am told several other musicians have begun to come in the evenings to play with the cello man and Electra said there is talk of a final concert for anyone who wishes to attend. She has made it her project to learn how as many people as possible will spend their last hours. Some evenings she comes to sit with me and reads what she has learned.

"We are witnesses of the end," she said, tapping my battered journal.

For me, of course, the fact that I am old and have pancreatic cancer means the end of the world holds no great terror for me. I had already accepted the reality of my own not too distant specific personal death, so the idea of a more generalized extinction seems almost an elegant reprieve from what I fear would have been an ugly, painful death. Lacking regrets or fears, I have been removed enough to be, as Electra puts it, a witness. Like her, I have enjoyed making my notes for an article that will never be written. I had originally thought that what I would like most of all to do at the end would be to be editing an article about the end of the world, honing and perfecting syntax and meaning. I had thought to take a final walk up to the top of the hill to one of the ubiquitous little Orthodox blue-domed churches that sits up there, and read my final notes through. But a foolish fall put an end to the ill-conceived plan. I am glad, for I wince a little at the image of myself inching up the steep path with my walking frame, white hair blowing in the wind.

That is vanity of course, and absurd, yet it does seem to be an inescapable part of the human condition.

I have a more humble plan now.

I do not think the end will happen quite so fast and dramatically as was thought initially. Nor do I think it will be an approach of darkness. I think non-existence will slowly converge upon us like the humidity that thickens some evenings until it coalesces into the strange mist that boils across the island in an endless eery rushing white tide. I think non-existence will come like that, from all sides, a beautiful clammy tide of cloud that will isolate us first from one another, turning us each into little islands of existence, then will envelop and consume us.

By my calculations, the end will come just before dusk this evening. I have been watching the vanishing of the stars and the rate of disappearance is quite steady; Electra's father, an engineer, concurs that it will come at about the pace of a slow stroll. He intends that he and his wife will arrive an hour or so before the end, so that they may enjoy a final swim.

When I see the outer Cyclades begin to go, I will go down to my bedroom and make a pot of tea on the primus I have been using. I will carry it up to the terrace to sit. I am hoping one of the little cats that Electra has been feeding and wooing will come and curl in my lap, finding the girl absent. I will give it some milk in my saucer as an enticement.

Electra is still lying on her terrace lounger listening to her music. She has been swimming in the little infinity pool of the hotel next door, and she is quite alone, her parents having left this morning.

They were initially distressed that Electra would not accompany them, but she told them decidedly that they must all do as they wanted, but that she wished to remain at home. They made her promise to come and sit with me at the very end, and she agreed. Of course she has no intention of staying with me. It was merely that she did not want her parents to imagine her alone at the end, and they know she is fond of me in her cool way. She told me what she intended to do when she brought up some fruit her parents had foraged last night. She was not asking permission, of course. That would have been absurd under the circumstances and in any case she knows me well enough to know it would not be necessary. But she offered me a few sheets of paper, saying with innocent offhanded egoism that I might like to read about all the ways that people told her they planned to meet the end. Hers was at the bottom. I read the last line and smiled up at her before I anchored the sheets under a lump of pumice, saying I would save them for later in the day. I asked if she would come and say goodbye before she left and she nodded.

She went a few steps then glanced back over her smooth shoulder to tell me she had discovered why the little Asian man had been rushing about. He had been looking for his wallet. "His wallet," she marveled, shaking her head.

At this point, everyone who accepts what is coming has decided how they will meet their end. Not the little Asian man, whom I saw hurrying up the steps again this morning with the same anxious expression. Not the old senile woman on the terrace below, tended to by her wizened older sister. Not Maria, who is even now down in her kitchen baking bread, as certain that the sun will rise on a tomorrow as she is that God exists. And truly it seems to me that meeting the end in a warm, ancient kitchen scented with rising dough is as good a way as any.

I THINK OF Adolphine and the affection in her voice when she spoke of Grigori. It is my hope and belief that she and the boy will see out the extinguishing of life that will result from his response to her grandfather's rage, together. Perhaps they will sit on her porch swing, holding hands and drinking homemade lemonade until the end.

The end matters, you see. How it is accomplished.

DREAM LONDON HOSPITAL
TONY BALLANTYNE

YOU CAN'T BE too ill if you want to get into Dream London Hospital.

The building has grown along with rest of the city, so the entrance now sits six stories up. Someone has built a concrete ramp—they're still building it, in fact: they pour on a little extra every day—so that people can spiral their way up to the entrance.

Standing outside the Victorian doorway, the moon enormous in the purple Dream London sky, you can read the words engraved into the stone of the lintel—Dream London Hospital—by the generous benefaction of the Healthy.

There are people hurrying up the ramp as I tell you this: a family by the looks of them. Father, tall and thin and out of breath from pushing a rusty old pram; Mother fat, red faced and panting as she hurries to keep up. She keeps one hand on the large egg squeezed into the mouldy interior of the pram that Father is pushing. Behind them comes Daughter, ginger hair in pigtails. She's holding on to Brother's hand. He's still in his pyjamas and carrying—how sweet—a teddy bear in the other arm.

I hold open one half of the wide double doors and Father distractedly thanks me as he hurries inside. I wait until the little boy is dragged by and I follow them in, unnoticed.

The reception area is crowded with people: the bruised, cut, scratched, bleeding, wounded and syphilitic human garbage that Dream London contrives to manufacture each and every night. I slip amongst them, just another refugee from the world of pain that lies outside the doors. I loiter a moment in the queue by the reception desk, listening as Father begins to explain:

"It's our Eldest, he's..."

"He's in the egg!" interrupts Mother, pointing to the pram. "I know it! No sound from his bedroom and I go up there and this great big egg is on his bed! Well, you hear stories, don't you? So I say to Father..."

The nurse behind the desk is having none of it. She's a big woman herself, grown fat on a desk job and too many biscuits. You can see the crumbs scattered around the desk. Yellow crumbs cover her starched white blouse, and yet she clearly doesn't care. Why should she? She is the Queen of the Waiting Area.

"I think," she says, oh-so-condescendingly, "that the *doctor* will decide whether or not your Eldest is in the egg."

"I don't need the doctor to tell me that," says Mother, leaning closer to the Waiting Area royalty. She drops her voice as she puts claim to a higher authority. "A mother knows," she whispers.

Score one to Mother. But Biscuit Crumb Nurse isn't so easily beaten.

"I shouldn't think you'd need a doctor to crack that egg open," she observes.

"Mrs Matthews did that," replies Mother with grim satisfaction, "and she found her son dead of suffocation. You have to let these things work their way through..."

Mother is so intent on the argument that she doesn't notice that Daughter has let go of Son and he's wandered off into the crowd, teddy bear under his arm. Daughter has been captivated by the louche young man with the sideburns who is turning his smouldering gaze on each of the females in the room in turn. Daughter is too innocent to notice the smell of ointment that tingles from the man's trousers. I would tell Mother—I should tell Mother—but it's not in my interests to be noticed.

There is a set of double doors at the back of the waiting room from which the nurses emerge, all starched linen and black stockinged legs. That's where I need to go.

I leave Mother and Father and take a seat by Husband and Wife, the better to watch the doors. Husband has no feet; he seems embarrassed by the way his legs end just short of his ankles. Two bloody rags are tied there.

"What happened to his feet?" asks a man in a motorised green hat. Husband shrivels under Wife's glare.

"He went for one of those fish pedicures," she says.

"Don't start that again!" says Husband, angrily, "how was I to know they were using piranhas? Anyway, the man said they would grow back."

The door opens at that point and I slide from my seat to slip past the emerging nurse. I leave the Waiting Area and enter Dream London Hospital's interior.

I smell antiseptic. Nurses move back and forth. Some of them are carrying bottles of pills, some are carrying ridiculously large syringes. Some of them push trolleys around but they do so without acknowledging their human cargo. The Dream London Hospital nurses are all busy busy busy doing the maximum amount of work with the minimum amount of empathy. I scan the pale blue corridor, I look through doors into tiny rooms containing single couches. Patients sit or lie in those rooms, waiting to be seen. They press cloths to wounds, they struggle to breathe, they hold their heads in pain, they gaze out into the corridor at the hurrying nurses, feeling as if they have been forgotten. I ignore them, I need to press on. I'm late for *her*. I have to find *her*.

Three sets of lifts lie at the end of the corridor, their doors painted the dark red you would expect to find in Hell's entrance hall. I don't like the look of those lifts, I resolve to take the stairs. I find a little door to the side of the lifts and I stand a moment in the cold, yellow stairwell.

It's pleasant in here. It's always nicer to be alone, where you don't have to hide. I could stay in here for hours, stay here in this no man's land. But there is work to be done. I have to decide which way to go.

Upstairs lie the private wards, the places where the rich of Dream London come to fake illness and gain sympathy, to have a little time out from the day to day. Upstairs are the places for people suffering from the vapours; the humours; from inflamed organs of sensibility and infected hermeneutics. Upstairs are rich women needing pampering and rich men having their sex addiction worked through by a series of nubile young nurses. *She* won't be up there.

I need to head downstairs. The lower you go in Dream London Hospital, the more serious the illness. Down the stairs, past the day wards; recuperation; in-patients; intensive care; keep heading down until you reached the deepest basements. There you find the furnaces, the place where they burn all the waste, the bloody bandages, the body parts, the dead. The very end of Dream London Hospital. That's the direction I need to go.

Just as I come to that decision, someone grabs my leg.

I look down into the eyes of Son, off exploring the hospital whilst Mother and Father and Sister fuss around their egg. He must have tripped, grabbed on to me to steady himself. Son nods by way of apology, lets go of me and then sets off downstairs. I wait for a moment to make sure no one else is around, and I follow him.

DOWN THE STEPS, fifth floor, fourth floor—I feel something on the third floor, and I leave the peace of the stairwell to look around. This floor is filled with little wards, eight beds to a room. The people here aren't so sick; they walk around carrying little clear plastic bags containing their bodily fluids, holding them up for the world to see. I make my way down to Ward 33a.

This ward is better than the others—it has windows. You can see a graveyard outside: broken gravestones overgrown with brambles; white tombs, their doors gaping open invitingly. The moon hangs heavy over the landscape, white as bone. It shines on the bodies of the gasometers that have drifted here on the Dream London tides, their metal tummies split apart where they have crashed into each other. Someone has flung the windows wide to let out the smell of sickness. It was a vain move, the thick smell of Dream London has poured into the room instead. Dream London smells of flowers and fecundity. The ward smells of gangrene and perfume. The mixture is enough to turn even my stomach.

I turn around, feeling for *her*.

There's a bird staring at me from the bed by the door. Her eyes are wide, her beak open slightly. Her soft, black feathers are dull and unhealthy, they have moulted across the white linen of the bed clothes. She recognises me.

"Leave me alone, Carrionman," she says. She scrabbles to sit up, and her clawed feet emerge from the bottom of the sheets, pink and scaly.

"You can't take me," she declares. She nods her head. "Yes. I'm not your prey. I fell down, but I got up all by myself. I'll heal on my own. These Dream Londoners, they brought me here against my wishes. I don't need their help!"

She's scared and proud and defiant, and I realise that she's right. She's not the one I'm looking for.

"I'm not here for you," I say.

"I think you're lying to me, Carrionman." She looks around the room. No one else is paying us any attention. "You have no jurisdiction here," she says.

"I have jurisdiction over people, not places," I say. "And I don't lie. I'm not here for you. Tell me, have you heard of any others like us in this place?"

Bird woman shakes her head.

"There's none of us up here in the daylight. You need to head down underground. You don't need me to tell you that."

She's right, of course. I look at her.

"You'll get better," I said.

"I'll do it on my own," she says, and I know she's right. I have no claim over her.

I leave the ward. There is a trolley full of legs waiting outside, they stand bent at the knee. A man is sorting through them.

"Get away from there!" shouts a nurse.

"But they cut the wrong one off!" he shouts. The nurse steps towards him and he hops off, down the corridor.

BACK IN THE cold yellow stairwell I take a moment to myself. I prefer it in here, I really do. But I have work to do, so I fluff my feathers and I descend to the last floor above ground.

The ground floor is lit by an eerie green glow. Down here the nurses wear thick lead aprons, they have dark glass visors covering their eyes. The air crackles with energy, and I jump at the two bright flashes that suddenly flare from around the corner. I'm looking around to see if there is a place to get my own lead apron when I hear a commotion behind me. An approaching rumble, a patter of footsteps...

"Out of the way! Coming through!"

It must be the strange energy that makes me so visible down here. Not that anyone cares. I'm jostled aside by Father and Mother, pushing their egg in a pram towards the X-ray machine.

"And about time too," says Mother to the nurse hurrying along at her side, pulled along by Mother's directed rage. "We've been waiting for hours."

Half an hour would be more like it, I think. Nonetheless, I follow them to the X-ray room, feeling less visible in the middle of the group of people.

The X-ray room is filled with chugging and rattling energy. Green machinery pumps and wheezes and glows all around us. The radiologist is waiting, his bones visible through his skin. He's completely hairless: no eyebrows, no eyelashes, no down on the back of his hands. He's much too thin, he looks as if he lives on radiation alone. His eyes are bigger than light bulbs and they sweep a green glow across the egg shell.

"You sink your son iz in here?" he says. "Put him in ze machine und I will see."

"Will we be able to see him through the shell?" asks Father, impressed by all the machinery.

"Ze machine does not see objects," says the radiologist,

impatiently. "It looks at people's souls und tells zem vot zey are really like. I vill tell you if your son is good or evil or just plain dead. Zis is acceptable, yes?"

"Bloody ridiculous," says Mother.

"Steady, Mother," says Father. "The man's just doing his job."

"You do not vant?" asks the radiologist.

"I'll bloody vell have vot's going," says Mother. "But there'll be complaints, I can tell you. People in this place don't give a damn about patients. It's all just about souls. You don't look after anyone in your care properly."

Funny she should say that just as Son is walking by unnoticed behind her. She doesn't see that he's having a great time in the hospital. Someone has given him a lolly and he sucks on it as he heads, with unerring bad sense, towards the large archway that leads to the basements. The engraving over the archway reads:

Abandon bodily fluids, all those who enter here.

I wonder if I should tell Mother, but I'm not here to help, nor to hinder, so once more I follow Son down the stairs. I can hear screaming. Or maybe it's just birds singing.

THE FIRST PLACE I come to under the earth is a ward the size of an aircraft hangar. Just like one of the really big ones back home where the powerful keep their Zeppelins. This ward has beds arranged in a grid pattern across the floor, each with a yellow light hanging above it, suspended from a cord nearly a hundred feet long.

The people in this ward aren't like those in Ward 33a. Most of them just lie in their beds, faces illuminated yellow as they stare at the ceiling. These people hardly move. In fact, I notice there is less movement the farther you are from the door. I wonder how far the nurses venture into the room.

But that's not my business. I tilt my head, listening for *her*.

On a bed nearby, Boyfriend sees Son wander by.

"Someone should get him out of here," he says. "A young lad like that? You don't want the Doctor to get his hands on him."

Girlfriend is watching. She's holding Boyfriend's hands. Actually, now I come to look properly, I see that neither of them have hands. Her arms lead directly into his. These two must be just *so* into each other.

"Little boy!" calls Girlfriend. "Are you lost?"

Son looks at her, sucking on his lollipop, his—how sweet— teddy tucked in his other arm. Girlfriend leans towards him, as best she can. Boyfriend is tilted off balance. Girlfriend continues:

"Little boy, you should head back upstairs if you can! This is no place for little boys."

Son gazes at her.

"What's your name?" asks Boyfriend.

"I'm not supposed to speak to strangers," says Son, and he turns around and heads off out of the ward.

A gong sounds. Matron appears in the doorway, beater in hand.

"The anaesthetist is coming," she says. "Sit up straight and answer his questions nicely."

I feel uncomfortable now, the only person standing in a ward where everyone is weakly struggling to sit up in bed. Everyone here is clearly in terror of the anaesthetist. I need to get out, but they're all looking towards the only exit. As I stand there, gripped in indecision, I suddenly feel *her*, there at the edge of my senses.

She's close.

There's a disturbance outside. Matron is called, and she hurries from the room. I take my chance and slip out behind her.

Son is sleeping peacefully on the corridor floor. The anaesthetist is bending over him, a fussy little man in a white coat.

"Ah, Matron," he says. "I found this young lad wandering the corridors. I can't see his ID bracelet. I suspect that he shouldn't be here. Would you be so kind as to check for me?"

"Certainly, Doctor Collins," says Matron, blushing. She pats her hair, she's clearly rather taken by the anaesthetist. "And if he isn't a registered patient?" she asks.

"Then I would be grateful if you were to load him onto a trolley and take him down to spare parts." The anaesthetist squeezes Son's middle and smiles. "There are some nice healthy organs in this firm little body. I'm sure they'd appreciate them up on the fourteenth floor."

"I shall get this seen to right away, Doctor."

Matron signals and a nurse runs forward, scoops up Son in her arms, and carries him off.

"Now then, Doctor," says Matron, "are you ready for your round?"

"Let us proceed, Matron."

They head off into the ward. Only I have noticed Son's teddy—how sweet—left lying on the black and white tiles of the floor. I pick it up and stroke it. Feathers on fur: it's an odd feeling.

But all this is just a distraction. It's time to go back into the cold yellow stairwell. Down a few more flights. *She's* getting closer, I can feel *her*.

Not on the next floor, or the next. Maybe here?

The corridors on this floor are padded with thick white cushions. I can hear giggling coming from behind a door. The patients in this soft white world wander around in straitjackets, they pick up pens with their feet and write letters in flowery script. They hold cups in their toes to drink their tea.

"Hello, Welcome!"

The man hugs me, he rubs his moon face on my feathery cheek, he holds my scaly foot in his pink hand and pumps it up and down.

"So pleased you could make it," he says. "I'm mad, you know."

"He's not mad," says Queen Victoria. She is standing at his side, holding an orb in one hand and a sceptre in the other. She is clearly not amused.

"I am mad," said the man. "Aren't I?" he winks at me. "Why else would I be talking to a huge crow? You are a crow, aren't you?"

"I'm related," I say.

"Don't listen to him," says Queen Victoria. "He's only pretending to be mad. He's spreading diseases to everyone in

Dream London Hospital. He pretends to be so friendly: a hug here, a reassuring pat on the hand there, a kiss on the forehead. Spreading germs all the time. He used to be on the second floor, but they all died of the 'flu. They say it sent him mad, being the only survivor, so they sent him down here. Really, it's what he had planned all along."

"How do you know that?" asks the man, suspiciously.

"You talk in your sleep," says Queen Victoria. She nods at me. "He sold his body to the influenza virus for one month of passion. One month of drink and debauchery and unending appetites. When all that passed and he was left weak and dying in the gutter, he was brought to Dream London Hospital and now it's the turn of the virus to have its fun. We'll all be dead by the end of the week."

"Don't listen to her," says the man. "She's the mad one."

Queen Victoria sneezes. Her nose is running, her eyes are running, she's even running a temperature.

"Have you told the nurses?" I ask her.

"What nurses? There are none here! They know what he's doing. They're hoping to clean out these wards. They want us all to die so they can get some new patients in."

"Oh hush," says the man. "Go and lie down. You're feeling weak and tired."

"If I am it's all your fault." says Queen Victoria, but off she goes anyway.

The man kisses me and heads off in the other direction. Now that I have some peace I tilt my head and listen for *her*.

She isn't here on this floor, I realise, but she is close. Not ten feet away, directly below me. It's an easy mistake to make. I am thinking like a bird, ready to swoop down on my prey. I can't be a bird in this human place, I have to take the stairs.

Down the stairs one last time and into intensive care. The patients here are joined to the walls by wires and tubes. Red and brown and clear fluids are constantly pumping, out of one body and into the next. These people share their kidneys with one another, one man lives on blood oxygenated by another woman. Orange and brown liquids bubble and squelch, into arms, out of tubes in their sides. The patients drip and gurgle and spread their lives out over several yards.

Funnily enough the first person I see is Son, lying on a bed fast asleep. I tuck his teddy bear underneath his arm. How sweet.

"What's the matter with him?" asks a red haired nurse. She's not talking to me, but rather to the nurse beside her who is wearing the smallest spectacles I've ever seen. You could see atoms through those lenses. You could see quarks.

"The anaesthetist put him to sleep," she says. "He's to be used for spare parts."

"The little mite." The red haired nurse leans closer to him. "He's such a sweet little thing. Poor, too. Look at the state of his clothes. Barely rags."

"You could say the same of nearly everyone down here," says Little Spectacles.

"And he's to be cut up so that some wealthy woman upstairs can have a new liver. And in three years time she'll have drunk that one into oblivion and there'll be another little boy lying here on the bed."

"So?"

"So I'm not letting it happen," says Red Hair. "Where's the sal volatile? That'll wake him up."

"You'll be in trouble if the Doctor sees you."

"I'm not frightened of the Doctor."

"Yes, you are. Everyone is."

Red Hair shudders, but she pulls a little green bottle from somewhere and opens the lid. She holds the bottle beneath his nose.

"Here we go," she says. Son coughs and splutters, and I realise I've been delayed here for too long.

I head into the next ward. The burns unit. And here *she* is at last, lying on a bed surrounded by all sorts of wires and tubes and things. Her feathers have been burned clear away, and her naked skin is pink and tender. The doctor is marking off her intimate parts with a blue crayon.

She sees me. She turns an eye towards me, the better to look at me.

"Carrionman," she says. "I knew you'd find me."

"You can't have her," says the Doctor, his back to me as he sketches out her internal organs on her skin. "She was brought to Dream London Hospital and so now she's mine."

He turns and faces me, and I feel a flutter of fear. He's a handsome man, every inch the doctor. Friendly, calm, professional, the very model of the bedside manner. A perfect healer. And yet I can see this for the shell that it is. Underneath all that, there is nothing. No emotion. He heals people because that's his job. He doesn't care. Pay him more and he'd be just as effective an assassin. He's the consummate professional. He couldn't sell his soul, he never had one.

"Well?" he says. "Must you take up my time?"

"If you cure her, then what will I eat?" I ask.

"I'm just doing my job," replies the doctor, smoothly.

"And I'm doing mine," I say. I turn to look at *her*.

"What happened to you?" I ask.

She looks embarrassed, she can't meet my gaze.

"I was staying in a guest house in Purley," she says. "It caught fire. I was trapped inside. They dragged me out, brought me here."

"She would have died if they hadn't done so," said the Doctor.

She looks down at the bed clothes. She knows its true.

"Do you want to die?" the Doctor asks her. She doesn't reply. But she doesn't want to die.

"It doesn't matter," I say. I tilt my head the other way to look at her. "You know how it goes. You can choose to live like a human, or you can choose to live like a bird. You chose to fly."

"Carrionman," said the Doctor, "you're just looking for your next meal."

So what if I was? Didn't the Doctor eat meat?

"Step away from her, Doctor," I say. "Turn off your machines. If she is meant to die, she will die."

"And then you'll eat her, Carrionman?"

"And don't you eat, Doctor?" I reply.

He looks at me, thinking, and then he shrugs.

"Plenty more where she came from," he says, and he reaches out and flicks a switch. The green wheezing machine dies.

"But I don't..." gasps the bird woman. We watch her die, the doctor and I. And then the Doctor leaves me in peace to enjoy my meal.

THAT'S ME DONE. There is no moral to this story, by the way, save that we all have to make a living.

I head back into the corridor, ready to go home.

I'm in the basement, at the very bottom of the Dream London Hospital. I can see the orange glow of the furnaces, just around the corner.

A dark shadow crosses the wall and Son turns the corner, teddy bear under his arm. He looks at me.

"Which way out of here, mister?" he asks. He is pale, his cheeks streaked with tears. He's clearly terrified: the fact that he is in trouble has finally dawned on him. "I want my mum," he says. It's enough to wring the heart of a stone statue.

From what I've heard, there are great men around the corner, naked but for loin cloths. They feed the furnaces. Covered in sweat, they hurl everything that comes their way into the fire, no questions asked. Rags, bones, strips of flesh, little boys.

I should leave Son to his fate.

But then again, I live by bird fate, not human fate.

"You're going the wrong way," I say, and I take his hand. "Come on, I'll take you back upstairs."

"Thanks, mister," he says.

I lead him away from the furnace, back up to his parents.

SAFE HOUSE
K J PARKER

"GENTLEMEN," I SAID, "please. Think about it logically."

The noose went down over my head, brushing my nose. They're surprisingly heavy, nooses, especially the low-grade hemp type. You really feel the weight, where they press on your collar bone.

"You can't," I said, "just kill sorcerers, everybody knows that. At the last moment they turn into smoke and vanish. So, if you hang me, it'll prove I'm not a sorcerer, and you'll have killed an innocent man."

The hangman scowled at me. "They all say that," he said, and pulled the bag over my head.

I hate it when they do that. Ever since I was a kid I've never been exactly wild about confined spaces. Inside a bag is about as confined as you can get. *Oh well,* I thought. The hangman was wearing a knitted scarf round his neck; imagine his wife giving it to him. *There you are, it'll keep you nice and warm when you're out hanging people.* My toes were clenching inside my boots; I was trying to dig my imaginary claws into the scaffold floor, to get a better grip. The things you do.

(Getting hung always puts me in mind of when I was a kid, and my mother decided it was time I learned how to kill chickens. She showed me, three times (three chickens), patiently explaining, there's a right way and a wrong way; where to support the bird's weight with your left hand, how to feel for the junction of the spine and the skull with your forefinger and thumb, so that when you come to do the twist-and-lift, it'll all be as clean and easy as clicking your fingers. Now it's your turn, she said; and I tried, and I made a mess of it. No, she said patiently, like this; and she showed me again, and again (I was, what, eight years old at this point); now you do it, go on, don't be such a baby. I remember, the chicken looked at me, and I looked at it. I'll swear, that bird was *sorry* for me. So I tried, and she had to grab it out of my hands and finish it off. No, she said, you're not *listening*, you never *listen*. So she caught me another clucking, thrashing, round-eyed chicken and subdued it with her big, flat hands (she could subdue any living thing, the way I imagine only a god could) and thrust it into my arms; and I crushed it to me, and got my right hand round the bird's neck, and tugged so hard that its head just came off—

I can't click my fingers, either. There's some things you just can't learn.)

You always believe in the last-second reprieve. It never comes.

THE THING ABOUT turning into a cloud of smoke is it *hurts*. In order to do it, you have to pull apart every fibre of your body while simultaneously raising your body temperature to the point of ignition. Not only that; you don't want to burn, you want to *detonate*. In effect, you've got the pain of being torn apart and the pain of being burnt alive, all crammed into a tiny fraction of a second of really, really intense discomfort. True, it's over in a flash—literally—but that's not the end of it. Think about when you bang your knee or stub your toe; you get the initial surge of pain, followed by a long, dull ache. Now think, every bit of you. And sometimes it can last for days.

THE THING YOU dread most is a sudden gust of wind. Thankfully, on this occasion I didn't have to deal with anything like that, which was just as well. A gentle breeze picked me up and carried me into a warm patch just below the clouds, where I hung for a while (catching my breath, so to speak) until the sun went past noon, and I was able to drift down to ground level and pull myself together.

The really skilful, show-off types can solidify with their clothes on and intact; not me. I wound up in a small wood somewhere with one shirt sleeve, which was jammed round my left leg so tight I had to scrabble round for a bit of sharp flint and cut it off before it stopped the flow of blood completely. I was dizzy, disorientated, freezing cold, nauseous, starving hungry—where the contents of your stomach get to during the dematerialisation process, nobody knows—and I hurt all over. I crawled under a bush, curled up into a ball and sort of existed painfully for quite some time.

Each time, it's like being born again, except that you're not some appealingly helpless bundle of joy surrounded by loving parents and doting relatives. Instead, it's a bit like coming back as a wolf cub. Very small animals are scared of you, larger animals want to eat you, and human beings know they can get threepence bounty on your skin at minimal risk. The talent, which got you into this mess in the first place, is no use to you at all, not unless you're one of those freaks who can recover from a total dislocation in ten minutes flat. What you really need at that precise point in your career is a safe place, with solid walls and a heavy door you can bolt shut, a warm fire and (if at all possible) something to eat.

I knew of exactly such a place. It was twelve miles away. Might as well have been on the Moon.

IN AP'ESANGELIA, THEY give you dirty looks, and when you want a bed for the night, everywhere's suddenly full. In ChorisAnthropou, you have to report to the Prefecture on arrival and swear a solemn undertaking not to try any weird stuff. In Callianis, soldiers wake you up in the early hours of the morning and give you a free cart-ride to the border. In BocFlemen, they kill you.

A man might be forgiven for avoiding these places. After all, they don't want you, so why put yourself out? Answer: it's the duty of a tenured adept of the Studium to go where he's sent and, generally speaking, if the Studium sends you somewhere there's a good reason. We—use of the first person plural makes it sound like I'm on the Faculty; I'm not, I'm third grade, a footsoldier, though with distinctions in military forms—have undertaken various responsibilities, unasked, unthanked. We regulate the use and misuse of the talent, wherever, whenever. We sort out untrained naturals who suddenly discover they can turn milk sour or command earthquakes. We track down rogue adepts who decide they've had enough of running errands and want to be gods instead. We research unexplained phenomena, in case there's something we should know. Some places they like us, some they don't. We don't get paid, or anything vulgar like that. We do the job, we go home, we get sent somewhere else, in my case usually somewhere they really don't like us at all.

Such as BocFlemen. Actually, I can see their point. They have an unfortunate history with the talent. A couple of hundred years ago, we—the talented community—did them the honour of choosing their country to fight a war in. The Studium put a stop to it, eventually. By then, however, the damage had been done. There's places in BocFlemen where the grass will never grow again, and the first thing women do when they've given birth is count the baby's fingers and toes.

I get sent to BocFlemen rather too often for my liking. They send me there because, deficient as I am in many aspects of our craft, I'm rather good at dislocations. It's one of those Forms that some people can do and others can't; nothing to do with intelligence, diligence, dedication or even natural aptitude, more of a knack, like wiggling your ears. A hint for young postulants trying to decide what to specialise in after second year. Don't opt for dislocations, even if you're really good at them. Otherwise, sooner or later some sadistic bugger will send you to BocFlemen.

* * *

YOU WILL HAVE gathered from the foregoing that my latest mission had ended in abject failure. Somewhere along a very short line (I'd only been in the country three days) I'd messed up and been found out, wasted a whole week being incarcerated and tortured, and then the whole dreary business of execution. I hadn't found the talented natural I'd been sent to deal with, I hadn't even tracked down the men I was supposed to make contact with. More than likely, someone would have to come in to get me out. I really hate it when I'm the one who has to do the rescuing, and I tend not to put too much effort into hiding my resentment. I wasn't, therefore, looking forward to having to face my saviour in due course.

YOU MAY RECALL that I mentioned a war.

When wars end, things get left behind. There's the obvious stuff, like the plough turning up bones every year in a particular field, or a helmet hanging upside down from three chains over a fire, full of soup. And there's buildings. As often as not, the briars and the nettles cover them up, or the locals smash up the masonry for hard standing. But there are some bits of military architecture that are too big to hide and too strong to break, and a classic example of this class are the blockhouse towers.

Both sides built them. They both copied the specifications faithfully from the same book, so you have no way of knowing from the outside which are which—unfortunate, since each side encoded their towers with heavy-duty guard forms, instantly and absolutely lethal to the other side. We—my lot—weren't on either side in that war, our order hadn't even been founded back then, but for some reason the towers of Side A—we don't know their names or anything about them—tolerate us, while Side B's towers kill us the moment we walk through the door. We have maps, of course, showing all the towers; where known, the towers are marked friendly or hostile. Roughly two thirds of them have been annotated in this manner. Naturally, since I seem to spend so much time in bloody Boc, I've studied these maps in great detail. I know where all the towers are, and their polarity (where ascertained). There was a tower twelve miles away. Needless to say, the polarity was unrecorded.

Great. However, if you can get inside one without it killing you, a blockhouse tower is your very best friend in a place like Boc. It will feed and clothe you, keep you warm, keep you safe until someone traipses out to get you. Boc people won't go near them, not for any money; I have no idea what they see when they look at them, but it's not what I see, that's for sure. A while back, they had a nasty habit of posting sentries round them at a safe distance, to arrest anyone trying to get inside; since the budget cuts, they haven't bothered so much. The tower was, therefore, my very best hope, provided I could get there and it didn't kill me. Fifty-fifty; in Boc, those are very good odds.

I GOT THERE.

Only just. The torrential rain was good, in that it kept people indoors, so I was able to move in daylight; not so good, in that I was soaked to the skin, and the ploughed fields turned into glue, and my eyes were full of rain so I couldn't see where I was going. But you don't want to hear about a naked man taking a very long, very miserable walk in the country. I got there.

Blockhouse tower 316N528W stands on the highest point of a hog's back dividing two river valleys. As is often the case, a dense wood had grown up all round it in the hundred-fifty-odd years since the war; the towers obviously did something to the ground they stood on, because grass, weeds, nettles, briars, all the usual ground rubbish simply won't grow within a three-mile radius, but oaks, beeches and silver birches go crazy. Ironic, in a way. They're desperately short of good lumber in Boc and pay through the nose to import it, and there's all this good standing timber they daren't touch.

Trees are good, though, if you don't want to be seen, so once I was inside the eaves of the wood, I was able to relax a little. It took me longer than I'd thought to find the bloody thing, but eventually I struggled up a steep slope and there it suddenly was, crowded by half a dozen of the biggest oak trees you ever saw, like a diplomat flanked by bodyguards.

Blockhouse tower describes them pretty well. They're square-footprint blocks, straight-sided, flat-topped, no battlements, crenellations or frilly bits. I read somewhere that they're built of brick faced with a special kind of concrete, the recipe for which was lost a long time ago—how anyone knows this I have no idea—because the facing doesn't weather, crumble or crack. What you see is a single black block about forty feet high, twenty feet square; sheer, smooth sides, slightly rough to the touch, and in the dead centre of the north-facing wall, the crumbling remains of a single steel door.

I stood and looked at it. This one was in better shape than most; it was red with rust but still in one piece, and someone had left it slightly ajar. It's going through the doorway that kills you. I went all thoughtful. The only people who use the towers nowadays are our lot. A partly-open door would therefore suggest that someone had tried to get in and been struck dead on the threshold. But I looked and there were no signs of a body—meaning nothing, since there are wolves in Boc, not to mention badgers, foxes and rats. Or it could be that the last person to use the tower had neglected to shut the door, or the door latch no longer worked. I stared at it for a very long time. Then, feeling more stupid than ever before, which is really saying something, I walked up to it and sort of winced sideways, slid past the door and went in.

There are few sensations like that of still being alive. I felt about two stone lighter, and suddenly and instantly exhausted, like if I didn't sit down right away I'd fall down where I stood. It goes without saying, it's as dark as a bag inside a tower (who needs windows when you've got *lux in tenebris*?) I sort of melted down onto my knees and stayed there for a while, relishing breathing. Then I heard something.

Another feature of the blockhouse towers is sanitation and pest control. Dust doesn't gather inside a tower, and there are positively no rats, mice, cockroaches, spiders, vermin of any sort. I dread to think what happens to them; they just aren't there. The only thing that makes a noise inside a tower, therefore, is people.

I kept very, very still. I hadn't moved the door coming in, so maybe the noise-maker didn't know I was there. Logic, that annoyingly unhelpful friend, was telling me that it could only be one of our lot, since nobody else would go inside a tower in Boc. Also, stupid Logic insisted on telling me, even if it's someone nasty, inside a tower, you're enormously powerful; the tower will enhance any offensive or defensive form you care to use, and will of its own accord shield you from any physical attack from a non-adept. There's nothing to be afraid of, Logic said. Well.

"Hello?" said a voice. "Is there someone there?"

In my defence; it was a female voice, and she sounded terrified. It's a sort of assumption you make; that the enemy is never scared. The enemy, as we imagine him, is a sort of ice-cool, nerves-of-steel super-predator, every fibre of whose being is concentrated with absolute intensity on killing you. So, you tell yourself, if the voice sounds petrified with fear, it can't be the enemy. Bullshit, of course. I've been the enemy loads of times, and I'm permanently terrified.

"Hold on," I said. "I'll get us some light."

Towers are really good at some things. I'd got as far as *lux*, and the lights came on.

A BRIEF DIGRESSION on the operating system of blockhouse towers.

As previously noted, we know almost nothing about them, or the people who built them. The leading hypothesis says that the interior of a tower isn't real-time physical space. Instead, when you walk through the door, you're automatically transported to a Room—third-floor, most likely, since that's where most of the shareable Rooms are; also, the few characteristics of towers we know about are consistent with the behaviour of third-floor environments. Take, for example (the hypothesists say) the furniture issue. When you enter a tower and turn up the light (possibly before, but how would you know?) the interior furnishes and decorates itself according to your wishes or, more usually, your preconceptions—just as a third-floor Room does. The alternative explanation (that the tower-builders had forms capable of materialising solid, real tables, chairs, curtains, footstools, bookshelves, candelabra, dinner services and spittoons out of thin air) is basically untenable. Anything solid you find in a tower is therefore only Room-real, which is why you can't take it outside with you. Quite convincing, except it doesn't explain how you can live on the food.

THE ONLY WORD to describe it was—

"Hello," I said.

She looked at me. Her eyes were so wide open, it must have hurt. Twenty-seven or so (but I'm useless at women's ages); thin face, mousy hair, very pale.

"It's all right," I said. "You're perfectly safe."

—*vulgar*. As in ghastly taste, as in tart's boudoir, as in—Well. Pink marble floor, for crying out loud. Little spindly-legged occasional tables, painted white, with ivy leaves. Enough red velvet to make curtains for the sky. Those pink-blue-and-white porcelain vases. Even a silver-gilt incense burner in the shape of a begging dog.

"I'm so sorry," she said. "I really didn't know I was—"

"Trespassing?" I gave her an idiot grin. "Me too. How did you get in here?"

"The door was open. I—"

It suddenly occurred to me that I was wearing a lot of mud and not much else. On the third floor, you just have to think, and—

She screamed. Well, fair enough. I'd just materialised a knee-length pale grey Brother's habit out of thin air. My trouble is, I don't consider the consequences of my actions.

"It's all right," I said. "It's not how it—"

"You can do it too."

IT'S NOT THAT I mind being stupid *per se*. It's the embarrassment that gets to me, the frustration at the time I waste, the idiotic messes I get myself into, the long, dreary business of sorting them out, explaining, trying to undo the damage.

Why had I been sent to Boc in the first place? To track down an untrained natural. Well, then. A man of normal perspicacity, a non-idiot, would've made the connection as soon as he heard a noise inside a blockhouse tower. Only a talented could get inside a tower. At any given time, there are very, very few talented in Boc, and we know all about them; we go to inordinate lengths to find them and get them out of there safely. Therefore, a talented discovered unexpectedly inside a tower in Boc *must* be an untrained natural—probably some poor kid from a village who knows he's different but not why; terrified, of course, desperate; as a very last resort, he makes a run for it and holes up in a tower, without the faintest clue what a tower is or what it does. True, her being a she might tend to confuse the issue, since it's an article of faith that very few women have the talent; but it's far from unknown, probably much commoner than we're led to believe. I should've figured it out much, much earlier. What can I say? I'm an idiot.

"IT'S ALL RIGHT," I repeated. "You're perfectly safe."

(See above, under idiot.)

"You can," she said—a curious blend of terror and triumph, a real collector's item. "You can do—"

"Yes, but we don't call it that. Certainly not in BocFlemen." I paused for breath. "You and I can both do some stuff that other people can't. It's no big deal. It's like some people are double-jointed. That's all it is."

She looked at me.

"But," I went on, "your people have a—well, let's say they have a different attitude. It's not like that where I come from. I'm from the Studium, in Politeia Thaumasta. Actually, I came here to find you."

She blinked, as though I'd shone a bright light in her face. "Me?"

I nodded. "We look after our own," I said. "I came to find you and ask if you'd like to come back to the Studium with me. The people there are all like us, so you wouldn't have to be scared any more. If you want—it's entirely up to you—we can show you how to control the gift you've been born with, and use it to do good, useful things. Obviously you don't have to come with me, but I really do think you should. I know it's difficult to accept, but you're not safe here."

"I know *that*." Well, I have The Speech off by heart, and I get all tongue-tied and hopeless if I try and adapt it to circumstances. "You'll take me away? To—"

"Thaumasta. It's on the far side of the mountains. We could be there in four days."

She frowned. "What would I have to do? I haven't got any money."

One of the Frequently Asked Questions; much better. I knew what to say. "That's perfectly all right," I said. "The Studium pays for everything. You get board and lodgings and clothes to wear, and like I said, if you want to learn we'll teach you, no charge. It's what we're for. We've been doing it for two hundred years, so we know how to look after people." I paused. She was still looking at me. "I don't want to hurry you," I said, "and I know, you want time to think about it, but please don't take too long. We're perfectly safe so long as we stay in this tower, but outside it could be dangerous, so if you're coming, the sooner we leave the better." I never know how to finish that particular speech. I just tail off and try and look sincere. I suspect I'm not very good at it.

"I'm not sure," she said. "I've been here a very long time."

"You think you have," I corrected her gently. "These towers

are funny old places. Time doesn't work quite the same in here. It's like—" I glanced at her. The next bit should've been, *instead of time being a straight line, think of it as a spiral, a spring you can stretch out, or you can squash it flat and the coils touch each other*. The look on her face reminded me ever so much of a rabbit. "It's different," I said.

"I don't think I could leave," she said. "It wouldn't be safe."

"It's all right," I heard myself say. "You'll be with me."

ONE PROBLEM WITH wars between factions of the talented community is that they're unwinnable. Invariably, after a brief initial phase marked by high levels of spectacular activity and collateral damage, both sides retreat to invulnerable fortified positions and exhaust themselves engaging in long-range area bombardment, whose only effect (apart from general devastation of the surrounding area) is to make sure that the other side can't leave their bunkers. Only when resources and patience run out does one side take the fairly desperate risk of trying to storm the enemy positions with ground forces. More often than not, the side making this move loses; too many of its people die in the attempt, until the point is reached where the losses cross the threshold into unacceptability, and there's no option but to cede the disputed territory and withdraw. In other words, victory almost always goes to the side that keeps its nerve longest and is prepared to tolerate the most damage.

Which probably explains why we tend to fight our wars in other people's countries. It's so much easier to keep one's nerve when the villages and fields getting burnt into glass belong to some stranger. A strategist must, above all, avoid the distractions of sentiment and emotional involvement, which must inevitably cloud his clear view of the true objective, victory.

Another problem is that our wars never end. We tell them to, but they rarely listen.

* * *

"FINE," I SAID. "Let's just stay here for now, get to know each other a little better, and when you feel like you can trust me, we'll go. How does that sound?"

She looked at me with her head slightly on one side. "I don't think I can—"

"It's all right," I said quickly, "we're not going anywhere. For now. Meanwhile—" I tried smiling. I really shouldn't. "How about something to eat?"

It was as if I'd said something inappropriate. "I looked when I got here," she said. "There was no food anywhere."

"Ah." Big grin. "That's because you didn't look in the right place."

"But I looked everywhere."

"No you didn't."

All right, party trick. Cheap party trick. In towers, like in third floor rooms, there's always a stone jar (grey, ordinary looking, about yay high) in the east corner. Just think of what you want and lift the lid—

"Here we are," I said.

—except it can't do cheese. Nobody knows why. I put my hand down inside the jar and produced a loaf of bread, two of those air-dried Vesani sausages and four apples. "Here," I said, throwing her an apple. "Catch."

She didn't even try. It hit the wall next to her, bounced and rolled ridiculously across the floor. "I'm not hungry."

Impossible. Refugees and fugitives are always hungry. They snatch the food out of your hand and eat like dogs. "Ah well," I said, breaking the loaf in half. "I'll put yours here and you can have it when you feel like it." I'd just realised that I was a refugee and a fugitive, and I was starving. I crammed bread into my face and chewed violently until it was all gone.

Long silence. She was watching me. I hate that. I got up, crossed the room and picked a book at random off the shelf. It turned out to be Anthemius' *Principles of Metallurgy*. I'd read it before (obviously, or it couldn't have been there) I sat down beside the fire and started to read.

Literacy is a wonderful thing. Not only does it communicate the wisdom of the ages throughout all time, it also helps you avoid those soul-destroying staring matches when neither of you has anything to say. I read two whole chapters before she finally admitted defeat.

"Where you come from—"

I closed the book and smiled at her. "Yes?"

"They can all do—you know—where you're from?"

"No," I said. "Most people can't, like most people aren't double-jointed. But those who can aren't feared or persecuted. We all come together in the place where I live—the Studium—and we learn to improve our skills, we study, and we help people."

She frowned. "I was told you hurt people."

Ah yes, I thought. "We don't," I said. "I mean my lot, the Studium. But talented people—that's people like you and me, the ones who have the gift—sometimes they do some pretty nasty things; just because they have the power, because they *can*. They did some really bad things here, in BocFlemen, a long time ago. It doesn't happen any more, because the Studium doesn't allow it, but the Boc people don't trust us. Why should they, after all? One day, we hope, they'll change their minds, but until then all we can do is try and stay out of their way."

"But you're here."

I nodded. "I was sent to find someone," I said. "I was sent to find you."

Her eyes opened wide. "Me?"

I nodded. "I was told to come here and rescue an untrained natural—that's what we call people like you, people who have the talent but have never been taught to use it. If they're left on their own, they can hurt themselves, or other people—not through malice, but accidentally, or from not knowing their own strength. Or they're in danger just for being talented, like in Boc. Well, we didn't have much to go on, just that this untrained natural was somewhere in this part of Boc—"

"Someone told you?"

I shook my head. "We can sort of feel these things," I said. "It's a bit complicated. Anyway, I came, and here you are."

"You came to rescue me."

I didn't sigh. It takes a while in practice before you realise; talented doesn't necessarily mean smart. Especially your untrained naturals. Some of them are as thick as bricks. "That's right," I said patiently. "That's the only reason I'm here. To take you to where you'll be safe."

She shook her head. "I don't think there's any such place," she said.

It's a bit like getting the pig to go in the cart. The more you try and drag, shove, chivvy, crowd it in, the more it digs in its trotters and walks backwards. So instead you chuck a couple of apples in and go away, then sneak back two minutes later, when the pig's climbed aboard and is happily munching, and slam the tailgate shut very fast. I smiled at her, picked up the book and started reading. Curiously, the book was now *Themistocles on Animal Husbandry*. I turned to the bit about keeping bees, which I rather like.

"What sort of things can you do?" she asked.

I put the book down. "Ah," I said. "Now that's an interesting question."

She listened attentively as I did the usual spiel—what we can't do, followed by what we can, followed by what we won't do, followed by what we actually do. I no longer need to think while I recite, so I spent the time observing her reactions, hoping for a tiny crack in the ironclad reserve, into which I could drive the wedge of urgency. Something odd there. Normally—as in 99 times out of 100—the usual spiel is competing against inherent disbelief, distrust and fear: *Is this strange man really what he says he is, is he really going to help me or is he the kettlehats in disguise?* This time, it was as though she was ticking things off on a list, preparatory to making a decision that wasn't the one I was trying to get her to make.

* * *

I USED THE term *ground troops* earlier. I suspect I've misled you into thinking that it refers to adepts, talented, *us*, being sent in to slog it out toe-to-toe with the enemy. That's not actually how it works. Adepts—all adepts, even me—are valuable assets; a great deal of time, money and resources has been spent on us by the time we graduate, and there are few enough of us to begin with. We're simply too precious and rare to waste. Wars among the talented are utterly devastating and ruinous, but nobody actually *dies*.

None of us, at any rate. For any warlike activity that involves physical activity (such as actually being there, within a two hundred mile radius of the combat zone) we employ, conscript, commandeer suitable bodies from the local untalented population to act as our proxies. Naturally we prefer volunteers, lured by promises of substantial payments to them—or, more realistically, their next of kin—but it's rarely possible to get enough people of sufficient calibre to be useful. A proxy, after all, needs to have a mind big enough and strong enough to hold and withstand the things we need to put in it. There are also intense physical demands. A proxy must be capable of surviving sustained periods during which his heart beats at twice its normal pace and his ribcage is subjected to extreme internal pressure. Saloninus once said that acting as a proxy is the equivalent of running twenty miles up a steep hill carrying someone heavier than yourself in your arms without waking him. I have no idea if that's true, but nobody's seen fit to refute it in an official publication.

About eighty per cent of proxies don't survive. Those that do tend not to live very long, for which they and those close to them are probably quite grateful. A very few come out of the experience monstrously enhanced, both physically and mentally, and live to a ridiculously old age. It's fortuitous that most of these fortunate few go on to develop a remarkable level of serenity and inner peace, which many an adept would envy. Most of them.

Fighting a war via proxies is almost, not quite but almost,

as hard on the adepts who wield them. The mental strain, so I'm told, is debilitating. In extreme cases, it can lead to severe damage to, or even loss of the adept's talent, which must surely be the proverbial fate worse than death. You can see why even enlightened people such as us would go to any length to avoid it.

"WERE YOU IN the war?" she asked.

Not a question I'd been expecting. "No, of course not," I said. "The war was centuries ago and I'm not that old. Also, the Studium wasn't involved, I told you that. It didn't even exist back then."

She tucked a stray strand of hair behind her ear. I like it when women do that; it's either alluring or endearing, sometimes both. In her case, neither. "So your people didn't build this tower?"

"No, of course not. But we can use it, because we're talented. Just as you can. Because you are too."

She frowned. Then she went to the stone food jar and lifted the lid. She reached down inside—

"There," I said. "You see?"

—and took out a knife.

(WHICH IS WHY it's so important that, one of these days, someone gets to the bottom of this towers business. Are they third-floor Rooms, or are they something quite distinct and different? It's important because, as everyone knows, a merely physical weapon can't harm a properly-prepared adept; he simply uses *scutum* or *lorica* and the weapon skids harmlessly off his skin, or he dislocates and floats away to safety as a cloud of fine grit. But if the inside of a tower is a third-floor Room, it's not like that at all. Room weapons (as everyone knows) work in a different way. They cause Room-wounds and Room-death, the proverbial Fates Worse Than, and not even *lorica* is guaranteed to protect you against them. With a Room knife, skilfully handled, you can do so much more than just kill someone.

Worst case; you can cut off their fingers. No fingers, you can't turn the doorknob. You can't turn the doorknob, you can't leave the Room. Now that's—)

AND A LOAF of bread. She cut two thick slices. "Want some?" she said.

"No thanks," I said.

"Suit yourself." She took another dip in the jar, and came out with a small piece of bacon, the size of a clenched fist, and a slab of white cheese.

"Is there anything to drink?" she asked.

I was staring at her. As previously noted—

"Middle of the south-east wall," I heard myself say. "There should be some sort of three-legged table. Under it, you'll find a small horn bottle."

"Ah, right," she said. I heard liquid gurgle into a glass.

As previously noted, the jars in towers and Rooms can't do cheese. I stared at it. Maybe it's butter, I thought wildly. But butter isn't stiff and crumbly.

"So," she said briskly, "you aren't one of the original tower-builders."

"No," I said. "How did you—?"

"So," she went on, with her mouth full, "really, you have no right to be here."

Something sort of plucked a string in my stomach. "Excuse me?"

"You shouldn't be in here at all," she said. "You're an intruder."

The small and underdeveloped part of me that deals with self-preservation issues was waking up. All right, I was thinking, time to be sensible. In which case, let's bypass *scutum* altogether and go straight to *lorica*.

I couldn't do it.

You know what it's like in first-year; when they tell you to do such and such a form, and you just *can't*. You try and try till your eyes pop, but it's real thaumaturgical constipation, you simply can't make it happen. I was actually clenching my fists, white knuckles and everything. What that was supposed to achieve I have no idea.

"I told you I wasn't safe," she said.

Oh, I thought. Oh, I see. "I'm not sure what you mean," said my voice.

She gave me an oh-come-on look. "You're an intruder," she said. "You aren't on our side, so you must be the enemy. I'm really sorry, you've been really rather sweet while I was waking up, but I'm afraid I'm not allowed to make exceptions. So you see, I'm not at all safe. I'm dangerous."

The door is to the left of the centre of the north-east wall. Because of the need to maintain eye contact I didn't turn and look for it, just backed towards it, groping for the handle with my left hand. It didn't seem to be there.

She clicked her tongue sympathetically. "No door," she said. "Sorry."

And she was quite right. There was no door anywhere in the room.

"You can't hurt me," I said, in a loud, wobbly voice. "I'm an adept of the Studium, with distinctions in military forms. If you make me fight, you'll just get hurt."

She sighed. "I know you are," she said. "Luckily for me."

"Luck—"

"That's right." Slight nod. "Unlike me, you're an adept. A powerful one. Me, I'm just a proxy." She smiled. "The talent's so rare among women, as you well know."

"You're a proxy?"

Another nod. "That's right," she said. "Yours."

The wall felt very solid against my back. Evidence, now I come to think of it, against the towers-are-third-floor-Rooms hypothesis. At the time, though, my academic instincts weren't exactly to the fore.

"You're not making any sense," I think I said.

"Oh come now." She was smiling. "Don't you see the elegant simplicity? Towers defend themselves against enemy intruders by drawing power from them; the defending proxy is powered up and the intruder is weakened. It's a very slight modification of *ruetcaelum*, that's all. You know, the form that you people use to control us."

"*Ruat*," I said, "not *ruet*."

She shrugged. "I stand corrected. Anyway, that's why you can't do *scutum* or *lorica*. In fact, because you were so very sweet and opened yourself up so generously, you can't even make a door any more. There's no way out, I'm sorry. I'll try and make it as painless as possible, I promise."

She raised one finger, and I felt as though I was being gutted alive; as though all my insides were being pulled out through my ears. She'd taken practically all of my talent, and now she was holding it, balanced on the palm of her hand, a little glowing red egg.

"Sorry," she said.

"Please," I said, edging away down the wall. "The war's over. There's no need."

"Not up to me," she said sadly. "I just do what you clever men tell me to."

I was stuck in the corner. Nowhere to go.

"I'm not one of them," I said. "The Studium doesn't fight wars. We clean up after them. I'm on your side, really."

"No, you're not."

There was no use trying to argue with that. So instead, I stabbed her with the breadknife.

SHE TOOK SEVERAL hours to die. If I'd had my full talent, I could have saved her. I tried. But it took so long to come back (as life ebbed out of her and back into me); by the time I was able to do anything, it was too late. She started to cry. I wanted to ask her to forgive me, but a refusal often offends.

The moment her eyes went blank, a door appeared in the wall. I sat and looked at it. Stupid door, I thought. I know where you lead, and I'm not sure I want to go there any more. I could just stay here and—I don't know, defend the tower against intruders, or just sit and stare at the walls. Just exist; it's not much, but it's more than a lot of people can do.

But it doesn't work like that.

Some time (which doesn't pass, of course, in Rooms) later, I got up, brushed the dust off my trousers, opened the door and went outside. The clothes came with me, which was nice. I wandered around in the forest for a bit, distracted by a wide variety of thoughts, and eventually strayed out into the open fields. Which was where they found me.

I think they hit me with something from behind. When I came round, I was tied to a chair. The chair was on the bed of a cart. The tailgate was hanging open. The cart was under a tree. There was a noose round my neck.

"You again," the hangman said. He was still wearing the scarf.

I laughed. I felt so happy. "Gentlemen," I said, "please. Think about it logically."

HEY, PRESTO!
ELLEN KLAGES

ON A GRAY Thursday afternoon, the fourth-form lounge was crowded with girls studying for exams. "I can't make heads or tails of this," one said with a sigh. She tossed her chemistry text onto the couch. "I'm just not the school type." She looked down at her Giles Hall uniform with a grimace.

"Have you thought about running away with the circus?" another girl asked.

"Oh, wouldn't that be a dream? Spangles and spotlights and applause. That's the life for me."

Several girls nodded in agreement. Polly Wardlow bit her tongue and kept her head down, her short brown hair falling over her eyes. None of the others noticed her look of disagreement. She concentrated on her own chemistry book, happy to lose herself in the refuge of equations and numbers—reliable, constant, and utterly practical.

Unlike her father, the magician. That was the family business, arcane secrets passed down from the men of one generation to the next. Even now, she thought, Hugh Wardlow—Vardo! on his posters—was performing somewhere on the continent, astounding the gullible with his illusions and legerdemain.

Perhaps just a bit of that had rubbed off, because Polly had a trick of her own. She knew how to make herself invisible. She kept quiet, sat at the back of each class, and sometimes wore

131

a pair of window-glass spectacles, nicked from the props room after a pantomime in her second term. They hid her face and made her look more serious. With the exception of the cricket pitch—she was an athletic girl and quite a skilled bowler—Polly preferred her own company, and spent her time reading and preparing herself for university, where she would study science, not trickery.

"The post is here!" called a girl from the doorway. There was a mad scramble as girls leapt from couches and chairs and clustered around the table in the corner of the room. Polly waited until the crowd had dispersed before checking for a letter of her own. She was hoping to hear from her Aunt Emma, her late mother's only sister; Emma and her husband David taught at a small college in Sussex. Because her father was always traveling, Polly spent the summers with them and their three sons, exploring the woods and ponds by day, reading in their library each night.

But the only letter was from London, on Vardo! stationery.

She returned to her chair and opened it. Just a few lines, in bold blue ink, and they changed everything.

> *Your uncle has been offered a research position in America for the summer, a marvelous opportunity, and the boys have never been abroad, so they're sailing the end of May. Naturally, you will summer in London. Will meet your train on 7th June.*
> *—Father*

Polly read it once more, then gathered her books and retreated to her room. She lay on her narrow bed, gazing out the window at the sports field, but seeing in her mind the rolling Sussex pastures. She willed herself not to cry. She was fourteen, hardly a baby. And London did have the British Museum, and the Library. Besides, it was only for a few months.

She knew that if she told any of the other girls, they would swoon with envy. Their fathers were in shipping or insurance, barristers and judges, from all accounts stuffy, dull men, not dashing international celebrities. Who would understand that she viewed this summer with as much anticipation as a trip to the dentist?

Polly did not dislike her father, nor fear him. It was just that they were, for all intents and purposes, strangers. His face was familiar, but his habits and interests were mysteries. And he knew just as little about her.

Her visits during Christmas week were a mix of parties with his fashionable friends—from which she was dispatched early—and the occasional awkward supper. He was at the theatre until late, rose at noon, and spent the day at his club or at his workshop, tinkering with whatever it was that he did between performances.

It had not always been that way. When she was very young, he had delighted her with tricks—pulling shillings from her ears, making her stuffed rabbit appear and disappear, cracking open her supper egg and releasing a butterfly that hopped up onto the window sill.

Then her parents had gone on a tour of the Antipodes. Her mother contracted a fever and died on the ship home. Polly was seven. Her father locked himself away with photographs and grief, and a few months later, Polly was packed off to Giles Hall.

HER FATHER WAS on the platform when Polly alighted from the train at St. Pancras. As always, his dark hair was slicked back with brilliantine, and his moustache was trimmed to a stiff brush, but he was not in his performer's top hat and tails, just a business suit.

"Hello, my dear," he said, leaning down to pick up her valise. She could smell the bay rum on his breath. "Hope I'm not late. There was a meeting at the admiralty, and it ran long."

"Have you joined the service?" War was brewing. It was all Mr. Patterson, the history master, had talked about for the last month of the term, but surely they would not be drafting men as old as her father?

"In a manner of speaking. They're forming a rather specialized unit—Stars in Battledress, catchy name—and they've offered to make me a captain."

"Will you be fighting? If there's a war?"

"Hardly. We'd be charged with maintaining morale and entertaining the troops, that sort of thing."

"Oh," Polly said. "I'm certain they'll appreciate it." They walked toward the station entrance. After a moment, she said, trying to keep her tone neutral, "You'll be traveling, then?"

"Not right away. In September, perhaps. Ah, here's a taxi." He held the door open as she got in, then settled himself beside her. "Alfred Place, Bloomsbury," he told the driver.

Polly sat quietly, watching the city stream by.

"But in the meantime," her father said when they stopped at a light, "I'm putting together another show." He pulled out his briar pipe. "The premiere is in a month."

"How very nice for you."

"Yes, quite." He lit his pipe and leaned back against the seat. "We're developing a new illusion for it. I've had to put a man on the door to keep prying eyes away until we open."

"So the public won't know?"

"And so other magicians can't—borrow. It's a rather cut-throat business," he sighed. "Once we're finished, it should play well, but there are more than a few kinks to work out before we get it on stage."

"You're in rehearsals now?"

"Day and night. I'm afraid your old dad may not be home for supper much, but duty calls." He tapped the driver. "This is it. Number twenty-three."

"They also serve who only stand and wait," Polly said, hiding a smile. "I'm sure I'll get along somehow."

FOR THREE DAYS, Polly reacquainted herself with the house and the neighborhood, settling into a pleasant routine. She decided on an overstuffed chair in a sunny corner of the parlor as her reading spot, found a shop that stocked her favorite brand of sweets, and secured a library card. She dressed in comfortable trousers and a jersey and was out by the time her father woke, supped alone on soup and good bread, and was in bed reading or asleep by the time he came home.

So she was quite startled when she came down the stairs at half past eight, her mouth watering in anticipation of Cook's cinnamon scones, to see her father seated at the table in his bathrobe, the *Times* folded beside his plate.

"You're up early." She helped herself to tea and, after a moment's hesitation, sat down beside him. At close quarters, she could see that his eyes were a bit red, and he had not yet shaved.

"Yes, well—" He brushed a finger across his moustache, as if reassuring himself of its presence, and cleared his throat. "I have a bit of a problem, and thought I might ask your help."

Wariness and curiosity vied for Polly's attention. The tea slopped into its saucer as she set it down. "What is it?"

"How tall are you now?"

"Excuse me?" She had not expected that.

He looked at her, eyebrow raised, and she said, hesitantly, "Five—five feet four. And a half. I think."

"Excellent. Are you limber?"

"I suppose. I'm quite good at sports." Polly pinched off a bit of scone, but her stomach informed her that at the moment it was not inclined to receive it, and she put it down. "Why do you ask?"

"Well, you see—" He paused, turning the handle of his teacup, and Polly realized, another surprise, that he was as nervous as she. "Fact of the matter is, one of my assistants gave notice last night. Valinda Banks. Says she's been accepted to the Women's Auxiliary Air Force, of all things."

"I see," Polly said, as if it were a point in a debate. "But what does that have to do with—" she let her words trail off, because she was not yet entirely clear *what* they were discussing.

"Valinda is about your size, and well, the illusion has a

rather small trap, no one else fits, and we haven't the time to build another." He smoothed his hand across the unwrinkled newspaper. "What do you say?"

"Wait. You want me as your assistant?" Polly's voice squeaked. His few female performers were always vivacious, attractive blondes. She was none of the above.

"I suppose I could advertise for someone just like you—small, smart, and a quick study—" He smiled at her, his moustache turning up at the ends, "But here you are. And you're a Wardlow. It's in your blood."

She sat very still, her unswallowed tea acrid in her mouth.

"Now, now. It's not *that* difficult."

You wouldn't know. Polly thought. *You love to perform.* But he looked so earnest that she could find no excuse to refuse him. Finally she gulped and managed a weak, "I don't have any experience."

"No one does, not with this one. We're all learning from the ground up."

She took a deep breath. "All right. I guess I—"

He stood. "Splendid. That's just splendid." He leaned down and gave her a peck on the cheek. "You know how proud your mother would've been, seeing you in the act?"

Polly felt herself blush. She could not remember the last time her mother had been mentioned. Or that her father had kissed her. It felt both comforting and utterly alien. "I don't know what to say." *That* was the absolute truth.

"Say you'll come with me today, if only to have a look around. I'll give you a tour, show you the basics, then later I'll take you to supper at the Criterion, just the two of us." He gave her shoulder a squeeze and stepped back. "Well?"

"That sounds like a perfect day," Polly said, lying as convincingly as any actress. "Thank you, father."

THE ST. JAMES Theatre was in the heart of the West End, just off Piccadilly Circus, the streets clogged with black taxis and red buses. Every building was bedizened with electric-light signs and billboards as tall as houses.

The taxi dropped them in front of the ornate lobby doors. On either side were alarmingly large posters of her father—of Vardo!—dramatically backlit, hair and teeth gleaming, his hands cupped around an object invisible to the viewer.

In the middle of the day, the theatre was closed. Her father steered her around the corner into an alley. A man sat outside the stage door on a stool, smoking a cigarette.

He stood. "Afternoon, sir."

"Hullo, Alf. My daughter's down from school for the summer. I'm hoping she'll be a regular face around here."

"Anything you need, miss." He touched the brim of his cap and held the door open for them.

It took a moment for Polly's eyes to adjust from the brightness of a summer day to the dim corridor. Backstage, the theater had none of the glamour of its public spaces. It was a dark-walled warren of cramped passageways with worn wooden floors and exposed brick walls, hung with wiring and massive loops of rope. Ladders and stairs canted off at every angle. She tipped her head back until her neck creaked and still could not see the ceiling, obscured by forty vertical feet of catwalks, pulleys, lights, and hanging canvas.

"Down here," her father said, pointing to narrow wooden stairs. She followed him to a low-ceilinged basement. Wooden beams were strung with bare electric bulbs; painted flats and discarded props and scenery lined the unfinished walls.

Polly had seen a few of her father's shows from the audience, the flash and the dazzle, the polished lacquered tables with gleaming brass fittings, the silks and velvet drapes. This place bore no relation to that stage, as far as she could tell. Yet when he turned, she saw that his face was alight with excitement, like a small boy with a new toy.

"My workshop." He opened an unvarnished wooden door and gestured her inside. "This is where the real magic happens."

The room was long and reasonably wide, lined on one side by

workbenches covered with tools and pieces of metal and what looked like laboratory equipment. Large machines stood in the middle of the space—enormous saws and lathes and drills, the floor beneath them covered in sawdust.

Her father took off his jacket and hung it on a rack by the door. "It occurred to me that you know very little about my work," he said, rolling up his shirtsleeves. "I suspect that you'll find it rather interesting."

Polly had her doubts, but her father looked more casual and relaxed than she could remember, and it had already been a day of surprises. She recalled an adage from one of her textbooks: *The first job of a scientist is to keep an open mind.* "Lay on, MacDuff," she said.

They walked slowly around the room. He showed her boxes with hidden panels that opened and shut with levers and pulleys; pistons that raised and lowered vases and other props; mirror-lined boxes that, when turned at an angle, would appear to be empty. With each object, he gave a concise explanation of the mechanics, and how it affected what the audience saw—or didn't see.

Another table held tins of pigments and binders, liquid rubber, cans of turpentine and pungent solvents. He demonstrated paints that glowed in the dark, or were such a matte black they rendered an object almost invisible in dim light.

Next was a sort of chemistry lab, jars of powders and crystals, beakers and glass rods, Bunsen burners, all familiar friends to Polly. She picked up a jar marked $KClO_3$. "Potassium chlorate," she said. "What do *you* do with it?" At school they used it to produce pure oxygen, but there wasn't much to see.

"I'll show you." He spooned a little bit of the white powder onto a square of paper, then ran a finger across the shelf of chemicals until he found the jar marked SULFUR. He carefully sifted some of that yellow powder onto the white and covered it all with a second square of paper. "Stand back," he said.

Polly took a step away from the table.

He picked up a hammer and gave the paper a sharp blow.

BANG!

Polly jumped several feet.

"Effective, isn't it?" He wiped his hands on a rag. "The least bit of impact sets it off. I can dust an ordinary object with one, my wand with the other, tap once and—Hey, Presto!" he said in his booming, on-stage voice.

He leaned back against the table. "I don't suppose they've gotten to that part in your chemistry course."

Polly shook her head. "I have blown up a few beakers, though."

"Collateral damage. Part of many experiments." He replaced the two jars. "One of these days, I'd like to try and create an explosive paint. I have all the texts, I just haven't found the time." He pointed to a bookshelf in a dim corner. "Perhaps you could help with that. Your aunt says you're quite the scientist."

"You and Aunt Emma correspond?" This was news to Polly.

"Of course." He took out his pipe and lit it. "After your mother died, I'm afraid I just threw myself into my work, and distance became a habit." He smiled sadly through the smoke. "But never for a moment think that I don't care about you."

Polly felt her eyes prickle, and was at a loss for words.

"You're my daughter, Polly. More like me than you might imagine."

"How do you mean?"

"Well, you probably think that magicians create illusions," he said, crossing his arms. "But we don't. We study the same scientific principles you do, and use them to create a reality that supports *belief* in illusions. Like this."

He picked up a piece of mirrored glass and, began to show her how the angles and lines of sight changed what she saw. Polly was so fascinated that she did not hear the outer door open.

"Hey, boss," a red-haired man in coveralls said. "We got another one of those crank letters." He held up an envelope. "No return—" He stopped. "Who's the young chap? New hand?"

"In a manner of speaking. This *chap* is my daughter, Polly. Polly, meet Archie Mason, my right-hand man and chief engineer. I stole him away from the eggheads when he graduated from Oxford."

"You went to *Oxford*?" Polly stared. "And you're working here?"

"Didn't take much persuasion. This is loads more interesting than calculating bridge capacities." He pointed to a table with a metal base. "I invented *that*, by way of illustration."

Polly didn't think it was particularly impressive, but the man sounded awfully proud of it. The table's top was a wooden disc about half a meter in diameter and as thick as a manhole cover. It was mounted on a center post affixed to the floor. She smiled politely. "It looks quite—sturdy."

"It held Valinda," Archie said.

"That was the idea." The magician saw the puzzled look on his daughter's face. "Would you like a demonstration?"

"All right." Not much to demonstrate about a table, was there?

"Splendid. Climb aboard." He pointed to a step stool next to it. "Aboard the table?"

"The table? Ah, I see. No, my dear. It's a piston-driven platform." Polly shrugged and climbed up onto the disc. "Now what?"

"Look up."

She did, and saw a neat circle cut in the workroom ceiling. "Is that the stage?"

"It is indeed. Now stand very straight, hold your arms tight to your sides, and tuck in your elbows." He turned to Archie. "I'll run up top. Usual signal."

"Two raps. Right-o."

"See you in a moment my dear," her father said, giving her hand a squeeze, and then he dashed out the door. She heard his footsteps clatter on the wooden stairs, then silence.

"Is this—?"

"Safe as houses." Archie stepped over to a square metal box mounted on a support pillar a foot from the platform. He looked over at Polly, winked, and rested his hand on the lever protruding from its front.

A moment later, from right above her head, Polly heard two sharp knocks.

"That's the cue," Archie said. "Arms in tight, now." He pushed the lever up.

Beneath her feet, Polly felt the 'table' begin to rise, as if she were in an elevator with no walls or surrounding cage. Her stomach churned as it did on carnival rides, as the disc went up, rapidly and smoothly and without a sound.

She counted under her breath and before she had reached *three* her head was going *through* the ceiling. Suddenly, the theater was spread out in front of her, a vast bowl of gilt and velvet, rows of empty chairs stretching back and back into the dim reaches of the farthest balcony. In another second, the top of the disc reached the level of the stage floor and she felt it click into place, again without a sound.

"Bravo!" her father said from the wings. He began to clap. "Well done!" He gazed at her as if she were a rare treasure.

Polly stepped off onto the boards, her body a-tingle with the excitement of the ride, her cheeks flushed with the unaccustomed praise. She glanced down at the disc, its wooden top now nearly invisible amid the floorboards. "Is that what you wanted my help rehearsing?" she asked.

"Yes. What did you think? You looked like a natural."

Polly wasn't sure what she felt. This was not her world. But standing there in his shirtsleeves, a smear of dust across one cheek, hair hanging over one eye, her father looked happier than she had seen him in years. She wanted the chance to know that man better.

"I'll do it," she said.

POLLY HAD THE mornings to herself. She breakfasted with tea and scones and a book, so content in her solitude that for the first few days, rehearsals seemed like an interruption and she doubted her decision. Then she got caught up in the rhythm of the workroom, the flow of ideas, the easy conversations peppered with jargon that soon became second nature, like learning another language.

Each day she found herself more eager to get to the theater and work alongside her father—Hugh—and Archie. She was pleased to find that, although they had vastly more experience than she did in every facet of the work, they treated her as an equal when it came to solving the myriad small problems that came up in the creation of the show.

"*The Lady Vanishes* is a superb title for Polly's bit," Hugh said.

"It is," Archie agreed. "That's why Mr. Hitchcock used it for his latest film. And why *we* can't. The audience will think it's a publicity stunt."

"I suppose you have something better?"

"Not yet," Archie shrugged. "But we have a week to decide before—"

"*La Femme Perdu*," Polly said from atop the props trunk.

Both men turned.

"Huh?" Archie said.

"Didn't they teach French at Oxford?"

"I'm an engineer. Latin and German. What's it mean?"

"The Lost Woman."

"*La Femme Perdu*," Hugh repeated, rolling the words out. "It's good. It's better. *Lost* has such a melancholy mystery to it." He snapped his fingers. "We'll use it. Good work, my dear."

Polly nodded, pleased. "Thanks."

They began to rehearse the illusion on stage the next week. The set-up was simple: A woman in a gown and a man in a smoking jacket and fez are in a drawing room with flowered wallpaper, having cocktails. On stage is a drinks cabinet with six-inch wheels. Off-stage a shot rings out. "It is your husband!" the man shouts. "Hide in here." He opens the cabinet doors, she curls inside, he closes them, leaving one slightly ajar. The husband rushes in. The men argue loudly. The husband shoots. There is a puff of smoke—the other man disappears! The husband looks around, sees the cabinet, flings it open. The woman is gone! All that remains inside is the man's red fez.

At school, Polly had diligently attended cricket practice, and memorized logarithm tables and irregular French verbs, but nothing had prepared her for the repetition and endless detail of building an illusion. Everything was timed to the second. A single misstep would spoil it all.

The drinks cart had to be positioned precisely on the stage—over the lift and at an exact angle.

"I understand why it's over the lift," Polly said at the first rehearsal. "But that's a circle, so why is the angle so important?"

"Sit down in the audience," her father said. Polly went and sat in the second row. "What do you see?"

"The drinks cart."

"Anything between it and the floor?"

"No."

"Are you certain?"

"Yes. I can see between the wheels, see the wallpaper behind it."

"So no one could possibly get out through the bottom of the cabinet without being seen?"

"No." Polly frowned. "But isn't that how I—?" She stared at the drinks cart.

"It is." Her father turned the cart at an angle. "Now what do you see?"

"The wallpaper behind it has gone all wonky."

He laughed. "Come back up and take a close look."

Polly did. Kneeling in front of the drinks cart, she could see a false front between the two wheels, painted so that it matched the wallpaper, but only at a particular distance and perspective. Hidden behind the frontpiece, the bottom of the cabinet extended down, flush with the floor. Inside was a sliding panel that opened over the disc of the lift.

"What about the fez?"

"Collapsible. It folds up and hooks into the roof of the chamber, invisible from the audience."

"That's ingenious," she said with real admiration.

"It's what I do," he said. "And why I want no one sneaking in to take a closer look."

Polly learned by trial and error. She had to wait to give Archie the pre-arranged signal—two sharp raps—until the men began to argue and their shouts masked the sound of her knuckles. She lay curled on her side in the cabinet for an hour at a time, practicing and practicing her exit, a five-part ballet: slide the panel; climb onto the lift; unhook the fez; place it on the panel; and slide that shut again from below as she descended into the basement. Every single movement was choreographed.

Fortunately, *La Femme Perdu* was her only role. The other illusions were performed solo by her father, or with the help of Chaz Manning, his stage assistant, who also played the part of the jealous husband. After a week of rehearsal, she began to feel more comfortable with her part, although she doubted that performing would ever be her first choice. Upstairs required presence and flamboyance; downstairs, preparation and ingenuity.

When she had rehearsed to the point of exhaustion, she was excused to the workroom, curling up in a battered armchair with a text from the bookshelf, an eclectic mix of technical manuals and histories of magic. Archie often fetched them supper—meat pies and ale, a lemon squash for her—and she spent her evenings eating, reading, and making notes when interesting bits caught her eye.

Some afternoons, when the men were working on other parts of the show, Polly had quiet time to try out some of her ideas. She discovered that it was a very well-stocked workshop, more comprehensive than any of the school labs, and soon her table was covered with experiments-in-progress. Two weeks in, she abandoned her morning reading in order to get to the theatre early, to work before rehearsals.

The day before the show opened, she thought she had solved one of her conundrums. After many failed attempts—and two blistered fingers—she had finally calculated the correct proportions to make a dark sludge, the consistency of thin pudding, of potassium chlorate, sulfur, and a binding agent called British gum, mixed with a bit of water and some lampblack. She painted it onto a dinged-up wooden ball, one of several she'd found in a parts box of discarded props from previous shows. She gingerly set it on a square of oiled paper to dry.

"La Femme, you're needed up top," Archie said, coming in the doorway. He peered over her shoulder. "What's that? Looks like a little cannonball."

"Close enough. I *think* I've created an exploding paint. I'll know once it's dry."

"Hugh will be dead chuffed. If it works, you should get him to take it to the Magic Circle next month. Ought to be a big hit."

"If it works, I'll take it myself."

"Not unless you go in disguise. It's blokes only."

"Figures," Polly huffed, then grabbed the silky dress that was her costume. "I need to change."

"Fly, *mein fraulein*. Last rehearsal. Mustn't keep Himself waiting."

The lift was in its up position so she took the stairs to the dressing room. Once dressed, Polly observed her father from the wings. He was running through his patter for the first act, speaking to an imaginary audience. It was a full dress rehearsal—top hat, tailcoat, white tie — and the man on stage was no longer Hugh, but Vardo! His rich voice was so well-modulated that even his whispers carried to the back rows. He moved across the stage, waving his wand, his movements fluid but precise.

A few minutes later he stepped off for a glass of water.

"Why do you bother with a wand?" she asked. "Isn't that a bit of a cliché these days?" The tailcoat and hat, she now knew, were not just a costume, but were tools themselves, full of extra pockets and secret compartments that he used for his sleights.

"It's tradition. And it's useful."

"How?"

"With it, every move I make is dramatic. From the opening curtain, the audience sees grand gestures." He swept his arm out. "They get used to them, and don't notice when I whisk a card off the table, or drop it into a pocket."

"Aren't they watching the wand?"

"Yes, and that's it exactly. They watch the wand—not my *other* hand."

"Oh." Polly thought about that for a moment. "You use it to direct their attention."

"Precisely. *That* is my job, to distract them from what I'm really—" He paused, turned, and stared into the wings.

"What is it?" Polly followed his glance, but didn't see anything out of the ordinary.

He chuckled. "Nothing. Just another demonstration. I looked, so you looked. Human nature. And while you were looking—and listening to me prattle on—" he opened his hand. "Hey, Presto!"

"That's my watch."

"And that's my skill. It took me *years* in front of a mirror, learning how to look at one thing and manipulate another." He gave the watch back. "I've had to sack a few hands who thought this would be a cakewalk, and didn't like the discipline."

Polly gulped, wondering if she was about to be scolded.

He smiled. "Not you, my dear. You're a trouper. Now, if you're ready, we'll take it from the top again."

THE MORNING OF the show, Polly was nervous. More nervous than she'd expected. She could walk through her part in her sleep, had actually dreamed about it twice in the last week, and felt confident that she would get through it without mishap. And everything had gone well at the last rehearsal, with Archie and Chaz and the theatre crew as an audience. But performing for a packed house? Perhaps that accounted for the butterflies in her stomach.

She managed a piece of toast and some tea before closing herself into the parlor for a few hours with an Enid Blyton novel to keep her amused and distracted. Or so she hoped. But the fourth time she put the book down and went to check the clock, she gave in. If she was going to pace, she'd rather do it in the workroom.

Her father had not yet come down. She left him a note on the hall table, inside his hat, where he'd be sure to see it, and set off for the theatre. On rainy days she took the tube from Goodge Street to Leicester Square, but this particular morning was warm and sunny, not a cloud in the sky, and a walk might burn off some of the fidgets.

Polly strolled past the British Museum, threading her way through the throngs of tourists, then down Shaftesbury Avenue, stopping to look in shop windows along the way. With the fresh air, her appetite returned, and she bought a cream bun at a bakery, wiping the last crumbs off her blouse when she reached the stage door. As usual, Alf tipped his cap when he saw her.

"Will you be leaving again, miss?"

"I don't think so. Archie's bringing supper. Why?"

"I need to pop over to the chemists and pick up a tincture for the wife. Won't be gone long, but—"

"It's all right, Alf. I'll hold down the fort."

"Thanks, miss." He held the door open for her.

As she expected, the theater was dark, just the ghost light that was always left on, center stage. She flipped the switch next to the basement stairs and went to the workroom.

The black-painted ball sat on her table. She turned on a lamp that illuminated the surface, but left the rest of the room in shadow, and touched a finger to the paint. Dry. She grinned to herself. Time for a test. She looked around for a suitable object, one that would allow her to strike a blow but not be *too* close, just in case. A brass rod the diameter of a cigarette and nearly a meter long fit the bill perfectly. Polly hoped her experiment wouldn't render it useless for its actual purpose, whatever that was.

She settled the ball into a toweling nest so that it wouldn't bounce or roll, and stepped back until the edge of the rod was just above the sphere. "One. Two." She took a deep breath and raised the rod a foot in the air. "Three!"

BANG!

She jumped, her ears ringing, as the rod jerked and clattered to the floor.

It worked! Polly capered around the workroom in a most unscientific way, shaking out her stinging hand, all of the morning's nerves gone. She had done it! She could hardly wait to show her father.

When her adrenaline had settled to a more normal level, Polly picked up her log book and recorded the results. She retrieved the rod, inspecting it for damage: just a small black smudge where contact had been made. And the ball? She tilted the lamp and looked closely. Except for one star-shaped grayish spot, it also appeared unchanged. She jotted down these findings, returned the rod to Archie's workbench, then, thirsty from her exertions, polished off the last of a rather flat lemon squash from the night before.

Her watch showed a little after noon. It would be hours before Archie or her father arrived. She pulled a book from the shelf and settled into the armchair to wait. She was deep into an account of Robert-Houdin using magic to avert a war when she heard a man shouting upstairs.

What was going on—?

Her thoughts were interrupted by the sound of running feet overhead and her father's loud stage voice: "Get away from that!"

Bits of dust fell from the ceiling as two men pounded across the stage.

Polly leaped out of her chair.

"Sack *me*, will you?" The unknown man was shouting. "Now you'll pay, Wardlow!"

"You're mad, Jim." Her father. "I'm going to—"

In a terrifying echo of the act, she heard a shot, and her father cried out.

Polly stood motionless, in shock. But a moment later, from the stage floor, she heard their signal: two sharp raps.

After a month of rehearsals, her response was swift and automatic. The lift. Draw attention. Misdirection. She looked around for a suitable prop, or a weapon. Nothing.

Except the black ball.

She scooped it up, thought for a fraction of a second, then grabbed another, unpainted ball as back-up. She slid them into the pockets of her trousers, then climbed onto the disc-topped lift. She knelt, stretching an arm out to the control lever, and flipped it with her fingertips.

The disc began to rise silently. Polly straightened up, tucked her arms against her sides, and counted. One... two...

At *three* she reached up to slide the panel of the drinks cabinet open, and tucked herself into its interior. One of the doors was ajar. Across the stage she could see her father, lying on the floor, holding his arm. A bearded man with a gun stood over him.

Then Polly Wardlow took control of the stage.

She eased the black ball out of her pocket, cradling it in her right hand, and took a deep breath.

"Hey, Presto!"

She sidearmed the ball toward the back of the theater.

It bounced over the boards, and with each impact, a sound like a shot rang out: BANG! BANG! BANG! BANG!

The man jumped away, looking about wildly.

Polly rolled out of the cabinet and onto her feet. With the speed and skill she'd learned at Giles Hall, she threw the second wooden ball, aiming at his knee as if it were the stumps on the cricket pitch.

The ball hit with a resounding *crack* and the man fell with a thin scream.

Her father reacted swiftly, reaching out with his good arm to retrieve the gun, and got to his feet. He stood over the other man, the barrel pointed at his middle.

Without taking his eyes off the man, he said, "Are you all right?"

"I'm fine." Polly saw that her hands were shaking and put them in her pockets. "How badly are you hurt?"

"My left arm—could use some—attention," he said, his words coming out in small gasps.

"I'll call for a doctor." She pointed to the man. "Who is he?"

"Jim Finney. He used to work for me." He shifted his arm and grimaced. "You might telephone the police as well."

"Right-o." She turned toward the hallway, but stopped when he called her name.

"Yes?"

"That was a brilliant entrance, darling. Right on cue."

ARCHIE ARRIVED JUST after the police. He and Polly stood outside the stage door with Alf. They watched as the bearded man was loaded onto a stretcher and handcuffed to the rails.

"It's all my fault," Alf said, wringing his cap in his hands.

"Not entirely," Archie said. "Finney's been hounding Hugh for the last month, threatening to shut down the show. If he hadn't gotten in, he would have tried again tonight and who knows how many might have been hurt."

"With a full house, it could have been much worse," Polly nodded. She turned to Archie. "What did he do, when he worked here?"

"Nothing well. Thought he was the gods' own gift to magic, but he couldn't even manage a proper sleight. Bumbled any number of set-ups before he was sacked. I thought we'd seen the end of him."

"Sounds like a nutter."

"Through and through." He shook his head. "But he was no match for you, I hear. I gather your magic paint worked?"

"Like a charm." She grinned. "More like a whizz-bang, actually."

"You're a right wizard, Polly. And I want the whole story, soup to nuts. But now I have shows to cancel and meetings with the press—and you need to go and see how Himself is getting along."

Polly found her father sitting on a cot backstage, his left arm in a sling, bandaged from elbow to shoulder, his eyes closed. The doctor beside him looked up when he heard her footsteps.

"So you're the young heroine," he said. "Quick thinking." He handed her a bottle of pills. "I gave him a shot for the pain, but he'll be wanting two of these before bedtime."

"Is he going to be all right?"

"In a few weeks. It went through muscle, not bone, nothing broken."

"Will he still be able to—?" she gestured at the stage.

"I expect a full recovery. He'll be a little stiff for a while, but there's no need to worry." He patted her on the arm. "No need at all." He shut his black bag. "Do you want me to call a taxi for you?"

"No, thank you. I can manage."

When the doctor had gone, Polly sat beside the cot. She leaned over and kissed her father's cheek. His eyes fluttered open. "Polly."

"I'm here, Dad."

"You were very brave."

She looked away for a moment, her face reddening. "I mightn't have moved if I hadn't heard my cue."

"But you did. Although I must say I was expecting a diversion, not a cavalry charge." He took a breath and stood, swaying only slightly. "Let's go home, shall we?"

She took his good arm and they walked slowly across the stage. "Hold up a tick," Polly said. She leaned over and retrieved the black ball, its surface now mottled with gray stars. She slipped it into her pocket.

"You're going to tell me all about that?"

"Yes," she said. "I suspect you'll find it rather interesting."

"Exploding paint?"

She nodded.

"Genius!"

Polly smiled. "I'm a Wardlow. It's what we do."

THE CHANGELING
JAMES BRADLEY

HANNAH IS NOT certain what wakes her: not a sound, she thinks, more a sense someone or something has passed through the room.

For a space of seconds she 't move, just lies, listening. Outside it is dark, silent save for the sound of the stream. She can smell woodsmoke, the sweet scent of the thyme over the fire; next to her in his cradle Connor sleeps, his breath slow and shallow. Somewhere in the distance an owl cries out.

Rising she crosses to the door, the shock of the cold making her gasp as she opens it. The moon high overhead, darkness pooling in the runnels of the grass beneath the trees. Although it is still she cannot shake the feeling she is not alone, that a presence hovers nearby. After a moment a fox emerges from the blackberries by the stream, its lean shape separating from their shadow to jog quickly through the moonlight; as it disappears again she turns inside, only to notice the horseshoe that usually hangs over the doorway lying in the dark by her feet. Kneeling she picks it up, and places it on the table before she lies down and draws the blanket around her shoulders.

When she wakes again it is already light, the sound of the birds outside loud. Sitting up she is surprised to see Connor is already awake, his eyes focused on the roof overhead. For a few seconds she watches him, wondering how long he has been lying there like that, something in the way he stares suddenly striking her as peculiar. As she reaches for him he flinches, his body stiffening, but as he finds her breast he relaxes, Hannah closing her eyes as the pressure of his mouth opens her inside, the feeling blunt, like desire. Like grief.

Once he is fed she dresses, then, drawing her shawl about herself, heads out into the quiet of the morning with him in her arms. Outside it is still, grey mist between the trees; down by the water the shape of a heron is visible and the quick plop of the otters as they flick and dive can be heard, but she barely notices as she hurries on, up the path toward the road.

Now she is on her own she is not sure how she feels about living so far from the village. Brendan built the cottage when they were courting, spending his evenings cutting wood and daubing the walls. It had been his gift to her, a demonstration of his belief in their future, yet Hannah had never cared for the house; instead it had been the place she loved, its proximity to the river and the woods, the curling brambles and wildflowers. Although it was only half a mile from the village, it was possible to step off the road and disappear down the path into a secret place, one that seemed to have a life all of its own. This morning she is mostly aware of the damp branches blocking her path, the way they slap her face and wet her sleeves, so that by the time she reaches the road and begins the walk to the fields she is wet and Connor is wailing.

Today they are harrowing, breaking the cold ground for the seed. Sometimes when they work there is merriment, laughter and singing, but not today, for it is hard, dismal work, an icy drizzle misting across them, the freezing soil turning their hands red and aching, so they work in silence, the only sound their breath, the sudden cries of the crows each time one of them rises to cast stones at them.

With Connor's weight against her Hannah works more slowly, meaning the others are already gathered by the fire in the field's corner when she leaves her work and joins them for the morning meal. Ill-tempered with the work, they barely acknowledge her as she seats herself, shifts Connor's weight so he may feed. But as she unties her bodice he suddenly pulls away and opening his mouth begins to shriek.

It is not a sound she has heard before, not a sound any child should make. Less a cry than one continuous note, high, piercing, horrible. Startled she looks up, sees the others staring at her. Unsure what to do she tries to adjust his position, jiggling him to calm him, but nothing seems to work, until at last she stumbles to her feet and retreats across the field, away from the others.

When at last he stops she is shaken, more shaken than she could have imagined. In the sudden silence she sits trembling, frightened to move in case he starts again. Finally she summons the courage to turn him, but as she shifts her weight he suddenly tenses and begins again, the sound louder this time, more sustained, continuing on and on and on until it seems it will never cease.

IN THE DAYS that follow the sudden bouts of shrieking grow more frequent, Connor's high, inhuman cry often leaving her so shaken she can barely think, barely function, so it is all she can do to draw water from the stream and gather the wool for spinning. On the fourth day it is too much, and she runs from the cottage in tears and stands in the forest with her eyes screwed shut, chanting wordlessly to herself to try to drown out the sound of his screaming.

When she returns he is lying quietly in his crib, his eyes fixed on the ceiling, but as she approaches he flinches away from her, as if frightened she means to touch him, and staring down at him she finds herself certain some distemper has crept into him without her noticing, something she does not know how to name or control.

SHE WAS NINE when Brendan arrived in the village. The master had been visiting the Duke at Chatterton and when he returned

Brendan was walking behind him. Later they learned there had been an accident in the Duke's stable, that Brendan's father had been killed, and for reasons that were never fully clear the master had offered to take him into his service.

Brendan's father had come from over the water, and Brendan had the dark hair and black eyes of his father's people. Yet he was a good lad, clear and kind and open-faced, and although at first some of the men resented him they could not hate him for long.

The first time Hannah saw him she was surprised by how tall he was, how handsome. He was leading one of the master's bays, moving lightly as the horse danced and whinnied, his face alight. Although the horse had been expensive it had proven wild and unmanageable, refusing all riders and charging at any who approached it. But as she watched, Brendan took its halter and pressed his forehead to its face, stroking its neck and murmuring quietly until it finally grew calm.

As Brendan grew he became more handsome, his good looks and graceful charm meaning all the girls wanted him for a sweetheart. Sometimes Hannah watched the way they fought to dance with him at the festivals, saw the generous way he accepted their hands, his habit of giving each his attention no matter whether they were pretty or not.

Yet somehow Hannah never danced with him. Not because she didn't care for him, but because something held her back. Occasionally she would catch him looking at her, and he would look away, but not before he had smiled.

Then when she was fifteen there came an afternoon when she was out on the road and she heard a horse behind her. Turning she saw it was the bay, Brendan astride it. Reining it in he stopped beside her.

"Hannah Wilkes," he said. "I had not thought to see you out here."

She turned to look at him. He was smiling, carelessly beautiful.

"Then you cannot know this road. I walk this way often."

He hesitated, and for a moment she regretted the sharpness of her tone.

"I'm sorry," he said, dismounting. "I did not mean to offend you."

She shook her head. "You didn't."

"Why do you come here?"

She shrugged. "I like the quiet," she said, aware of the intentness of the way he watched her, his attention to what she said.

"And you?"

He smiled. "She needed riding and it seemed a fine day to take her out."

Reaching up Hannah stroked the bay's long nose. "Is she still wild?"

Brendan patted the bay's neck with one hand. "Not for me."

While they were speaking they had reached the shadow of the great oak that stood between the road and the wood. Looking at it Brendan grinned.

"Come with me," he said, looping the horse's halter over a branch and opening the gate. When she hesitated he held out his hand.

"Don't worry," he said. "There's nothing to be afraid of."

Taking his outstretched hand Hannah allowed him to lead her down the hill into the wood. Beech trees grew there, tall and green, and beyond them a stream. By the stream he slowed, placing his hands on her waist to lift her over, then, taking her hand, he led her on, into the wood.

Beneath the trees it was quiet, the only sound the wind in the trees, the cries of the birds. Brendan moved quickly, quietly, a smile on his face. Then, as they reached the edge of a hollow he stopped, motioning to her to keep quiet.

At first she did not see what he was pointing at. Then she saw a litter of fox cubs, playing in the hollow. The cubs were small, jumping and pouncing on each other and rolling here and there. Surprised, she smiled, and turning saw Brendan smiling back.

"How do you know they were here?"

He shrugged, and placing a hand on her arm pointed to the ridge behind the cubs where the vixen had appeared, a rabbit in her mouth. Perhaps catching wind of them she stopped, sniffing the air. Down below the cubs began to mewl and cry, racing toward her. Then, as the cubs reached her, the vixen lowered her head and, with her cubs jumping around her, jogged down into the hollow.

"Does Old Hughes know?" she asked, and at the mention of the gamekeeper's name Brendan shot her a conspiratorial smile and shook his head.

"What if he finds out?"

Brendan shrugged. "He'll not mind about a few foxes."

Looking down at the mother tearing the rabbit apart for her cubs Hannah remembered how many times foxes had stolen chickens from the farms nearby.

"Are you sure about that?"

This time he grinned. "No."

That evening, when she arrived home, her father saw something in her manner, and, suspicious, asked her where she had been.

"Nowhere," she said, "just walking."

But her brother, Will, snorted. "Young John Bradley said he saw her walking with Brendan O'Rourke on the village road."

She shot her brother an angry look, but he just folded his arms and smiled unpleasantly. Across the table her father looked up, his face suspicious. The Bradleys owned the farm that bordered theirs, and he had long intended Hannah would marry Old John Bradley's eldest son, Young John. Yet she did not care for Young John, thinking there was a coldness in him, a resentment that made him small.

Her father removed his pipe from his mouth. "Brendan O'Rourke?"

"He was out riding," she said, perhaps too boldly. "It didn't mean anything."

Her father sat staring at her for a long moment. "You be careful of that boy," he said at last. "I'll not have you as some Irishman's whore."

*　　*　　*

SOMETIMES SHE WONDERS whether things might have been different if not for her brother and father's determination she wed John Bradley. For as the summer progressed she found herself meeting with Brendan in secret.

It was intoxicating at first, to have somebody so obviously in love with her. He was so handsome, so kind, so in love with the idea of her it was almost impossible to resist. Yet still some part of her held back. It wasn't that she didn't care for him: she did. Nor was it that he didn't make her happy, or that his presence didn't make her spirits lift: indeed when they were together she could almost convince herself she loved him as he clearly loved her. But each time they parted she felt that feeling slip away, replaced by a sick feeling she was betraying someone, although whether it was him or her she was never quite sure.

Sometimes she wondered why he couldn't see it, couldn't tell, and then she felt wicked, certain that it was her doing, that she was deceiving him. More than once she decided to break it off, and once even did, yet each time she saw him again, and her doubts fled. It was as if his love were enough for both of them when they were together.

Meanwhile Will watched her, seeking to catch her out. They had never been close, something in his nature making him jealous of her. Sometimes she wondered what it was that made him want her to marry John at all, although she knew the truth was simple: that he wished her to conform to his wishes, to do as she was bid.

And then, on the evening of the harvest, she and Brendan slipped away into the forest together. The night was warm, and as they walked they could hear the sound of laughter and music from the feast over the back. Yet as they reached the stream they heard a noise behind them, and turning, saw Will standing there.

"Will!" she said, in surprise. "What are you doing here?"

He laughed. "I would rather know what you are doing here, although I do not think it will take much unravelling."

"Where I go is my affair."

"Not when you go with this one."

"It is not your concern, Will. Go back to the feast."

He laughed. "Oh but it is my concern, sister. For you have been forbidden to walk out with this Irishman."

At this Brendan stepped forward. "I have no quarrel with you, Will."

Will looked at him as if seeing him for the first time. "No? Well I have a quarrel with you. Have you forgotten my sister is promised to another?"

"Promised by you," Hannah said.

"Promised by our father. Or have you forgotten him?" Will said hotly, stepping forward. Beside her Brendan extended an arm, shielding Hannah from her brother, and as he did Hannah felt something shift, felt the way things moved around her. Perhaps Will felt it too, for he hesitated, then shook his head, and snorted.

"So it's to be like that, is it? Well you've made your bed, Hannah, I hope you enjoy lying in it."

AS THE DAYS grow longer she visits the village less and less. Although Connor's fits of screaming have grown less frequent he has grown increasingly difficult in other ways, only rarely sleeping, his moods alternating almost without warning between jags of hysterical crying and a curious, empty state where he lies staring at the wall or the ceiling, as if seeing something there that she cannot. The nights are the worst, when he will not sleep for longer than an hour, demanding food and screaming in the dark or lying staring into the black in silence. Occasionally she tries to convince him to sit, for he is almost eight months old, and should be crawling soon, but he turns rigid at her touch, or lolls away.

Yet despite it all Connor continues to grow. Sometimes when he is asleep she looks at him and sees the child he once was, the beautiful baby she held the day he was born, and in those moments she is filled with love for him. But when he is awake these moments pale in the face of his anger and screaming.

In the village it is worse. It is common knowledge there is something wrong with her child, yet no one speaks of it to her. And so she goes through her days alone, tending to Connor and avoiding the gaze of people she has known all her life.

Even when she works alongside them she is like one apart. In the fields, the others fall quiet when she is there, or make awkward conversation, so much so that she takes to working on her own, bent over in a patch of field a furrow or two removed from the others.

And then, one afternoon in July she is with the Widow Thirlwell in the kitchens, preparing the food for the men's dinners. All week they have been bringing in the hay from the western fields, the men and many of the women labouring through the afternoons and into the long, high evenings, eager to take advantage of the warm, dry weather; and although it is hard work there is cheer in it, and in the meals they eat, often after ten, when the sun finally dips low and the dusk comes. As they begin bundling the food the Widow pauses and looks at Connor for a long moment before returning to her work.

"You should not blame yourself," she says after a few seconds, not looking up as she speaks. "Some children do not thrive."

Startled, Hannah pauses, a rush of emotion rising in her throat. A moment later the Widow lifts her face and looks at her. She has round cheeks that are burnished apple red by the sun, and her eyes are small and bleary blue, yet there is a sharp intelligence behind her laughing manner.

"Some of the women say it was the shock of losing that husband of yours, others talk of bad blood, or witchcraft. Don't listen to them: I had three children who did not thrive and I never lay with the devil or any foolery like that."

Still Hannah does not speak. Part of her wants to weep with relief, but another part is angry and upset she has been a subject of discussion.

That evening, when she takes the food out, she watches the others talking and laughing, sees the children chasing each other, and, her head singing with exhaustion, finds herself gripped by a sudden fury, too afraid even to speak for fear she will shout or scream like a madwoman.

A WEEK LATER she is out by the field when old Maggie appears out of the trees. Hoping to slip away Hannah averts her eyes but the old woman is too quick, calling her name so Hannah must turn and acknowledge her. As Hannah turns Maggie smiles unpleasantly, aware she has won this small contest of wills.

"What is it?" Hannah demands, although she knows the answer well enough.

"You did not pay me," Maggie says.

Hannah doesn't flinch. "Why should I pay you for witchery?"

"Perhaps you should ask yourself that question. After all, you're the one with a child who will not thrive."

Hannah takes a step toward the old woman, her fists clenching. "Did you curse him, witch?"

Maggie snorts. "Calm yourself, girl. I had nothing to do with what ails your child, though I would have been within my rights."

When Hannah doesn't step back, Maggie smiles. "Are you telling me you haven't guessed the truth already?"

"What truth is that, witch?"

"Your child: he is not human."

Hannah hesitates. "Not human?"

"It is the work of the little people. A baby as fair as him is easy prey for them. Was there never a night you did not feel their presence?"

She does not reply, just stands, looking at the old woman. Maggie smiles unpleasantly at her.

"Yes, now you see. The child you rear is no longer yours. Your Connor is gone, stolen away. And in his place a changeling."

"No," she says in a strangled voice. Maggie does not move, just stands, staring at her. Not for the first time Hannah sees the delight the old woman takes in causing pain.

"Is he as other children? Does he speak? Does he walk or play? Does he cry out when you touch him?"

She shakes her head.

"It is because he is not human, he is a thing made of wood by fairy hands."

Something in Maggie's words makes Hannah pause. "Wood?"

Maggie smiles and nods.

"And my Connor?"

Maggie shrugs. "Gone."

"And how do I get him back?"

"Drive out the changeling. They fear fire and water: if you push him under the creature will leap free rather than drown, and once the enchantment is broken your child will return."

Hannah stands looking at the old woman. Somewhere in her she knows this pleases Maggie, that the old woman sees a way to have her in her power, that this is itself a vengeance of sorts.

"I must go," she says. "I will be missed."

Connor is sleeping when she returns, although she sees by Jane's face the time he was not was not easy. Taking a penny from her apron she presses it into her hand, but Jane pushes it back, telling her to keep it.

"You have enough to worry about," she says.

She does not argue, just nods, dropping her eyes as Jane leans close and kisses her cheek before she slips out the door and away.

Left alone with Connor she stares at him, hearing Maggie's words echoing in her ears. Could it be that this creature she calls her own is nothing of the sort? That this thing she holds in her arms and feeds at her breast is nothing but a copy of a child? Part of her knows these fears are madness, that the old woman's words were meant to disturb and frighten in precisely this way, yet as she looks at him lying there she cannot put the idea out of her mind.

SHE AND BRENDAN had been married a year when she went to Maggie. Brendan did not suggest it, nor would he have wanted her to if he had known, but she knew her failure to be taken with child worried him. It was not for want of trying: although afterward she often felt lonely, lost, she could not help but take pleasure in the way their bodies moved together, in Brendan's delight with her, the rapt intensity of his desire.

Maggie's hut was quiet when she reached it, although in front of it a fire burned, a pot suspended over it. Over the door hung rabbit's feet, the skulls of animals. Seeing them Hannah hesitated, stepping back, behind a tree, but as she did old Maggie emerged, and looked her way.

"Who's that?" Maggie called. "Don't worry, I know you're there."

A moment passed then Hannah stepped out to find the old woman staring at her.

"So," she said, "it's you. What brings you to my hut?"

Hannah did not answer, just stood rigidly, and after a moment Maggie snorted.

"I see," she said, and turning motioned to Hannah to follow her into the hut.

Inside it was dark, thick with the stink of smoke and herbs and the old woman's body.

"You would be with child?" Maggie asked, and Hannah nodded. For a long moment the old woman stared at her. Then she reached out a hand, quick as a snake, and shoved it into Hannah's skirts. Hannah cried out, in shock and shame, but she did not pull away. The old woman's hand was hard, her fingers rough. As she poked and felt Hannah fought the urge to look away, unwilling to give the old hag the pleasure of seeing her distress.

"He loves you, I think."

Hannah looked at her in surprise and found Maggie watching her.

"And you?" she asked, "Do you love him?"

When Hannah did not reply immediately Maggie chuckled, a cold smile on her face.

"No matter. Here, drink this, then lie with him under the full moon. A child will come."

Hannah took the herbs in her hand. Maggie was watching her.

All at once she felt a kind of revulsion toward the old woman, her prying smile.

"What, witch?" she asked, the anger in her voice surprising her.

"You should be careful," Maggie said. "He is touched by the fairies, that husband of yours. And they are jealous of those they favour." As she spoke she reached out a hand for Hannah, but Hannah jerked away, suddenly filled with loathing. Maggie smiled in something like triumph, but shaking her head Hannah backed out of the hut, not turning back when she heard the old woman behind her, calling her name, demanding her coin.

She waited a week, then on the night of the full moon she made the soup Brendan liked and drank the herbs, wincing at their bitter taste. And when they were done she took him to their bed, and with an urgency that frightened her, drew him into herself. But when they were done and he lay spent on top of her she felt the old emptiness return, and with it a loneliness that sang through her like regret.

As JULY PASSES she works in the fields in the days, sleeps in her cottage at night. While the other children run and play by the hedgerows and on the furrows, chasing the birds under the care of their older siblings, Connor lies and stares at the clouds or the leaves overhead. Other children his age are walking, speaking, yet although his body is strong, the muscles in his back and neck holding him rigid when she touches him, he does not sit, and on those occasions she rolls him onto his belly the violence of his fury and screaming quickly convinces her to return him to his back.

It is a blessing, in a way, for while he lies still she can work uninterrupted. Once she might have joked and laughed with the others as they worked, but as the months have passed the other villagers have become cautious around her; although they still laugh amongst themselves as they work, they keep their distance from Hannah, only speaking to her when they have to.

It pleases her to be made separate like this. For she does not seek their company, and in truth she has little energy for it. For although Connor is calm in the daylight, he is not at night. Instead, when the darkness comes he begins to cry and thrash, his voice rising in the high-pitched scream she has come to hate and fear, the sound of it keeping her from sleep night after night.

Were he another child she might be able to comfort him, to lull him to sleep. Yet her touch only makes it worse, provoking cries of fury and distress. The only thing that will work is feeding, and even that works less often with each passing week. More than once she has found herself seated outside, in the dark, listening to his cries inside, and wishing only for sleep.

Unable to sleep at night she takes to curling up in the shade of the trees during the warmth of the afternoon, while the others rest and talk, dozing amidst the smell of the grass and the soil, the high song of the insects.

Thus it is that one afternoon she wakes to the sound of voices, and sitting up sees the others have made their way to the side of the road. Lifting an arm to shade her eyes she sees a man leading a wagon along the road below, some object secured beneath tarpaulins atop it.

As she hurries across the field to join the others she sees the object on the back is a machine, a monster of a thing made of metal and timber, with great pipes protruding from it.

"It's the threshing machine for the master," Bill Egan says as she draws level with him, not taking his eyes from the road. Hannah nods, remembering hearing the talk about this machine, the way it has put men out of work in towns all over the county. But as she stands, watching the wagon wind on toward the big house it is not the machine she is looking at, but the young man on the horse, who has stopped and is conversing with old Tom Moore, his face relaxed and filled with an easy good cheer.

IN THE DAYS that follow the thresher is the only subject of conversation in the fields amongst the men. The women, by contrast, are more interested by the young gentleman, whose name it seems is Thomas Middleton. He is an engineer, and has the manners of a gentleman, although he is often in the field with the other men. Jane claims to have heard he will be here a month, which means he will be here for the harvest dance, and for a time they amuse themselves by imagining who he might dance with.

She does not join them in their chatter. Yet she watches him. He is handsome, but she does not see that, or not only that. Instead she sees somebody who has come from the town, somebody who moves in a world larger than this one. There is a lightness and an ease to his manner, an openness in his smile she cannot help but notice.

Once, only a few years ago, he would have noticed her. Now though she pauses in her work to stare at him, aware of the way she has been made invisible. One afternoon, down by the road she pauses by the trough where the horses are watered and takes in her reflection, saddened by the sight of her sunburned cheeks and unruly hair, the coarseness of her skin.

But then, a fortnight or so after he arrives, Old Tom Moore calls her to him in the east field and bids her bear a message back to the master's house for the Widow Thirlwell. Because it is hot Hannah takes the path past the old dovecote by the stream, hoping to keep to the dappled shade of the beech trees that spread there. The dovecote has been abandoned for as long as anybody can remember, its structure home to wild birds, disturbed only by the children who come here to steal their eggs. But as she rounds the bend toward the road she is surprised to see Mr Middleton standing in front of it. Suddenly uncertain she comes to a halt, and is about to turn away and up the slope, but as she does he turns and looks at her.

"I am sorry," she says, "I did not mean to disturb you."

He smiles. "You have not disturbed me. I was just wondering how long this has stood empty. Do you know?"

Hannah shakes her head. "It was empty when I was a child," she says. "And even then it was old."

Mr Middleton looks back at the structure, as if considering

her answer. "And would the local people use it if it were not abandoned?"

Hannah hesitates, uncertain about what he is asking. "It is not ours to use," she says. "It is the master's."

He nods and looks at her again. "But if it were yours to use you would use it?"

"I suppose."

Perhaps seeing her discomfort Mr Middleton shakes his head and grins.

"I'm sorry," he says. "I sometimes forget myself. It's just it seems strange, you all toiling in the fields while something like this stands empty."

Hannah nods. "Perhaps you should speak to the master."

He looks at her. "Perhaps I should," he says, then pauses, looking at her. "Do you have a name?"

Hannah looks at him. Seen close up he is younger than she had thought, his eyes green beneath brown hair.

"Hannah O'Rourke."

"A handsome name," he says. "And what brings you this way?"

"I am taking a message to the kitchens."

"I see. I am heading back there myself. Might I walk with you?"

For a long moment he stands, watching her. Then, surprising herself, Hannah smiles. "Of course," she says.

WHEN SHE RETURNS to the field she does not tell the others of her conversation with Mr Middleton, although she knows some busybody will make sure they hear of it soon enough. But for now it is enough to have this thing for herself, to feel the way it swells within her. Perhaps Connor senses it as well, for as she makes her way back home that evening he lies against her quietly, without fighting or complaining as he usually does, and when it comes to sleep he passes easily into unconsciousness. Yesterday he screamed and fought and moaned and she wept with frustration, until she looked at him and saw what others saw, that there is something unnatural about him, something not-human, as if he were a distorted reflection of a child. Yet now, as she lies on the edge of sleep and hears him breathing next to her she does not know what to think. For although he is barely there, a dumb thing, still she knows somewhere within herself his flesh is of hers, his warmth is wound into her being, and to think otherwise is sinful, hateful, a denial of herself as much as of him.

JULY FADES INTO August, the days coming high and hot so they work faster against the threat of the storms they know will come. As they cut the wheat she watches Mr Middleton directing the men, teaching them the operation of the machine. Although they have not spoken again since that afternoon she has seen his eyes seek her out across the field, seen the way his manner changes as she passes. So have others: although they are wary of teasing her about it some of the women have taken to whistling at her when he passes, although she will not give them the pleasure of responding.

The machine is a monstrous thing. Steam-driven, it roars and hisses, belching steam and smoke into the air as it grinds and creaks. The first time it started Connor began to scream, beating his head into the ground so hard she was afraid he would do himself harm. That first day she bore him away down to the stream where it was quiet and spent half an hour trying to calm him, a response that has not altered, meaning she has spent much of the past fortnight with him screaming and beating his head, the merest murmur of the machine enough to make him grow rigid and begin to fight.

For the others the machine is a constant source of wonder. Even though the men still mutter darkly about how many have been put on the road by similar machines this one is a source of constant fascination, so much so that at any given moment a group of them are to be found standing near it, watching as the wheat is fed into its maw and discussing its operations.

And then, all at once, the harvest is over, and the celebrations are upon them. Although it is two years since she went to the harvest dance, this year she finds herself as giddy about it as she was when she was a girl of fourteen.

The Widow Thirlwell offers to care for Connor while she is at the dance, and so on the evening appointed she brushes her hair and takes the shawl Brendan bought her when they wed and walks the half a mile into the village to leave him with her and then on, to the back barn, where the dance is to be held.

It is a warm night, and although the storm that has been threatening all day has held off clouds are gathering to the west, lightning dancing on the horizon. Perhaps sensing she meant to leave him, perhaps simply because he was uncomfortable in a strange place, Connor had begun to whimper as she bid the Widow farewell, and although she hesitated the Widow had placed a hand in the small of her back and pushed her out into the warm night, leaving her anxious; but now as she approaches the barn that unease falls away, replaced by a strange, giddy delight in the possibility of her freedom.

Although it is still early a crowd has already gathered, some seated at the tables that stand in the yard, others laughing and talking. To one side a group of the younger men are gathered around the barrels, drinking; as she enters she glimpses her brother and Young John Bradley, and for a moment she and Will's eyes meet, before Will looks back to John and raises his mug. In the trees lanterns have been hung, giving the place the feel of a fairy kingdom.

Now she is here she is not certain she should be. Once these people were her friends: now she is a stranger amongst them. For a while she lingers by the oak tree, looking out over the crowd. By the barn Tunny Brown and the others are tuning their instruments, in front of them some of the children are chasing each other, darting back and forth across the area that has been set aside for dancing. From somewhere in the distance thunder rumbles; without thinking she tightens her hand about her shawl.

And then, just as she is deciding to slip away, to go back and spend the evening in the Widow's kitchen, she feels somebody beside her, and turning, sees Mr Middleton, the sight of him causing her to step back in surprise. He smiles.

"I'm sorry, I didn't mean to startle you."

She shakes her head. "You didn't."

"Are you sure?" he asks, and for a moment she hesitates, then laughs.

"Maybe a little."

"Perhaps I could fetch you a drink to make up for my rudeness?"

At first Hannah does not know what to say, then she nods, quickly, as if this moment might end. "Yes," she says. "I would like that."

He extends his arm, and together they walk toward the tree where the barrels stand. As they approach several of the men glance at the two of them and turn away but if Mr Middleton notices he does not show it.

"That man with Young John Bradley, he is your brother?" he asks as they wander back toward the tree.

Surprised Hannah glances over her shoulder. "Yes," she says. "How...?"

Mr Middleton smiles and gives a little shrug. "I heard some of the men talking."

"And what else did they say?" she says, the flash of anger in her voice surprising her.

If Mr Middleton is surprised by her anger he does not show it. "That you were married to one of the stablemen but he died. That you have a child who is touched."

Hannah stares at him, searching for some sign of mockery. "And if it is true?"

Mr Middleton looks at her, his green eyes clear. "All villages are full of gossip," he says. "In my experience it is best not to pay it too much heed."

Still Hannah does not move.

"Although I am sorry you have suffered such grief."

His voice is so calm, so kind that Hannah cannot speak, and

so for a long moment they stand in silence. Then over by the barn Tunny Brown and the others strike up a tune. With a smile Mr Middleton extends a hand. "Perhaps we should dance?"

If Mr Middleton is used to more elevated pleasures it does not show, for he is light and quick on his feet, bowing to the women in a playful way that makes them laugh. But it is Hannah he returns to whenever he can, holding her hand and watching her. And when, after half an hour the two of them stumble off again, to lean against a tree, he bows to her with a flourish, provoking her to laughter one more time.

"You dance well," she says, and he laughs.

"And so I should. My father is a dancing master."

Hannah looks at him. "No," she says. "I do not believe you."

Mr Middleton laughs again. "Most assuredly. A good one as well."

"Then how did you become an engineer?"

Mr Middleton shrugs. "It seemed a good profession."

"The men say the machine will put them out of work."

Mr Middleton pauses. When he continues his voice is less careless. "They are right. But it will be for the best."

"How can it be for the best if they are without work?"

"There will be other work in the towns or the cities. But it's not about them, it's about the future. We have the chance to change people's lives, to bring them ease and opportunity. We cannot not take it."

Hannah does not reply, and after a moment he continues.

"This village, your village, it is a good place, but its ways are of the past. People here talk of witchcraft and fairies and ghosts. This machine and others like it are the beginning of the end for those old ways."

Hannah glances at him, looking for some sign he has divined her fears, that he is speaking to her of more than just the village and its ways.

"I am sorry if I have offended you," he says.

She shakes her head. "You have not offended me. Yet I think you underestimate the difficulty of the task you describe. People here do not think their ways are old-fashioned, they think they are right. The idea of changing frightens them."

As she speaks a cry goes up from some of the men, and glancing over she sees the harvest princess has appeared.

"And you?" Mr Middleton asks.

Hannah hesitates. "I do not know. Now come, we must throw flowers with the rest of them."

There are more dances and songs and drinking, so it is after midnight when the storm arrives, the cool air sweeping in over the trees and sending plates and glasses tumbling. Taking Hannah's arm Mr Middleton draws her away, and with his coat over her head the two of them run back toward the Widow Thirlwell's cottage. By the stile at her gate they pause, the rain clattering down around them.

"Thank you," he says.

"For what?" Hannah asks.

"For tonight."

To her surprise Hannah laughs, and reaching up kisses his cheek. "You are a fine dancer."

He laughs. "As are you."

She can feel his eyes on her as she runs down the path toward the Widow's door, the possibility of his presence making her step light. But before she is halfway there she hears Connor scream and her belly clenches. On the doorstep she pauses, eyes closed and listening, willing this moment to continue even as she steels herself for the moment when she opens the door and it begins again.

He lies on a blanket, his body rigid and face contorted, his head beating rhythmically on the floor. The air stinks of shit. The Widow is slumped in a chair on the other side of the room, her face pale and drawn.

Crossing to him Hannah kneels, but he jerks his body away from her, redoubling his screaming.

"He's been like this since you left," the Widow says. Hannah does not answer, just nods, and reaching down she gathers him up, pressing his rigid body to her.

"I am sorry," she says but the Widow only shakes her head.

"It's not your fault."

Hannah doesn't answer, just turns toward the door.

"You can't go out, not when it's like this," the Widow says, standing, but Hannah only shakes her head.

"Thank you," she says again, and pressing Connor's stinking form to her chest she hurries out into the rain.

SHE WAS COOKING when they found Brendan. She heard the cry, and running out she saw them gathering around the stables.

He might have been asleep, save for the trickle of blood that ran down his forehead, and the way his body lay slackly. As she approached they stepped aside to let her pass, but some impulse made her stop before she reached him, stand looking at him lying there.

Looking up she heard a horse whinny. "It was the bay," she said. "Wasn't it?"

Old Bill Tompkins hesitated. His face was stricken. Then he nodded.

"Aye."

Behind him she could see the horse's face, its eyes calm, unconcerned, as if its actions had barely ruffled its consciousness. Sometimes, in the weeks that followed she would see the horse standing in the yard or grazing in the field. Each time she watched it, waiting for some sign it understood what it had done, yet all she saw was its impassive gaze, the glint of madness that had always been there. Sometimes, when she was alone, she tried to imagine what it must be like to be a horse, a bird, to move like that through the world.

If she had thought Brendan's death would heal the rift between her and her parents she was wrong. On those occasions she saw her mother or her father in the village they would turn away from her, as if ashamed. Her brother did not turn away, instead he stared at her, smiling, as if she had proven him right in some way.

And so when Connor came she was alone, left to fight her way through the labour without help or guidance, his tiny body wrenched into the world in the soft dark of the summer evening, the floor around her thick with blood and fluid, the taste of her own flesh sharp in her mouth as she tore the cord, and afterward, his small, angry life pressed against her as they slept.

It was two days before she was well enough to walk to the village. Her body weak, still thick with pregnancy yet loose and shattered as well. As she entered people stared at her, at the way she bore Connor against herself, and she saw the way she was no longer one of them.

SHE IS DRAWING water when Mr Middleton appears, wandering along the path beside the stream in the half-light of dusk. Setting the bucket down she straightens, pleased to see the way he smiles when he sees her.

"Miss O'Rourke," he says, "I had not thought to find you here."

She nods toward the hut. "I live here," she says.

Glancing up at the cottage he nods.

"So far away. Does it not get lonely out here on your own?" As he speaks he smiles, and Hannah blushes, afraid he is teasing her.

"I like it. Why are you here?"

He glances back the way he came. "I thought to see where the stream led."

Perhaps she looks disappointed because he smiles again. "And you? Are they not working in the high fields today?"

"I'm not shirking," she says, and he laughs.

"I did not think you were." As he speaks she stoops to lift the bucket and he steps forward.

"Let me take that," he says. As he speaks his hand closes on hers, and she looks up, sees his face close to hers. For a second or two they do not move, then he pulls gently on the bucket, and she releases it.

She directs him to place the bucket by the door to the cottage, then turns and looks back down the slope toward the stream.

"This is a fine aspect. A man might do well to look at it in the evening."

Hannah looks at him, sees he is grinning. "I thought you a man of the town."

He nods. "Indeed I miss the town when I am away. But the country has its compensations."

As he speaks he smiles, and she feels herself blush.

"It would be nice to be able to compare them," she says.

He laughs. "Perhaps you could visit me one day."

She stares at him, trying to tell whether he is teasing.

"What?"

"I think you are teasing me."

Again he laughs. "And if I were?"

"That would be most unkind."

For a long moment he stands, looking at her. Then he looks down.

"I am sorry it is only now we are having this conversation," he says.

"Why?"

"Because we shall not have a chance to continue it. I leave tomorrow."

"Tomorrow?"

He nods. "I have been called back unexpectedly."

"But you will be back, will you not?"

He looks at her for a long moment. "I cannot see when."

For a few seconds neither speaks. Then he steps back. "I am sorry," he says, "I have taken up enough of your time already."

"No," she says, surprising herself with her boldness. "Please, stay." But he doesn't answer, just lifts a hand and touches her face with his fingers.

"I am sorry, would that I had come this way sooner. If you are in the town you should look for me though." For a moment she thinks he will lean forward, kiss her, the touch of his fingers on her cheek almost painful. But then he steps back, moving away into the fading light.

For a long time she does not move, just stands, staring down at the stream and the space where he stood. All her life she has wanted a reason to leave, to go to the town, and here, now, one has slipped away from her. Perhaps it might have been different if she were a wanton, if she had convinced him to stay, but somehow she thinks not.

Reaching down she places her hand on the bucket, meaning to lift it, but even as she does she feels herself falter, and releasing it sinks back against the doorframe. How did she come to be here, she thinks, alone out in the woods, without a husband or a family or anyone for conversation? How is it that she does not live in the town, have fine clothes, live by the light of candles?

It could have been different, perhaps, if she had not married Brendan, if she had simply left, sought a place in one of the great houses or service somewhere, for then she might have met another man, one who might have lifted her out of here, away from here, a man like Mr Middleton perhaps, kind and good and full of life. What a life that might have been. And then the thought comes to her: might that not still happen? After all, he had asked her to call on him; perhaps she might leave too, follow him to the town. There is something between them, she is sure of that, something good and true, and he would make a fine husband.

And then from behind her she hears Connor begin to cry, his high-pitched wail piercing the quiet of the evening, and as he does she knows this is just idle fancy, no matter how fine he is no man would take a woman with a changeling for a child, no man would want that screaming lump of wood if he did not have to. For a moment she imagines just standing up, beginning to walk, the way her steps might carry her down, away from the cottage to the bank of the stream, then on, along, through the forest to the road, and on, to Bath. She could, she thinks, nobody would know, nobody would miss her, she would just be gone, the thought so liberating she actually gasps. Yet as she gets to her feet it is not the quiet she hears but Connor, screaming, on and on, the sound crowding her mind, filling it, and despite herself she turns, goes in to him. When will it stop, she thinks as she reaches out to lift him, when will it ever get better? As she lifts him to her shoulder she hears his breathing change as he gathers himself for another round of screaming, the sound of his cries filling the cottage until she puts him down again, and turning, walks back out into the gathering dark. Yet as she does she remembers Maggie's words, her description of the ways the spell might be broken, the thought stopping her in her tracks, making her turn, walk back in to where Connor lies, his tiny face screwed up in fury. For a long moment she hesitates, not sure what to do, then she reaches down and gathers him up, and half-walking, half-running, stumbles out the door, down the slope to the stream, the shock of the water cold as she hits it and wades out into the flow, the weeds slopping about her legs and insects skittering before her. In her arms Connor's cries falter in surprise before he begins to scream again, louder this time, but as he does she grasps him with both hands and pushes him down, into the water, his eyes widening in shock as the water covers his face, his mouth opening and closing as he thrashes and pulls, his distress so plain she has to fight to resist relenting, letting him go. It is strange she thinks, the way time has grown elastic, the way she is in the moment and without it, as if she has stepped out of this world and into another. Beneath the water Connor is still struggling, his face contorted and screaming. Any moment now he will change, she thinks, any moment.

Now.

MIGRATION

KARIN TIDBECK

EDITH THINKS ABOUT what was up top, as she sits on the edge of her bed waiting for worktime.

It was a desert, dunes shaded in sepia. They lived in little houses on a wooden platform. Edith would dive for spiny shells in the sand and give them to the bowl-maker.

Sometimes, though, she dreams of an ocean, of crawling out of a little cave to stand in the surf. The water is warm like blood. The ocean feels as real as a memory. She once mentioned these things to Irma, who merely shook her head. *I don't know what you're talking about,* she said. *This is our home, you silly thing.* Edith asked, *Then where did we come from?* Irma's face went blank, and then she shrugged.

Gregor's voice rings out on the other side of the door, "Wash your clothes, wash your clothes!"

Edith slips into her cardigan and gently shakes the worn bedsheets out. A seam has split along the cardigan's right shoulder. She'll have to take it to Irma for mending. Maybe after delivery, because today is delivery day.

THE DOWNSTAIRS FLIGHT yawns at her, darkness seeming to seep up from below, and she has to look away briefly. When she turns back, it's just a set of concrete stairs. Gregor lives down there, after all, and more neighbors below him, and below them, all the way to the bottom, so it's said. Edith starts her upstairs climb.

Most of the doors in the stairwell are propped open, and people are sitting and standing in doorways and on landings, already at their tasks.

Edith greets her neighbors, chanting as she goes, "Mend your things, mend your things?"

"Wash your clothes?" comes the response from above, and she catches up with Gregor, laundry basket in his thin arms.

He nods at Edith, who waves back. A neighbor hands him a frock for washing. Edith and the neighbor look on as Gregor drops the garment into the empty basket. He stirs it around with his stick, picks the garment up again, shakes it out and folds it neatly.

"All done," he says, and the neighbor thanks him kindly.

Only Otto needs something fixed today: his shelf has chipped, and Edith taps her hammer on it to fix it. She gets all the way to the janitor's room at the top landing without another customer. The janitor's door is closed, and Edith's first in line. She sits down at the top of the stairs, gazing idly at the painting on the flat wall where the next flight of stairs should have been. It almost looks like a real set of stairs, gray and crumbling slightly at the edges. It's easy to imagine them switchbacking all the way up to the surface. On the wall between the stairs and the janitor's door, the elevator is still inert. It could ding at any moment now. The janitor will come out of her room and open the elevator door in a gust of fragrant air. Inside will be stacks of brown boxes, one for each of the neighbors. Edith's mouth waters at the thought of fresh mushrooms, crispy little insects, chewy lichen.

It finally happens when the line of neighbors snakes down the stairs as far as Edith can see, and Irma who is right behind her in the queue has just fixed the seam on Edith's cardigan. The janitor steps outside, tall and magnificent in her blue dungarees. She greets the neighbors with a raised hand and a smile. As if on a signal, the elevator dings. The stairwell falls quiet. With a flourish, the janitor reaches for the handle and pulls the heavy door open.

The elevator is empty.

MEALTIME CONSISTS OF the last mushrooms. They've gone soggy and smell rank, but Edith forces them down. She sits down on her bed to wait for bedtime. The window-painting on the far wall needs touching up; the blue part of the ocean is flaking. Edith ran out of the blue color halfway through, and painted the rest green. It's a place where two oceans meet. It'll be all green when she's done it over, as if the window has shifted.

All the janitor had said was *the elevator is empty*, and the words had traveled down the stairs. The neighbors had looked at each other in confusion, then meekly returned to their rooms. Edith had lingered for a moment. The janitor had merely closed the elevator door and gone back to her room. Edith tried the door handle to the elevator. It was locked.

Edith finds herself walking around the room, picking things up and putting them in their place, wiping the table and the shelves, folding her clothes, shaking out the bed sheets. She puts the rubbish in the small bucket and sets it down outside the door, where it'll be empty before morning comes. The stairwell is quiet now. Everyone is waiting for bedtime. There's a strange acidic tickle in her stomach. It shoots tendrils into her legs.

Edith sits back down on the bed, but her stomach is churning. Something is about to happen. It's never good when things happen.

IT BEGAN IN the colonnades under the town on the platform in the desert. Someone saw a pale and unfamiliar figure leaping from shadow to shadow.

Then came the horde.

As the invaders caught the villagers and tore into them, they made soothing, crooning noises that somehow drowned out the shrieking. They strangled the villagers, tore their eyes out, opened their throats with sharp teeth. They rolled the bodies over the edge of the platform, into the sand. When they couldn't find any more victims, they went into the little houses and closed the doors.

EDITH WAKES UP in the middle of the night and retches over the side of the bed. She manages to crawl out and find the chamber pot before her bowels empty themselves in a long, excruciating spasm. When it finally subsides, she slides off the pot and onto the floor. The stink of her own waste makes her retch again, dribbling bile on her shoulder.

Then someone is banging on the door, and she must have blanked out, because the vomit on her shoulder is cold. Three bangs, then silence, then three more bangs. Voices outside, many footsteps marching down the stairs. They're going somewhere, and she should be going with them. They're going to leave her all alone. But every joint in her body hurts, and her bowels empty again before she manages to find the pot, and then she's standing at the edge of the platform, gazing out across the desert.

SOME OF THEM managed to escape. Edith persuaded them to hide in the silo. They watched the massacre from a little window on the loft. When the light faded and the invaders hadn't moved for a while, Edith led the refugees out and away from the village. They walked for hours across the hot sand, until they came upon a structure in the middle of nowhere. It was a little concrete shed, perhaps three meters on each side. The heavy door stood ajar. The villagers went inside after very little hesitation, into the cool gloom of a stairwell. The door swung closed behind them. Inside, neatly ordered rooms, as if they had been waiting just for them. They took a room each and sat down to wait for bedtime. When the lights went out, Edith thought she heard a stranger's voice complaining in the stairwell, *They're much too early. It's not right.*

WHEN THE CEILING lamp comes on, it's weak and flickering. Edith sits in a puddle of shit and vomit next to the bed. The stink is thick like a fog. Her joints still hurt, but not as badly as in the night, and she manages to stand up on shaky legs. She dries herself off with an almost-clean towel and puts on her dress, thick stockings, cardigan, slippers. There's still a little water in the jug on the table. It eases the burn in her throat.

The slight groan of the door hinges is very loud in the quiet stairwell. It seems somehow larger than it used to. The downward stairs gape at her.

"Hello?" Edith calls weakly.

No reply, save for a faint rustle below. She hobbles across the landing to Irma's door and knocks. Nothing happens. She pushes the handle down: it's unlocked. Inside, Irma's room is tidy and unoccupied: the bed is made, the table empty, her sewing tools sit in a neat row on the shelf.

Edith starts to climb the stairs but her legs refuse to carry her upward. She sits down on the lowest step, heart pounding in her throat.

"Hello," comes a faint reply from upstairs.

Gregor comes shuffling downstairs behind her. His face is very pale and his eyes wide. He gasps as he sees Edith.

"I'm so glad to see you. I thought I was alone." He sits down on the step next to Edith; his nostrils flare briefly but he doesn't comment on her smell.

"What's going on?" Edith says weakly.

"They're all gone, Edith." Gregor gestures upward. "I was just upstairs. No one's here. Not even the janitor."

"Someone was at the door last night," Edith says. "I wanted to go outside, but I was so sick."

Gregor runs his hand over the wall with a rasping noise. "I was afraid," he mumbles. "I wanted to go too, but it was pitch dark and the noise outside. It scared me. And now… they're all gone."

"Everyone?"

"Everyone. We shouldn't be here. Can't you feel it?"

Edith swallows. Gregor's right. It feels like when she once overstayed her welcome at Irma's, and Irma left so that Edith would take the hint and go home.

"We have to go find them," she says.

Gregor looks nauseated. "I'm still afraid."

Edith reaches for his hand and squeezes it.

THE FIRST FLIGHT of stairs down to Gregor's flat is easy enough, especially for Gregor, of course—he lives there. Gregor finds Edith some water and a handful of dried beetles, and her legs become slightly more steady. The next flight of stairs feels slightly more ominous, but still, it's where Gregor's under-neighbors live, and he knows them well. They knock on one door each, but no reply. The rooms beyond are tidied and empty. No one seems to have brought anything with them. They have left their tools behind.

They both stop short at the next flight of stairs. The light is distinctly dimmer. For a second, Edith thinks she sees shadows rushing up at them, but then she blinks, and they're gone. Gregor grabs her hand.

"I've never been this far," he says.

"Neither have I." Edith pauses. "Do you know how far down the stairwell goes?"

Gregor shakes his head.

The doors on the next landing are identical, and the next. Even though she's counting them, it feels as if Edith and Gregor aren't actually going anywhere, just arriving in the same place again and again. The fear that spreads cold tendrils through Edith's face and ears makes her light-headed, almost giggly. They stop knocking on doors, instead just opening them gingerly. On the ninth landing down, the rooms are no longer furnished, just gray-walled cells. The walls become first damp and then wet to the touch, and the air slowly warms up. Gregor's breathing has a slight squeak. Edith's knees ache. The smell of wet earth creeps up from below.

On the seventeenth landing, water seeps out from a crack in the wall and trickles across the floor. A shadow around the little stream tells of an ebb and flow, like in that dream, by the ocean: the water would draw back to reveal a beach pierced with thousands of little holes, each holding a pale and tiny crab. The trickle runs down to the next landing, where the concrete bleeds more water. When water starts seeping into Edith's slippers, it's warm, like blood.

On the twenty-second landing, the stairs abruptly end. Where the next flight of stairs should have started is a blank wall. One single door stands next to a broken wall sconce. The handle glints in the faint light from upstairs. The floor here is dark and soft and squelches with runoff. Edith takes a deep breath and pulls at the door handle.

A bulb in the ceiling bathes the room in yellow light. It's furnished and cluttered with tools of all sorts. The bed is rumpled, the sheets smell heavily of sour musk. At the far end of the room is another door. Edith's knees are throbbing. She sits down on the bed. Gregor closes the door behind him and crosses the room to try the other one. It's locked.

Warm fatigue creeps up along Edith's legs. "I need to rest," she says.

Gregor's fingers drum an uneven rhythm on the tabletop. "What do you think about, when you think about where we came from?"

Edith blinks. "I thought no one did but me."

"Of course not," Gregor says. "I talked to Adela about it every now and then. We could never agree. She says it was a desert."

"It was," Edith replies.

"No, it wasn't, and I don't understand where you got that from. It was a forest. Tall trees with dark trunks like pillars, and high up there, straight branches covered in little needles.

The canopy was so dense that nothing grew on the ground. We lived in spheres hanging from the branches. They were pretty, all coppery metal and with big round windows. We didn't like touching the ground. We ate needles and bark, and we were happy like that."

Edith considers. Then she starts telling Gregor of her own memory, but the light goes out, and sleep takes her.

IT IS DARK and Edith is in bed, under blankets, Gregor curled up next to her. She has woken up because someone just gently pulled the blanket from her shoulder. A presence is looming over the bed.

"Who are you?" Edith whispers.

The sound of lips parting and a dry tongue unfastening from the palate. The words are laden with clicks and smacks. "I am the caretaker. And you're late for your migration."

"Where did the others go?"

"Downstairs."

"Why?"

"It was time."

"I don't understand," Edith says. "Are you the one who makes the boxes?"

"No more questions," the caretaker replies. "All you have to do is move on."

"But where are we supposed to go?"

A brief pause. "You should know that. Haven't you had dreams?"

"I dream of an ocean sometimes."

The caretaker smacks its dry tongue. "That won't do. No. You're heading for houses. Remember that. Houses in a circle, with lanterns over the doors."

The caretaker pulls the blanket off the bed and drops it on the floor. "You'll know where you're going. It'll feel right. Now go. You'll be late. It's the other door."

It moves away. The door to the stairwell opens with a groan.

The caretaker's silhouette against the faint light of the stairwell doesn't look quite right.

"First too early and now too late," the caretaker mumbles. "Something's not right."

Next to Edith, Gregor stirs and sighs. "What was that?"

"We have to go," Edith says.

THE OTHER DOOR opens onto a tunnel through raw rock, walls glowing faintly with blue-white larvae. The echoes of Edith's and Gregor's footsteps are very faint. Edith's heartbeat is slow and heavy. Their breath and the shuffle of their feet on the rough ground count out a rhythm that sucks her in. She almost doesn't notice when the tunnel widens into a cave, not until whatever is crouching by the little pool moves slightly and Gregor lets out a little squeak. Backlit by the luminous water, the pale figure looks almost like a neighbor. It suddenly turns around and looks up at them. Small eyes glitter in the waterlight. It lets out a small whimper. Edith leans on the wall, because her heart is rushing and her knees are buckling. They stare at each other. The other bounds away into the dark with a rasp of naked feet on stone.

Gregor sits down with a thud. Edith rests against the wall until she can feel her legs again. Then she pushes herself to her feet and walks over to the little pool. The water is full of little glowing specks that tastes strongly of minerals. Edith splashes the water a little, to break the silence.

"It seemed to be afraid of us."

"It was alone," Edith replies. "Maybe next time it won't be."

STALACTITES EXTEND FROM the tunnel's ceiling, leaving just enough room to crawl through. After a while, they can't see the tunnel walls anymore, just irregular pillars stretching in every direction. Winged insects with glowing abdomens crawl over the pillars. They're easy to catch. Bitter and sour juice bursts over her tongue when Edith bites down on them.

Gregor slips on a loose stone and twists his ankle so badly that his foot hangs limp at the end of his leg with a fist-sized lump on the ankle bone. Edith wraps it with her stockings as well as she can, and helps him climb onto her back. They continue in silence, Gregor occasionally wheezing in pain.

"There was a storm, a firestorm," he says after a while.

"I woke up because my house was rocking back and forth. I opened a hatch and looked outside and there it was, a glow between the trees, and all the air was rushing toward it. People were climbing out of their homes, screaming. Someone banged on the walls and made them ring. We threw out ropes and climbed down to the ground. Some people panicked and just jumped. I'll never forget that noise.

"We picked up the children and the frail and ran, but we couldn't run fast enough. The fire was catching up with us, eating everything in its way. We heard the pops and bangs as houses exploded or fell to the ground. A woman shouted, *Save us! Save us!* Soon we were all chanting, *Save us! Save us!*

And there it was: a tree, the biggest tree I had ever seen. The same woman who had led us here banged on the bark and screamed, *Let us in! Hide us from the fire!* We all echoed her: *Hide us! Hide us!*

"A door swung open in the tree. We crowded inside. Inside was a stairwell. And the reason the stairs are blocked is that either the danger hasn't passed, or... because we asked the tree to hide us, but we forgot the rest. We forgot to tell the tree that it should let us out again once it was safe. It's just doing what we asked."

Gregor pauses.

"We should be going in that direction." He points into the murk.

"How do you know?"

"I just know."

Edith doesn't feel any such thing, but does as he says.

* * *

HER BACK IS hurting badly when she realizes that the stalactites are trees, and that grey light is filtering down from above. The floor is a carpet of brown needles.

"Gregor," she whispers.

From where he clings to her back, Gregor lets out a small sob. "I know these trees."

He slides down from Edith's back and hobbles over to a tree, resting his cheek on the bark. He turns to Edith, and tears are running down his face. "We're home."

He points upward, and there they are, spheres hanging in branches. Rope ladders trail down from their hatches. The spheres look pristine, waiting for new occupants. Silence is complete.

"We're home!" Gregor shouts.

Edith frowns. "You said this place burned."

"Obviously it's here now," Gregor says acidly.

Gregor waves at the spheres. He hobbles over to the nearest rope ladder.

"Hello? Hello?"

The soft silence eats the sound of Gregor's voice. He tries to tug at the ladder, but the rope somehow slips out of his fingers. He grabs futilely at it.

The silence makes Edith's ears ring. The spheres have no dust on them, no dirt. There's no trace of the firestorm Gregor talked about.

"I'm not sure we should be here," Edith says.

"I don't understand why I can't get the…"

Gregor throws himself at the rope ladder. He somehow manages to miss it by an arm's length. He lands on the ground with a huff.

Edith scoops up a handful of soil and pine needles and sniffs it. Her hand might as well be empty. "Gregor. Shouldn't the trees smell like trees?"

"Of course they do," Gregor replies absently, staring at the ladder. "Look, I'm staying. The others are here, we just have to wait for them to come out."

Edith shakes her head. "I don't want to be here. It's all wrong. And it's not home."

The look Gregor gives her is full of pity. He's never looked at her like that before. "I'm sorry." His right hand is still grabbing for the rope ladder. He doesn't seem to notice.

"I'm sorry too, Gregor. I'm leaving."

"I'll be here," Gregor replies. "I'm climbing up and I'm going to find out what to do. A weaver, maybe. A singer. It depends on what the others are."

Edith turns around. She doesn't look back. The forest seems to push at her back as she leaves.

THERE'S NO WAY to tell whether she's walking in the right direction. The stalactites spread out in an irregular grid. She should have a feeling of where to go, like Gregor did, but she doesn't. Occasionally, she finds traces of others passing through: a scarf, some chewed insect carapaces, dried excrement. She follows them like a trail at first, only to end up where she started. Eventually she just pushes forward without thinking much.

At last, the rushing in her ears is more than her own blood. It rises and falls, rises and falls, and in the distance shines the warm yellow circle of a cave mouth.

IT'S AN OCEAN, far below, and Edith is standing on a ledge high up on a cliff wall. The sky is bright blue, fading into white; somewhere behind the cliff is a sun. A path snakes down toward the water. The ocean is green. Edith knows it must be warm, like blood. She steps out onto the ledge and follows the little path down. The path ends in a beach, dotted with thousands of tiny holes. She crouches down next to a cluster of them just in time to see a little crab run for shelter. Dark recesses sit in the cliffside. Edith looks into the nearest one; inside is a narrow bed, a little table and two chairs. No dust, no sign that anyone lives there. The only sound is that of waves. Just like Gregor's rope ladder, it proves impossible to climb into the caves. Somehow her foot falls short of the threshold again and again. She's not supposed to be in this place, or the place isn't ready for her. She climbs back up the path.

THE GLOW OF a lamp lures her out from between the stone pillars. It's a lantern with glass walls, suspended from the cave ceiling. It lights up a wall of grass that grows higher than her head. It parts before her easily enough, giving off a sharp and herbal scent as she touches the blades. It eventually parts onto a circular clearing. The sky is dark; the only light comes from the lanterns suspended on curved poles over the doors of little houses standing in a tight circle around a high central lamppost. Someone is scuttling between the houses, their movement pattern human but somehow not quite. The caretaker is setting down little brown boxes in front of the door of each house.

It's delivery day.

Edith watches as the caretaker scurries into the high grass, and the sky brightens into a uniform blue, brighter at the edges. People come out of the houses and wave at each other across the lawn. They pick up the boxes, tearing them open with delight. Edith recognizes none of them. They're dressed just like her but they're tall and gangly, their skin slightly darker than her own, and with large, shining eyes. She backs away into the grass before any of them can see her.

EDITH FINDS HER neighbors in a huddle among the stalactites, holding each other and whimpering. Everyone is there. They look at Edith in astonishment as she approaches. The janitor, who no longer has a janitor's bearing, slowly gets up on her feet.

"We tried to go home," she says weakly. "Someone was already there. Are you here to help us?"

Irma is leaning on the stalactite closest to Edith and hugging her legs. She doesn't seem to recognize Edith at all.

"Irma," Edith says, but Irma doesn't react to her own name. Edith looks at the others. "What happened to you all?"

They merely gaze at her.

"We need to go home," the person who once was Irma whispers.

"Then why aren't you walking?"

No reply, just uncomprehending stares.

"Come," Edith says. "We have to go."

They meekly get up and follow, shuffling blindly forward. The janitor, if it still is the janitor, takes her hand and holds it so tightly it hurts.

And finally, a slight tug in Edith's chest. A direction: this way.

THE STALAGMITES BECOME thick and rough and stand on upturned blocks with carved faces, and this is a familiar place at last: a colonnade, and the metallic scent of granite and sun-warmed wood, and the sound of voices. Home.

"This is it," Edith says. "We're here."

"But there are people here," the janitor whispers, and points at a person walking further ahead.

Edith recognizes the gait, that strange grace. They walked just like that when they came to invade and take over. Here they are, usurpers, living in a place that doesn't belong to them. Someone is living in her house, sleeping in her bed, playing at her profession.

She looks at the others. Their faces are blank. They have no memory of this. But they do have hunger. It shines out of their eyes.

"It's our turn," Edith says. "This is our place. Let's take it."

And she starts toward the usurper at a walk, and it turns around and sees her, and when it breaks into a run, her heart floods with a wild joy.

THE BED IS very soft. The hut has just enough room for a bed and a table with chairs. There is also a shelf with some interesting objects. One in particular is very smooth and comfortable to the touch: a bowl edged with soft thorns.

Outside, the sun has risen almost all the way to zenith. The others are already up, wandering among the houses, picking up objects and talking about them. Their faces are different, and so are their gaits; they have already started. By the platform's edge, gazing out across the desert, stands a man.

"Hello."

The man turns around. "Hello." He smiles. "I'm not quite awake yet. You know how you wake up some mornings, and you have to tell yourself, 'Here I am, Urru-Anneh is my name, and I dive in the sand for shells.' It's one of those."

"Exactly one of those. I woke up, and I had to remind myself, 'I'm...'"

Urru-Anneh waits patiently.

"Arbe-Unna," she finishes.

"And where are you going this fine morning, Arbe-Unna?"

Arbe-Unna hesitates. "I'm on... an errand."

"Good luck with your errand then." Urru-Anneh smiles and turns back to gaze at the desert.

Arbe-Unna wanders off into the village, where the others are greeting each other and helping each other remember who they are and what they do. A silo stands at the edge of the platform. Inside, it's very quiet. In the middle of the floor sits a crate on wheels. The crate is filled with little brown parcels. An enticing smell rises from them. Arbe-Unna catches a glimpse of something moving in the loft—a head, an arm?—but when it doesn't happen again, decides it must have been nothing.

Arbe-Unna grabs the edge of the crate and pushes it outside. The other villagers throw their hands up in joy when they see the crate and the parcels.

"Good morning!" cries Arbe-Unna. "It's me, Arbe-Unna, your janitor."

The others cheer, and form an orderly line as the janitor hands them each a parcel. Arbe-Unna chats with each of them, finding out their names and professions. They are more than happy to talk about themselves, sometimes helping each other to remember details. At the end of the ceremony, they're all good neighbors, although they don't all agree on how old the village is or who's related to whom. But that's how people are.

It does feel as if someone's missing, but that might also be because of the dream she had last night. A cave, a forest, a friend who stayed behind. Something had gone wrong. It was a relief to wake up and find everything alright with the world, everyone in their right place.

ON SKYBOLT MOUNTAIN
JUSTINA ROBSON

"THAT IS QUITE enough," Lettice said firmly as she took hold of Missy Bancroft by the long brown curls at the nape of her neck and reached over to detach her hand from Esther Mann's blonde plait.

The hand was sticky with jam and repellently moist with heat from the fighting and the late summer day. It came free only because twelve year old Missy hated the notion of the Widow Lettice Beaverley touching her even more than Lettice hated doing so. Rumour in Far Ashes said Lettice Beaverley was a witch, which was incorrect, but useful at certain moments.

Missy shrieked at a pitch that would deafen cats and Lettice released her. The child zipped to a safe distance at the centre of the tent leaving Lettice beside the display of jams with the other milling adults. Lettice glanced down at the ruins of Lyda Prufrit's black cherry compote which had come via wagon and the copper jam pan of Mistress Tyvalt, confectioner and confiturisse to Lord and Lady Bonfort at Wast Castle. There was no trace of an imp in it now. She regretted her choice of sabotage, though not the act itself, as Missy began to shout loudly,

"The Widow Beaverley has cursed the Prufrit jam! There was a familiar doing something to it. I saw it! I had it in my hand."

"It was you in the jam, Pigface!" Esther screamed in retort, hand on her head. Lettice saw sly triumph in her eyes beneath the tears. Esther followed Missy, determined to win the fight regardless of any truth, particularly since it was now a proper spectacle. "And your mother says every year that Miz Prufrit cheats!"

At that moment every eye in the tent was on the two yelling girls or looking out for an adult to take charge. Lettice glanced down and saw that the jam-marks of the imp's feet were distinctly visible in two three-clawed footprints on the white linen where Missy's hand had grappled with it. Missy went for the plaits again and in that moment Lettice took the corner of her apron and made a blithering attempt to clean up. Adults were unable to see The Least Things. If they did they had a way of rationalising any evidence that they existed, which usually worked very well on its own, but she didn't want to give any substance of any kind to Missy's claim. Better to be thought an idiot for trying to clean up jam on linen with a dry cloth.

The event closed with Miz Prufrit taking her jam and her ribbon home, smug and much-consoled through the late afternoon sunshine. Missy and Esther were reconciled as if nothing had ever happened, their hands full of biscuits. They cast dark looks in Lettice's direction as she put her marmalade away and she knew that she'd made a terrible mistake. Ten years she'd lived here and controlled her sense of fairness and, for the most part, her tongue. She'd done everything to present her best face, knowing stories followed her around like stray dogs, even going so far as to borrow a pan and concoct overly sugary marmalade that was sure to go unplaced at the summer fair so that its appearance would render her the more invisible. Now however, incensed for a moment by the smugness of Lyda's presentation, she had let her sense of justice get the better of her.

She spent a little more time circulating among the stalls and then walked home along the roads to where her rented house sat in the lee of the Ivystead farm. All the way she regretted her actions even as she felt righteous of them. She could not abide a cheat or petty cruelty. It was not the first time she had done something that would take root and be the eventual cause of her having to leave somewhere. She was particularly angry because she liked Far Ashes. It was close to the border of Nazuria—the land of the ice warriors, where the people were paler and their customs strange and bizarre, their gods terrifying and their magical practices heretic and cruel. Nazuria was a high land of sorcerers and mountains. It was beyond the edge of the world for the civilised of the Cascar Empire who had surrendered their ancient ways to the Holy Writ after the conquest of the Empress Aturin a century ago.

Lettice had long since given up on hopes of such things bringing a change for good. The Holy Writ was a man's words on a paper though it pretended to have divine authority and power. It was the product of people who wanted to stamp out magic by denying the existence of it, Lettice thought, sympathetically, though it had left the unmagical at the mercy of every passing Greater Aspect. Children were innocents under the Writ and could not be held responsible for speaking of arcane matters until they came of age. Missy was well below age. She had seen and she *would* talk, most likely until someone took notice enough.

Lettice studied her house after she had lit her rush light and saw nothing in the tiny one-roomed home that she could not leave, save for the basket in the corner. The idea of leaving irked her however—she was no threat. She was the very opposite of a threat to anyone.

She lit her fire and put water on it to boil for a hot drink in the cold hours before bed. When she had settled in her chair and warmed herself she reached for the basket and took off the waterproofed hide that was its fitted cover. She lifted out the doll inside and set it on her knee, tidying the embroidered silk shawl that wrapped it before she brushed her fingers once across its featureless cotton face. She felt much calmer then.

She spent a comfortable hour dandling the baby on her knee, loving every moment of the sweet company, the dark eyes which smiled at her when she smiled and the little hands which reached out in delight to touch her face, never knowing she was not young any more. Chuckles filled the smoky air. The love she felt then was so pure and all-fulfilling that the vagaries of the day and her temper left her. Here at least was a spell well spent, though it cost her twenty years. But later, when she had put Annett back to her basket and herself to her straw mattress she could not help but consider it a foolish decision to linger and then the anger came again, fierce and hot. Beneath the anger hid a weariness from years of moving on that she could not face and so she was still there a month later when Lord Bonfort's man came and knocked on the door.

He was dressed in a neat livery that she recognised from having worked on the embroidery of the cuffs and borders for sixty sets the previous autumn—it had paid well but seemed a mighty extravagance for footmen and soldiers to her. He was young and held himself away from her a little, looking over her head as though she was literally beneath notice as he said, "Widow Beaverley, you are requested to attend the Lord of Wast at the Castle on pressing business."

"I cannot imagine what for," Lettice said, hoping to prise it out of him as her heart sank. Mentally she was already packing.

"Word of your abilities has reached his Lordship's attention and he has a proposal for you that might spare you the inconvenience of a hanging."

Lettice felt her mouth hanging open for a good second before she snapped it shut. Though entirely expected the implied accusations and sentencing still hurt. Since the fair she had kept herself apart, dealing only on market days to hand in her sewing and shop for food. Her behaviour had been impeccable. She had even paid alms through the Temple Gate to priests that were little more than the Papess' beggars, resenting every copper. In their dull eyes she'd seen only the satisfaction of unimaginative men whose lives had been signed away in return for a roof and regular meals—entirely the fault of the Wastern temperament and its love of repose. That they would prosper, smothering the survival skills of generations, while she must run like a rat for the rest of her days hurt bitterly.

She knew herself her own worst enemy, of course, always. To refuse the summons, to delay, all these things were impossible for a woman alone. "I'll get my things."

With the basket on her back and her best coat on, the old cloak left to decorate the empty room, she set out after the squire's pony. To her relief its grain-fed paces soon left her behind before they had even passed Far Ashes. On the way she dropped off the mending for the village tailor that she had already finished. The servant said there could be no pay until market day, which she had expected. She asked for it to be retained. Although she knew she would not be coming back she saw no reason to give any satisfaction about it to anyone. The only one to miss her would be the farmer when his rent was unpaid but he would have her firewood and her matching cream pottery bowls that she so loved, so it was not all bad news for him.

As she left Far Ashes she watched her shadow step before her and walked until it had begun to stretch behind. At that point she looked for a resting place and sat on a fallen trunk that had been pushed to the roadside, sure to stay away from the reaching shade of the trees. At the trees' feathered edges where they lay dappled across the stones she saw mountains, high and far, and a cold distant peak that bore no visible paths.

Between the grey trunks two dryads stared at her. In the past she would have had to hunt them if she wanted them. Now that they were used to people not being able to see them in broad daylight they took almost a minute to realise she was staring back at them. They waited to see if she would be afraid but when she gave them a firm look they melted back into the trees. They were not the first Minor Aspects she had seen lately, though most of these were relatively benign forms which were simply looking for recognition and had no interest either way in human affairs. The mountain, on the other hand, bothered her. She could feel its presence beyond the trees and over the hills. Mountains have long roots and longer reaches. What thrives there are the stripped-off things, the lees of those who tread the slopes, the remnants of those who reach the heights where the wind winnows all but the raw soul away.

Lettice made a note to buy new boots. If there was to be winnowing she wanted to have good feet for it.

The walk took two days. She stopped at inns she knew of along the way, where a cot in a warm room was available in exchange for her stitching skills. The meals she paid for from the last of her wages and at the final stop, a wealthy village just shy of Bonfort, she sold all she had of fine lawn handkerchiefs and embroidery and the sickly marmalade. She had been there before, some years ago, and had left when the rumours of a baby had spread, because it was not seen out always but only now and again, and seemed not to grow. She hoped not to be recognised and kept her hood down.

She had been suspected of taking children from parents in the countryside for coin—as town baby farmers did—and then drowning them rather than minding them. She supposed there must be a precedent for doing such a thing, though it was an evil she could only have punished rather than plotted. But the chatter of ill deeds sped faster than a fire and she had fled, much as she was doing now. A few faces seemed to recognise her, but most did not, occupied with their own business. She saw no sign of menace until the evening came and found her at the inn's snug, tucked in the corner with her hood down, drinking a toddy as she passed her final hours of freedom.

As night drew on she listened to a conversation between two men who sat as close to the log fire as they could without roasting themselves. A foul steam came from their clothing as they dried, though it had not rained all day in town. They wore the black outer robes of the Simple Friars but beneath that she saw the leather boots more like those of Nazurian reavers and their belts held several blades apiece. Their chests were crossed with baldrics of black tanned leather that supported narrow-headed axes and coils of rope that they would not put down. In the firelight their hands were revealed sore and cracked with cold, though it was a mild night. They spoke with distant accents, different ones, though the symbols about their necks branded them as brothers of a kind. Lettice did not know the sign but it was not hard to interpret—a twisted knot that could not unravel because it was a single strand. They were some kind of sorcerer-warriors and they had reached Bonfort from the bitter cold hills to the east within a single day. To do so required a considerable magic—striding—which Lettice did not possess and had only heard of. She surmised it was striding or riding at least, upon the kinds of horses or pantherkin that few but the Queen commanded. They did not bear her arms however, only carelessly hung wooden tablets at the waist with the Holy Writ scripted on them as any pious layman might wear. One had them the wrong way about, which confirmed to her that they were merely for show.

As Lettice slumped, cup aslant in her relaxed hands, pretending to sleep, the conversation delved swiftly into fearful mutterings about the mountains, from which it became apparent they had fled. They spoke of shadows on the land that followed them, the sound of wings in still air, the blocking of the sun without a cloud and of choughs that watched for their steps to fall on poor ground and then scattered tiny pebbles at them from on high. Stone slides took the path out under their feet.

This was immanent magic Lettice knew very well. In certain places it required only the merest push to take form, there was so much of it about. In these places the Eightfold Wall was thin and any Greater Powers might pass.

The men glanced often at the door, and shivered when it shut with a thump against the air outside. They talked about someone who had followed them, not only on the mountain, which might have been a wight or a ghast, but off the mountain where such things could not tread, even across the running spread of the Wasterling River where it was whited water that nothing should be able to span that was not alive and true, part of the holy creation.

Lettice shivered, but sternly reminded herself it was the careless wizard who mixed his doctrines with such freedom.

You did not suppose creation holy and susceptible to the Writ if you also supposed it chaotic and interleaved with the Eightfold Plane. If the former then all your ghasts were demons that you must fight like a warrior but were categorically separated from, and if the latter then they were wild creatures beyond the ken of human minds that you dealt with at your peril but with which you shared a fundamental common existence. The first declared one being over all in mimicry of human rule. The second knew only the necessities of survival and the hunt. Lettice knew the latter truer than the former, for which she might rightly be hung for heresy tomorrow should she prove a disappointment.

The men spent Bonfort gold on fine food and wine and finally were joined by a third returned from the Castle itself, the glow of pride in it still about him. He was dressed as they were except for a red cord at his waist and he was sober. He pushed his hood back and revealed a head groomed and hair tied in tight rows that gathered at his nape, beard the same and beaded with scarlet and silver clasps.

"I said we advised against it," he informed them, taking his seat between on the bench and quite blocking the heat. "But he won't be swayed."

"Did you agree to accompany him?"

"He says to pay us from the hoard," their leader said.

"No dragon, no hoard," the one with the strangest accent said, so quiet she thought for a minute that she had misheard but the curl of flame in the grate agreed suddenly, painting the man's face with a meandering yellow line.

"Nah. No *dead* dragon, no hoard," the other corrected him, wincing as he touched a deep crack in his knuckle. "I ain't goin' back on that mountain."

Lettice felt she had heard enough. She must get out before the last of her spirits failed her. She got up quickly, knocking her cup to the tiles and smacking her lips as if she had startled from a deep sleep, then shuffled around the three and around the traders lingering in the heat. Outside the room the chill evening air was biting for the first moments and her breath misted in front of her as she turned in the passage, looking for the way to the stairs. She had to struggle not to be dismayed at this sign.

"Bloody beldames," she heard said as the door closed after her.

In the morning she made herself as respectable as she was able with the help of a kind farmer's wife who brushed out and sewed up her hair. Then after a breakfast of eggs and milk to fortify her for what must come she left and went to present herself at the Castle. There was a long wait and then a maid of a level deemed suitable for escorting nobodies into the Lord's receiving rooms was sent for. Lettice was taken to a waiting room and after another hour of staring at a tatty tapestry of unicorns and maidens she was permitted to enter a wood-panelled chamber.

If it hadn't been for the unicorns perhaps she might have been able to contain her memories of the war. No images or reminders of it were permitted anywhere, which is why in every innocent, bland depiction she saw the razing of Wast as it had been, before the Cascars. In each thread of pretty hair and poised hoof there was fire and blood, in each virtuous face the screaming mouths of those who did not die quickly enough. In and out the weave Least Ghosts formed, lost and looking for a home.

What should I have done? she thought. *I am only one against the armies of the East. I could have... but no, I could not. What would dying have achieved? But then again, what has living achieved—they are still here and what I know will die with me after all.* The unicorns and the maidens stared into serene emptiness. It took all her strength to sit. Finally she was shown to the Lord's study.

Lord Bonfort, attired in black and silver, sat with a quill in his hand as if he was interrupted in the middle of his letters. If the page before him had been added to in a month she would have been surprised, but she affected to look and wait for such a learned, powerful man to pause in his necessary duties.

"The Widow Beaverley," the maid announced with a curtsey, her face downcast.

Lettice did not curtsey and angled her head as if to peer at his paper and correct his spellings. "Lord Bonfort. You wished to speak with me." She couldn't even make that sound polite.

The scrape of the guard's boot at the door was met with a gesture of one of the Lord's ringed fingers. It slid back and the maid departed down some mousehole or other, Lettice supposed, or would have if this man had his way. He was tall and relatively handsome, with only the hints of grey coming to his temples and into his neat black beard. His grey eyes set at her with a frown of patriarchal disappointment and a little pity, which is what her motes of rebellion had sparked in him, she saw—how very toothless she must be. He spoke quickly, fortunately, or she would have lost her temper.

"They tell me you have some talent with the fell arts," he said, as if they were discussing ordinary business. Beside his hand a copy of the Great Writ lay in leatherbound perfection, the silk ribbon place markers aligned in position for Exorcism. He rested his fingertips on it lightly, as if it could earth him against some shock or other. "Is this so, or merely the moitherings of jealous chattels?"

"What do you want of me?" Lettice said. Let them do what they would, she would not bow to inferior minds. After the initial jolt of terror at this decision she felt a calm take over. She composed her hands on the handle of her basket and waited patiently for his answer.

Lord Bonfort looked her over for a moment. It must be hard for him to decide whether she was being rude or acting from a position of real power, she thought. He did not have a good eye for these things, which explained his state here at the edges of civilisation in Wast; it was the kind of place that minor royalty was sent to prove itself or be erased. "I want you to cast a curse, a hex, for me, at a certain time. If you really have poisoned foods and blighted crops, sold the souls of innocents and brought winter storms you must be able to manage this?"

This fresh listing of her 'crimes' rather took her breath away. She thought hanging would probably not be enough for such as her. They had burned children for crying out of turn when the

Writ was introduced, to scar the face forever. Some died of the shock. She held fast to the basket. "What am I to curse, and for what?"

"We are leaving tomorrow on an expedition to the mountains," Bonfort said, his hand sliding off the Writ and onto his desk. "There is word that the dragon of Mount Nazur has died."

"I do not see my part in this." She held her breath. He could not be serious.

"There is a hoard, of course, that should be reclaimed," Bonfort said, watching her closely. "And always a danger that it is not as deceased as it might be. In the event that it is not you will curse it."

This notion was so preposterous that Lettice found herself smiling and had to struggle to suppress it. The only thing which distracted her was the knowledge that he was hiding something, though if this is what he was prepared to say aloud what he concealed must be impressively foolish to a degree she could not imagine. She wondered if he were trying to start a war with Nazuria, or if they were manoeuvring him there by feeding him nonsense. She was about to say she had never heard anything more ridiculous when she understood that those might be her last words. "I see," she managed to say. 'So what would you be employing the wizards of the Red Circle for, then?"

The atmosphere of the room changed at that point. From a semi-amiable tolerance to an icy agitation in less time than it took her to draw breath.

"That is not your concern, witch," Bonfort said after a moment in which his advisors and he exchanged glances. "Are you able to do your part or not? That is all you need worry over."

"Indeed," Lettice said faintly, wondering why he didn't consider that the Red Circle had not proven itself able to deliver a curse. Then she remembered that they pretended to abide by the Writ. Officially they were scholars and friars. She, on the other hand, was already damned.

She was escorted out and given a room and gear for the expedition which she must make fit by dawn. In the evening she was given a supper in the servants' hall, alongside a group of women who were not going at all but who had spent the last month labouring to produce food and clothes for the journey. They assumed Lettice to be a freewoman from outside the town and treated her to all their opinions of the Lord and his household, in particular the Lady Bonfort: "A woman of ambitions—he's completely her creature, down to the last idea in his head—t'was she who came up with the dragon talk, first of the mountain, then the treasure and then the Kingship. She brought them wizards into it, and all that goes with it."

"Why?" Lettice said.

"To see 'im dead for bringin' that slavegirl 'ome," muttered one.

"She's eyes on the throne," her neighbour told her confidently, barely able to be heard over the hubbub of voices and the clatter and slam of plates and cutlery. "And she has a lib'ry full of books of Nazurian warlockery. Eh-em, I mean, fireside stories of course, not a word of truth, but she have faith in 'em. And she's got a spyin' glass. My sister is 'er second maid and she's seen it. A ball the size of a man's 'ed. She's from Keltrad that Lady Bonfort. They're primitive down that way. Until last autumn and the Glory they burned the Writ and any who spoke of it, though she's taken to it lately at chapel in town."

"Do you think there is a dragon in the mountains then?"

Lettice looked around at the woman, opened and shut her mouth a couple of times. "I can't say I ever really considered it," she replied.

"Them Red wizards was brickin' it yesternight so I think there must be—though they go stirrin' it up and we'll burn for sure," another woman put in, emphasising her point with a chicken bone that caught Lettice's attention. She felt a sensation that she had learned to dread —a conviction that what she was about to understand was absolutely true; that she was about to know a fragment of the future. It didn't matter what she did next, the vision would form.

She looked at their dishes. Among the heaps of plates, the spilled wine, the broken bread, the tumbles of tough sinew spat out and the vegetables scorned for meat in the midst of plenty there was but one bone. *Only one to return*, said the voice in her mind which spoke unbidden and whose words she disliked to hear. It had told her many things over the years, had never faltered. It had warned her about the Cascars years ago and she had listened, and fled.

"I am sure there is nothing there at all but a lot of rocks and empty caves," Lettice said firmly and got up. "Please excuse me, I am not used to so much rich food and I fear I must lie down."

Her companions looked dismayed at her, because she had given very little in exchange for their talk. "Better be somethin' up there or we'll all suffer come the return."

She went to her room, shadowed by a guard, and composed herself for a sleepless night. Hex a dragon indeed. This is what life came to when people without a shred of magical sensibility took it on themselves to interfere with things. She could no more have hexed a dragon than she could leap to the sun. As long as her life depended on their believing it, however, she found that she was prepared to pretend she could. Given that she was also happy to spit in a Lord's eye this intrigued her, for it felt like two opposing forces propelling her in the same direction, one to preserve her life and another to spend it. Either way, there was no avoiding the journey.

In her room she took Annett out from her basket and slept with the warm, fat baby cuddled in her arms; an unexpected stay of execution. In the morning she put her back in the basket. Where they were going there was no place for living children.

Her reservations about the journey proved well founded. The roads were hard and unforgiving and the weather still cool enough in the valleys to make it taxing. By the time they had crossed into the borderlands of the Nazurim and began to ascend, ever fearful of spies and assassins, it was properly cold and the winter clothing had been brought out. Lettice walked or, when she was tired, rode on one of the covered wagons.

The foothills were bare and unceasingly desolate after the meandering valleys of Wast. Their heather, bog and rocks was unbothered by farmers and most other things too, save the odd hare or hawk. A few dells held dark knots of trees and the kind of Lesser Spirits that held such gloomy places precious and dwelt in their shelter so they were not blown to bits by the wind.

That night the wagon and the horses abandoned the path and turned for home. Chatter and high spirits were replaced with silence and concentration. Sore feet stepped onwards, the porters carrying the luggage now and breathing heavily as they crawled steadily up the lower slopes of Nazur, the Skybolt. The peak was a jagged strip of white against the cobalt blue.

Lettice trod carefully, placing her feet between stones and lightly on rock. Scatterings of dust and tiny pebbles were all that covered it instead of earth. Black ice coated the sunless sides of boulders, shiny as scales. In the click of pebble on rock, the twist of stunted thorn trees, bent all in a single wave by wind, in the overreaching vast vault of the sky an overwhelming, exacting power lay massed. The black birds the Red sorcerers had spoken of floated out their lives on its high currents. They were not really birds.

So she crept, hoping to go unnoticed as if that hope had any chance when she walked within the thing she sought to avoid. The emptiness demanded she pour herself out. The weariness that had kept her in Far Ashes yearned towards it.

At the evening camp they were so few there was only one fire for all. The men's faces were deadly serious and the fatted-bullock looks that they had sported in the lowlands were now grizzled edges and deep lines. Forced to observe them at close quarters she was not surprised to see that many of them were not real people; empty incomprehension lay behind the blacks of their eyes as they huddled and ate. A lot of them filled Waṣt now, more year on year. She sat alone at the midst of them, wrapped in her cloaks, looking at the ground or her soup cup but eventually Bonfort called on her to speak.

"Were the Red sorcerers right? Is there a dragon here? Is it like those from the tale of the Dragon Kings?"

Here it was then, the focus that she had longed not to hear, the one he had kept to himself. "You speak of the Journeys of the Dragon Hero," she said, not asking a question. "It is a sorcerer's story, much misunderstood."

In the tale two brothers went up into the mountains in despair after the sack of their kingdom. They spent thirty days alone in the wild, surviving, starving as their bodies shrank and their spirits were eaten by the hungry ghosts of the high plateaux. Eventually they were so empty that when they came upon the bones of a dragon hidden in a cave they ground them up and ate the dust before lying down to die. The dragon spirit filled them and they returned, powerful beyond measure, to wreak their revenge. They were not men, but they ruled for centuries, tyrants and unassailable, until sorcerer warriors slew them— those the Red Circle presumed their forebears. Lettice had never paid much attention to this story, since there was a terror at its core which disturbed her so greatly she sought never to lure its attention. Now as Lord Bonfort spoke she felt a circle close to a knot within her.

"But is it true?"

Lettice looked up, furious. "All I did was put an imp in the jam!"

They all stared at her. She shook her head angrily. "Did you come here for that, then? To eat dragon bone?"

Soon the mountain would bare the graves in her heart and then—she did not know what then and started in reaching for the basket as a kick on her ankle gave sudden pain.

"Mind your tongue, witch."

Lettice had had time on the path to ponder the worth of the human lives around her; those she left behind in Wast, the greater masses she had heard of, those left long ago in the earth and herself. For all her efforts she had not resisted the mountain. Stripped of the world they had left she could no longer hide in its solidity from the knowledge of how it had been built. From these heights overlooking all of Wast the village beneath the lake that had fascinated her as a child with its plaintive ghosts shone like a tiny mirror, white as the cloud, bright as the sun.

She looked at the guard's boot that had delivered the kick and the things she had seen came creeping out of memory to stand around her; the murdered girls and the slaughtered boys, the butchered men and the blood of women taken to be used until they died and left without burial or mention again, the Writ a slab of rock across her friends that crushed them into dust.

She had always known the dragon was here.

"Aye they are right," she said, reaching down to rub her ankle.

The men shivered, but Bonfort ignored them. "I have seen no signs of a living dragon. Is it alive?"

"Yes," she said, drinking her soup.

"Where?"

Lettice turned her head and looked up to the brilliant white summit, one of many, that rose far above them. A little below it black rock broke the perfect blanket and steadily showed its harsh edges in a scatter of ridges. "There is a cavern up there. That is where it is."

Uneasy bickering and dispute. They were not sure whether to believe her.

"If we go up and there is nothing you will pay dearly." Bonfort clenched his gloved fist and his jaw muscle flickered.

As if it was her fault. She sat up and lifted her head, looked directly at Bonfort. "You can no more take its power than you can build a butterfly. That is the only advice I have for you. Your Red mages would go no farther. In that, at least, they show wisdom." She gestured at the tattered cloth and the red coil of thread holding it fast to a stone that marked the small lee in which they rested. "Even I long to be out of this place. There is nothing good here. Go home."

She felt rather than saw the hand raised to belt her. "The ramblings of a mad old woman. You cannot allow it!" But a glance from Bonfort had it taken down.

"The river ferryman at Cold Sidens swore that you kept his boat afloat though it had a hole in it a hand wide from rapids. The villagers at Tornscrap say you lifted a tree more than two ton off a house just to save a dog with no more than a word.

You raise the dead." He made a gesture and she started as the guard beside her seized her basket. With a jerk he tore off the cover and scattered everything it held onto the stony dirt. The few personal items and the white cloth doll tumbled out and the booted foot kicked through them: a spindle, a distaff, some wool, a leather reticule of sewing needles and threads, a golden ring.

"Women's nothings. What kind of a witch are you?"

Bonfort did not correct the guard this time. Lettice reached down for the doll. The booted foot kicked it away. It bounced heavily and landed at Bonfort's feet. He picked it up and brushed it off, apparently without thinking, then studied it briefly— featureless head, simple arms, simple legs, no hands or feet.

"If you continue up the mountain none of you will return," Lettice said.

"She curses us!" one of the men spat, standing and moving towards her. Bonfort held his hand up and the man stopped. He toyed with the doll, Lettice watching his every move. "What is the dragon that lives here?"

"Death," she said, though this was true of all dragons. "Do you still want its treasure?" She reached out to reclaim the ring, but the same boot trod down on it and she had to snatch her hand away.

"Many rich men have sought it over the years," Bonfort said, his lips looking thin and bitten as he contemplated the least success. "Their bones and their fine weapons are still on the hills for the taking. And the skulls of their sorcerers."

"Did you not think it strange that the Nazuri allowed you here without argument?" Lettice tried her final, desperate tactic. "They won't walk on its ground."

"Your business is to hex the creature to prevent peril," Bonfort told her shortly. "See you manage it or your skull will be sooner collecting more rain than you would prefer. We ascend to the cave at first light." He got up and tossed the doll onto the fire.

The guard bent and took the gold ring. The other items were left where they lay. Lettice did not pick them up. She watched the doll burn and thought, *I could never have left you on my own.* Lettice had put Annett, her daughter, beyond the world a long time ago, to spare her the ravages of black water fever, and now she was entirely beyond return's gate. She gave nothing away in her expression about this, nor moved, until all but the guard had gone to sleep. Finally he slept too, thinking he watched the same night stars pass slowly over the black tooth of the mountain and Lettice climbed the frozen road up and over the boulders and the crags to the cavern.

The night was clear and bitter. After hours of effort she fell a final time of many in the darkness and did not get up again. The sun found her and she opened her eye to its bright light as the rim of it crested the horizon below. Voices came from close at hand, men, and those of the Greater Powers that circled them, hungry and unseen.

Lettice stretched out her hand and the Greater Powers scattered. She got up from her cold bed and the mountain shifted a little, enough to loosen stones that had teetered on the brink of falling for over a year, held by ice and the winter lately. They gave with a sudden gush of smaller rocks and then boulders were tumbling and bouncing down the slopes, breaking on each other as the fall became an avalanche of stone moving like water in a single wave, roaring. The men were swept away and she watched them go, tiny toys thrown about jauntily until they lay buried under the foot of the crag and the last stones trickled down over them and came to rest.

She went down there to the edge of the fall line. The night's camp was there, a few yards beyond the last pebble. She picked up the golden ring from where it lay on the bare stone, pocket-fallen. There were embers in the fire, and soup, still warm. She took out the clothes from the packs and dressed herself in Lord Bonfort's silver, red and black with the fancy borders. Her old clothing she tossed on the fire, careless of whether it burned or not. In the reflection of melted snow she looked at her own face and saw it become his face. She straightened and surveyed her terrain, from Nazuria, where they rightly feared the mountain and the creatures thereon, to Wast, whence a woman called Lettice Beaverley had come to be shriven.

At the edge of the cliff she slipped the gold ring onto her finger and turned her face towards the south. Above her the black birds spiralled on the rising currents and she opened her dark, leathery wings and made her descent into Wast in the low country, Cascar as it was known then, though it would not be known that way for long.

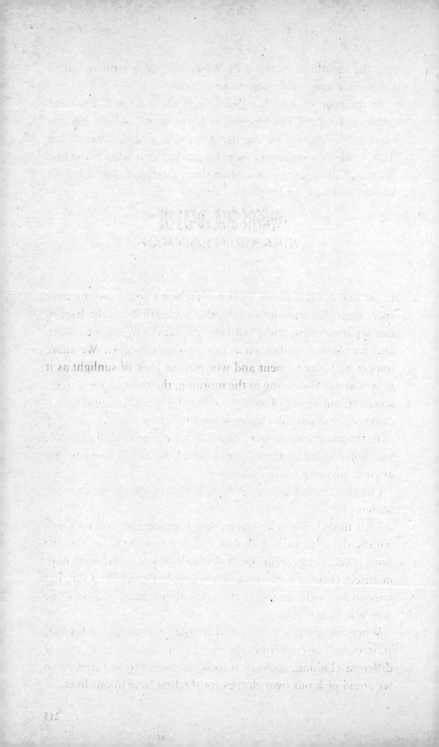

WHERE OUR EDGES LIE

NINA KIRIKI HOFFMAN

IN MY EARLIEST memories, I can't tell where I begin and my twin sister ends. We stare into each other's eyes through the bars of our separate cribs, and I fall into her mind and she into mine, and we swim together on a tide of our thoughts. We share hunger and contentment and wonder, the look of sunlight as it moves across the ceiling in the morning, the taste of apple juice, so sweet and bright, the one foot that feels cold because a sock came off, and we don't know whose foot it is. Ours.

To the frustration of our parents, who wanted gifted children, we didn't speak until we were three. We didn't need to tell anyone anything outside ourselves.

I forget who broke silence first. When we spoke, we said full sentences.

I felt interchangeable. Damia and I answered to each other's names, did each other's chores, laughed or didn't laugh at the same jokes. We were one in a world full of others. We were both intensely curious about how other people experienced life, but only so we could share our thoughts about them, and why our way was better.

When we were ten, Dad had us put in separate fifth-grade classrooms, over Mom's protests. He insisted we choose different clothing, too—even took us shopping at Penney's so we could pick our own clothes for the first time in our lives.

It made me nervous when Damia and I went into a dressing room and tried on two different things. I felt as though we were in separate slices of time. She got itchy, too. We wanted the same clothes. Dad despaired, but bought us three matching outfits and said we had to wear them on different days.

That September, when I went to a classroom without my sister for the first time, I felt lost. I couldn't pay attention to the teacher because I missed my twin so much. Her absence made me stupid.

A month later, though, I had a sneaky feeling of happiness. Everyone in class called me Cosima or Cozy. Sometimes it was, "Cozy, you idiot!" That hurt without the instant comfort my sister could supply, but I learned to live with these small wounds.

My classmates never called me "Damia."

Damia still cried every night after we turned out the lights. I did, too, if it seemed like she wasn't going to stop. I buried my secret happiness deep down inside, where my sister would never sense it.

I SAT ON the wall by the school's front steps, hugging my green backpack and staring at sparkles in the sidewalk. Damia's teacher wanted to talk to her about a science project, so she was late. Most everybody else had walked or biked or bussed off already. I wished Damia would come out so we could fall into step with each other again. A school day was too long a time apart, even broken in half by time together at lunch.

Someone paused in front of me. The first thing I saw about the woman was her pointy-toed cowboy boots. They were black, with red leather flames up the sides.

I glanced up, past her crinkled turquoise skirt and the white shirt embroidered at the yoke with flowers. Her hair was blue-green. Her eyes were pale green, like the bottom of a Coke bottle. Her mouth had the short upper lip and the pillowy lower lip I saw whenever I looked at Damia or a mirror, and her angled cheekbones looked like ours, too. The tips of her ears poked up through her hair, like fox ears. I wondered if she were a cosplayer.

"Cosima," she said. Her voice was low and thrilling.

"Do I know you?"

She sat beside me in a flurry of blue skirts and took my hand. Hers was cool and dry and almost reptilian. She smelled like jasmine and honeysuckle and dust. "I'm your real mother," she whispered.

An arrow of ice shot up my spine.

"Are Damia and I adopted?" I whispered back. I had never suspected it for a second. Our little brother Lars looked a lot like us, a lot like Mom, same high cheekbones and gray-green eyes and streaky brown hair. I remembered when Mom was pregnant with him (she was so cranky with morning sickness!), and when we first got to see him, two days after he was born, in a basket in Mom and Dad's room.

We couldn't be adopted.

"I'm not Damia's mother. Just yours."

That totally made no sense. I thought of Damia's and my shared baby album—pictures of Mom, twice as big as she had been with Lars, and pictures of us minutes after our birth—Dad was a maniac with the cell phone camera, and could bore anybody with an excess of pictures of the same thing over and over. He'd gone so crazy snapping pictures on our zeroth birthday he ran down the battery and had to borrow someone else's phone to call Grams and Gramp and let them know we'd been born.

I shook my head at the green-haired woman.

"I stole Cosima when she was a week old and left you in her place," whispered the woman. "She has been a boon to us under the hill. Still, I missed you, flesh of my flesh, spirit child."

My back twitched with shivers.

She lifted my left hand and slid a ring onto my ring finger. Vines of gold and red gold twined around a small green stone, with green gold leaves woven in. She released my hand, leaned forward and dropped a cool kiss on my cheek, then rose and walked away without looking back.

The kiss left a tingling in my cheek like the touch of ice or flame. "But—wait—but—" I tried to say, a stir of confusion and anxiety constricting my throat, and then the school door opened and Damia rushed out, and the warmth of being two who were one reclaimed me.

"Did you miss me?" she asked, which was what we always said to each other whenever we were separated and came back together.

"More than the moon and stars," I said, a ritual response.

She smiled my smile and I stood and we walked home side by side, our steps matching each other's.

After supper, when we were at our twin desks side by side in our bedroom, doing homework, Damia said, "Where'd that ring come from? You didn't have it at lunch."

I tensed. I had almost forgotten the stranger and her frightening story. "Somebody gave it to me while I was waiting for you."

"Who?"

"No one I know." I wished I had never spoken to the woman who said she was my mother.

Damia took my hand and stared at the ring, then twisted it and tried to pull it off. It wouldn't come. "Some stranger gave you a ring and you put it on?"

"Uh," I said. "She put it on me. It doesn't come off." Though I hadn't known that until this moment. I had felt the ring's presence, noticed it once or twice during dinner, and thought how pretty it was, but I had not thought more about it.

Damia frowned, making two upward furrows in our forehead. "It's really pretty," she said in a low voice. "I wish I had one like it."

My mind flooded with money-making schemes so I could buy her a ring. I'd never seen one like it in a store. But maybe I could get her a different one. Ask Mrs. Radich next door if she had any chores I could do for money, like grooming her Persian cat, and Mr. Alexi down the street, who sometimes hired us to weed his vegetable beds. Maybe Dad would let me draw something for him.

Damia touched the green stone in my ring, then turned back to her math.

It was the first crack in the mirror.

WHEN WE WERE fifteen, we got learner's permits, and Dad took us out to practice driving. Damia wore the Black Hills Gold ring I had bought her, with some help from Mom, for our twelfth birthday, and I wore the one given me by the woman who had messed up my mind. It didn't come off. Sometimes, it tingled, and strange thoughts came into my head, and that was when I tried hardest to slip it off, but soap and Vaseline didn't do it. It stayed just the right size, even as my fingers grew.

Saturday afternoon, Dad took us out to a parking lot at a mall that had closed ten years earlier. Weeds grew through the cracked asphalt, and faded herringbone lines marked parking spaces. Here, we could drive in circles, backward, fast, slow. We practiced parallel parking against the curb by the boarded-up hulk of the mall, between red lines Dad had spray-painted on the pavement.

Damia asked me to get out while she practiced parking. She said I distracted her.

"How can I distract you when I'm sitting silent in the back seat?" I asked.

"You're thinking too loud."

I got out. I figured she was pissed because this was one area where I didn't have the same trouble she did. She always parked two feet from the curb. I had tried beaming helpful thoughts at her while she was backing and forthing. Mistake.

I kicked a can on the sidewalk, watched it bounce off a patchy green concrete wall, and tried to fold my thoughts into myself instead of sharing them. My eyes felt hot, and the ring burned on my finger. I rubbed it, trying to ease the heat.

Through the windshield, I saw Dad speaking to Damia, his eyebrows pinching his eyes narrow. I hated that look, especially when he turned it on me.

Something flashed past the edge of my eye. I turned and saw the green-haired woman. She stood still as glass in the shadows near the mall's main entrance. This time, she wore dull gray-green clothes that blended with the peeling paint on the concrete walls of the mall's outer skin. Her boots were dark gray, and her hair was green-gray. She smiled and blew a kiss. I felt a flutter against my cheek, as if a moth brushed me, and then something like pain or freezing, as if the kiss seeped through my skin and spread out inside me. She edged into deeper shadows and was gone.

Damia slammed the car door. I turned and saw her standing by the car, staring toward me.

"Damia, you need to park again," Dad's voice said.

"What just happened?" Damia asked me.

I glanced toward the place where the woman had stood, then at my twin. "Nothing."

ON OUR SIXTEENTH birthday, I woke feeling strange. Damia opened her eyes at the same moment and we stared from twin bed to twin bed at each other, the way we did most mornings. Early morning sun lightened the curtains at the window, brought out the color in our pale green walls and pale blue ceiling so our room felt like an underwater haven. Small round mirrors we had glued to the walls like bubbles here and there showed pieces of our room and our self to each other.

Sometimes we waited to see who would smile first, and sometimes we both smiled at exactly the same instant. Those were the good mornings. Sometimes we were both distressed by dreams we had shared, or things that had happened the day before. I would see Damia's frown and know my face wore the same expression.

"I dreamed you left," Damia said. She breathed deep and pressed her fist to her sternum. Her eyes looked too bright under her half-lowered eyelids.

"I didn't dream." I twisted the ring on my finger, a nervous habit I'd developed in response to twinges the ring sent through my hand once in a while.

We were out of sync. That had started when we were ten, and the gap between us grew wider all the time.

"Happy birthday," I said.

"Is it?" She slid out of bed and went to the closet, came out with identical pale green blouses. She tossed one to me. It was what I would have picked. I got up and dressed, and we went down to breakfast together, our steps hitting the stairs simultaneously, so it sounded like only one person descended.

Lars was eating Cheerios, shoveling them into his mouth. "Hey," he said, puffing Cheerios and milk back into his bowl, "look!" He pointed toward our places at the table.

Between our cereal bowls lay a small package with a gold bow on it, a thing the size and shape of a can opener. Mom and Dad were sitting at the table, and for once neither of them was hiding behind a section of newspaper.

"That's a promise. We can't give it to you yet," Dad said. "But we have it waiting."

Damia and I sat. We consulted silently, then nodded. She picked up the package and unwrapped it. It was a car key.

"Oh, Daddy!" she cried, and leapt up to hug him. I got up a moment slower and embraced Mom.

"Thank you so much!" I said.

"Look in the driveway," Mom said.

We rushed to the window together and stared out at the car we'd own when we got our licenses. A dark blue Honda Fit. We jumped up and down and squealed as if it were the one we'd pick over all other cars.

"It's perfect!" Damia said.

"Just right!" I said.

The whole family went outside. Damia and I climbed into the front seats, and Mom, Dad, and Lars crowded into the back seat. Damia and I took turns sitting behind the steering wheel. Lars supplied *vroom vroom* car noises.

Dad took custody of the key when we climbed out again.

After breakfast, Damia and I ducked into the downstairs bathroom together to check our reflections before heading to school. My ring sent a jab of pain into my finger, so I stared at my hand instead of my image. When I looked up, I saw a stranger in the mirror.

Damia and I had had our hair cut short a couple months ago. Now it was in an in-between state, brown and shaggy with blond streaks, long enough to touch our shoulders, with bangs that covered our eyebrows. Mom wanted us to get it cut again.

In the mirror, my hair looked green instead of brown. Furry red fox ear-tips poked up through it. My eyebrows had thinned and angled up from the inside edges, and my eyes looked farther apart, a grassier green than they should be. I reached a hand toward my foreign face and saw much longer fingers, almost spider-leg thin, coming toward mine in the glass.

"Cosima!" Damia cried. My new eyes met her gaze in the mirror. "Where did you go?" Her breathing came fast and harsh, and her hand lifted, reaching for me, then stopped before we touched.

"I'm the same as I've always been," I said. I wondered if that were true.

Damia shook her head, her mouth drawing into a grimace of fear. "You're not you," she whispered. "I feel sick. You—" She gripped the pointed tip of my ear as though it actually existed. She pinched.

"Ouch!"

"Cozy!"

"Let go. That hurts."

She let me go, and pressed her hands over her mouth. Our hearts beat out of sync, hers much faster, and our twin bond thinned, snapped back, stretched. My stomach churned.

I cupped my soft, furry ears in my hands and squeezed.

My ears shrank back to normal. The green drained from my hair, and my face filled out until I looked like myself again. Like Damia.

"What just happened?" Damia asked. She was gasping. She gripped my shoulders and stared into my eyes.

"I don't know." I stared back, memorizing her eyes, her face, her expression, making mine match it exactly.

"That *didn't* happen," she said. "It's not going to happen again. You won't let it."

We looked at each other. She was everything I loved, and I could be just like her. There was never anything else I needed.

We nodded.

"Girls! School!" Dad called, and we raced out and grabbed our jackets and backpacks.

NOW THAT WE were high school sophomores, Mom and Dad didn't dictate our class choices anymore, but we ended up taking different classes anyway.

The ring zapped me while my social sciences class was watching a documentary about World War Two. The classroom was dark, curtains closed, Mr. Abel at the back semi-monitoring the laptop he was streaming the video through. I had a desk nearest the window wall, toward the back. Soft snores came from the desk nearest mine. Scott Rankin was always short on sleep and usually slept through anything he could, even though the voiceover was talking about war atrocities, and there were images of skeletal concentration camp survivors on the screen.

The ring sent a warm tingling that spread through my hand, up my arm, and on into the rest of me. I tasted chocolate and caramel, and felt like I was wrapped in warm velvet. Happiness and well-being bloomed in me. I stretched, and felt strength in my muscles.

I heard music. It was a quiet melody that hid under the soundtrack of the film and the soft snores of my classmate, the whispers from a couple of girls in front of me. Flutes, drums, and some kind of string instrument, a web of sounds that connected everything. I blinked. The world shimmered. Rainbows edged everything, and a rustle of wings whispered from everywhere, as though I were surrounded by angels.

My fingers looked longer, and gold glowed through my skin.

I laughed and stood up.

"Cosima?" said Mr. Abel.

I turned a different kind of sideways so everything faded to smoky outlines, then walked through the nearest wall. People were black skeletons against the wavery black edges of furniture. I had to get out of the building, out where there was sunlight and plants.

The walls were only smoke. I walked through them to the schoolyard, went to an oak tree and embraced it. Under its rough, wrinkled gray skin, life moved. I kissed the tree, and it fed me green. I fell into a dream of green and sunlight that warmed and nourished me, where every flavor of air, every breath of wind, excited me, even as I held still; I basked in thrilling contentment.

I was still embracing the tree when school let out an unknown length of time later. Damia came to me, but I couldn't understand what she said, until she said, "Are you going to stay like that?"

"Yes," I said.

"No," she said. "You promised." She gripped my shoulders and tried to pull me away from the tree.

I clung to the tree, then remembered: This was Damia, my beloved sister for whom I cared more than anything or anyone else. I didn't want to hurt or distress her. I let her pull me free.

She turned me around so we faced each other. She stared at me. Her face paled. "Cosima. Who are you now?"

I looked at her, the self I had been until the middle of social studies that afternoon, the person I loved. "I'm your sister," I said. Your other self.

"You're not," she whispered. "Allie said you stood up and turned into smoke during social sci. What was that? That's not my sister."

I hugged her, embracing the shape I should be, and thought what that felt like from the inside, and called that reality back. The soft gleam left my skin. I blinked and lost my shadow vision. My ears crinked as they retracted into themselves; my fingers shortened and stubbed; everywhere in my body I felt a thickening, a heaviness. I had not known how dense we were until I had the chance to be otherwise.

I felt tired. All the green and glow the oak tree had given me was gone. "Let's go home."

Damia pulled out of my embrace and stared at my face. Her smile was slow in coming.

THAT NIGHT, AFTER the surprise birthday party with cake and five of our friends from school in our living room, after Lars sticking his finger in the frosting on the remaining cake so no one else would want to eat any more of it, after Mom's and Dad's hugs and wishes, Damia and I went upstairs to bed.

She slept as soon as the light went out. That didn't make sense. I wasn't sleepy at all.

My real mother came then, veiled in darkness, smelling of jasmine and honeysuckle and book dust. She sat on my bed in a welter of skirts. "Did you enjoy your last day here?"

"What do you mean?" The ring tingled and burned on my finger. My ears stretched. Soft gold glowed from my arms as they lay on top of the covers.

"Time to come home with me," she said.

"I don't think so."

"Now that you know what you can do, how could you possibly want to stay here?"

"Why did you exchange me?"

She smoothed her dry hand over my cropped hair, tweaked the tip of my ear. "Every so often, we need fresh blood."

That didn't sound good. "If I go home with you, will the real Cosima come back?"

She stroked my hair and said nothing.

I couldn't abandon my sister. "I'm staying here."

"You'll lose all that makes you special," she said. "Everything you enjoyed today. I'll take it with me. I can't let you do things like that where others can see."

I closed my eyes and remembered sliding through a wall, seeing people as shadows, knowing I was invisible. The worldsong, shifting and embracing. Walking into the web of life, learning what sunlight tasted like, and how it felt to be rooted in the eternity of Earth. I swallowed a bitter taste.

She whispered, "At home, you can be your true self all the time. You can fly, and our sky is full of games. You'll be able to use your powers to your heart's content—others will teach you how much you can truly do, things you've never even imagined were possible. You will make so many friends, my beautiful daughter, and have so many adventures—we have buildings made of glass and magic. Creatures that are only myth here run wild there. The trees in our forests have voices, and the grasses whisper, and the seas speak. The tastes there—berries as big as your hand, with all the sweetness of summer; cakes made from clouds; drinks crafted of nectar before the bees get to it. You will learn things humans never know."

My heart twisted with longing.

I opened my eyes and stared through the darkness toward my sister. No one else would ever be such a good friend.

"Come on," said my real mother.

I sighed and gave up the future she offered. "No."

She plucked the ring from my finger. I felt as though I were going to crash right through my bed, I was so solid.

"You will regret this the rest of your life." She rose and faded, her scents, her sounds, her presence. All I heard was my sister's soft sleeping breaths, like a gentle tide brushing across a beach.

I STARED INTO my sister's eyes the next morning.

"I dreamed—" she said. "Wait. What did *you* dream?"

"I dreamed I stayed," I said. I sat up. I felt so heavy and slow, and already tired, though I had just awakened. Was life going to be like this? Had I always had some of my mother's lightness inside, and now it was gone?

Damia came to me then and hugged me. Even her hug felt heavy, but I didn't tell her so.

DEVIL'S BRIDGE
FRANCES HARDINGE

"THAT MAN." LAUREN peered across the street, eyes narrowed. "He was outside school when we came out. I think he's following us."

Petra felt a familiar tickle of apprehension. A quick glance across the road showed her a silver Honda with a male driver. Despite the greyness of the day he wore dark glasses.

"We need to get you home," said Lauren. Despite being only fourteen she was nearly six foot, and her heavy-featured face had an Easter Island solidity and solemnity. "Actually... maybe we should just head straight to the police."

"Yeah," muttered Petra. "Because that always helps." She flashed Lauren an edged, rueful smile.

Petra was not the sort of person others believed. Shop assistants watched her like hawks. Teachers assumed that she was the cause of all trouble. Everyone's gaze snagged on the whitish stubble across her scalp. She was fidgety and restless, her eyes evasive and too wise. Everything she said came out sounding like a jibe.

But it was worse when people *did* take her seriously. Now and then care workers asked her to roll up her sleeve, so that they could look for puncture marks or bruises, and make sure that the strange spider-like freckles swarming over her neck, arms and shoulders weren't tattoos. School nurses dropped in quiet questions about how everything was *at home*.

"We'll lose him, then," said Lauren. She scowled belligerently at the distant car, as if tempted to throw it down the street.

The two girls cut through the mall and the churchyard, then took the tree-lined route back to Petra's house. Even when they reached Petra's front door, Lauren was reluctant to abandon her friend.

"You call me, yeah?" she said. "If that man shows up and turns out to be one of those weirdos."

Petra nodded hard, and to her huge relief saw Lauren's tall, clumsy figure stride away into the descending dusk. *Get out of here, Lauren,* was all she could think. *Before things get creepy again.*

Petra unlocked her door, and entered the darkened hall to a host of home-smells—mildewed trainers and the ghost of long-dead ravioli dinners. She closed the door behind her, put it on the chain and drew the bolts. Stepping into the lounge, she shrugged off her anorak and flipped on the light.

The stranger from the car was in the lounge, sitting on the tea-stained sofa.

He was about forty, with jowls that thought he was fifty. Petra looked at his gold-faced watch, long charcoal coat and trim haircut, and she smelt money. He had the soft, pouched mouth of somebody who gets his way too often.

In spite of his comfortable plumpness, Petra's instincts were screaming. His small grey eyes had a clammy brightness, like stars drowning in glue. The hands resting on his knees had a tensed, braced stillness. Petra cursed herself for bolting the front door. If she sprinted to the hall, he would catch her before she could pull back the bolts.

"Where's my uncle?" she asked instead.

"I gave him fifty pounds." answered the stranger. His accent was posh, his voice rather deep. "He said he had friends to see and would 'leave us to it'."

Petra ground her teeth. It was all too believable. Her uncle's one magnificent gesture, the adoption of his sister's child, seemed to have exhausted his life's supply of goodwill and responsibility. Ever since, uncle and niece had been bound together in a briar tangle of resentment, guilt and lacerated affection. In her imagination she screamed at him for leaving her in the lurch, but knew exactly what answers would have flown back at her.

You think food pays for itself? Would it kill you to pull your weight? I don't invite these people, but when customers are breaking the door down trying to give you money, don't expect me to kick them out.

Could Petra slip a hand into her anorak pocket, and text for help? Unlikely. And who would she text? There was no cavalry, just an uncle who kept alley-cat hours, a hospice-bound mother who no longer knew her and a hole where a father used to be.

There was another means of escape, but Petra did not want to consider it unless there was no other choice.

"It was *you* I wanted to talk to," the stranger continued. "You are the Bridgekin, aren't you?"

And Petra could not lie. She gritted her teeth and tried to keep her head steady, but the nod happened anyway.

"And is it true? That you can create bridges to anywhere? Absolutely *anywhere*?"

"For a price. Yes."

The man let out a long breath. There was a world of emotional investment in that sigh.

"My name's Carlton," he said, getting out his wallet, "and you don't need to be afraid. I'm just here to do business. Now... what kind of price?"

"I never said I'd do it," said Petra. Even as the words left her mouth, she felt the atmosphere become arctic. The man was still pulling notes out of his fat, fawn-coloured wallet, spreading them on the coffee table, but she could see a dangerous tension in his jaw.

"Listen," she said quickly. "Just listen. You know where the bridges come from? The old story?"

"The legend of Devil's Bridge?" answered Carlton. "Yes. I know it. An old woman found her route home blocked by a deep gorge with a fast-flowing river. The Devil came by and offered to build a bridge for her, on condition that he could have the soul of the first creature to cross it. He assumed that she would cross first, but instead when the bridge was finished she sent her dog across ahead of her. So she escaped, and the Devil was thwarted—"

"He bowed," interrupted Petra. "He didn't yell or throw lightning bolts. He bowed to her, and winked. Because he already knew he was going to get the last laugh. The old lady found out afterwards that she *still* had the power to make bridges to anywhere she liked, and so could her daughters, and so could *their* daughters. And their granddaughters, and their great-granddaughters, blah blah, until you get to me. But there's a price for every bridge, and the further the bridge, the higher the price. And who do you think that gets paid *to*, Mr Carlton?"

"Are you saying that I would have to pay with my soul?" For the first time Carlton looked genuinely taken aback.

Petra wanted to say 'yes', and scare him into leaving. But the power that bound her tongue was having none of it.

"No," she said with bitter reluctance, and saw him relax. "I... don't think it's really the Devil, with horns and stuff. I think that's, you know, apocryphal. But there's something out there, and it wants everything that's precious to us. And it believes in bargains.

"Money won't cut it. Not for you. I bet you could drop a couple of thousand quid and not even feel it, so that's not worth anything. You'd have to pay something that really mattered to you. Something that *hurt* you to lose."

Carlton seemed to be weighing this up.

"How long would the bridge last?" he asked.

"Only until you've crossed it. Then it'll vanish."

"So... if I wanted to come back here again, I'd have to pay a second time?"

Petra heard him with an icy sense of deja vu, but could not stop herself answering.

"You can't make a bridge without me. Once you're on the other side, you're on your own."

Carlton slowly put away his wallet, and sat very still for several long, dangerous seconds.

"I wouldn't be 'on my own'," he said at last, "if *you* came over the bridge with me." He pulled something out of his coat pocket.

Before now it had always been knives. Kitchen knives in shaky hands, stupid little penknives, once a Kukri, all waved by men and women with frightened eyes full of need. This was the first time Petra had found herself staring down the barrel of a gun. Guns were from films. The sight of it filled Petra with an electric feeling of the not-quite-real.

"I'm sorry," said Carlton, "but I need this bridge."

"Yeah." Petra's voice sounded raspy, and there were drums in her ears. "Yeah, they always do."

IT WAS ALWAYS 'need'.

Strange needs, sometimes. *I need to walk your bridge as a rite of passage. I need to visit the building in this engraving, in a realm with two yellow moons.*

But more often the needs were simple, sordid and mundane. *I need to get into the hospital pharmacy, where the drugs are kept. I need to get out of the country before the police find me.*

"I need to see my wife," explained Carlton. "She's in New Jersey—and she's leaving me. She won't see me, won't talk to me on the phone. This is my last chance before divorce proceedings go through. But nobody will give me her new address. Can you still build a bridge to her if I don't know exactly where she is?"

Petra reassured him that 'my wife's house in New Jersey' *was* an address as far as the bridge was concerned. She hadn't needed to know about the background either, but perhaps it was a good sign that Carlton wanted to explain. Maybe it meant he was still thinking of Petra as a person.

But does he, really? Has he even wondered why I didn't run off down a bridge of my own when a stranger showed up in my house?

"I'm ready," said Carlton.

Petra let out a long breath. Bracing herself against a chair back, she closed her eyes and thought of bridges. Not bricks and wood, but stitches in geography, binding places together. Bridges as nowhere zones where the rules broke down. The hearts of towns, the mouths of castles. Troll-roofs.

As always, something responded. There was a pulling sensation that made Petra feel sick, like a gravitation of the spirit. She forced herself to yield to it. She became a conduit, a meeting place for the negotiation. Bid and counterbid rushed through her like gale winds.

The deal was sealed. She did not know what Carlton had paid. Whatever it was had streaked past, leaving a smell like hot summers in its wake. She suspected it was probably a bundle of memories that had once been precious to him. Perhaps his life would be less rich for the loss of them. Perhaps he would be a different man without them.

Petra opened her eyes, stretched out with her hands and mind, and let the bridge into the world.

Wrought iron snaked out of the carpet, forming palings, ornamental curls and banisters. Ghostly slabs of white marble appeared between them, translucent as moonstone, each higher than the last. They floated unsupported, drifting and shifting slightly from side to side as if in a breeze. The strange steps led upwards and disappeared into the ceiling, which had melted into a gently churning smog.

At the same time, the living room darkened and flattened. The posters lost their colour. The bookshelf might have been painted on the wall.

When Petra placed her foot on the lowermost step, it dipped slightly like a raft on water, then righted itself. The next step did the same. As she climbed her home shrank and dulled below her, then vanished.

Carlton was a step behind her, but Petra did not look around. She hated him for being so stupid, for throwing away a precious piece of himself and making her responsible. She was stingingly aware of all the parts of herself that were lost forever. The colour from her hair. Her ability to lie. Her singing voice. An hour of sleep each night. She was a sponge-like mass of holes.

Every bridge was different. Carlton's bridge was unusually grand and formal, but there were odd little dissonances. Stained silk ties fluttered pennant-like from the palings. Some steps were frosted with fractured bottle glass. Jointed brass dolls dangled from the curls of the balustrade, like dead birds caught in a fender.

Below the floating slabs were mist and the distorted sound of water. Dun-coloured things that might have been boats flitted past with uncanny speed. Without looking, Petra knew that the digital display on her watch would be unchanging.

"Where are we?" asked Carlton. "Another world?"

Petra shrugged. "You planning to go swimming? If not, it doesn't matter."

"You're not curious?"

"My Mum was," Petra muttered. "She liked making people bridges to... strange places. Places with blue suns and singing stones, that kind of thing. You know what happened on her last trip?"

"No. What?"

"I don't know either. But Dad went missing that day, and Mum came back broken."

And that's how it'll be with me too if I let anyone matter to me. Some day I'll panic and use them to pay for a bridge.

The steps were descending now, and heading into a denser darkness. At last they ended in a prosaic wooden door, with an ornamental chrome handle. Petra turned the handle, pushed it open... and stepped out of a closet door into a lavish bedroom.

Petra halted, dazzled by all the floor-to-ceiling mirrors, the expensive-looking gowns draped over the bed, and the stained glass windows looking out upon wide lawns and yellow maples. Before she could muster her wits, Carlton grabbed her by the shoulder.

"Don't move a step till I get back," he muttered, his eyes bright and hard. "I'm your bridge-fare home, remember? And if you run out on me... I'll know where to find you." With that, he barrelled out through the bedroom door onto the landing.

Petra was still gaping at this sudden departure when she noticed the photographs on the dressing table. Most showed a beautifully turned out woman of middle years, hugging dogs or sitting with what appeared to be family members. She had high cheekbones, careful makeup, and a face that Petra had seen on TV dozens of times, and more recently in all the newspapers.

The celebrated female news presenter. The snowballing rumours of domestic violence followed by proven facts. The imminent divorce. The disputed millions...

Petra's face grew hot. She raced out onto the landing, just in time to see Carlton running downstairs with his gun in his hand.

He never wanted to talk to his wife. He just wanted to commit a murder with a perfect alibi.

The nearby landing window looked down onto the lawns. Glancing out, Petra spotted a woman walking over the grounds back towards the house, hair tucked under a knitted hat, her stride casual and comfortable. She was throwing a ball for a large shaggy wolfhound, which bounded, lolloped and fetched.

Petra yanked the catch and threw open the window.

"Run!" she screamed as loudly as she could. "Run for your life!"

The woman shielded her eyes and stared up at her, chin dropping in shock. While she was still motionless, a door crashed open below. Carlton charged out onto the lawn, directly beneath Petra's window. He raised his gun, and levelled it at his wife.

The TV presenter stared aghast. Petra could see incomprehension, shock and nothing more. Not a will to move, run or be somewhere else.

The wolfhound started to sprint towards Carlton. It was too far from the gunman to be useful, but Petra could feel its jowls rippling with speed and its eyes bulging with effort. Its wish was as simple as rain.

Need to be there. Now. Reach him. Save her.

Petra gave it a bridge.

Nobody else saw it. Nobody felt the wolfhound pay all it had without hesitation, without a whimper. Nobody saw it leap onto a glimmering bridge of rabbit bones and race with the beauty and purity of selflessness.

All the others saw was the wolfhound teleporting twenty feet, then leaping onto its enemy, bowling Carlton over backwards. Carlton's gun fired, and the dog took a bullet through its chest.

It bought its mistress a handful of precious seconds. Seconds in which to fumble a rape alarm out of her pocket and trigger its siren. Seconds in which men in private security firm uniforms sprinted round the side of the house, drawing their own guns. When Carlton pushed away the dead dog and struggled to sit up, raising his gun again, they shot him repeatedly.

The TV presenter ran to the wolfhound and dropped to her knees beside it, cradling it in her arms. One of the security guards, however, spotted a young face up at a second floor window, and gave a shout.

Petra ducked back from the window, and fled to the presenter's bedroom. She could hear the back door being flung open downstairs. People were stampeding around below, shouting things like "room clear!", the way they did in films. In panic she reached out for a bridge, the way she had every other time she had been kidnapped.

Just get home, forget it happened. What can I pay this time? What have I got left? The ability to see the colour yellow? But what if that means I end up totally blind? I could give up more of my skin—let the spider-spots leak up onto my face. But then there'll be doctors for sure...

As feet thundered on the stairs, a sly voice seemed to murmur in her brain. *You could give up your friendship with Lauren. It would be the best thing for her too.*

"No!" hissed Petra aloud. "Not that. Never that. I'd sooner get shot dead right now." Her head was full of the image of the wolfhound, leaping to its death for sheer love.

And so when the security guards burst into the bedroom, Petra was still there, hands raised above her head. They trained their guns on her, yelled, made her lie down on the floor and secured her wrists behind her. But they did not shoot her.

As she lay at their feet sobbing, they could not have guessed that she was weeping uncontrollably for the death of a dog.

THE POLICE INTERVIEW went badly. At first Petra managed to limit herself to truths that *didn't* sound like crazy lies. Carlton had kidnapped her at gunpoint, and forced her to go to New Jersey with him. She hadn't met him before that night. She hadn't really known where they were going. She hadn't known that he wanted to hurt his wife.

However, other questions naturally followed. How did they get to New Jersey? Why was there no record of them passing through an airport? *We travelled through darkness on a bridge made from the power of his wishes and bought with fragments of his essence... oh never mind.*

She might even have been suspected of being Carlton's accomplice, if the TV presenter had not interceded, testifying to Petra's desperately shouted warning from the window. Having seen her dog teleport, the woman may even have guessed that Petra was telling the truth.

The authorities compared notes, re-assessing all the cuts and bruises in Petra's medical records and the various claims that she had been followed or kidnapped. Her story about Atlantic-spanning phantom bridges was reinterpreted as a 'cry for help'. With dread inevitability, it became clear that she would be taken away from her uncle, who received the news with a devastated calm. Petra felt just as numb, even when Lauren's parents swooped in and asked to have her stay with them, 'for now and then we'll see how it goes'.

She only cried when she was alone with Lauren, half-crushed in the taller girl's hug.

"It's my fault the dog died," was all she could say.

"He knew what he wanted," Lauren said at last, after letting Petra cry herself out. "He wasn't sorry, either. Was he?"

Petra shook her head, and sniffed messily.

"He knew what was important to him," Lauren went on. "And that's the big thing, isn't it? Knowing what to keep, what to throw away. We all make choices like that, and mostly we don't even notice. Picking which dreams we give up. Choosing the people we spend time with, and the ones we don't."

"But I don't get to keep anything!" exploded Petra. "I just lose things. The bridges are eating me, one bite at a time."

"You *don't* just lose things," said Lauren, who was big, stubborn and right about everything. "All the weird places you've seen—they're making you smarter, tougher and stronger. You're beating the Devil every day, Pet. You're growing faster than he can prune you. Some day soon, nobody will be able to force you to do anything any more. You'll be the one calling the shots.

"And I'm so proud of you for not bridging back from New Jersey. Because for years you've been holding things together like a broken jam jar. You've dropped it at last, and *that's good*. After this you'll have a *home* with *food,* and the weirdos won't know where to find you. I'm sorry, but there are some things you're better off losing.

"Just... don't lose me, OK?"

Petra held on tight, with both arms and all of her considerable will.

"I won't," she said.

THE NURSERY CORNER
KAARON WARREN

NOW THAT I am old myself, with grandchildren, one dead husband and a lover of twenty years, I feel odd twinges of pain that cannot be explained by anyone but myself. I know that somewhere in the Nursery Corner Mario Laudati is playing a game with a part of me I will never get back.

IT WAS NO secret that my father died violently.

"He was under the table and it was like a fountain," I told everyone at school. "Blood gushing up and banging under the table and coming back on top of him. He was so covered in blood, he kept slipping out of the ambulance men's hands."

I squeezed my hands together. The other kids all thought I was fascinating, anyway. I lived in a bigger house than any of them, and my mum worked in the old people's home there, and I always had stories to tell. I was popular because I took them stuff from the home, like little sugars and soaps. I took them hand lotion and packets of biscuits. They didn't mind the old-people's-home stink, but I tired of it, and I kept clothes at a friend's place, wanting the smell of the place off me, out of my hair. I used a highly perfumed shampoo my mother didn't approve of, *it's so bloody expensive, just use the home stuff,* my mother said, because everything we had was taken from the home. Shampoo, soap, biscuits. Chips, sometimes, frozen meals, medicine, plates, glasses. I hated the supply cupboard, though. The old people would corner me and try to hug me, they'd make me hold their teeth, they'd make me hold their dry, weak hands.

I didn't miss my father. He'd been away a lot, mining (and yes, I had a nice collection of rocks but I didn't know what any of them were) and when he was home he was nasty to be around. Falling asleep, drunk, under the kitchen table. I'd sit there, eating my cereal before school, his snores shaking my bowl, his stink making me ill. Only the cat sitting on his chest, enjoying the rise and fall, could make me smile.

He wanted us to move to Far North Queensland, so he didn't have to fly in fly out. He wanted us to be with him, up among the dust and rocks, where women and children stayed home unless they went to the movies on Saturday night or sometimes shopping.

Mum talked to the patients, not really thinking they'd understand, needing someone to vent to. "He really expects me to pack this in? Move up north, live in a tin shed? What's Jessie supposed to do? She needs good schooling, lots of friends," her voice strong, full of courage.

"God's country, this," one of the old men said, but many Australians say that about their hometown. Our quiet Sydney suburb was pleasant enough, but God's country? That was pushing it.

Dad didn't like what he overheard, and I slept with my pillow over my ears and my cat curled up against my cheek because I hated the shouting.

Mum was cheery the next day, with bruises up her arms, one on her chin, one on her throat, and it was the same every time he came home.

We smiled through it, and I hardly ever saw her cry, but even at six years old I knew this was not how things should be.

She had a job to do though; looking after them and me and she did it so well we all adored her.

The *compos mentis* old people gossiped together. I learnt most of what I know from listening in. The old men were the ones who decided. You wouldn't think they could manage it, and no one else believed it, but it was them. He was weak and pathetic, snoring under the table like he did, bottle spilt out beside him and it was a simple matter, they told me, to slit the bastard's throat. They left the knife in his hand and it would have taken a family member to push for a real inquiry, and that didn't happen.

These men had been to war. They'd killed before. They told me all this from the age of six, competing to horrify me with stories, giving me nightmares about the enemy begging for mercy, and watching souls rise like steam.

They saved us from my father, and I was always kind to old men because of it.

AFTER DAD WAS buried, Mum signed a four year contract to manage the home, and there was a little party to celebrate. The gossipers said she got it because the owners felt sorry for her, but no one seemed to care what the reason was. I was happy. I liked it there most of the time, with the old people being kind to me when they remembered who I was and when I was too fast for their grab hands, and where my mother felt confident and safe.

She set up special places for me here and there. A windowshelf with knickknacks, like a snowdome from Darwin, which made us all laugh because snow in Darwin! And puzzles carved from rainforest wood. And there was a bookshelf with a secret stash of lollies. And a place she called the Nursery Corner, which had a soft blanket, toys and some of my pictures pinned to the wall. It was a dull place, really, and none of the children who came to visit sat there. Mostly they hunched near the exit, trying not to look at the residents.

Things happened I would never tell a soul about. The bodily fluids that seemed to appear out of nowhere, and the evil things

241

they'd say, some of them. Bile spewing out of their mouths, telling me awful things a child shouldn't know. We took the people other places rejected. Reform School for the Elderly, my mother joked.

She started to bring in entertainers for the patients, and I could invite friends along and often the room would be filled with children sitting on the floor, the buzz of them making the place so much brighter, so much further from death.

Mostly the entertainment was awful. The old people didn't mind it except Aunt Em, who hated everything.

"You can call me Aunt Em," she said when she first moved in, as if hoping a friendly name would soften her edges. Nasty woman with pursed lips disapproving all the time as if she thought life doled her out something wrong, as if everyone around her was wrong. She liked me most of the time, though.

I avoided the entertainment when I could. Elderly magicians. Singers, dancers. There was nothing wrong with being old, but these people had always been crap.

The musicians in particular were tragic. They played slow music, the old people clapping out of time, vague memories lapping at them of what it used to be like to listen to music. To dance. To be moved by the notes. Some wept and instantly forgot why they had wet cheeks.

Doesn't it take you back, they said. Listening to songs from fifty years ago. *Doesn't it just! Remember that as clear as a movie.*

Some remembered nothing, or were stuck in a single moment in time.

"Wasn't that marvellous?" the residents would say afterwards, as if they'd seen the Bolshoi Ballet.

All the entertainers flirted with my mother. "Look at Matron blushing," because they wanted more work and she was charming. Even as a kid I knew that, and she was at last free of Dad's rules, his disapproval and his desire she be nothing but a cipher for him.

Mum rarely got someone back twice.

That changed when I was about twelve and Mario Laudati appeared, with a magic chest of goodies, bright clear eyes, a warm, strong handshake. He had one earring; a flashing LED light.

He said, "I'm an all-rounder. Take a tape measure and you'll see. One hundred centimetres all the way around. Can't get much rounder than that!"

They loved him, including Mum. He was a bit older than she was. *Save me a chair,* he said, *I'll be moving in here before long,* clapping his hands, bright and breezy, and they all chuckled because clearly he would never be old enough to sit with them, unmoving for hours. He was so lively, hopping from toe to toe.

He made me nervous, thinking he wouldn't like me. He asked odd questions, as some adults do, trying to disconcert me.

"Is this place haunted? Any nasty ghosts I should know about?" he asked me.

I nodded. Thinking on the spot, I said, "It's haunted by all the people they've killed."

He laughed. "Are there many?"

I counted on my fingers, holding them up like a child in kindergarten showing how old she is. I looked sideways to see if he found me funny and he was smiling, a big, genuine grin I wanted to see all the time.

He set me up in the front row to be his assistant. It was all about light and dark.

Somehow he seemed to have control over our electricity because the power went out, leaving him in the dark, standing with a swinging lantern. The old people were quiet; was it the first time ever? He walked around us, telling a story I can't remember, making cats appear in the shadows, and children playing with a hoop. "There I am!" Aunt Em said. "That's me with my hoop!" and others clamoured to be the one.

If it wasn't hypnotism, it came very close.

For a moment, between the flickering lights, I saw him with a different face. He looked like a teenager, like one of the boys I admired at school, perhaps. The ones on the train my mother would tug me close to avoid. She seemed to think teenagers were the worst things on earth and would have kept me locked up if it would stop me becoming one. She didn't accept that some of the old people she looked after were worse. Mr Adams, with his hysterical scratching. Martha Jones, who could shift from a quiet mouse to a woman so filled with fury she tore opem the throat of a patient one time. These were not the only ones.

When their attention wandered Mario drew them back with a sharp clap of his hands.

When the lights came on people had shifted around. Some had lost their socks, others found a rose on their lap. For them it was mostly meaningless because they were used to the disconnect of change. They were used to appearing at the breakfast table and having no idea how they got there.

"Isn't it magic?" the residents said. "Isn't he wonderful?"

I had seen that other face, though, and I couldn't look at him in the light. I went to the corner where Mum kept my box of rocks, and I ran my fingers through them, thinking of my father before he died, when he would show me the rocks and tell me their long-forgotten names.

"What's that you've got there? A boxarox? I know a lot about rocks."

Mario picked up a pale blue one. "This one is called a poo pellet." I giggled. This was silly. He went through my box, naming them all. He was so rude, so outrageous, that I wept with laughter and the old people, those who could move, came to watch.

This was the moment, I think, that they came to consider him a suitable boyfriend for Mum.

She kept a lot of secrets. I remained unaware of their changing relationship, even as he came to perform again and again.

He had yellowed fingers but told me he hadn't smoked for a long time. He lit a cigarette, "Don't smoke," he said, "Don't you ever," and he held it up. "I love the smell and the burn," he said. "That glowing red tip." He touched it to a patient's hair, which flared brightly before fizzling out. It was our secret.

* * *

I STARTED TAKING my friends on private tours of the place when I was fifteen. Like most kids, we were obsessed with ghosts and killers, with creepy people and disgusting things; we loved to be scared. I'd lead them through the hallways, making up stories about what the residents had done. Showing them where my father had died, lifting the table to show them his blood. I asked the old people to lend me a dollar and you should have seen them, searching for wallets or purses they no longer owned or, if they still had one, opening it again and again and again, looking for money that wasn't there. My mother didn't notice until the man who called himself John John moved in.

John John would cut himself with anything. Plastic forks, the edge of the drink trolley, a sugar spoon. It was a challenge for him and it was terrifying for my friends to watch him. If you took his weapon away he'd scream like a hyena. He'd attack the nurses or anyone who got close, so we stood far away. Until one of my friends snuck up to him, wanting a closer look at all his scars. John John roared, stabbed the boy with a key he'd stolen. The boy was fine but it meant Mum finally found out.

Jesus, when Mum found out. It was her disappointment that got me more than anything else. "I can't believe you could treat them this way. Such disrespect," she said, her voice flat, depressed, as if I made her very tired. She laid her head on Mario's shoulder. We sat in her office with the door shut, the old people shuffling outside, wanting to come in.

Mario said, "Jessie has the greatest respect. She's allowing them to entertain, one of life's great privileges." He was on my side; he understood me. He'd comforted me when one of them threw shit at me. He'd said, "It's okay to be upset, but I know you want to be strong for your mum. You don't want to freak her out." He'd brought me shampoo, a secret supply, stuff that didn't smell like the home. He really did understand.

The old people scrabbled at the door, and my mother had to call for backup to get them all settled down.

Once they were all drugged and asleep, Mario said, "I've been thinking of something for a while now, something that might work here. Let me play with the Nursery Corner. I've done it before. I'll make it a place for calm reflection. You'll see. It might help with people like John John."

"It's Jessie's corner. Your time. It's up to you two."

"What do you think, Jessie? Do you mind if I mess your corner up?"

I didn't mind for a second.

HE WAS BACK a couple of days later, laden with a carpet, a chair, other stuff. He stacked all my toys from the Nursery Corner into a box and handed it to me. "Bin it if you like," he said. The residents started to gather as they often did when he was around. The drugs made them slow, made them flap their gums, suck on their teeth. The sound of it made me ill.

Mario moved around among them, talking, building his corner.

"Keep watching!" he said, and it seemed to me as if the residents stiffened, lost control of their ability to move.

First, he rolled out the carpet. It was bright yellow, like a sun, with purple edges and a large dark stain in the centre. "I was born on this carpet," he said, "right there, so it symbolises the beauty and the miracle of birth. The beginning."

They barely reacted, except Aunt Em, who had no children yet loved to judge those who did.

"I can still see the bloodstain."

"It's possible I top it up every now and then. For the sake of a good story."

He placed the rocking chair on the carpet. It looked rugged, unpolished. There was a crocheted cushion cover, filled with a thin cushion, and a white fluffy blanket.

"I've travelled the world with this chair," he said. "It's all that is left of the place I was happiest in all my life. School." Some of them shifted in their seats. Others were asleep. One ground his finger into the back of the woman in front of him; she acted as if it wasn't happening.

"Imagine a time," Mario said, "before we had light at the flick of a switch. He remembers, he was there!" pointing at Jerry Everard who, at 98, remembered very little.

Some chuckled. I sat on a chair with my knees tucked under my chin until a nurse told me *down*. They usually used single syllable words with me, as if I was a dog. They mostly didn't like me there; they thought I was a distraction, that I upset the patients. It wasn't true; the patients liked me. The staff were jealous, more like.

He set a bowl of jelly beans down on a small table beside the rocking chair. I did not ever see that bowl empty.

"That's when my school was built. It was a place for the lost, the lonely. It was the place we could go when our families didn't want us and nobody could teach us. It sat out in the bush, bright, with impossible gardens around it."

Were they listening? It was hard to tell. Jerry smiled, but that was his default expression. "It was full of lost children. All of us being given a future. And then... it burnt down."

There was no more reaction to this than to anything else he said. "How did it burn down?" I asked.

He closed his eyes and tears squeezed down his cheeks. "A horrible bloody accident." He swung his lantern. "No one's fault." He didn't try to make it funny; he'd stopped entertaining.

"But you survived."

"I did. I was the only one who came out alive."

He gave the rocking chair a push. "Who would like to be first? Who wants to experience the pure calm of the Nursery Corner?"

I did. "Me first!" I said. He glanced at my mother, who nodded indulgently.

He said, "Not yet for you. Not yet. You're happy, and innocent, and have a life to live. There is nothing to calm in you."

John John, up the hall in his room, screamed as he did every five minutes or ten, often enough to make me want to scream myself.

"Let's start with him," Mario said. He wriggled his fingers like a puppet master. Two of the nurses wheeled John John down the hallway, his arms strapped to the chair but his fingers reaching for them as if they could stretch beyond their means and scratch eyeballs out.

Four nurses lifted him into the chair in the Nursery Corner, one for each limb to keep him still. Mario set it rocking as they held him down. The rhythm of it did calm him, and one by one, the nurses tentatively let go. John John sat quietly, eyes closed, rocking, rocking, finding muscles he hadn't used in months.

This seemed to quieten all of the residents, and they mimicked his movement back and forth, back and forth.

"How long does he get to stay there?" Aunt Em said. She'd elbowed others out of the way to stand in front.

"As long as he likes."

It was over an hour before the man stirred and lifted his head. His face seemed gentler, and there had been silence from the moment he sat in the chair.

"He's happier now," Mario said. "Now, who is good at sharing? Sharing is Caring!"

THE NURSERY CORNER worked on all of them. If they started to throw a tantrum, if they screamed, became violent, if they attacked a staff member, they were placed in the Nursery Corner and they would come out softer, quieter. It was a godsend, my mother said, and she said that Mario was a godsend as well.

I didn't like it. To me, it was like they became puppets. Diminished.

"Where did you go?" I asked when they came out. "What did you see?"

Many forgot instantly, their eyes clouding over. Others remembered long enough to say, "The air was fresh," or "I saw my father there," before memory was gone. I didn't keep a record, but I reckon many of them gave up the ghost not long after a visit to the Nursery Corner. As if they'd seen heaven and no longer feared it.

*   *   *

ONE NIGHT, I heard a creaking sound. I crept out to have a look at the Nursery Corner. The hallway was lit only by the floor lights set to guide the staff in the dark.

The Nursery Corner seemed to glow, but I knew that wasn't possible. It made me think of when the circus was in town, set up in the school's playing field. From home, at night, the lights of the circus set a halo of light around the school, and this was how the Nursery Corner seemed, as if there was something bright and exciting beyond it.

I heard *creak creak*. It was Aunt Em, gently rocking. She clutched the soft white blanket and her mouth drooled.

There was a noise behind me and it was Mr Simons, completely naked, pulling at his penis in a way I have never seen since, stretching it almost to his mouth. I was enthralled, and that's where my mother found me, staring, open mouthed, and Aunt Em, rocking and drooling, and Mr Simons, tugging and tugging.

She bundled me up and put me to bed. She stayed and talked with me for an hour. My sleepiness, and the shock, and her quietness as I was talking led me to say more than I should have about the things I saw and heard.

"I hadn't quite realised. I'd forgotten how young you are," she said.

"It's okay, Mum. It doesn't bother me," but still she spoke to my teachers, and to the nurses, and between them they decided the home was not a good place for me, at least until I was older. Mario said he was jealous I was going to boarding school; best years of his life, bar none.

"Until it burnt down," I said.

"You be careful. No smoking in the cupboards," he said, and I shook my head, because I knew what smoking did and that I'd never do it. He was a private school boy and Mum was too. Fancy schools, they both went to. My father went to the nasty local, my mother said, and she always said it in that way of knowing.

"You'll make connections for life at these schools," Mario said, but he appeared to have no friends from childhood at all.

I had time to say goodbye to all my substitute grandparents, but none of them really noticed. Aunt Em complained that her arms hurt. She held them out, weeping, and the nurse in attendance said, "There is nothing wrong," like the doctors told her to say, but gave Aunt Em pain relief nonetheless.

So many of these old people felt pain others saw no reason for.

My cat was old and slow and I couldn't consider taking her. Besides, she loved it there; so many laps. So many hands to stroke her. And she knew, she had learnt, when a person was about to turn nasty.

She knew when it was time to get off a lap.

BOARDING SCHOOL WAS not all that, but it was okay. It was boring compared to the old people and what they told me. Those secrets and outrageous stories.

My mother's letters grew increasingly bizarre, listing all the deaths, first up, before anything else. Then it was all about Mario and how wonderfully the Nursery Corner worked to calm people down.

She spoke of aches and pains her patients suffered that the doctors couldn't identify. *The doctors never listen, is the problem. They think these people are making it up, but none of them have the imagination any more. Mr Simons left us the watch collection he was always talking about. Turns out it was worth money after all.*

At first, I visited every term break; less often as I got older. Mario looked after Mum and he wanted me to understand that, to the extent that he kept his hand firmly on her arse, as if to let me know the story, in case there was any doubt. Mum looked happier every time, less severe, more full of genuine laughter. She worried over her patients, always, but she somehow seemed to believe they were safer now.

"He's a wonder," everyone told me. "What he does for these

people," and truly, the place was far quieter. They all sat in their chairs, smiles on their faces. Some played with toys, holding them weakly in their laps. Others gazed at the TV, especially if a singing show was on.

WHEN SCHOOL WAS done I moved back home. After starring in the drama productions for two years I thought my path was set, but finding work as an actor proved to be soul-destroying ("Lose some weight and get back to us") and not what I thought it would be. I moved back to help Mum out and bide my time, waiting for Hollywood to call.

"How's my favourite audience member? My favourite movie star?" Mario said most mornings, winking at me. He knew I was worldly wise, now, not the innocent I once was.

I wondered what he got out of it all. What he gained. Was it just the adulation? The love of a good woman like my mother? He still travelled, giving shows around town and sometimes further afar, but he was always there for her, he always called if he was late.

The staff still rolled residents into the Nursery Corner if they got a bit bolshie. The nasty ones, the whinging ones, they'd get sat there every few days, because after an hour, they'd come out child-like. Happier. More willing to work at the repetitive tasks and activities that were supposed to help them. Vaguely useful things, like making lavender bags or packing candles. Sometimes they tied bows for funeral homes, black ribbons needed in the hundreds. Cruel but they have to face it, Mum said. She didn't think you should pretend death isn't going to happen. It wasn't like other places, where people simply 'went away', as if they moved to a pleasant place we'd never visit. Here, we had wakes.

We had a lot of wakes.

There was always movement in the Nursery Corner. A trick of the light, the nurses said (the doctors were never there long enough) more so at night when the whole floor flickered with shadow as if there were candles but there were none.

Sometimes I watched it like a movie, straining my eyes to identify shapes.

Sometimes my old cat curled up on the chair, emerging hours later with fur ruffled and a wild look in her eye.

No VISITOR WANTED to stand in the Nursery Corner. Sometimes it happened by mistake and they'd shiver, look up and down for a draught, a fan, an explanation. But there was also a sense of comfort. Of well-being. Like the good days of childhood. Warm summer holiday mornings. Nights when dinner was your favourite meal. A birthday when you liked every present so didn't have to lie. Those moments when your mother was her real self, laughing like a young girl. This is what they told me; I never stood there myself. The breeze of the corner, and the scent I smelled there put me off. Sometimes it was new books. Sometimes it was boiled cabbage.

Grandchildren and great grandchildren brought in to visit were sent to the Nursery Corner as if it was a treat.

They sat on the edge of the rug, bunched up. "Go on, have a rock in the chair," but you couldn't get many of them to step into the corner or sit in the chair. Those who did would come out quiet, very quiet. What would a child see, if an adult saw childhood? Past lives?

I HEARD THE chair rocking late some nights and wondered who was in it. I'd find out the next day; the one who was the most vacant.

I thought they sank into dementia with greater speed and less resistance once they'd been in the Nursery Corner.

"What do they see?" I asked Mario.

"Lots of friendly people; you've never felt so welcome."

"Have you ever been?"

He said he hadn't, but I knew he had. I'd seen him rocking there at night, especially on nights my mother was out shopping, or visiting her sister. Not often.

"Are there other places like this one? Other Nursery Corners?" He still travelled to perform, but rarely spent more than a night away.

"A few. I like to help where I can." He listed them and there were more than a few. He had Nursery Corners set up wherever he visited.

Mario told me that, depending on the sort of person you are, you'll find peace or sorrow in the Nursery Corner. "You might see battered children, lost to a parent's fury. Or tiny babies, sucked from life like metal filings to a magnet. Or a train filled with laughing families, or a table laden with sweets. Each of us sees something new in there, something different. You, I think you will see a thing of great beauty. You will feel more loved and needed than you have ever felt before. You will be at the very centre of the universe. A star. Like moi."

I'd missed out on a dozen auditions ("lose some weight") and was beginning to think I was kidding myself, so this fantasy of his resonated with me.

I never bothered Mum with my audition woes. Tried to help out where I could. We attended to Mrs T, who had stripped naked and was attempting to climb onto the table.

"Come on, now, into the Nursery Corner. Let's have a nice sit."

Mrs T sat in there, folded into a blanket, rocking, tears coursing. "They're good tears," Mum said. "Best to have something to remember with sadness than to have no memory, no sorrow at all." She looked me straight in the eye as she said this. She thought I needed to get a life, or I'd have nothing to cry about when I was that age. "You're twenty-four, Jessie. What have you experienced? Who have you loved? You need to take chances."

I thought, *I'm going to see what I see when I sit there. See how I feel.* I wasn't sure if she was right or not. Had I lived, yet? Was Mario right, and I'd feel fulfilled after sitting in the corner? Would I come out knowing what to do with my life?

I'd wanted to try for a long time, had been tempted to send my friends in when we were younger, just to freak them out. But it had never happened.

* * *

I SAT DOWN on the chair in the Nursery Corner and began to rock.

Within moments, I heard music, but so faint it was like an echo. The smell of soap, age and toilets lifted and it was dusty, mostly, outside road dust, pollen and, I thought, frying bacon. We had bacon twice a year at the home, on Mothers' Day and Fathers' Day. It made them cry every time. "It's like the old days, going back," one told me, "it's as if all the rest of my life hasn't passed yet."

I could still feel the press of wood against my arms, the scratch of wool from the blanket on my leg, the soft give of the cushion, but what I saw was far different.

Lit by bright sunlight, shaded by ancient oak trees, the two buildings sat low and long in lush, green lawn. One painted red, the other yellow, even at a distance I could see they were well maintained.

My feet were bare and as I walked towards the buildings (because where else would I go?) the softness of the lawn tickled my soles and I began to run, filled with a sense of pure joy the like of which I had never felt before. The sun was so bright my eyes teared up.

The sound of laughter, and voices chanting, the smell of baking bread and of rich, red roses led me on. Children played on swings and slides and as I watched a boy fell off and sat in the dirt, dusting himself off. One girl seemed to hurt her arm badly and if I hadn't seen the other children helping her, I would have run over.

I reached the red building. A sign by the door said, 'St Lucia's School' with the motto beneath: *There is a Light at the End of the Tunnel* and I thought, *This is the school I would have loved to go to.*

I pushed the door open.

"There you are, Jessie!" It was a girl I didn't know but who seemed familiar. She had clear blue eyes and her cheeks were flushed. "Come on, come and play. We have to do Maths soon, yuck, but we can play for a while."

She took my hand and led me to a vast playroom. Many other children were there, and they all looked up at me and smiled. "It's Jessie!" they said, as if I was a long-lost friend. They seemed happy but, on closer inspection, some had marks around their wrists, bruising around their eyes. All of them looked tired.

My new friend led me to sit among the toys. Robots, hoops, pirate costumes. 'SHARING IS CARING' a handwritten sign said.

I wondered why the children would welcome me, an adult, so delightedly, then realised that I, too, was a child. Was I eight? Six? My father was alive, then, and I wondered if I could find a phone and call him, just to hear his voice, see if he was sorry.

There were no phones, though. No television, no computers.

In the corner sat a large beanbag, jellybean print. The small table beside it had a box of jellybeans and some tweezers next to it. I wanted one of those jellybeans, wanted to have the taste of sugar, the memory of home. My friend stopped me. "That's Mario's. He'll give you one if you wait till he gets here."

Time passed. I don't know how long. I slept. I ate. There was custard, hot dogs, there were cheese sticks and there were beautiful peaches. I watched the others playing and sometimes joined in. Sometimes they would stand in one place for hours as if waiting. Or they played skip rope for hour after hour after hour, tears running down their cheeks as their arms tired. They didn't respond when I told them they should stop, have a rest. My cat was there, young again, chasing butterflies and purring so loudly you could hear her in the other room. She didn't know me, though. She wouldn't sit on my lap.

Sometimes I would rock on my heels and remember; there is another place. Not this one. I knew that in that place, people had to be shaken awake, physically carried out of the Nursery Corner, and I wondered if anyone would do it for me.

They did, at last. My own mother, giving me a poke in the Nursery Corner.

On my lap was the banana I had been holding when I sat in the chair and it was rotten, after being a perfect piece of fruit. "You've had a good nap!" Mum said, as if I'd been gone only moments. "You look so peaceful I barely wanted to wake you. But I need to sit Mrs Allan down. She's a bit agitated."

Mrs Allan winked at me. "See you there," she said.

I stepped away, feeling shaky, but with a deep sense of peace.

"DID YOU LIKE my school?" Mario asked. He sat closer to me than he normally would, as if our relationship had changed.

"I had a pretty weird dream."

"Not a dream. Ask all of them." He waved at the room, all the old people and, I thought, the wall of the dead, all the photos of long-gone and recently departed. I walked along the wall until I found her, my new friend. A woman who'd lived with us for only two months before she died of an infection. I remembered her as being a great lover of the Nursery Corner. I remembered her clear blue eyes.

There were others, too; they played as children, fell, sang, learned, ate as children in that other place.

"A little piece of you with me forever," Mario said. "In my place, waiting for me, with all the others. I don't take it all. Just a glimmer, an echo, a hint."

He was a hypnotist, and he had finally managed to crack me. I backed away from him, my eyes downcast. I knew I could clear my head of him, and of that place, that I would not be diminished by it.

I also knew I wanted my mother to get rid of him. That he shouldn't be among these people.

"You didn't say if you liked my school. It's an exact replica of the one that burnt down."

"It was fine. Quite lovely, actually. No sign of flames, or burning."

He had tears in his eyes. "Thank you. Thank you. None of them ever remember."

I thought of the patients, how much emptier they seemed. He thought he stole very little but I thought he stole the last of them. He took any dreams they had of their own heaven and made them vanish completely.

MUM WOULDN'T GET rid of him. She said he made her happy and this was true; he adored her, treated her like a princess. He adored her so much, he never asked her to sit in the Nursery Corner. He never tried to take that part of her.

She'd stand there sometimes, saying, "Sit! When do I have time to sit?" and he'd say, "On the toilet!" and she'd screech with laughter at this.

I asked him what he was creating that place for; what was the point. "Filling it up again salves my conscience."

Because children had died in the fire; I'd looked that up. The lights had failed and they had stumbled in the darkness. Handprints were found; you could see them online. Tiny handprints, some of them, along a hallway leading to a storage cupboard. A dead end. "And I will live there forever, one day. When the place is full."

"It *is* full," I said, although I knew perfectly well the walls rang with silence and that there was room for hundreds more. "Seriously, you couldn't fit anyone else in there and have it still be nice to live there."

"Did they talk about me when you were there? Ask about me? Because when I'm there... well. You see how people are with me here. You see how much people love me."

At that moment, he lost all that made him lovable; his humour, his cleverness, his confidence. He exuded a desperate lonely neediness I hated to be around.

In the Nursery Corner, the whole world revolved around him. "Yes," I said. "They talked about you a lot. Laughing, you know, like people do here when they mention your name, because you're funny."

My neck hurt when I awoke the next day. I rubbed it as I

walked the ward, and the residents nodded at me. "Sore neck? Sore neck? There will be more."

IN THE END, he rocked himself to death. He left a note, saying he was ill and not able to cope with the pain, and he said he was sorry, and that he loved us all.

I wondered if the old men had stepped in to defend us again; if they had killed another predator for me. But I had to accept that this was not the case, that Mario Laudati had chosen to go and therefore had won.

After Mario died, the residents tried sitting in the Nursery Corner and it made them angry. They got nothing out of it, rocking rocking rocking with no transformation, no good feeling. I thought, *Good. I'll burn it all, the carpet, the chair, cushion, blanket. Then his school will burn again, and we'll be free of him.*

MY BONFIRE ACHIEVED nothing.

OVER THE YEARS the Nursery Corner sat empty. It lost its glow and all feeling. Mum did, too. She turned the age many of them were when they went in, and she knew, she was absolutely sure she did not want to be among them. I took her to live with me and my family; this was inevitable and worked well for all of us.

I never told her about the sudden pains, the aches, the unexplained twinges. I never told her it meant that Mario was playing with me, in the school, that he was making me skip rope, or eat chili, or climb a tree, that he was wanting more from me that I would ever have given him here, on the other side. She had no aches and pains of her own, not really, until she caught pneumonia at 92. She went quickly after that.

* * *

I WILL NOT go quickly. I'm in no hurry. Because I know where I'm going.

Back to school.

ABERRATION
GENEVIEVE VALENTINE

YOU'LL SEE THEM someplace you're going when you're trying to make the most of your time. They're standing at the top of the steps to the public library (the amazing branch where they do the photoshoots, not the squat concrete one you go to), or they're on the balcony at a concert you overheard someone talking about. They'll be at the greatest altitude you can reach while still seeming effortless; they like being able to look down.

You'll notice them a long time before they notice you, though they seem to stutter in and out of sight. They're dressed the way you've always wanted to dress. Sometimes you'll glance back and not see them, but they're nowhere else either, and a second later something catches your eye and it's them anyway and you feel like an asshole. You never get a sense of what they look like.

If they smoke they'll barely keep hold of their limp-dick cigarettes, wrist angled hard enough to crack. If they laugh it's parted lips but teeth close together, two straight rows, a furrow between their eyebrows like they're already finding reasons it's not so funny after all. One of them touches the other one right at the small of the back, cigarette a cinder between their fingers, and you get the impression of pushing even though nobody's moved.

They're awful, they don't even pretend otherwise, and when you look at them the hair on your neck stands up, and the word

Rotten unfurls inside of you. (You couldn't say it if anyone asked, your mouth is too dry, but it sits there sharp-edged, like you swallowed a name tag.)

One of them peels away, finally, passes you on the way to the bar or around the bottom edge of the steps towards the street; shoulders pinched, the shadow of the other one already falling across both of you.

"Don't look," she says, so low that music or traffic swallows it up. When they disappear, you're still standing right where you were, staring at your own shoes, and it's fucking stupid, but as soon as the words were out your gaze dropped.

It wasn't like you did it because you were embarrassed to have been caught out; it was the urgency, some terror in the snap after the T and the K, and you know a warning when you hear one.

"OH," SHE SAYS at the top of the bridge.

There's little else worth saying—she's gotten so tired of languages lately, which would feel like a defeat if she cared more about losing—but a sound of surprise still falls out of her sometimes, some gut punch of feeling that gets a death rattle.

The last time she vanished from this city it was a ruin and you couldn't get within five miles of it, nothing left but a few plaster-roof islands and the last few wooden fingers of the pier. Appearing in it now is visiting a grave to find the departed eating an apple on their headstone.

She feels desperate already, so desperate as to be fully solid, and she grips the stone and waits for someone to run into her. No one does. No one can really see her for long; she's been so many places she's not really anywhere any more.

The stone's at her hip. It's quiet when she touches it, though she feels it all the time anyway, a phantom heat right through to her spine.

One of the vaporettos is sinking, nearer to the sea. But it's early, only just dawn, and no one will realize in time for the alarm to do any good; half of them will drown. It won't take long. She watches.

When it's over she walks through the smaller streets, catches half-sentences and the windows of shops where the things in the very front have gone a little dusty and it doesn't matter because they're only tourists. Someone is napping in a piazza, and after she touches his shoulder he has no more use for his camera. She takes three photographs: the slime easing up the edge of a canal, the curtains in a house where someone is very ill, the shadow of a flight of birds that looks like a monster underneath the water.

It's a city of corpses, like every other city, and she walks across the bridges and thinks about drowning.

HE CATCHES UP with her under one of the abandoned billboards for Lunar Enterprises that looks out over a dark stretch of desert. She's crossed her arms to keep from looking for a cigarette. Nobody makes them any more; there's no point looking.

She's carrying a camera, one of the instant ones that's back in vogue. She's holding the pictures like a hand of poker, five snapshots of the city at the edge of the valley as the lights went out and out and out.

"They came out nice," his voice is a thousand years weary with telling her.

"They did." They're already fading, though; she only looked at them once. Soon they'll start to disappear at the edges, and by the time they leave here there won't be anything left to take.

He used to tell her to give it up, but she's not the only one who has hobbies, and he stopped asking a long time ago.

He reaches for the pack in his pocket, taps out two, lights the second one off the cherry from the first. They give off just enough flare to remind them how pitch dark it is. She can see the hollow above his top lip, that's all.

"I don't smoke any more," she says.

He raises his eyebrows, smokes both cigarettes at the same time.

The last of the smoke feathers from his mouth as he drops the butts; they vanish before they ever hit the ground, and he grinds his boot into the dirt like he's trying to spite them. Their kind leave no traces.

Still, hers just vanish; his all gathers somewhere, waiting for him, everything he touches, everything he does. He's always going home.

"Been hoping to run into you," he says.

She's been in eight places since she saw him last, or ten. In a couple of places there was only a day. She spent a week in the mountains, staying clear of a black bear that got more agitated the longer she stayed—it could tell something was wrong, right up until it died. She hopes it's all right now, but it's the same way she hopes everyone who drowns in Venice centuries from now fought until the very last; you get cruel eventually.

Maybe she started out cruel. She suspects that the very first time she opened her eyes and was elsewhen, her sympathy had vanished. Something she was born to.

(She's thought about it, that maybe anyone becomes like this if you give them long enough and show them what they've seen. Doesn't bear much reflection.)

From the city there's a siren. The blast that comes in the dark will kill three hundred people, give or take.

He made friends all the time. Said they held on more fiercely, which she knows; said they loved more deeply, which she doesn't doubt. But he loves them back, loves women and men and the sort of child who can actually see you, who stares you right in the eye and ignores you when you say, "Don't look," and then gets angry at all once as it realizes it's been robbed and it's looked too long at the thing that will kill it.

Lucky, she says when he tells her. He never asks her what she means.

"Good to see you," she says.

The first of the rumblings begins. They look across the darkness, where the edge of the city is just beginning to separate from the dark with a layer of smoke and flame.

Her heart is a thousand stairs with nothing at the top, and she's afraid all the way up.

IF EVERYTHING WORKED as it was meant to, you were always there just before the worst of it, the birdsong before the bomb. But aberration doesn't always listen, and she appeared too late, sometimes, or a year early, or a hundred years. Sometimes she'd shown up in the middle of a war, and when the stone in her pocket warmed and creaked and pushed her to wherever she was going next, it was the only sound on a field without graves, the ground swallowing blood as fast as it could.

Once, by some mistake, she'd been spat out before there were people at all, and she'd sat on a tree trunk and watched the sun stain the leaves, and the ferns at her feet rustle with animals that seemed like her: mammal at first glance, but reptile if you knew what you were looking for. She lifted her hands before she remembered she had no camera. It got colder eventually, warmer again. The ground underfoot stretched an inch or two. She wondered if she'd be sitting there for a hundred million years, waiting. She didn't mind.

There was a white vulture, and as it tilted its head to her, black eyes in sickly-blue sockets, it was the most beautiful thing she'd ever seen. She's forgotten the thing that died.

She had no camera. When she appeared next (Morocco, maybe), her hands sat in her lap a long time, framed by nothing.

LENS ABERRATIONS IN a camera, in order of disaster:
Distortion: a warp across something you thought was holding steady. Tilt shift: makes your subject fall away from you, every house teetering on the verge of collapse. Bokeh: a cheat in the shape of light, turning light into spheres of nostalgia that hover behind whatever you're trying to capture, a hostage of a good time. Chromatic: the edges of your colors burn into something they aren't, and you can't trust your

colors any more, but that one is subtle, and you won't know until it's too late.

Curvature: the thing you want most is sharp and bright, and everything else slips out of focus by degrees. That one you can live with. It's close enough to life. Can't blame it for that.

None of it works, of course. If it did there would be chaos. You can take all the pictures you want. Their face will be gone— some lens flare that wasn't there before, or a dove taking off in the foreground with two feathers spread over where they used to be, or obscured behind a cloud of someone's cigarette, even if you've never smoked and they never have. If there's no excuse that the frame can find, you'll just see a vanished face where the picture's been eaten away, someone lifting a disappearing glass to lips that don't exist anymore.

THE INVADING ARMY of a country that doesn't yet exist piles the corpses of the vanquished outside the camp. The straggling forces of the occupied wait until deep night before they set the bodies on fire. Their attack on the camp comes in the middle of the chaos, and takes hundreds of enemy lives; the contagion that was already sickening the dead wafts equally across friend and foe. Both armies will be decimated soon, and the germ will crawl victoriously over the countryside for longer than anyone remembers the war.

He's leaning against the tree trunk, barely touching her left shoulder; his hair makes a sound against the bark when he turns to look at her. "If you take the tragedy out of it, it's pretty funny."

This is why she gave up on languages. "If you take the tragedy out of anything, it's funny."

He smiles and rolls his stone across his knuckles, a skipping stone shaped like a coin. She's seen it a hundred times. She's never laid a finger on it.

A deserter staggers past them, close enough to death that when he looks up he's startled to see them.

"Don't look," she says, and the soldier opens his mouth, drops his gaze to the ground. It's too late for him, though, and he doesn't even make it past the tree before he crashes to the ground. He's facing them, eyes open; she looks away.

He looks back and forth between the corpse and her, and for a moment his face gets fond; it does that whenever something happens that he can take for her having some kind feeling.

She lets him think what he likes.

(He was the one who explained her aberration, the first time he ever found her, when she was occupying the last of her mind and he looked like he knew how thin that thread had gotten. He must have been looking for her; she wonders, sometimes.)

His trajectories seem like real journeys—every time she sees him she knows he's come from a place and is going to another, moving through the world and witnessing everything he can. Hers is a slow, suspended spiraling-down, and it's possible to tell at which points he came back by clocking when things skidded violently to one side, a kite that's been shot.

He watches her for a while, unblinking. She wonders if he's descended from the vulture, the way she's a child of that half-changed reptile.

SHE'D SEEN THE sun rise over the valley once. It hit the top of the mountains first in a line of gold, and crept over the fields in a dozen shades of green—there had been sheep, only a handful, someone had been careless and would lose them before the sun was fully up. Pines ringed them in now, a jagged mouth that cast long shadows. At the edge of the green was the drop, and the lake underneath dark as a pool of oil.

The hill she stood on was clumps of heather that smelled rotten despite the dried-out grass, and with every step she sunk an inch as if the hill was going to give. There was a village at the bottom of the valley, just at the horizon, but no lights were on at all; she was the only one awake, watching the sun as the lake hid from it, as the sheep moved closer to the fall.

I want to keep this, she thought. There was no reason, there was never a reason to keep one thing that passed over another thing that passed, but this she loved more than she could remember loving anything. She was breathing just looking at it, hard enough that she could feel ribs.

She took a dozen pictures with the box camera she'd stolen from the city she'd walked away from, knowing none of them would hold this, knowing she was losing the moment when the heather looked alive with light. When the first two sheep fell she watched them go and had to sit down to keep from reaching forward over the edge of the drop to pull them back and try to catch it in the frame.

They made a noise as they fell, all of them, the same anguished cry that was more human than any sound a human made, but she's forgotten it. It was a long time ago, and there are no pictures.

"IF I CAN AFFIX myself, I will," she tells him the next time she sees him, which if she averages out the time in between her moves forward and back, near as she can tell, is two hundred years before the last time she saw him.

He doesn't have any cigarettes, and his thumbs twist at the edges of his pockets. His eyes are black, his skin is dark; she wonders what he looks like to the rest of them—a shadow, a hollow, the silhouette of someone they'd forgotten who will suddenly spring to mind just before terrible news comes in. He'd told her once that she's the color of the clay everyone walks over, but they were fighting then. No way of knowing.

"This is a terrible time to make a decision that terrible," he tells the bridge over the river. "Look at this place. Won't be worth living in for another seven hundred years, and you can't get anywhere else until they discover the waves."

"I don't want it now. I'll wait for the right place."

He looks at her from the corner of his eye. She wonders why she's hard to look at.

"You'll waste it," he says, like he sympathizes. "You'll throw yourself from the first tall thing you find. Staying anywhere turns into a circle of things that are never quite what you wanted. You like to see it and be finished."

That seems cruel for someone who has a place he can return to. "I can't keep hold of a camera," she says. "I don't like it to be finished. I just can't bring anything back home."

"You'd be wasted at home, too." He smooths his hands over his chest pockets. Empty.

"I found the place I really wanted. I know I'll never get back there, don't worry, that's all gone. But I've been looking."

"That sounds exhausting."

She thinks that's a little rich, coming from him. She doesn't say anything.

"So have you picked the lucky grave?"

She says, "I know what I'm waiting for."

To feel anything, she thinks. As soon as I open my eyes and feel anything at all, I'm going to bury this rock in the ground and live out my days and die. Any magic has to fade if you bury it in the ground; it leaches out through the water and the air, it becomes a village of people who live a long time but can never stay put, it becomes a herd of deer who cross a continent.

Then there will be time enough to find a high place, if she wants one. There will be a hill with a lake like oil at the bottom, and a sheer drop that no one climbs out of.

"Don't do something stupid just so I'll miss you," he says.

She turns to him. "Promise me you'll find me and tell me if it works."

I want you to know where I am, she doesn't say. She doesn't say, *I want you to look at my grave just once.*

"If it doesn't work, I won't have to find you. You'll open your eyes and a locomotive will run you over and you'll know, and when you open them again you'll know, without any help from me."

"Promise me you'll find me," she says.

Her eyes sting, looking at him. Maybe that's the first sign of something changing.

He meets her eye; her heart is a thousand stairs with nothing waiting at the top.

To REMEMBER, SOMEONE had told her as they touched her hair, before she ever learned about a camera and what it could do for anyone who wasn't her. To make you appreciate home, someone had told her as they pressed the stone into her hand—she'd been all night wandering, and it must have been an offense. They must have been afraid of her; she hopes she was frightening.

Don't do this to her, he'd said.

She's forgotten if he was always there or if he found the moment and tried to intervene; she only remembers his breath between her and the shadows the trees were casting. It was the last thing she ever heard, standing in that place.

She suspects it was meant to be a place she'd come back to, that her heart and the stone in her hand would draw her back there when the traveling was over, but the first time she opened her eyes all that was gone.

She doesn't remember where or when, or anyone she left. The ground that could never be filled had taken them all in its mouth, and if she went back in time enough to meet them, she wouldn't know their faces; she wouldn't know where to stand to call it homecoming.

Maybe she's stood there already, and all she saw was the little circle of the box camera, a field inverted, a picture that was going to be devoured any second.

When she closes her eyes and tries to conjure it back, she sees a drowned pier, and his face in a wreath of smoke, and a vulture's eye, and a camera lens that was grasping to hold on.

It TAKES SIXTEEN moves before there's a worthy place. (One of them had seemed beautiful, but she was only there an hour before the stone got warm and she grit her teeth and felt the sick-stomach lurch that reminded her she had a body. It had been an hour of red dust so bright the sky looked purple next to it; chromatic aberration.)

But this is a quiet town, big enough that she can steal a camera, near enough to a river that she can follow it into the meadows, and be alone just past the bend. There's no high ground here, but the world is wide.

At the top of a sloping hill that's as close as she can find, there's a tree that reminds her of the place where they watched the beginning of the plague, and she presses her lips into a thin line, counts backwards carefully from ten as she gets closer. He never makes much noise. If she didn't always expect him, she'd never know when he'd appeared.

She stands beside the tree for a long time as the sun crawls over everything. The branches look like a man smoking, they look like someone reaching out for her, they look like a map of Venice. Below her is the little town and the river, and she looks as far as she can for a ship that could be carrying him.

At sunset the branches look like the veins on the leaf she looked through once as the things that would become mammals skittered across her feet. In the dark the branches make cracks in the sky as she looks up at the moon, asks it nothing, counts to a hundred thousand thousand.

It's dawn when the stone begins to get warm around the edges. Panic clenches her tight for a moment, and she thinks about plagues and cities and deserts and no, it has to be here, she has to risk it, she'll grow old waiting but she'll wait, when he finds her he might laugh but she can't stand the idea of ever again moving, she's breathing like her chest will burst, she's staying here.

She drags a few inches of earth off from the ground beneath the tree, shoves the stone into it, scrapes in her tears and breathes against it and spits for good measure, buries it in a single two-handed shove of dirt like a door slamming shut.

She closes her eyes, feels nothing, opens them. The bank of the river is shrinking; tide's coming in.

This is the ground then, she thinks. Whenever he finds me, he'll know where I'm buried.

It's sunrise when the light hits low enough that she sees the place where the ground is risen, a little burial mound grown over with a hundred years of moss and little blue flowers she's forgotten the name of.

It's a small grave. It's barely big enough for a small, flat rock she could roll between her fingers like a coin.

YOU'LL SEE HER when you go someplace trying to be alone— dramatically, romantically, the sheer hill that hangs over the bay, the kind of place where poets go. Somewhere you can look down on everything.

She'll be standing near the edge of wherever it is, not close enough that you'd feel right about crying out, but close enough that you keep glancing out of the corner of your eye as you sit down, try to let the moment wash over you. She seems like she's waiting for someone, though she's not moving, her arms crossed tight over her chest, everything about her looking pinched in, stretched out.

You never quite catch her face, however long you look at her; when you try to get her attention you just remember some dark unblinking eye and then something going fuzzy at the edges like a bad photograph. When you look out at the bay you always forget she's there until you move.

You'll begin to think that poetry's a bit much after all. It's not like you went through anything so bad, and it's awfully windy to be in a place so high. It's too windy to be as close to the edge as she is.

You'll stand up to reach her, start to move and then freeze, some prey instinct that holds you where you are.

"Be careful," you'll say.

She'll say, "Don't look."

ICE IN THE BEDROOM
ROBERT SHEARMAN

1

SIMON PAINTER HAD at last found a way of getting through the nights. Balancing his head on two pillows, the sheets pulled up to his neck, he would take a third pillow in his arms and hug it against his body tight. One arm over and one arm under, he would spoon with the pillow all night long—and if he got too hot, or too uncomfortable, or if he just had the urge to stare sleeplessly at a different patch of dark, he would turn over and he would take the pillow with him, lifting it in his arms, then somersaulting it over his body, allez-oop! Like it was a dance. One arm over, one arm under—and the arm under would never get numb as it had when he'd cuddled Cathy, so really, cuddling the pillow was better, wasn't it? Wasn't it? And he never pretended that the pillow was Cathy, that would have been daft, and besides, she may have been short but not as short as all that!—he had called her sometimes his 'little lady', and she had laughed at him, and only occasionally found it annoying—he never *believed* the pillow was Cathy (it wasn't *belief*, at any rate), but he would sometimes stroke it, he would run a finger down the very centre of it as if it were a human spine, and he might sometimes kiss it, he might wish it good night.

So, Simon coped with the nights, even if he hadn't yet worked out how to fall asleep, but that would come, give it time, he couldn't expect miracles.

The doctor asked him if he had been thinking about suicide. He told her he had been. It seemed a little blunt of her, he was only after some sleeping pills, but he was by nature a polite man and was willing to oblige her queries.

"That is a concern," said the doctor. The doctor was a short, pretty woman, who nonetheless in no way resembled Cathy.

Was it really a concern, Simon asked her. He had thought it better to confront these thoughts head on, that's what his friends had told him, that's what they'd said on that video he'd rented from the library. He told her not to be concerned, please, not on his account, and he gave her his very best reassuring smile. But she remained stubbornly concerned, and wasn't that just typical.

Of course he'd been thinking about suicide. He'd been puzzling at which way would be the most painless. He'd read somewhere that drowning was quite a nice way to go, that it even gave you a sense of euphoria (but then again, how would they know?). Falling from a great height wasn't too bad—and he'd heard that the body fell so fast that there wasn't time for the brain to process it, in effect you'd be dead before you knew, in effect you'd die in ignorance. But the thought of the impact. With all your internal organs smashing into one another. With your heart bursting pop against your ribcage. That was, on reflection, less appealing. And when it came to it, at the very precipice, just seconds away from oblivion, could he really swing himself over the edge? Could he ever be that brave? He thought not.

He'd always assumed pills would be the best way to go. In a funny way, when he'd found Cathy's body, still warm, but still so dead, he'd felt a tiny flutter of relief. Along with the panic, the way that his insides were turning over, the way he'd gone so very cold—relief, wasn't there, a little bit? The relief making things better. At least she'd opted for an easy method. At least she'd done it in a way there wasn't any blood. But then—oh, he'd made the mistake of reading up on the subject—in the days after Cathy's death there had been so much to do but so little incentive to do it—and he read of the horrible things a drug overdose would do to your insides, there was nothing clean and tidy about it. Really, the descriptions alone made Simon gag. And he remembered the way he'd found her, on the floor, twisted, and *not* in her favourite armchair, *not* with a composed smile upon her face. He supposed it hadn't been such a peaceful way to die after all.

He probably shouldn't have told the doctor any of that, it did nothing for the concerned expression on her face. And he didn't get to go home with any sleeping pills. So.

There hadn't been a suicide note. Simon didn't know why Cathy had done it. He supposed she'd been unhappy. Shouldn't he have known she was unhappy? Shouldn't she have told him she was? He felt like an idiot. He didn't know what to say to anyone when they gave him their condolences. He didn't want to admit she'd seemed perfectly okay to him. He had to lie about it, give her death some extra depth. There'd been a trauma they'd been battling together for a while. And he'd failed her. He'd failed.

He wasn't going to kill himself. He would never kill himself. But if he ever did. If he ever decided to bite the bullet, as it were. He promised himself he'd leave a suicide note.

He'd hug the pillow close to him, and he thought he could smell Cathy's hair on it. Even though that was unlikely, he'd washed the sheets after he'd found the body, he'd given the whole flat a good spring clean, he'd wiped away every trace of her and he could kick himself for that now. He sniffed at the pillow. He smelled fabric conditioner, and pretended it was the scent of Cathy's shampoo.

And he'd stare out into the blackness of his bedroom, and minute-by-minute, and hour-by-hour, but eventually, at least eventually, he'd get through the night.

* * *

1

THOUGH HE MUST have slept, because the cold woke him.

He didn't want to open his eyes. He refused to open them. He grabbed for the sheets, the sheets must have fallen off. The sheets hadn't fallen off, he was already tugging them as close to his body as he could, he'd cocooned himself within them, and still he was shivering.

And he smelled the fresh outdoor air.

He opened his eyes, and stared up at the moon.

He goggled at the moon for a moment. In turn, the moon stared down at him, and maybe it was just as surprised. Who knew?

At first he thought that the roof of the house had blown off. Maybe there'd been a storm? Some violent storm, but one of those quiet storms, so he hadn't noticed. And it wasn't just the roof that had gone, it was the house around him, it was the entire bloody world.

And the moon, not so distant as he would have liked. It hung in the air above his head, it was bearing down on him. It filled the sky. It glowed. He shielded his eyes from that glow. When he looked again, the moon seemed even larger, he could make out the craters on it, could see how rough and pitted was its surface. He thought that if he stood up on the bed he might even be able to reach it. He knew he couldn't really. He was fairly sure that was impossible. He didn't try.

He hoped that whatever was fixing the moon into place wouldn't give way, because then the moon would fall down and squash him flat, and then he'd die.

The glow above him. And beneath him, another glow reflecting back. He looked over the side of the bed, and saw that it was sitting upon a lake of ice. More than a lake, the ice was everywhere—and it was clear, so smooth, no one had set foot upon the ice, its surface was in such contrast to the jagged coarseness of the moon, it was perfect. And yet that smoothness, it scared Simon all the more. Not a single mark upon this ice world, untouched, unspoilt, what would it feel when it woke up? Because Simon suddenly knew that it *would* wake up, he was so dazed and so tired and he knew nothing, but he knew *this*, it was a single primal truth he had been given: the ice would wake, and find him there, him and his bed sitting ridiculously on its too smooth skin, and it would open up and swallow them whole. With nothing but the pockmarked moon as a witness.

He looked about him, and it was ice as far as he could see. Nothing else in any direction. An entire ocean of it, no relief from the cold hard grey.

"I'm asleep," he said out loud. Of course he did. But it didn't feel more real for the saying, and his breath came out as steam.

Neither the glow of the moon nor the glow of the ice were enough to burn away the night. The night ran its way between them, a thin ribbon of the densest black. Simon's head was in the black, he thought it might choke him.

He forced his eyes closed, but they wouldn't stay shut.

And he thought that if he could confront the fantasy of it, that he might still be all right. If his body could come into contact with the world, and see that it made no sense. He looked over the side of the bed once more. The ice seemed grim and so so cold—but it couldn't be there, could it? He climbed out from the sheets. They weren't doing much good anyway. He sat up cross-legged on the bed, he took a deep breath. He swung one bare foot over the side, he slowly lowered it down onto the ice.

He suddenly remembered doing this as a child. The way he'd dread having to get up in the night, setting his feet down onto the carpet. Hoping he wouldn't disturb the monsters he knew were sleeping under his bed.

His toe touched the ice. And he felt nothing, there was nothing. Encouraged, he pressed the whole ball of his foot down hard. And there it was, at once, the cold *burned*, and it was all Simon could do not to scream, he pulled his leg up to safety with both his hands and did it so clumsily that he nearly unbalanced himself, he nearly fell off the bed, he nearly fell on to the ice that looked so cool but burned like fire.

He rubbed at the foot. Tried to rub away the pain. He looked back over the side. "No, no," he said. Because where his toe had touched the ice there were now cracks. "No!" he said, because he could hear those cracks splitting, as the ice broke underneath the weight he'd put on it, thin jagged lines snaking their way from the pressure point across the ocean in all directions like a spider web.

Thank God, the cracking stopped. Thank God, the ice held. It took Simon a while to get his breath back, and he couldn't tell whether that was the cold or the panic. Gently he peered back over the side. The legs of the bed stood firm upon the ice surface. He leaned over a little further to work it out, why such a heavy object as the double bed they had got in the sales only a couple of years ago, with the big brass headboard that Cathy had thought looked like it belonged in a palace—"It'll be like we're royalty," she said, "as we sleep, or watch TV, or anything else we might get up to," and even then she'd blushed, she looked every inch the little lady right then—how could this bed, so heavy that he never thought they'd even get it up the stairs, how could this bed balance so exactly upon the ice? And as he leaned the crack in the ice began to splinter again—as if his looking alone had caused it to break, or his even *questioning* the situation. "I'm sorry," he said, "sorry!"—and quickly he sat back up. He tried to find the exact centre of the bed, huddled in it, tried to make himself small and light and hoped that was enough to keep him safe.

He made himself shut his eyes again. His eyes were wet. He realised he was crying.

Friends said he hadn't cried since Cathy had gone, and that wasn't true, he had cried a lot. He just hadn't cried whilst they were watching, so how were they to know? He admitted he'd forced the tears out somewhat—he'd stared at the bathroom mirror and told himself he was going to have a really good cry, and he'd set his face nice and taut in preparation—and he'd thought of Cathy, hard, and he'd frowned, even harder. The effort gave him a headache. Sometimes water came out.

Sometimes it didn't. He'd tried to cry at Cathy's funeral, but he just hadn't been able to get the concentration right. He thought he'd let her down.

Now the tears flowed so easily, and they just wouldn't stop. He was so lonely, and full of despair, and he didn't know if he wanted to live or to die. And he tried to cry as gently as possible, he didn't want to move about or make too much noise, just in case it set the ice breaking once more—but pretty soon he was almost slapping the tears from his face, and that *hurt*, and there was a strange moaning sound coming out of his mouth that didn't quite sound human.

It seemed as if he heard the moaning echo back at him, from long long away.

It pulled him up short. He listened again. Strained to listen. And just as he was giving up, there, there it was again—the same moaning noise, a cry in the distance. As if the ice itself was mocking him. It made him quite angry. It made him want to shout out and tell it not to be so rude. And he listened to the noise harder, and he realised it wasn't a moan. It was a howl.

He scanned the horizon once more, on all sides. He lowered his head away from that dark ribbon of night. And, out there—a black dot. He'd have thought it was nothing, just a speck, a trick of the eyes—but as he tried to focus upon that speck, Simon could see that it was moving.

He didn't know how long he watched that speck. For a while he couldn't tell whether it was getting any closer, but it was definitely in motion—if Simon kept his head straight, really straight, and didn't move a muscle, he could see it quiver. And after an hour or so, maybe much more, the speck no longer seemed to be part of the horizon, but a chunk broken off from it and running free. And the howling was getting louder.

By the time Simon could see that it was indeed a wolf it was quite clear that the wolf had already seen *him*, and long ago, and that it was making straight for the bed, and it wouldn't stop until it reached him. And Simon thought about making a run for it, he really did—maybe the other side the ice would be stronger, maybe the ice wouldn't burn. He'd long since stopped crying. But he still hid under the covers.

When he dared to check, he saw that the wolf had stopped, no more than ten feet away from him.

Simon thought he had seen a wolf before. At a zoo, surely? He'd thought they were like pet dogs. This wolf was nothing like a pet dog. Maybe it was surprised to see him, all this sudden concentration of flesh and blood right in the middle of nowhere. It was tilting its head to one side in what looked like intellectual contemplation of the matter. Then it grinned, and just for a moment the grin looked welcoming—but the grin just kept growing, it got wider and wider. Drool leaked from the mouth. When it hit the ice it sizzled.

"Go away!" said Simon. Thinking that if he sounded angry enough, it might be convincing. "There's nothing for you here!" But that wasn't strictly true, was it?

The wolf began to circle the bed. With every lap it took, it seemed to Simon that it was closing in. It was unhurried, nonchalant even. A wolf of sophistication, making plans.

And Simon kept shouting at it, and swiping ineffectually at it with his arm. At one point the wolf stopped, and seemed to look over its shoulder, in deadpan to an invisible audience— what does this guy think he's doing? Simon would have laughed if he hadn't been about to die.

At length the wolf settled down on its haunches and watched him.

Simon watched it back. He thought that if the wolf broke eye contact it might give up. Or rather—he thought that if *he* broke eye contact, the wolf would leap up at him and bite open his throat. He wouldn't blink first. He mustn't blink.

God knows how long this went on. And in the distance Simon heard more howling, and his heart sank, but he didn't dare turn round to look.

The wolf closed its eyes. For a moment Simon thought that maybe it had died, maybe he'd stared it to death. Could you stare a wolf to death? But the wolf's body stirred in sleep. Its fur looked so thick and warm and cosy. Pretty soon the wolf started to snore.

This would have been a chance to escape, if Simon had had somewhere to escape to.

The wolf squirmed deliciously, it was dreaming. And though Simon didn't want to take his eyes off it, he found that they were getting impossibly heavy. And he was dreaming too.

3

WHEN HE WOKE up he was back in his bedroom, but his pillow was wet with tears, and his foot still ached from the burning cold.

He decided not to sleep in his bed the next night. Instead he lay down on the sofa and watched television. It was uncomfortable, he didn't fit on the sofa properly, and the quality of the television programmes was, frankly, poor.

On the third night he went back to the bedroom. But this time he'd come prepared. He put a sharp knife under the pillow. At the bottom of the bed, wrapped up in a plastic shopping bag, he placed a pound of raw meat. If he couldn't fight the wolf, then maybe he could distract it.

He wasn't sure if he slept that night or not, but if he did, the sleep was dreamless, and there was no return to the ice world.

One evening he called the Samaritans. The man on the end of the phone sounded smooth and professionally concerned. "How can I help you?" he asked.

Simon was quite rude to him. "You've got the wrong name."

"I haven't told you my name."

"The Samaritans. The whole point of the Samaritans was that they were uncaring shits. That's why they talk of the *good* Samaritan, the one who stood out from the crowd, because the rest were so bad. Do you see? Like a good Nazi. Or a good member of the Taliban. Just calling yourselves the Samaritans, it's stupid. You might as well call yourselves Nazis."

The Samaritan said, very gently, "Is there something else you'd really rather be talking about?"

"No, there bloody isn't," said Simon, and hung up.

A few more days, and he took the raw meat away from the bed. It was beginning to stink. The day after that, he took away the knife as well.

A month to the day after Cathy had killed herself, Simon went back to work.

Everyone seemed so pleased to see him. And so sorry for his loss. Lots of brave smiles shot at him from the cubicles of the open plan office, one or two people gave him a thumbs up—good for you, we're thinking of you, buddy. A couple of the women hugged him, and that was nice, but the hugs weren't very tight, and were taken back pretty quickly, as if maybe Simon had some infectious disease, as if by touching him too close their loved ones too might start topping themselves. "Hey hey," said the boss, open arms but not quite offering a hug, the arms being opened was gesture enough, "it's good to have you back!" There was lots of paperwork piled up on Simon's desk; "Don't worry, we've taken care of all the urgent stuff. Just to get you back in the saddle, okay?" Simon looked at the paperwork. Some of it needed filing. He filed some of it. He began to cry. He filed some more paperwork, he cried a bit more, he went to lunch. When he came back from lunch he sorted some more paperwork for filing, cried, and the boss asked if he could see him. "It's too soon, isn't it?" said the boss. He looked so sympathetic. And only the smallest bit impatient. "How about you try again when you feel better? Why not take another week? Another week won't kill us." Simon thanked him. He left. He did it without fanfare. No one noticed. No one looked up from their cubicles and waved goodbye.

He phoned the Samaritans again. He apologised for being rude last time, but he'd got a different Samaritan, or the same Samaritan didn't remember, or the same Samaritan didn't care. Simon told the Samaritan he was depressed. The Samaritan asked for his name, and Simon gave him one.

"It seems to me that you loved Cathy very much," said the Samaritan at last. "And maybe there's no explanation for why she left you. Maybe you can never know. But you sound like a kind man. And you sound like an honest man. I can tell you've been straight with me, and that's so brave, you're open and sincere, and I'm sure you were to Cathy too. You're a good person, Ben. Ben, you'll be okay."

Simon thanked him.

"And just remember this important truth," said the Samaritan. "The flames of Hell don't burn."

"I'm sorry?" said Simon. "What was that?"

"You heard," said the Samaritan, and the line went dead.

That night, when Simon went to bed, he took the knife with him, and put it back under his pillow.

4

HE WAS BACK, just as he knew he would be. The moon above, the ice below, the darkness all around. The wolf was there too. It got up from its haunches, stretched, heaving itself to attention, the holiday was over and it was time to get back to work. Simon wondered whether the wolf had been waiting for him all this time. He supposed it had. He almost felt sorry for it.

The wolf padded across the ice towards him. Closer than it had ever come before.

"Go back!" said Simon. And when that didn't work, "Stay!"

The wolf leered.

Simon fished underneath the pillow. He grabbed the knife. He should have brought a carving knife, but he'd worried he might cut himself accidentally whilst sleeping—this ordinary dinner knife looked pathetic. He gripped it hard by the hilt, waved it in the wolf's direction. "Stay," he said. "I *will* hurt you." The knife caught the glow from the moon, it twinkled bluntly.

And incredibly, the wolf seemed deterred by all this. Or maybe it was just confused? Either way, it backed off a few steps, and that was good. It lowered its head, as if ashamed. But then—then, the body tensed, the wolf gave a growl, and all too late Simon realised what it was doing, it was preparing to attack—head still low, but now the legs rising, and now sprinting across the ice, the growl a shriek, and the wolf was in the air leaping straight for Simon.

For the *knife*—Simon saw the open mouth coming towards him, he stabbed clumsily at the air—but the wolf didn't want him, it wanted the *knife*. Simon felt the wolf's jaws snap as teeth bit into the blade, felt the full weight of the beast as it flew over him with inches to spare. The wolf was so close and then it was gone. It had stolen the knife from out of Simon's hand and now it was making its getaway, its back feet didn't even touch the bed as it jumped clean over it and landed nimbly on the other side of the ice.

Simon felt a damp on his neck, and wondered what it was, and thought it might be blood, that the wolf had bitten him after all, that he was going to die—but it wasn't blood, his fingers came back from the wetness clean—it was drool, he'd been splashed by the stream of flying drool.

He stared at the wolf, and the wolf, shamelessly, stared right back. Simon's knife still clamped tight between its teeth. It was panting, maybe with the effort of the leap, maybe as some mocking triumph.

The wolf gave a warning growl.

Simon thought it would drop the knife then. The wolf shook its head, fast, from side to side—too fast, and for too long, it seemed the wolf's head blurred with it. And then the knife was out of the mouth, and into the air. Not dropped, but thrown—high up, it looked as if it might hit the moon.

And the wolf got onto its hind legs. It raised up its body tall. It looked like a performing seal. Sat beneath the knife. Opened its mouth as wide as it could go.

The knife arced, it didn't reach the moon, it seemed to hang in the air with disappointment at that. Then it fell, fast, blade down.

The wolf caught the knife in its open mouth. It was like a circus trick. Simon got a ridiculous urge to clap. The knife dropped from sight, straight down the wolf's throat. A circus trick gone wrong.

Still on its hind legs, the wolf looked at Simon then. It grinned. From the peculiar angle of its head, the grin looked especially cheesy. And then, as Simon watched, it seemed that a dark shadow had fallen upon the wolf's stomach, and the shadow *grew*, it spread fast and thick and liquid, it spread right up to the throat.

And then—like a wet bag, the stomach split open. Guts splashed out onto the ice.

The wolf gave a little hiss that sounded like laughter, but couldn't have been, it was a death rattle that didn't work, it was hard to do a death rattle when a knife's cut through your insides. It seemed to wink at Simon, first one eye, then the other—and then the eyes stayed shut, and the wolf stopped hissing at last. It pitched forward, heavy, wet, and quite dead.

Was it deliberate? Had the wolf known what it was doing? Had it killed itself just to spite him? Simon turned, leaned gently over the side of the bed, and threw up.

He lay beneath the sheets, shivering, trying to keep warm, with the wolf carcass on the ground beside him. The blood leaked out until there was no more blood to leak. On the hot ice it began to bubble; when the bubbles burst they made funny little popping sounds.

It wasn't long before Simon could smell the meat. Some of the fur had burned away, Simon saw where the wolf's skin was turning crispy brown. His stomach gnawed. He remembered how the wolf had drooled. He was drooling too.

Simon didn't eat the wolf. He turned his head away, refused to look at it, stared out into the wilderness, tried to block out the smell of roast dinner cooking so close by. He ignored the way the head seemed to loll towards him so genially, as if inviting him to tuck in—the dead mouth fixed into a generous smile. He didn't eat the wolf, because he didn't dare to. He didn't dare reach across to take the food in case he fell off the bed, or in case he made the ice crack, or in case (in case!) the wolf even now was faking it, in case, in case, in case. He felt hungry. He felt ashamed he was a coward. He felt lonely, and wanted company, and wished that the wolf were still alive.

Soon the fur had all burned away. The meat lay on the ice, such a waste—good grub, and no one had wanted it. Burned black now, too tough to eat, and shrunken dry with all the juice boiled out of it. Simon found himself looking at the remains for a long time. Those few spoiled hunks of flesh, some bone. Is this what death was, really? Is this all that it amounted to? How could these fragments of limbs and this blackened fat ever have been part of something that lived and hunted and fed? It was ridiculous to think of. It made no sense.

And in time even these last stubborn pieces of dead wolf were absorbed by the ice. Just the knife was left, and it looked new and clean.

Simon slept.

5

HE ARRIVED AT the house punctually, as always, and yet when the front door was opened Arthur affected a look of delighted surprise to see him there.

"Simon! Hello, hello. Please come in."

"Thanks," said Simon.

"Are those flowers for us? How kind. Sarah! Sarah, Simon's here."

Sarah called out, "Hello, Simon."

"Why don't you come in? Please. So. How are you?"

"I'm doing okay, thanks."

"That's good."

"I'm not sleeping well, though."

"No. Sarah! Sarah, Simon's brought us flowers! Again. Do we have a vase?"

"I've got a vase," called Sarah.

"How are you, Arthur?" asked Simon.

"Oh, I'm all right. Come on through! Life goes on, doesn't it? Come on through."

"You'll love my parents," Cathy had said to Simon, and it was so early on, wasn't it, it was on the second date? The second date, and already she was wanting him to meet the family, it almost put him off his starter. "And they'll love you too, I know." Cathy had told him that she went to see her Mum and Dad every Sunday afternoon, without fail, and Mum would cook a roast, and Dad would pour glasses of sherry and make lots of bad jokes. It didn't matter that she'd left home nearly fifteen years ago, that she'd been married once (it hadn't worked), that to all intents and purposes she was now unavoidably classed as a grown woman. Those Sundays were still sacrosanct. And that was so alien to Simon, that a family *could* be that close; he saw his parents only at Christmas for a mutual exchange of indifferent presents, and the encounter was fleeting, and the atmosphere was strained. He envied the way that when Cathy took him for that first Sunday roast she was able to fling her arms around her mother without embarrassment, that she talked to her father like they were both proper adults. He envied it, but was charmed as well.

At the funeral he'd sat with her parents, of course. Sarah held Simon's hand throughout the service, squeezing it hard from time to time. And Arthur gave him a hug afterwards, still in the chapel, still in front of all the world, and wept without shame. "You will keep coming for Sunday lunch?" he asked. And Sarah, taking his hand again, was nodding fiercely. "It would mean so much to us," said Arthur. "And we can get through this together."

Arthur was a burly broad-shouldered man. He didn't look anything like Cathy. Sarah was slight and had Cathy's hair, and sometimes Cathy's expression if she were amused or puzzled, but Sarah wore glasses and the wrong kind of lipstick, and Simon thought her face looked crooked.

"Sherry?" asked Arthur, and Simon said yes, though he didn't much like sherry. "The weather's getting better," said Arthur. "I think next weekend I might be able to get out into the garden." Simon said that would be nice.

Sarah appeared, with Cathy's hair and the crooked face all her own. "Hello, Simon," she said. She hugged him briefly.

"Simon's brought us flowers," said Arthur, again.

"So I can see," said Sarah. "Thank you, Simon. Dinner's nearly ready." And she was gone.

"I'm sorry about Sarah," said Arthur. "She's a bit sad today."

"Yes," said Simon, though he hadn't seen a difference.

"It's Sally's birthday. You know." Sally was Cathy's older sister, Simon had only met her twice, and one of those times had been at the funeral.

"Is Sally all right?" asked Simon.

"Oh yes. Yes. But you know. Anniversaries. Gets the brain thinking. Any excuse. Top up?"

They took their replenished glasses into the dining room. Sarah brought out the food.

"This smells nice," said Arthur. "Doesn't it, Simon?" Simon agreed that it did.

"I hope so," said Sarah. "It's a different sort of lamb this week. I was in the supermarket, there was a different sort on offer, and there was a label saying, try it and see, so I thought we would. It comes with herbs on it."

"It smells great," said Arthur.

The lamb was very good, the herbs made all the difference. The carrots and peas were fresh and tasty, the mashed potato had fluffed up well. The gravy was a bit bland. "Mmm," said Simon, and as he bit into the lamb he thought of the dead wolf and it made it all taste better somehow. Arthur winked and nodded approvingly at him, and Sarah gave some trace of a smile.

"I might get into the garden next week," Arthur told his wife. "In the summer we can have a barbecue."

"It's Sally's birthday today," said Sarah. "Maybe she'll phone."

Arthur asked Simon whether he'd gone back to work yet, and Simon said he was toying with it, but he wasn't sleeping well, he shouldn't work until he was sleeping maybe. And Arthur said that it was good to work.

"Well, I thought that lamb was the best lamb ever," said Arthur.

"You say that every week," said Sarah.

"That's because," said Arthur, and he took her hand, "every week you just get better and better at cooking it." Sarah took her hand away.

"Please stop bringing flowers," said Sarah. She wasn't even looking at Simon, she was still looking at her husband.

"I'm sorry, what?" said Simon.

"Please stop. We don't need them. We have lots of flowers."

"Oh, I don't mind," said Simon. "But I'll stop. You know. If you want me to."

"I do," said Sarah.

She got up to clear the plates. Simon stood up to help her, but Arthur smiled and shook his head, and Simon sat right back down again. Sarah stacked all the plates on top of one another, one, two, three, pressing them together so the remains of dead lamb were squashed between them. She made her way towards the kitchen, the stopped, and turned. She said, "And she didn't say anything? She didn't give any explanation?"

"Sarah," said Arthur.

"No," said Simon. "I'm sorry."

"She didn't say a word? Give a hint?"

"No."

"You must have done something to her," said Sarah.

"Sarah," said Arthur, again.

"No. You must have done something. You can tell us. It's all right. You can say."

"Sarah," said Arthur. "Simon's a son to us."

"He's not our son," said Sarah. "You're not our son, are you, Simon?"

"No," said Simon.

"You agree you're not our son?"

"Yes," said Simon.

"If someone had to die," said Sarah. "And I'm not saying someone had to die. But if someone had to, why did it have to be Cathy? Why not you?"

She took out the plates.

"I'm sorry," said Arthur.

"No, no," said Simon.

"She's upset," said Arthur.

"It's all right," said Simon.

"Though she does have a point," said Arthur.

Simon said nothing.

"Six weeks you've been coming here," said Arthur. "Since Cathy went. Six weeks, and I'm not saying I thought it'd get better fast, but it's still a long time. And you never say anything. You never offer any reason for what she did."

"Maybe there wasn't a reason," said Simon.

"Bullshit," said Arthur, placidly enough. "Sarah's right. You must have done something. Or said something. Or, I don't know, not said something. So that Cathy was here and now she's not."

"Yes," said Simon.

"Sarah went to church last week," said Arthur. "Some woman told her that suicides go to Hell. That Cathy is now in Hell."

"God," said Simon.

"She said she was sorry about it, she wasn't being nasty. But facts are facts."

"God," said Simon. "That's horrible. I'm sorry."

Arthur shrugged. "If Sarah wants to go to church, why not? Why not? If it gives her some closure. Christ knows, I'm still looking for mine. And don't bring us flowers. For Christ's sake. The flowers keep dying. Why do we want to deal with all your dead flowers? Think a little."

"I can't sleep properly," said Simon. "All I do. Is try to work it out. Work out what happened. What I should have done. I think I'm making myself ill. I think I might be very ill, really."

Arthur smiled then, and it wasn't a cruel smile, it seemed

forgiving and true. He waved Simon closer. Simon leaned forward.

"The flames of Hell don't burn," said Arthur.

"What?"

"The flames of Hell don't burn," he said. "They *freeze*."

He sat back in his chair, the smile never left his face.

"I should go," said Simon. He got up.

And at that moment Sarah came back. Her face was wet. She had been crying, she seemed to have stopped for a while. "Simon," she said meekly. "Oh, Simon." And she put her arms around him. "Simon, I'm sorry."

Simon put his arms around her too, felt her crooked face bore into his shoulder. "I won't bring any more flowers."

"Oh, bring as many flowers as you like!" she said. "Really. Putting them in vases, taking them out of vases when they die, it's something constructive, isn't it?"

"You won't stop coming, will you, Simon?" Arthur was still smiling, but the smile looked pinched now. "We still want you here. You're the only part of Cathy we have left. We need you. We need you. Please. We need you. Please."

Simon said of course he'd continue to come. He enjoyed seeing them. He enjoyed his Sundays. Arthur and Sarah were family to him.

"And in the summer," said Arthur. "In the summer, we can have a barbecue."

6

AND ONE NIGHT, Cathy got into bed beside him. It was too dark for him to see her, and he wanted to turn on the light, but he knew that if he did she would go away. And he knew one day he'd have to let her go, but not just yet, not now. He recognised the shape of her body. He smelled her hair, and it was nothing like the fabric conditioner.

She whispered to him. "I'm cold."

"Yes."

"Can I cuddle up? You make me warm."

"Yes," he said. She tucked her feet against the back of his thighs, she craned into his back, her head was at his neck. She was freezing. He winced at it.

"Cathy," he said. "Cathy."

But she didn't say anything else. He couldn't tell if she were sulking, or if she'd fallen asleep. He thought she was asleep. Although her body wasn't moving at all, he couldn't feel her breathing in and out, he'd always liked that, he'd regulate his breaths so that they matched hers, that had always made him drowsy. "Cathy," he said, a little louder, as loud as he dared, because he didn't want to disturb her after all, he didn't want her to answer him. She wasn't getting any warmer. The skin felt hard, like ice, and now the ice had taken hold of his body, it was slowly stealing over him and where it reached he felt numb. He tried to wriggle free, but Cathy held him too close, or maybe they'd been frozen together, maybe they'd be together forever now and those fingers digging into his chest were really icicles— Oh God. Even her breath was freezing, a blast of cold air at his neck that never eased, was it even breath? Because where was the in and out he'd liked, there was no in or out to it, and it was roaring now like the wind. "Cathy," he said, one last time, but it was too quiet, she'd never have heard him over the storm. And he wished Cathy wasn't there, he wished Cathy were gone. He'd rather take his chances with the wolves.

He closed his eyes tight.

When he opened them, he was back upon the ice. The moon hung so low that Simon instinctively ducked so he wouldn't scrape his head on it. A dozen wolves sat in a circle around his bed. They whimpered to each other in the cold, and they licked their chops.

Simon felt happy to be there.

And then the circle was broken, the wolves parted to make way for their mother. Simon didn't understand where she could have come from so suddenly, why he didn't see her approach.

She was beautiful. Her fur was long and black. She was the size of a lion. Simon heard each paw thud hard against the ice as she walked towards him, and the ice wouldn't crack.

If Simon was to be killed by a wolf, then let it be by this one. It was only right. And with the other wolves watching, he wouldn't even die alone. There was something to that, it was right and it was good. Simon gazed into the she-wolf's eyes, and they were yellow and green and blue and more colours besides.

One of the little wolves growled. At Simon or the she-wolf, who could say? Maybe it just wanted attention. Its mother swiftly picked it up in its jaws and lifted it clean off the ground. The wolf looked so startled, it was really very funny. It looked proud too, it was getting all that attention it had asked for! Mummy bit down hard, Simon heard the crack. The head didn't come quite off, it listed brokenly to the side. And then gently, so gently, the mother lowered her dead child to the ice, she opened her mouth, out it tumbled, she let it free. She nosed it tenderly, and then lifted her head and didn't ever look at it again.

The other wolves seemed to learn from that, and backed off.

The she-wolf padded over to the bed, as lightly as its bulk would allow. Simon felt his chest heave in fear, but he would not shut his eyes, he would never again flinch. Her breath against his face was so very warm.

He reached out and stroked her. In turn, she put her head down on to the bed. He put his arms around her neck. She let him. He knew that at any moment she would bite, but until then it just felt good to be holding on to someone again, and it felt good to be warm. The fur was rough against his skin, but that didn't matter, it didn't scratch him, it tickled.

Simon and the she-wolf stayed close for a long time. He didn't want to let go. Didn't move a muscle, didn't give her any sign he wanted the intimacy to be broken.

And, at last, she was the one who pulled away. Because they're always the ones who pull away first, aren't they? But she didn't run, she waited for him patiently.

He tore the sheets into strips, knotted them together to make them strong. He tied one end of the rope to the brass headboard Cathy had liked so much. With the other end he made a noose, and put it around the she-wolf's thick neck.

The she-wolf got into position at the front of the bed. She strained hard. Soon, but very slowly, the bed began to move. She was encouraged by this. She pulled harder, stronger. She lurched into a trot, dragging the sleigh behind her.

Simon laughed. The other wolves howled, he thought they were laughing too.

And on she ran, picking up speed now, the giant wolf taking him across the ice. And the wolf pack was running by their side, sometimes sliding over in the excitement, trying to keep up.

On toward the unchanging horizon.

1

SOMETIMES THE JOURNEY would make Simon drowsy. And he'd fight it as hard as he could, because he didn't want to go back to those pointless dreams. Of days spent being bored at home, eating food, watching television, feeling sad. But the bed sleigh was so soft and comfortable, and he was warm too, he could stretch out his hands and bury them within the coat of the she-wolf. He didn't want to sleep, but he knew it was all right, the dreams weren't pleasant but sooner or later he'd wake from them and he'd be back with his friends on the ice where he was happy.

The wolves still ran by the bedside to keep him company. He'd got to know them. He'd given them all names. He hadn't called a single one of them Cathy, and that made him feel a little proud of himself.

Once in a while the she-wolf would come to a stop. She may have been running for days without a break. She was exhausted. And Simon would tell her it was all right, she could rest. Or even stop for good, if she wanted—after all, where did she think she was taking them? Living on this patch of ice would be as good as any other, this may be the best bit of ice in the whole world. The she-wolf seemed to understand, or maybe she didn't, maybe that was wishful thinking. She refused to give up. She just needed a break, and something to eat. She would scoop up one of the wolves in her mouth, she'd bite it open. She would share the food with Simon, and Simon wasn't always very hungry, but he didn't want to seem impolite. He would cook his wolf meat on the burning ice until it was good and tasty. The she-wolf would eat her supper raw.

In his dreams he would still visit Arthur and Sarah, and sometimes he thought his visits made them happy. Sometimes he even made them laugh. He could be good company in dreams, he discovered. He could be strong.

He went back to work, just to give himself something to do whilst he waited to wake up.

And one day, and this was months later, there were no more wolves left to eat. The she-wolf was spent. She couldn't go on. Simon listened to her breath, and it sounded old and raddled. Her fur was threadbare.

"No further," he said to her. "We'll stop now. Promise me we'll stop."

The wolf fixed those eyes upon his, and there wasn't much colour left to them now. She lowered her head. A nod? Or a gesture of defeat. She allowed him to take off the leash. He hugged her for a long while.

And then, when she had had enough, or just couldn't bear the parting any longer, she moved her head from his. She bared her teeth. She growled. One last act of ferocity. And she bit down, savagely, she tore through skin and she shattered bone. Out came the blood, her own blood, she had bitten into her own flank—and from the gash she pulled out gobbets of meat, she dragged them onto the ice where they sizzled and cooked.

Simon wished she hadn't done that.

He ate her. And what he couldn't eat, he pulled up onto the bed and wrapped under the sheets so they had been given some sort of burial.

He used her sharp teeth to cut out two large patches of fur. He put his feet within them. He got down on to the ice, and he didn't burn. He left the bed, and he walked onwards.

He didn't have much further to go.

8

AND, JUST AS the ribbon of dark seemed at its densest, as the moon was as low as it had ever been. There, Simon thought the ice seemed clearer than before.

He peered down and it was like looking into a mirror.

He was so old. His chin was a forest of bristles, grey and set in, he'd never be able to shave them off now. His cheeks sagged. In his eyes he saw something flinty and hard he'd never noticed before. He supposed it ought to have made him feel ashamed, he'd got so old. But it didn't. He was glad, that in spite of everything, he hadn't given up yet, he'd kept going. That old grizzled face was the evidence of it.

He remembered how he'd once stared into his bathroom mirror and made himself cry. He hadn't needed to do that for a long time, tears came so much more easily these days. But he decided to try it again, even if only for old time's sake. He stared hard so that his eyes were bulging. He furrowed his brow. He thought of Cathy.

And there, just beneath his old tired reflection, he saw her.

Of course, he didn't believe it was really her. Not at first. She was too perfect, too much the image he'd always kept in his head. The face gazing up at him, and so *light* somehow, like it was full of soft air—that smile she'd had, that favourite smile, the one which showed the tip of her tongue. The eyes.

No, she was there, she was there, under the ice.

He stared at the face, but it didn't move. It couldn't move, it was frozen stiff. (It was dead.) She was dead, and that smile wasn't going to get any wider, that tongue was going to remain an unfulfilled promise, it wasn't coming out to play. Frozen still, like the photographs he had at home, the ones he swore he'd throw out but somehow never did.

And Simon thought to look about him. And he realised Cathy wasn't alone.

Beneath the ice there were more faces, bobbing to the top like apples. And the faces had heads, and the heads had bodies—he could see now the limbs splayed out, arms bent upwards as if trying to break to the surface. All caught in thick sheets of jagged ice so livid they looked like flame. He had been walking across the ice all this time, the dead only inches below his feet, and he hadn't even thought to look. Bodies stacked on bodies stacked on bodies, bodies all the way down.

He looked back to Cathy. "I'm so sorry," he said. And Cathy blinked.

He stomped hard upon the ice then. It wouldn't break. He jumped up and down with as much force as he could muster, trying to be the heaviest he had ever been, willing every single ounce of him to be focused upon the spot where his foot hit the surface. He shouted loudly at it, and when that did no good, he swore at it too, he told the ice what he thought of it, that it was a cruel fucker. He got down on his knees. He pounded at the ice with his fists, he tore at it with his fingernails. The hands burned, and he wasn't sure he could stand the pain, but soon he stopped caring, on he pounded. Open up, you bastard. Give me her back.

He did this in love. And love is terrible, and makes the heart hurt like Hell itself. But it can also do extraordinary things.

Simon broke through the ice. He grasped at Cathy, but she was too slippery, or Hell was too strong. He put his head under the water. He put his whole body in. He pulled her free.

He dragged his little lady up to the surface, and there on the ice he stretched her out, and he lay there panting, and she didn't pant because she was dead. Or because she was frozen, or because she didn't want to, what did he know what she wanted? Had he ever known, really? She did nothing but blink at him, and at last he cradled her on his lap, and she was so very, very cold.

"Why did you do it?" he asked her. "Didn't you love me? I thought you loved me. Didn't I love you, wasn't it enough?" He held her and he cried.

She tried to move her mouth. The face splintered with the effort. Hairline fractures ran from her lips down her body. Water began to leak from the cracks. He felt her start to break open. He saw how much pain even attempting to talk caused her.

"No," he said. "No. Don't speak. I don't need to know."

He kissed her on that shattered mouth then, and her lips seemed to press hard against his in turn. And the cold ran down his throat, as refreshing as an iced drink on a hot summer's day.

"I'll never love anyone the way I've loved you," he told her, and even as he said it he wasn't sure it was true. So he held her tight, he wrapped himself around her, one arm over, one arm under.

It took her several hours to melt away. He stayed with her right to the end.

9

AND THEN HE woke up—or fell asleep, he could no longer tell the difference. And in that dream, or waking state, he was in a lot of pain, and it took him a while to realise, and at last he went to the hospital.

And later that night, when he fell asleep—or woke up, whichever—he went to some place entirely new.

His blistered hands mended, in time they even got some feeling back.

10

AND THINGS GOT better after that. Things got worse before they got better, as things have a way of doing. But, in the end, things improved.

But there was one night that was terrible, and Simon was overcome with such a tremendous sense of pointlessness that it seemed like a weight pressing down upon his chest. He could feel it, his chest hurting with it, he could feel his heart thumping away just below the surface. He went to the bedroom window. He opened it. It was a cold night, the blast of chill seemed welcoming somehow, he'd forgotten how comforting the cold could be. He would crawl out of the window. That would take care of it. He could crawl out of the window, and he could let himself fall, he could go headfirst if he really wanted to be sure. And he didn't do it. And it wasn't because he was stayed by any powerful force—no hand of God from on high, no wolves, Cathy didn't come back and urge him to live. No one was there to help—just as, he supposed, at the moment she'd needed it, no one had helped Cathy. But he understood suddenly that to kill himself would be the work of a moment, how quick it would be, a single decision taken in an instant. And that no one should be defined by a moment, not even a terminal one. Simon had his moment then, just as Cathy had had hers—they chose differently, that was the only thing between them, and it was all right, it was really all all right. He stayed by the window for a long while, enjoying the cold, enjoying the possibility that the cold might still be the last thing he'd feel. And at last he yawned, and got back into bed, and went to sleep, and he never seriously considered taking his life ever again.

He still went to visit Arthur and Sarah on Sundays. But not every week, maybe one week in three. He didn't take them flowers. He sometimes took wine.

One Sunday Arthur sat him down before the lamb roast and told him he had some news. Arthur had cancer, and he wasn't going to fight it. It was okay. He accepted it. " I'm not prepared to struggle," he said. He told Sarah and Simon that he loved them both, and that his only sadness was leaving them behind, and Sarah cried a little, and Simon mostly just felt proud he'd been included.

Again, Simon sat with Sarah during the funeral. She squeezed his hand during all the difficult bits.

She said to him afterwards, "I like to think that Arthur is with Cathy now. Is that silly?"

"No," said Simon. "It isn't silly."

"But what if they've gone to different places? I don't know. I can't help but think. Arthur died naturally, but Cathy..."

"I have no idea where Cathy is now," said Simon. "But I can promise you, she isn't in Hell."

Sarah kissed him. Simon asked whether she would like him to come and see her next Sunday, and Sarah said she didn't think she would. Not now, not any more. But she smiled and she kissed him again. And then they went their separate ways.

He only went back to the ice the once. And it was years later, and only for a little while. He didn't think he was even fully asleep, he was just dozing.

Simon hadn't even thought about the ice for such a long time. He'd met Debbie, and things were good with Debbie. She didn't do any of the Cathy things he had once loved, but that was fine, because in retrospect Cathy hadn't been good at any of the Debbie things either. Debbie laughed a lot more than Cathy did, and she made the cutest face when she was tired, and when she got excited her feet wouldn't stop tapping.

Debbie wasn't there that night. She'd gone to visit her mother. And Simon quite enjoyed having all the bed to himself again, but missed Debbie all the same, and cuddled the pillow.

The cold of the ice was a shock, as was its brightness. But it wasn't unpleasant. Simon breathed in the air, and he liked the way it felt so fresh, and he liked the puff of steam he was able to blow out.

Ice as far as he could see, but wasn't that something? That the ice was never ending, that it just went on forever, that nothing got in its way. You had to admire something that just refused to give up.

He threw off the sheets. Yes, it was cold, but he'd get used to it. You could get used to anything, given time and patience. The moon was close above him. He stood on the mattress. He wobbled a bit on the bedsprings, but he steadied. On his tiptoes, he stretched his arms as high as they could reach. And he touched the moon. His fingers caked with soft crumbly moon dust.

He knew he was saying goodbye to the ice world. And he was all right with that. Because to get to say goodbye at all, that is a privilege.

He couldn't see anything on the horizon, there were no black specks dancing about in the far distance. But he heard the howling, from so far away, the sound carried across the silence. Simon smiled, he threw back his head. He took a deep breath. And he howled too, as loud as he could, and hoped the wolves could hear him.

ABOUT THE AUTHORS

Tony Ballantyne (www.tonyballantyne.com) is the author of the *Penrose* and *Recursion* series of novels as well as many acclaimed short stories that have appeared in magazines and anthologies around the world. He has been nominated for the BSFA and Philip K Dick awards. The idea for 'Dream London Hospital' sprang from his latest novel, *Dream London*, which was described by the Financial Times "...as strange and unclassifiable a novel as it's possible to imagine, and a marvellous achievement." He is currently working on the follow up, *Dream Paris*, due to be published in September 2015.

James Bradley (cityoftongues.com) is a novelist and critic. His books include three novels, *Wrack*, *The Deep Field* and *The Resurrectionist*, anthology *The Penguin Book of the Ocean* and most recently the novelette, 'Beauty's Sister'. His fiction has been shortlisted for or won a wide range of literary awards, including the Miles Franklin Award, the Christina Stead Award for Fiction, The Age Book of the Year and the Aurealis Awards for Best Novel and Best Science Fiction Short Story. In 2012 he won the Pascall Award for Australia's Critic of the Year. His new novel, *Clade*, will be published in 2014. He lives in Sydney, Australia and blogs at cityoftongues.com.

Isobelle Carmody (www.isobellecarmody.net) is the award winning author of over thirty books and many short stories. She has just returned from living more than a decade in Europe to do her PhD at the University of Queensland in Brisbane. 'Grigori's Solution' is the first of a collection of stories she is working on, called *The Beach at the End of the World*.

Frances Hardinge (www.franceshardinge.com) was brought up in a sequence of small, sinister English villages, and spent a number of formative years living in a Gothic-looking, mouse-infested hilltop house in Kent. She studied English Language and Literature at Oxford, fell in love with the city's crazed archaic beauty, and lived there for many years. Whilst working full time as a technical author for a software company she started writing her first children's novel, *Fly by Night*, and was, with difficulty, persuaded by a good friend to submit the manuscript to a publisher. *Fly by Night* went on to win the Branford Boase Award, and was also shortlisted for the Guardian Children's Fiction Award. Her subsequent books, *Verdigris Deep*, *Gullstruck Island*, *Twilight Robbery*, *A Face Like Glass* and *Cuckoo's Song* are also aimed at children and young adults. Frances is seldom seen without her hat and is addicted to volcanoes.

Over the past thirty years, **Nina Kiriki Hoffman** (ofearna.us/books/hoffman.html) has sold adult and YA novels and more than 250 short stories. Her works have been finalists for the World Fantasy, Mythopoeic, Sturgeon, Philip K. Dick, and Endeavour awards. Her fiction has won her a Stoker and a Nebula Award. A collection of short stories, *Permeable Borders*, was published in 2012 by Fairwood Press and a new young adult novel is due from Viking in 2015. Nina does production work for the *Magazine of Fantasy & Science Fiction*. She teaches writing through Lane Community College and lives in Eugene, Oregon.

Ellen Klages (www.ellenklages.com) is the author of two acclaimed YA novels: *The Green Glass Sea*, which won the Scott O'Dell Award, the New Mexico Book Award, and the Lopez Award; and *White Sands, Red Menace*, which won the California and New Mexico Book Awards. Her short stories, which have been collected in World Fantasy Award nominated collection *Portable Childhoods*, have been have been translated into Czech, French, German, Hungarian, Japanese, and Swedish and have been nominated for the Nebula, Hugo, World Fantasy, and Campbell awards. Her story, 'Basement Magic,' won a Nebula in 2005. She lives in San Francisco, in a small house full of strange and wondrous things.

Garth Nix (www.garthnix.com) grew up in Canberra, Australia. When he turned nineteen, he left to drive around the United Kingdom in a beat-up Austin with a boot full of books and a Silver-Reed typewriter. Despite a wheel literally falling off the car, he survived to return to Australia and study at the University of Canberra. He has since worked in a bookshop, as a book publicist, a publisher's sales representative, an editor, as a literary agent, and as a public relations and marketing consultant. His first story was published in 1984 and was followed by novels *The Ragwitch*, *Sabriel*, *Shade's Children*, *Lirael*, *Abhorsen*, the six-book YA fantasy series "The Seventh Tower," the seven-book "The Keys to the Kingdom" series, *A Confusion of Princes* and, most recently, the Troubletwisters series (co-written with Sean Williams). A new novel set in the Old Kingdom, *Clariel*, is due out in 2014. He lives in Sydney with his wife and their two children.

K J Parker (www.kjparker.net), who lives quietly in exile in the south-west of England, has written three trilogies, four standalone novels, four novellas (two of which won the World Fantasy Award, a fact of which Parker is shamefully, embarrassingly proud) and a small hatful of short stories; all of which (as they say on Broadway) everybody loved except the public. When not writing, Parker does strenuous things in the woods. K J Parker is a pseudonym designed to conceal the true identity of someone nobody's ever heard of.

Justina Robson (justinarobson.blogspot.com) was born in Yorkshire, England in 1968. After completing school she dropped out of Art College, then studied Philosophy and Linguistics at York University. She sold her first novel, *Silver Screen*, in 1999. Since then she has won the 2000 Amazon. co.uk Writers' Bursary Award. She has also been a student (1992) and a teacher (2002, 2006) at The Arvon Foundation, in the UK, a centre for the development and promotion of all kinds of creative writing. She was a student at Clarion West, the US bootcamp for SF and Fantasy writers, in 1996. Her books have been variously shortlisted for The British Science Fiction Best Novel Award, the Arthur C Clarke Award, the Philip K Dick Award and the John W Campbell Award. A collection of her short fiction, *Heliotrope*, was published in 2012. In 2004 Justina was a judge for the Arthur C Clarke Award (best SF novel of the year published in the English language), on behalf of The Science Fiction Foundation. Her novels and stories range widely over SF and Fantasy.

Christopher Rowe (www.christopherrowe.typepad.com) has published more than twenty short stories, and has been a finalist for the Hugo, Nebula, World Fantasy, and Theodore Sturgeon Awards. Frequently reprinted, his work has been translated into a half-dozen languages around the world, and has been praised by the *New York Times Book Review*. His story 'Another Word For Map is Faith' made the long list in the 2007 *Best American Short Stories* volume, and his early fiction was collected in a chapbook, *Bittersweet Creek and Other Stories*, by Small Beer

Press. His Forgotten Realms novel, Sandstorm, was published in 2010 by Wizards of the Coast. He is currently pursuing an MFA in writing at the Bluegrass Writers Studio of Eastern Kentucky University and is hard at work on *Sarah Across America*, a new novel about maps, megafauna, and other obsessions. He lives in a hundred-year-old house in Lexington, Kentucky, with his wife, novelist Gwenda Bond, and their pets.

Robert Shearman (www.robertshearman.net) is probably best known for bringing back the Daleks in a Hugo Award nominated episode of the first series of the BBC's revival of *Doctor Who*. But in Britain he has had a long career writing for both theatre and radio, winning two Sony awards, the Sunday Times Playwriting Award, and the Guinness Award for Theatre Ingenuity in association with the Royal National Theatre. His first collection of short stories, *Tiny Deaths*, won the World Fantasy Award; its follow-up, *Love Songs for the Shy and Cynical*, received the British Fantasy and Shirley Jackson Awards, while third collection, *Everyone's Just So So Special*, spawned his craziest idea yet. His most recent book is collection *Remember Why You Fear Me*. Coming up is a new collection *They Do the Same Things Different Here*.

Born in 1977 in Stockholm, Sweden, **Karin Tidbeck** (www.karintidbeck.com) lives in Malmö where she works as a project leader and freelance creative writing instructor. She has previously worked as a writer for role-playing productions in schools and theatres, and written articles and essays on gaming and interactive arts theory. She's an alumna of the 2010 Clarion San Diego writers' workshop. She has published short stories and poetry in Swedish since 2002, including a short story collection, *Vem är Arvid Pekon?*, and the recent novel *Amatka*. Her English publication history includes noted short story collection *Jagganath* and stories in *Weird Tales*, *Shimmer*

Magazine, Unstuck Annual and the anthologies *Odd?* and *Steampunk Revolution*.

Genevieve Valentine's (www.genevievevalentine.com) first novel, *Mechanique: A Tale of the Circus Tresaulti*, won the 2012 Crawford Award and was nominated for the Nebula Award. Her short fiction has appeared in *Clarkesworld*, *Strange Horizons*, *Journal of Mythic Arts*, *Fantasy*, *Apex*, and others, and in the anthologies *Federations*, *The Living Dead 2*, *The Way of the Wizard*, *Teeth*, *After*, and more. Her story 'Light on the Water' was a 2009 World Fantasy Award nominee, and 'Things to Know about Being Dead' was a 2012 Shirley Jackson Award nominee; several stories have been reprinted in Best of the Year anthologies. Her nonfiction and reviews have appeared at *NPR.org*, *Strange Horizons*, *Lightspeed*, *Weird Tales*, *Tor. com*, and *Fantasy Magazine*, and she is a co-author of *Geek Wisdom* (Quirk Books). Coming up is new young adult novel, *The Girls at the Kingfisher Club*. Her appetite for bad movies is insatiable.

Bram Stoker Nominee and Shirley Jackson Award winner **Kaaron Warren** (kaaronwarren.wordpress.com) has lived in Melbourne, Sydney, Canberra and Fiji. She's sold many short stories, three novels (the multi-award-winning *Slights*, *Walking the Tree* and *Mistification*) and four short story collections. *Through Splintered Walls* won a Canberra Critic's Circle Award for Fiction, two Ditmar Awards, two Australian Shadows Awards and a Shirley Jackson Award. Her story 'Air, Water and the Grove' won the Aurealis Award for Best SF Short Story and will appear in Paula Guran's *Year's Best Dark Fantasy and Horror*. Her latest collection is *The Gate Theory*.

FEARSOME JOURNEYS

THE NEW SOLARIS BOOK OF FANTASY

Edited by **Jonathan Strahan**

Featuring original stories by

Daniel Abraham
Saladin Ahmed
Elizabeth Bear
Trudi Canavan
Scott Lynch
Glen Cook
and more

How do you encompass all the worlds of the imagination? Within fantasy's scope lies every possible impossibility, from dragons to spirits, from magic to gods, and from the unliving to the undying.

In Fearsome Journeys, master anthologist Jonathan Strahan sets out on a quest to find the very limits of the unlimited, collecting twelve brand new stories by some of the most popular and exciting names in epic fantasy from around the world.

With original fiction from Scott Lynch, Saladin Ahmed, Trudi Canavan, K J Parker, Kate Elliott, Jeffrey Ford, Robert V S Redick, Ellen Klages, Glen Cook, Elizabeth Bear, Ellen Kushner, Ysabeau S. Wilce and Daniel Abraham Fearsome Journeys explores the whole range of the fantastic.

 WWW.SOLARISBOOKS.COM

Follow us on Twitter! www.twitter.com/solarisbooks

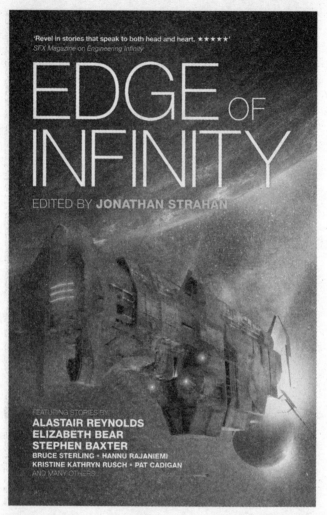

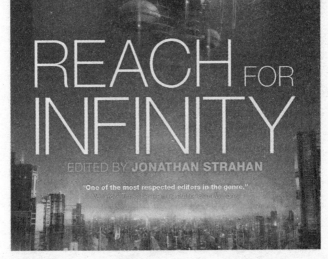

FEATURING STORIES BY **KEN MACLEOD** • **PAT CADIGAN** • **ELLEN KLAGES**
ALASTAIR REYNOLDS • **KAREN LORD** • **GREG EGAN** • **LINDA NAGATA**
ADAM ROBERTS • **HANNU RAJANIEMI** • **ALIETTE DE BODARD** AND MORE

REACH FOR
INFINITY

EDITED BY **JONATHAN STRAHAN**

"One of the most respected editors in the genre."

What happens when humanity reaches out into the vastness of space?
The brightest names in SF contribute new orginal fiction to this amazing
anothology from master editor Jonathan Strahan.

Including new work by Alastair Reynolds, Greg Egan, Ian McDonald, Ken Macleod,
Pat Cadigan, Karl Schroeder, Hannu Rajaniemi, Karen Lord, Adam Roberts,
Kathleen Ann Goonan, Aliette de Bodard, Peter Watts, Ellen Klages & Linda Nagata.

 WWW.SOLARISBOOKS.COM

Follow us on Twitter! www.twitter.com/solarisbooks

'A cliché it may be, but
there really is something
for everyone here... an ideal
bait to tempt those who only
read novels to climb over the
short fiction fence'

*– Interzone on The Solaris Book
of New Science Fiction, Vol 2*

THE NEW SOLARIS BOOK
OF SCIENCE FICTION

SOLARIS RISING

EDITED BY
IAN WHATES

FEATURING
NEW WORK BY

Alastair Reynolds
Peter F. Hamilton
Stephen Baxter
Ian McDonald
Paul di Filippo
Ken MacLeod
Adam Roberts
Pat Cadigan
AND MANY MORE

Solaris Rising presents nineteen stories of the very highest calibre from some of the most
accomplished authors in the genre, proving just how varied and dynamic science fiction
can be. From strange goings on in the present to explorations of bizarre futures, from drug-
induced tragedy to time-hopping serial killers, from crucial choices in deepest space to a
ravaged Earth under alien thrall, from gritty other worlds to surreal other realms, *Solaris
Rising* delivers a broad spectrum of experiences and excitements, showcasing the genre
at its very best.

 WWW.SOLARISBOOKS.COM

Follow us on Twitter! www.twitter.com/solarisbooks

FEATURING
NEW WORK BY
Paul di Filippo
Paul Cornell
Sarah Lotz
Gareth L. Powell
Adam Roberts
Mike Resnick
Tanith Lee
Aliette de Bodard
Phillip Vine

AN EXCLUSIVE EBOOK
OF NEW SCIENCE FICTION

SOLARIS
RISING 1.5

EDITED BY
IAN WHATES

"Highly recommended... a very strong eclectic anthology with
something to please any lover of contemporary sf."
Fantasy Book Critic on Solaris Rising

An anthology of nine short stories from some of the most exciting names in science fiction today. From both sides of the Atlantic - and further afield - these nine great writers offer you everything from a mystery about the nature of the universe to an inexplicable transmission to everyone on Earth, and from engineered giant spiders to Venetian palaces in space.

So settle in, and enjoy yet more proof of the extraordinary breadth and depth of contemporary SF. Featuring Adam Roberts, Aliette de Bodard, Gareth L. Powell, Mike Resnick, Sarah Lotz, Phillip Vine, Tanith Lee, Paul Cornell, Paul di Filippo.

 WWW.SOLARISBOOKS.COM

Follow us on Twitter! www.twitter.com/solarisbooks

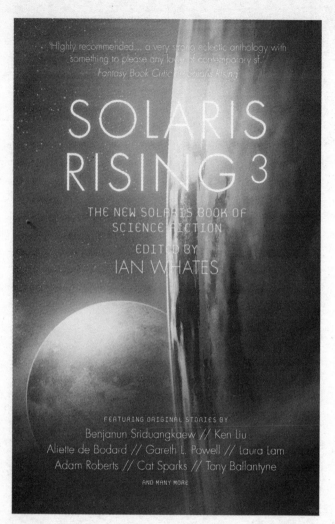

'Highly recommended... a very strong eclectic anthology with something to please any lover of contemporary sf.'
Fantasy Book Critic on Solaris Rising

SOLARIS RISING 3

THE NEW SOLARIS BOOK OF
SCIENCE FICTION

EDITED BY
IAN WHATES

FEATURING ORIGINAL STORIES BY
Benjanun Sriduangkaew // Ken Liu
Aliette de Bodard // Gareth L. Powell // Laura Lam
Adam Roberts // Cat Sparks // Tony Ballantyne
AND MANY MORE

Award-nominated editor Ian Whates showcases the best in contemporary science fiction, celebrating new writing by a roster of diverse and exciting authors. Here you will discover how this 'literature of ideas' produces stories of astonishing imagination and incisive speculation.

Solaris Rising 3 thrillingly demonstrates why science fiction is the most relevant, daring and progressive of genres.

 WWW.SOLARISBOOKS.COM

Follow us on Twitter! www.twitter.com/solarisbooks